C0-DVZ-958

DATE DUE

AP 21 '03			
NO 30 '04			
FO 26 '05			
FE 9 '6			
MR 6 '07			
MY 2 2 '08			
MY 3 1 '9			

DEMCO 38-296

Writing In Between

R

Writing In Between

Modernity and Psychosocial Dilemma in the Novels of Joseph Conrad

Beth Sharon Ash

St. Martin's Press
New York

Riverside Community College
Library
MAR '00   4800 Magnolia Avenue
Riverside, CA 92506

PR 6005 .04 Z55245 1999

Ash, Beth Sharon, 1953-

Writing in between

WRITING IN BETWEEN. Copyright © 1999 Beth Sharon Ash. All rights reserved. Printed in the United States of America. No part of this book may be used or reproduced in any manner whatsoever without written permission except in the case of brief quotations embodied in critical articles or reviews. For information, address St. Martin's Press, 175 Fifth Avenue, New York, N.Y. 10010.

ISBN 0-312-21483-9

Library of Congress Cataloging-in-Publication Data

Ash, Beth Sharon, 1953–
    Writing in between : modernity and psychosocial dilemma in the novels of Joseph Conrad / by Beth Sharon Ash.
        p.   cm.
    Includes bibliographical references and index.
    ISBN 0-312-21483-9 (cloth)
    1. Conrad, Joseph, 1857–1924—Criticism and interpretation.
    2. Literature and society—England—History—20th century.
    3. Psychological fiction, English—History and criticism.
    4. Modernism (Literature)—England.   5. Social Problems in literature.   I. Title.
    PR6005.04Z55245   1999
    823'.912—dc21   99-12662
                                                                         CIP

Design by Binghamton Valley Composition

First Edition: September, 1999
10 9 8 7 6 5 4 3 2 1

For Brett,
who made this book possible

Contents

Part Three
Disappearing Landmarks: "Revolutionary"
Social Change and Psychobiography

Acknowledgements

My parents, Allan and Marilyn Ash, have been constantly supportive of this project, always encouraging my every scholarly endeavor. Sadly, Edward Clarke did not live to see this book in print; the project, focused in many ways on the mourning process, helped me to understand the depth of my own loss and is partly my tribute to him.

I want to thank Professor Thomas Leclair at the University of Cincinnati for helping me to envision the manuscript in its final form. Thanks, too, to Professors William Veeder and Lisa Ruddick at the University of Chicago for providing me with constructive criticism on earlier drafts of the project, and for their continuing interest.

A fellowship from the Beineke Library at Yale University enabled me to research the Joseph Conrad Collection and make use of excerpts from the original manuscript of *Under Western Eyes*.

The Psychosocial Contexts of Conrad's Authorial Subjectivity

At the end of 1906, Joseph Conrad was deeply depressed, afflicted with a variety of physical ailments and writer's paralysis that together prevented him from completing his novel *The Secret Agent*. Though such depressions were more or less chronic for Conrad, the illness in 1906 was both unusually severe and uncanny in its timing. In mid-December, after his forty-ninth birthday, Conrad wrote to his intimate associate John Galsworthy that he feared a "nervous breakdown"; later in the month Conrad mentioned to Galsworthy that he had just reached his forty-eighth year, when in fact he had just turned 49. Biographer Frederick R. Karl suggests that Conrad misremembered his age in part because his father, Apollo Korzeniowski, had died at the age of 49. Apollo succumbed to tuberculosis, as his wife Ewa had done several years earlier. Both deaths were direct consequences of their shared decision to remain together as a family (with their son Konradeck) while Apollo served his sentence of exile in Russia, where he had been sent by a Tsarist court as punishment for his activities preceding the 1863 uprising, and for his role as a revolutionary and as a politico-religious writer serving the cause of Polish emancipation from Russian oppression. Ewa died in exile. Apollo survived to see his sentence commuted, only to travel to Cracow and live in isolation with his young son Konrad, waiting to die as Konrad looked on. Near the end, Apollo cast the pages of his uncompleted manuscripts into the fire—an act, and image, of spiritual desolation that would stay with Conrad all his life. Thus in

1906, at age 49, in thrall to a paralyzing depression, and drifting blankly through his own unfinished manuscript pages, Joseph Conrad unconsciously identified with his own father at the threshold of death. And with good reason he made himself a year younger, paralyzed against the many terrible meanings that completion might have for him.

This glimpse into Conrad's psychological life, important as it is, shows us only one highly personal dimension of his experience. Even as he was burdened in the latter months of 1906 by his personal past, he also had to cope with the swiftly changing social and literary scene in Edwardian England. Active revolutionary politics in Russia began in 1905, creating an international movement that provided British voters with a powerful impetus to sweep away the Tory imperialists after their nearly 20 years in power. The wave of populist sentiment carried the Liberal party to a spectacular victory in the General Election of 1906, and set the stage for the emergence in Parliament of a Labour party independent of Liberal control for the first time. The political landscape was changing in dramatic fashion. Furthermore, due to a new openness toward Russia, England's literati were actively translating and studying Tolstoy and Dostoevsky; and many, including Edward Garnett (whom Conrad counted as a close friend), idealized the newfound Russian literature, attributing to it prophetic insights into what revolution in general could mean in the new century. The conjunction of 1905 and the broad movement of progressive opinion in Britain seemed to promise a new era of emancipatory politics; but this, unfortunately, was not to be. During the later Edwardian period the old Liberal party, struggling with the conflict between its humanitarian ideals and its imperialist proclivities, could not work as a viable centrist position to reconcile the competing claims of social classes and groups. The internal contradictions of British Liberalism, whether "old" or "new," were compounded by the rise of alternative ideologies, and liberalism lost much of its philosophical force as the discourses of technocratic functionalism and socialism became increasingly dominant. Conrad attended to these changes with great interest, sometimes with passion, not uncommonly with irritation or outright despair. Raised as he was in a world of personal and political instability, Conrad could not but be affected on many levels by the social turmoil that shaped England in the prewar.

These social circumstances—the Russian "invasion" of English political and literary culture, and the systemic political changes occurring in British society—figure importantly in *Under Western Eyes*, the novel Conrad wrote between 1907 and 1911, precisely because of *who* Conrad was. For him, the present was running in directions that dangerously paralleled his

Polish childhood, evoking many of its themes and conflicts, both personal
and cultural. This novel, I would argue, is not about either Russia or
England exclusively, but rather about the seeming irreconcilability of past
and present experience, even as that experience demands and exacts repetition of what has come before. It is, moreover, about psychosocial contradiction, about the matrix of relations, over time and in present identity and
social process, that make meaningful the appearance of aporias, disavowals,
and efforts to at once make and conceal meaning. And it is about Conrad's
reactions to the impossibilities of his relations both past and present, private and public, conscious and unconscious, and about his impossible relation to his own text. In this sense, the novel (like all of Conrad's texts) is as
profoundly ambiguous as it is probative, patterned according to the double-
bind of "neither this . . . nor that."

All of Conrad's most significant work is written "in between"—
between various necessary yet untenable options that can neither be realized nor abandoned. Why this should be so is the subject of this study:
being in between impossible psychological options and/or social commitments is what drives Conrad's narratives, even when the writing seems
designed to obscure rather than illuminate the underwriting, blindly to
enact rather than comprehend the reasons, the *relations*, that motivate irresolution.

Yet how does one construct a coherent critical narrative that
accounts for the complexity of overdetermined relations and circumstances
that emerge in Conrad's novels? And more broadly, how does one read a
text, any text, as the aesthetic locus of both social and psychological configurations, as a human event that recapitulates and refigures multiple
meanings and levels of meaning, such that it is impossible to claim that
either the psychological or the social referent is the "real" cause that shapes
the text's production? Indeed, given the dialectical interplay among all of
these factors in Conrad's texts, one does well to adopt a hermeneutic suspiciousness about causal language altogether.

To tell such a story is, by my way of thinking, to do some version of
"psychohistory" or, as I see it, "psychosocial dialectics." I am dissatisfied
both with the older models of psychohistory (e.g., those fashioned by
Erikson and Sartre), and with the newer ones, broadly designated "social
constructivist," which in negating the authority of the "subject," also tend
to negate human relational particularities. This occurs, for example, when
one begins with Lacanian psychoanalysis, and extends Lacan into the social
field via Althusserian Marxism (Fredric Jameson), or via Foucault (the postcolonial theory of Homi Bhabha).[1] My readings are fundamentally guided

by how I think about, and attempt to resolve, this central problematic of how best to investigate complex relations between the various contexts that constitute Conrad's situation as author. The theoretical aim of my book is to demarcate a "middle ground" that positions agency without erasing it, and allows for a coherent interarticulation of psychoanalytic and cultural criticism in the study of literary texts.

Both Erikson and Sartre share my goal of locating the psychological and socio-historical elements that underlie character structure, and that might be inferred from textual production and biography. Yet neither Erikson (in *Young Man Luther*) nor Sartre (in *The Family Idiot*)[2] succeeds in drawing personality and culture into genuinely dialectical relationship with one another. Erikson's study is marred by uni-directional psychological determination. He tends to reify human agency inasmuch as he sees identity as something one searches for or loses, and he presupposes that the seeds of adult personality are forged almost exclusively in the crucible of the family, unfolding from childhood to adulthood in a fairly predetermined way. Since Erikson focuses primarily on the idiosyncratic and familial dimension of Martin Luther's experience, he is moreover unable to account for how the resolution of Luther's identity crisis could ignite a mass movement.[3] I believe that Luther provided solutions to questions of social and personal identity that made sense to others because the culture had been woven into his personhood from the beginning, and he had never ceased responding to it. Great men and women must live somewhere in order for their greatness to have meaning.

Erikson does not take social interpretation far enough, but Sartre goes to the opposite extreme. Using a Marxist perspective to focus on the role of the family as the conduit of social institutions, Sartre shows how persons are fabricated by the shaping force of social environment. His analysis of Flaubert hinges on the highly dubious claim that when the primary psychological relation with the mother does not engender in the subject a sense of spontaneity and freedom, he can only conform to the shape of the social vessel into which he has been poured. Flaubert somehow becomes for Sartre a purely negative example of the existential "project" of self-realization—a perfectly impotent center of intentionality, rather than an exemplary model of singular freedom and responsibility.

Erikson and Sartre fail in opposite ways, but both rightly affirm some belief that people create themselves to some extent from the basic material of their given conditions. Without a notion of personal choice and subjective coherence, analysis reduces life to a collection of learned roles, the enactment of others' expectations and desires, the mere habitation of "subject positions" dictated by ideology. Foucault's "subjectification" by discourse, Lacan's description of "the alienation of the subject in the signifier," and Jameson's (Althusserian) deconstruction of "the myth of the self," all risk overdetermination of the subject by social forces, and hence displace self-reflexive consciousness, but only through various dissolutions of subjective agency. It follows that such decentering rules out in advance reciprocity and consensus in human relations. I do not, however, wish to restore humanistic subjectivism (the subject treated as the origin of meaning or the locus of radical freedom). My aim is to recover "the subject" in all of its existential unpredictability and psychological density, but also to insist on human situatedness in cultural and material contexts of life. In what follows, I want to map my reading of Conrad in his context(s), and then to briefly suggest the theoretical commitments that allow for my relational view of subjectivity, this middle theoretical position between the unitariness of humanist identity and the various post-subjectivities (constructed via social discourse).

Conrad as a Psychosocial Subject

To conceptualize the interpenetration of socio-psychological process and the worlds of shared social practices and meanings in Conrad's novels, I situate his work in three historical contexts: the late-nineteenth-century breakdown of organicist ideals of social order; the entrenchment of a fully organized imperialist culture; and the political strains that afflicted British society during the later Edwardian period. My descriptions of social context are largely consensual (that is, many historians understand these aspects of the period in the ways I adopt), for my point is not to offer new historical interpretations, but rather to highlight shared meanings, specific institutional practices, responses to historical events that are influenced not just by political or moral blindness, for example, but by *unconscious* process. Such an understanding begins from the theoretical assertion that social formations are open to psychoanalytic reading when the subject is conceived in relational psychoanalytic terms, and when the fit between the subject and his or her social matrix is seen as necessary and dynamic.

Using the idea of "relational subjectivity," I analyze Conrad both as a creature of culture and as a psychologically discrete subject acting within and interpreting selectively defined cultural horizons. As a theoretical concept, "relationality" is a hermeneutic and psychoanalytic principle that allows me to reconceptualize human agency. As I conceive of it, the "relational subject" is dialectical and dialogical: dialectical because it is defined by the continual interplay of relational matrices (the personal is bound to the interpersonal and the social, but cannot be reduced to them); and dialogical because the subject, in its selective reliance on assimilation and internalization, expresses itself by talking back, for example, in symptomatic conflicts with, and critical interpretations of, its world. The idea thus allows me to tell a coherent story about Conrad's texts and about the author as biographical subject according to the interplay of psychological and social experience. This ongoing exchange is especially apparent in Conrad because he is so uniquely positioned both inside and outside British culture and its turn-of-the-century transformations, and because of his vulnerability to loss and social marginalization.[4]

At the most basic level, I understand Conrad's texts as complicated responses to modern trends toward secularization and industrialization, and to resulting disruptions in the role of traditional authority in shaping social relations. In this broadest of social contexts, the novels can be seen to disclose a historically specific, not simply personal, sense of loss, disappointment, and vulnerability. In my effort to historicize psychoanalysis, I argue that shifts in social structures and cultural values might engage (at once repeat and influence) private psychological experience, and that the primacy of issues of attachment and separation, narcissistic wholeness and disintegrative anxiety, disillusionment and idealization, become focal when investment in shared meanings is challenged by socio-historical change.

For example, in texts like *The Nigger of the "Narcissus," Heart of Darkness,* and *Lord Jim,* Conrad is fundamentally concerned with what the psychoanalytic cultural historian Peter Homans calls the disturbance of "man's inmost self" in the face of modern industrial society.[5] But why should "the self" be thus dislocated? Homans observes: "The shared social experience of increasingly mechanicalized modes of production always tears self-consciousness out of its traditional modes of connectedness to supportive natural, social, and cosmological worlds, and in doing so inflicts a *historically specific narcissistic blow* to the universal human, spontaneous sense of, and wish for 'the whole' " (*ATM,* p. 230, my emphasis). The loss of shared meanings due to economic, political, and social change is experienced as object loss, as having to be or do without something upon which we depend for a sense of self-coherence, purpose, and worth. As social psychologists Fred Weinstein and Gerald M. Platt explain, one's connections to social ways of life, and even to cultural abstractions, are also "object" relationships. "By object relationship we mean the ties that exist between and among individuals and aspects of their selves (e.g., a sense of efficiency and mastery), and between individuals and *such abstract associations and arrangements as political authority, economic institutions, occupational groups, social statuses and roles, and cultural ideals"* (*PS*, p.102, my emphasis). Thus, to be deprived of familiar and meaningful ties to culture, sometimes even when these have oppressive dimensions, is to suffer a challenge to what Homans calls "primary self-definition," or the narcissistic sectors of personality.

Further, according to psychoanalysts Heinz Kohut and Didier Anzieu, shared group experience and fantasy function in the deepest sense to bring members into unconscious contact with the "mother" of infancy, and with the wish for that state of inviolable interconnection that is associated with her. Threats to the permanence of one's place in the social matrix can arouse fears of abandonment, which might be experienced as separation or fragmentation anxiety.[6] Thus, in a very basic way, cultural losses are also personal losses, and can lead to a general sense of inner disorganization, rage at the injury to self that loss inflicts, and emptiness.

As Homans says, disillusionment must be followed by an adequate experience of mourning if subjects are to move toward "new knowledge of self, new ideals, and consequent new ideas" (*ATM*, p. 24). If mourning fails, however, then apathy, anger, and despair are more likely to persist, or the experience of loss is more likely to be disavowed altogether through a defensive program of false restitution. In the latter case, lost ideals and traditions are often replaced by regressive external structures—"new revitalized group formations and new systems of ideas, such as are found in sect formations, ideological rigidity, and massive remythologizations" (*ATM*, p. 126). In this way, bourgeois society subsumes old structures of value for ideological purposes, and symbolic objects and cultural sects are created to control (not to transform) aggression, as well as to gratify antisocial fantasies mobilized by feelings of powerlessness and dislocation. To the extent that such cultural forms rigidly obstruct the capacity to risk interaction with "otherness," they are *not* what psychoanalyst D. W. Winnicott calls "transitional" forms. That is to say, they are not symbols that enable the subject, in cultural play, to discover the (negotiated) distinctions between fantasy and reality, identity and difference, and so on. Rather, such forms, which are enlisted solely to defend against a primary sense of ontological insecurity, serve merely as fortifications against change. This distinction between transformational and purely defensive forms is central to my reading of turn-of-the-century British culture, and to appreciating Conrad's portrayal of that culture's psychological and institutional dynamics.

Conrad's novels, in assimilating and responding to significant cultural transformation, show themselves to be organized around relational contradiction. On the one hand, they scrutinize with astonishing critical force the social ambiguities and ontological insecurities aroused by the modern scene; on the other, they reenact these same problems. Conrad struggled throughout his life, and in his art, with fundamental psychological issues (such as loss, restitution, attachment, and self-coherence) in ways indicative of being "in between," of a self organized around irresolution and deferral, the imperative to mourn and the failure to do so, and therefore around impasse. These psychological predispositions place him in relation to his social world in particular ways, and invariably with a deep and insistent ambivalence toward those aspects of the world that he finds most necessary to self-identity, whether these be evident through acknowledged or disavowed internalized aspects of his personal history, ongoing identifications or disidentifications with important contemporaries, or broader political and ethical commitments or objections to institutions, ideology, and cultural myths. As a result Conrad's texts can leave readers with the disorienting sense that he is both a critic of and apologist for his subject. It is precisely in the quality of its irresolution, I believe, that Joseph Conrad's work gives voice to the central relational dilemmas of modernity.

In part one, I focus on organicist social ideas and ideals in two different ways. First, I consider the longstanding notion that existing class distinctions had a "providential dispensation," and examine British culture's powerful theodicial urge to protect the earthly institutions that upheld such distinctions. I then investigate how imperialism used organicist ideals (e.g., ideals of communal unity) and traditional values of duty, honor, and loyalty to underwrite an advancing industrial economy. The older forms of life decayed even as pre-capitalist mandates and values seemed to be recovered, thus creating a framework for social division and contradiction. In this context, I interpret *The Nigger of the "Narcissus"* as a semically double and contradictory text—a work that at once legitimizes (what Conrad recognizes to be) the obsolete and distorted traditional mandates of British paternalism, and anatomizes the ways that mechanicalized modes of production disrupt the traditional social individual's sense of self-coherence, purpose, and worth.[7]

The crew of the "Narcissus" makes James Wait, the black "other" who has been reified as an imperialist symbol of blackness (at once degenerate and magical), the center of their own cultish mythologization. The crew thus attempts to allay their rage and satisfy their desire for narcissistic wholeness—ends that cannot be reached through rationalized and impersonal social arrangements alone. As a symbolic object Wait is used to repeat and protect existing patterns of alienation. What is more, both the novella's preface and conclusion work to circumscribe and sustain Conrad's portrayal of contradiction and irresolution. Like the crew, the author seems unable to forge productive relations to traditional institutions (whether a relation of reliance or opposition), or to fashion an individual social identity capable of traversing the problematic terrain of modernity without having to make deferral itself the locus of security, and hence of identity.

In the book's second part, I again look at the problems of contradiction and disavowal, now in the specific context of British imperialism. I begin by exploring imperialist ideology and various cultural practices, including nineteenth-century attitudes about race and important features of late-Victorian education. I then move to read *Heart of Darkness* and *Lord Jim* against the background of imperialist culture. The British were chronically ambivalent about allying national identity with archaic, grandiose fantasy and its rationalization, and struggled with the confusion of condoning certain ideals and policies that violated the ethical foundations of British self-definition. Selfhood and ontological security were premised on the survival of both poles of this irreconcilable contradiction, making strategies of disavowal necessary.

The Marlovian narratives at once enact and critique imperialist fantasy and rigid dichotomization and are both wedded to and critically distanced from the terms of imperialist selfhood. Marlow continually accommodates self-knowledge to its opposite, defensive ignorance. He understands Kurtz's and Jim's misguided idealism, their ignominy and confusion, but then commits himself to what he criticizes. But how does one address the thorny problem of where Conrad himself is positioned? Interpretation of the novels stands or falls on how the critic deals with the fact that Conrad is only an implicit voice in these first-person Marlovian fictions (none of which are easily identified with Marlow nor emphatically distanced from him) and on what sense is made of this ambiguous positioning. When we take the double voicing of authorial irony into account, while also reading for the affective inflection of social experience in the stories, we see that Conrad as author "inside" the text is hopelessly entangled in Marlow's perspective, and that the implied author can no more escape the novels' ubiquitous conflicts than can the narrator. Thus, while the grandiosity of imperialist policy and mythmaking is shown to be structured by identifiable destructive fantasies, and imperialist practices and mandates are seen as injurious and corrupt, what Conrad defers is the psychological process of working through loss. In effect, the emotional work necessary to establishing a sustained critique is hindered by a failure to mourn, to accept having to be without heretofore meaningful cultural ideals and affiliations with a powerful social fraternity, and to come to grips with an unalterable fascination with personal grandiosity.

In part three, I focus on aspects of the Edwardian political and literary scenes, and in this context explore prominent psychological themes in Conrad's novels *The Secret Agent* and *Under Western Eyes*, and in his personal history, with special attention to how each conforms to the dynamics of irresolution. I investigate Conrad's representative relationships, including his highly conflicted relation to his father, his acrimonious literary rivalry with Dostoevsky, and his relatively close, though ambivalent, associations with the radical H. G. Wells and liberal aristocrat John Galsworthy. I employ these relations (familial, literary, personal) to suggest how the larger context (political, economic, and social) is directly interwoven with biography, and to argue that what is happening in later Edwardian society provides a remarkable analogue to the primary psychosocial patterns of Conrad's experience, and of his late major works.

The potentially polarizing forces in Edwardian culture (for example, nationalist-imperialist and labor-socialist groups), and the increasing erosion of nineteenth-century liberalism as a viable doctrine of social mediation, provide a social parallel to Conrad's "in between" position. That is, they call into relief his acute sensitivity to loss, his struggle with the psychic polarities of extreme ambivalence, his writerly idiom of deferral, ambiguity, and defensively reconstituted ideals, or alternatively his idiom of irony as a response to acute depression. Hence, his texts struggle continually and in countless ways with an inability to create the negotiated middle of stable relatedness. After 1905, his writings not only thematize political instability, the forces of "revolution" arrayed against those of "reaction," but also treat social disorder with corrosive irony, perhaps Conrad's most desperate defense against depression or worse. *The Secret Agent* introduces the complicity between Conrad's here-and-now consciousness of cultural and personal loss and the morbid feelings of childhood abandonment and bereavement. *Under Western Eyes*, in telling a "Russian" story that is also about Conrad's conflicted experience of British culture and his Polish past, sustains an increasingly unstable and shrinking space for negotiating identity—caught as it is between the perpetual struggle with the barren contradictions of the present and the danger of disappearing into the childhood world of lost objects.

What Conrad called the age of "disappearing landmarks" had marked him as its own. In negotiating the fit between the exigencies of his most central interpersonal relationships and those of his social world, Conrad's genius captured British culture's most fundamental discontinuities and non-resolutions, while the culture, in turn, evoked and reinforced his reliance on deferral and impasse, making them necessary aspects of his character as "homo-duplex," the man of the in-between.

Theoretical Commitments

What allows for this interpretive narrative about Conrad is a synthetic critical position, one that is based on connecting post-Heideggerian hermeneutics, specifically Gadamer's theory of meaning and historical analysis, first to the interpersonal and process-oriented ideas of relational psychoanalysis, and then to immanent and critical social theory. Philosophical hermeneutics, relational psychoanalysis, and immanent ideology critique (which takes account not only of domination, but also of participation), allow for a coherent and sophisticated description of dynamic psychic and historical interaction that neither radically decenters the subject nor uncritically affirms its freedom. (Indeed, part of the interest of reading Conrad from this position is noticing just how his need to belong so often blocks his capacity to claim a relatively autonomous vantage point.) This synthesis is also an approach that, in practice, preserves a commonsensical appreciation of psychologically inflected close reading, a style that is responsive to the social and political without turning textual interpretation into a would-be sociology of surveillance techniques or ideological interpellations.

Gadamer's "coherentist" model of knowledge tells us that meaning is a relatively determined and determinate product of hermeneutic dialogue, and that our standards for justifying our arguments are the rational, political, and ethical norms of our cultural heritage. Such norms are of course open to modification and innovation; and while they establish knowledge as historically contingent practice, they are also the basis for illuminating, critiquing, and in this relative (and non-viciously circular) way, for overcoming our contingency. A significant corollary to Gadamer's epistemic model is his interpretive view of self-reflexivity. Interpretation allows awareness, though never full awareness, of how, as Richard Rorty puts it, one has been "described" by a preexisting world. Interpretation allows for self-redescription—taking a position on one's situation—and in this way achieving relative autonomy in the world.[8]

Gadamer's view of human activity as mediated process (a continual interpreting and being interpreted) underpins my approach to psychoanalysis and social theory. Yet I want to acknowledge that Gadamer's philosophy is in no sense psychoanalytic and provides no specific form of social theory. In giving a sophisticated account of the dialogical constitution of reflexivity and agency, however, Gadamer encourages an awareness of psychological and social modes of explanation as mutually informing, interrelated narratives. Or again, within the epistemic context of "the living circle," one cannot rest content with a monocausal view of things. The psychic and social domains of life are interdependent: neither can be explained without the other.

The psychoanalytic model that fits best with philosophical hermeneutics is, broadly speaking, "relational" in type. Psychoanalyst Stephen Mitchell, editor of the journal *Psychoanalytic Dialogues*, has put forward an argument for the theoretical coherence of object relations theory, self-psychology, and interpersonal-culturalist views, and in doing so has shaped an integrated relational model of psychoanalysis.[9] Relational psychoanalysis is somewhat like Lacanianism in that both emphasize that the subject and the other exist within interpersonal and social structures of interpretation. However, Lacan's relentless insistence on the negative in his three experiential registers (the imaginary, the symbolic, the real), his stark emphasis on the irremediable "méconnaissance" of the subject, its alienation and captivation by others and by "the big other" of language, radically decenters the subject by being radically undialectial about the processes of social exchange. In this way it virtually precludes intersubjective acknowledgement and crucial socio-linguistic practices of adequate dialogue and negotiation.[10] In contrast, the balanced structure of mediation in relational theory, its focus (in Mitchell's words) on psychodynamic process "within a multifaceted relational matrix which takes into account self-organization, attachments to others ('objects'), interpersonal transactions, and the active role of the analysand in the continual re-creation of his subjective world" provides a continuous circle of mutual influence between interpenetrating frames in which subjectivity is formed and is continually negotiated. (*RCP*, p.8) In so doing, the relational model finds in hermeneutic dialogue (the "horizonal" character of Gadamerian understanding) a cogent epistemology for justifying psychoanalytic claims.[11]

Relational theory establishes a notion of self that is, by the very nature of its formation, open to social analysis. But what is true in theory has been underdeveloped in practice. I have taken up this challenge to historicize relational insights. First, I extend the cycle of mutual influence between the intrapsychic and the interpersonal to include the socio-historical situation(s) of self-formation. Second, I investigate the psychic and the social as heterogeneous but interdependent variables. This investigation depends not just on psychoanalysis, but on appropriate theories of social formations of power and participation, on ideology critique and the like.

In extending relational theory, for example, I interpret the subject's original relational matrix as it emerges from historically specific caretaking arrangements, and also suggest how aspects of this matrix are continually affected—solidifed, evaded, modified, transformed—by the subject's later interpersonal relations and attachments to larger cultural meanings and institutions. In thus expanding Mitchell's notion of a "relational matrix," I use object relations theory, as represented by diverse theorists (W. R. D. Fairbairn, Harry Guntrip, D. W. Winnicott, Wilfred Bion, André Green, Julia Kristeva, Christopher Bollas, Thomas Ogden), and self-psychology (Heinz Kohut and Robert Stolorow), as a coherent body of work to interpret subjectivity as a *psychosocial* problematic. Relational psychoanalytic concepts allow exploration of the depth-psychology of the social individual according to themes such as differentiation (separation, relative autonomy) and fantasies of reunion (de-differentiation, merger), disillusionment (loss, mourning) and idealization (fantasizing security or resisting change by idealizing), and issues of self-esteem and self-coherence (narcissistic issues), and illuminate the interplay between relational dynamics and social-historical forms. Such themes open us to an understanding of how the play of repetition and change in historical process is linked not only to ideological mystification and its reflective critique, but to social identifications nourished and lost by individuals; and this is possible precisely because subjective identity, fantasy, and need are built upon the social significations (models of authority and hierarchy, ethnic heritage, institutional symbols) that define collective identity.

In describing the interplay between the heterogeneous realms of psyche and society, I draw on the neo-Marxist, quasi-psychoanalytic formulations of the intellectual partners Claude Lefort and Cornelius Castoriadis. Like Gadamer, Lefort and Castoriadis believe that social inquiry must take the form of immanent analysis. Hence, they reject Marx's analytical metanarrative (of economic foundationalism), but still make use of specific Marxian descriptions of the distinctive historicity of modern, bourgeois society; and they borrow and modify elements from poststructuralism's view of signifying practices as forms of domination (Foucault), but without giving up the relative autonomy of historical agents. In my discussions of nineteenth-century organicism and early twentieth-century imperialism, I use Lefort's neo-Marxist definition of ideological mystification (namely, "the projection of 'imaginary community' under the cover of which 'real' distinctions are determined as 'natural,' the particular is disguised beneath the universal, and the historical is effaced in the atemporality of the essence"). I also adopt Lefort's view of pedagogy as a central model of power in the nineteenth century.[12] While Lefort is certainly indebted to Althusser and Foucault, he doesn't carry forward the idea that performance of an ideological or discursive position is constitutive of the subject as such.

While many of my critical descriptions depend on Lefort, I view Castoriadis as the theorist who endows the idea of social identity with real psychological force. With his term the "social imaginary," Castoriadis argues that "imaginary" does not just designate functional ideological distortions, but also includes a core of significant representations—symbols, myths, traditions—by means of which a society distinguishes itself from other societies and from nature. Thus Castoriadis goes beyond merely impersonal, functional explanations of the social by taking into account, in the very constitution of social identity, the creative potential of persons as this is rooted in their psychological constitution. And if the social imaginary conveys innovativeness, it also expresses irrationality, for example, in the incredible proliferation of details and complications that characterize the central stories and symbols of any culture. Such proliferation can be traced to an unconscious desire for "total unification," an archaic fantasy of primary unity in the mother-child dyad.[13] Such formulations lead to Castoriadis's broader claim that "the social individual, as society produces him, is inconceivable 'without the unconscious'; the institution of society, which is indissociable from the institution of the social individual, is the imposition on the psyche of an organization which is essentially heterogeneous with it—but it too, in its turn, *'leans on'* the being of the psyche . . . and must, unavoidably, 'take it into account' " (*IS*, p. 298). Hence, whether we are concerned with social structures of participation or domination or both, we must be concerned simultaneously with the psychic needs of persons to connect with or separate from such structures (as well as with intricate patterns of defense for fending off recognition of affiliation and/or differentiation). Though Castoriadis invokes as a starting point classical Freudian psychoanalysis ("which we are not about to improve upon or overhaul" [p.274]), his overarching principle is one of relationality within the social field. There is, I think, an unnecessary theoretical inconsistency here. Indeed, the revisions developed by relational psychoanalysis fit nicely with Castoriadis's view of how our subjectivity is at once relationally embedded and fraught with dialectically contending forces and perspectives. Hence I start, both epistemologically and psychologically, from a relational rather than a strictly Freudian conception of personhood.

* * * * *

In the preceding, I have wanted to suggest an inherent fit between the book's theoretical orientation and its practical readings. Of course, theory cannot validate interpretation, but it does clarify why and how we can construct narratives that illuminate various mediations between social practices/identities and psychologically inflected texts, as well as connections between these and possible versions of the author's life. These narratives focus on different aspects of the entire relational matrix of subjectivity, and in multiple ways reveal how Conrad inhabits and writes from a position in between contradictory commitments, a psychosocial assemblage of necessary yet untenable oppositions (ambivalent forms of attachment, the perils and comforts of isolation) that cannot be entirely actualized or avoided. While both Gadamerian hermeneutics and poststructuralism, specifically Homi Bhabha's postcolonial theory, describe variants of in-betweeness, Conrad's position as both writer and social subject is distinct from either of these.

For Gadamer, our understanding is mediated and processual, and in this sense in between.[14] For Bhabha, the in-between is an "interstitial" space of representation or enunciation where cultural difference operates under the aegis of Derridean *differance*; and the structuring operations of "mimicry" and "hybridity" are deployed as subversive repetitions, reversing and dislocating the "symbols" (the "signs taken for wonders") of the dominant order.[15] Despite their obvious differences, both of these theorists overlook psychological experience, and hence seem to take for granted the self's capacity to play with boundaries—for example, what must occur in the back-and-forth dialogue of Gadamerian processual understanding, or in Bhabha's version of postcolonial "agency" as a morphing alloy of cultural categories (race, class, gender, geopolitical location and so forth), displacing any fixed center. Agency remains essentially abstract and disembodied, and hence in-betweeness is overlooked as a psychological idiom, as the experienced dilemma of being stuck or suspended in between. Dilemma in this sense belongs to the psychologically inflected self; it is a way of being-in-process that is embodied, has a unique history, and requires us to respond both unconsciously and affectively to the specifics of our sociocultural world.

Conrad's idiomatic negative refusal of choice, his viewing of the world in terms of irremediably opposed alternatives that cannot be embraced or given up, colors his relation to culture as chronically ambivalent and melancholic. It also suggests an internal world where conflict, the tension between mutually informing experiences of otherness and sameness within the self, becomes contradiction, the tension between disconnected aspects of self where mutual exchange and transformation become not only difficult but dangerous to the survival of needed psychosocial provisions. Conrad's commitment to such dilemma is an artifact of his inability, in a variety of ways, to properly mourn lost objects. Conrad's work, like his life, attempts to hold on to a sense of continuity, but often at the expense of the unfolding of discursive truthfulness. Instead he elaborates an aesthetic of irresolution, of denial and deferral, that comes from the need to balance or suspend contradictions, because such refusal of choice, paradoxically enough, provides for him the best possibility for "going on being." Understanding Conrad, in my view, begins here.

PART ONE

Industrialization and "Secular Theodicy"

CHAPTER ONE

Alterity and Emptiness:
A Psychosocial Reading of
The Nigger of the "Narcissus"

In the spring of 1897, after Conrad received the proof sheets of his new tale, he communicated to his literary friends Ted Sanderson and Cunninghame Graham his mixed sense of elation and self-doubt about his authorial career. To Sanderson, Conrad suggested the novella was a turning point, saying plainly, "It seems to me that I must sink or swim with that story."[1] Critics have long recognized the tale as the first in Conrad's oeuvre to realize his inimitable vision, but the author himself was feeling some urgency prior to the text's publication about whether his new project would in fact find a readership. Would the tale establish him as a presence on the literary scene, as he so fervently desired? Or would it, as he wrote to Cunninghame Graham, provoke in an unthinking audience "an instinctive disgust"? Conrad worried, justifiably perhaps, that the late-Victorian reader would find the tale's subject matter offputting, its complex and thoroughly unreliable narrative impenetrable, and its lack of incident and heroics frustrating. He anticipated the worst: "So be it. In my mind I picture the book as a stone falling in the water. It's gone and not a trace shall remain."[2] The desire to be accepted and admired burns as strongly as the need to say something subtle and dangerous, though the last, as Conrad feared, might relegate the story to oblivion. He hoped for a popular readership and the

attention of contemporary literary critics; and as we know, the tale has
received considerable scholarly attention over the last 30 years. Yet what
we find even among scholarly readers is, first, a continuing perplexity
about narrative point of view, and second, a certain critical surrender ("an
instinctive disgust"?) with respect to Conrad's classist and racist attitudes,
whether through shame-faced apologies for the text or contemptuous dis-
missals of it. Though we have salvaged some of its traces, this stone of a
tale continues to lie at the bottom of the water.

Critics writing in the 50s like Albert Guerard and Marvin Mudrick
faulted the story for its gross violations of point of view,[3] but Ian Watt in
the late 70s rightly pointed out that, though "Conrad certainly flouts the
modern shibboleth, there seems no reason to accept this or any other literary technique as an eternal and universal prescription."[4] The novella's narrative voice, shifting between the first-person plural (the fallible, placed
perspective of the crew) and the third-person (limited) omniscient, creates
a great deal of narrative inconsistency. The first-person narrator also shifts
wildly, sometimes within the space of a single sentence, between the time
of action (the innocent viewpoint of the crew) and the time of narration
(the wizened perspective, based on hindsight after the voyage has been
completed). Moreover, the third-person narrator, essential to Conrad's
critique of first-person subjectivity, is not itself immune to subjective illusions, to oscillating in the generalizing passages, as Robert Foulke has indicated, "between the extremes of rhapsody and denunciation."[5] William
Bonney in the 80s argued that Conrad, given his intent to circumscribe the
reader's identification with first-person subjectivity, has no choice but to
grant the third-person narrator a greater degree of perceptual acuity, but
also that the unreliability of this voice is entirely consistent with Conrad's
belief in the limits of consciousness. Because one can never escape the
coordinates of cultural belief, the "subjective fabrication of meaning,"[6]
there can be no infallible authority. However, while Bonney provides an
apt description of unstable point of view, he does not connect these instabilities with the ideological and psychological content of the tale.

Both David Manicum and Marshall Alcorn have taken useful steps in
this direction. Manicum explains that the alternation between first and
third person is "a subtle mimesis" because it displays Conrad's "central thematic concern" with "the dichotomy of altruism and egotism,"[7] while
Alcorn further specifies Conrad's ethico-psychological sense of that same
dichotomy. Alcorn writes that the novella carefully distinguishes between
"empathy," which is seen as "a narcissistic seduction (and attraction)," and
"the self-sacrificing demands of duty," or "altruism."[8] However, both critics

neglect the basic insight of the earlier scholarship: the "mimesis" is inconsistent. We might in a rough and ready way see Conrad valorizing duty as voiced by the third person, and as condemning the egotism and "deluded" empathy of the first person, but the complicated cross-currents of the tale cannot be revealed through a rigid dichotomizing structure of interpretation. Further, the thematics, given by the two different narrative perspectives, are not just of an ethico-psychological nature, but also political and historically specific to late-Victorian England. That is, the tale is as much about power (and how it can be used either to create or undermine solidarity) as it is about narcissism and self-sacrifice.

Even as such efforts emerged to read the tale's problematic narration and psychological themes, they were largely pushed aside by ideological readings. Here dissection of Conrad's prejudices (particularly of classist and racist assumptions) has tended to eclipse all other critical considerations; and this has resulted in far too many flat, programmatic readings of what in literary terms could only be described as rough, uncertain, even confounding terrain. Watt, for example, is stymied when it comes to Conrad's racism, and offers us apologies instead of analysis. He assures us, for example, that the "irrational projection" of the collective fear of death onto the St. Kitt's negro, James Wait, is ultimately overcome because "the crew learns that, behind [Wait's] mysterious and menacing authority, there is only a common human predicament" (CN, p.106). Yet in his effort to uphold Conrad's humanist credentials, Watt fails to investigate the meaning of the crew's "irrational projection," or how it is tied to the thematics of duty and narcissistic identification.

Further, cultural criticism in the 70s and 80s often simply refused to consider the tale as anything more than a prolonged conservative-reactionary tirade. Eagleton and Jameson agree that the tale feeds off stereotypical class prejudices, and both dismiss it out of hand. Having learned the Marxist proprieties of reading Conrad, Lawrence Hawthorn in the 90s condemns the work as "a tediously reactionary tract" that relies not just on class stereotypes, but on racist ones as well. The gist of Hawthorn's discussion is located in his rather vacuous conclusion that, while Conrad seems preoccupied in the tale with describing the flat and misshapen physiognomy of "the nigger" (James Wait), his later works are, fortuitously enough, not as racist as this.[9] While we all agree that every text lends itself to a multitude of potentially interesting readings, one feels with this sort of criticism that the tale has been looked at or sorted, but that it remains largely unread.

Homi Bhabha's postcolonial theory provides an important corrective to some of these earlier Conradians. In contrast to critics who assume that stereotypes are just simplistic negative images, Bhabha realizes, to his credit, that stereotypes function as discursive and psychological strategies.[10] He is not locked into the positive/negative binaries. For him, a stereotype necessarily influences how subjects, both dominant and dominated, see themselves; and hence he understands that its psychological effects can be crucial to the exercise of power. I would submit that, while Bhabha's theory does not provide an adequate integration of psychoanalysis and ideology critique, his view of stereotyping at least suggests a more promising direction.

The Nigger of the "Narcissus" is a story about conflictual psychological needs and the social exercise of power. Understanding this story depends on understanding how it is problematically situated within late-nineteenth-century organicist ideology, and its different versions of "secular theodicy." Indeed, such organicist theodicies established a nexus of capitalism and racism that is crucial to unpacking the novella's unstable and double point of view, as well as its recourse to social projection. Organicist ideology sought to "naturalize" capitalist expansionism by cultivating the sense of obligation to uniform standards of duty. But Conrad, who was at once a proponent of duty and a critic of capitalism, stood both inside and outside of this discourse. As a result of his uneven espousal of organicist beliefs, the author not only split his narrative into the double perspective of third-person narrator (who is very much aligned with the fixed standards of authority) and first-person (the proletarian standpoint of the crew), but also depicted both authority and crew in remarkably self-contradictory ways. The novella's racism, which is located in the crew's projective identification with the black sailor James Wait, is as fitful and self-contradictory as the novella's allegiance to organicism. Through Wait, Conrad not only figures a social fantasy that manifests the "irrational" hatreds and wants of workers burdened by the depersonalizing pressures of bourgeois capitalism, but also exploits that same social fantasy for the more or less violent purposes of authority. Destabilization of narrative point of view is thus a function of two central elements: first, that of Conrad's need to rely on traditional structures of obligation, even while recognizing that capitalism has intensively and systematically co-opted these structures; and second, that of the ethico-psychological conflict between the equally insistent demands of communal service and the unfulfilled desires of individuals. (If Conrad condemns his workers for their narcissistic desires, he also knows that capitalism incites and aggravates such brutality and leaves many needs unfulfilled.) Thus, even at this level of general observation, it is perhaps clear that Conrad is neither here nor there when it comes to bourgeois and racist prejudices, that he is, in fact, both critical of and loyal to the dominant order.

In order to open up the text in these ways, this chapter begins with a detailed account of Conrad's view of organicism. The primary purpose is to describe the interaction between received ideology and psychological dynamics broadly manifested in the thematics of the text, and specifically demonstrated in the characters themselves. The second section tackles the tale's central ambiguity, namely, its racist projection, and develops the overdetermined psychosocial meanings given to Wait. In Conrad's view, society at the transitional moment of *The Nigger of the "Narcissus"* can neither go back to traditional structures and moralities nor forward to the creation of new solutions. This vision of the world as stuck, turning over on itself, generates the ambivalence and irresolution of the tale. The narrative thus demarcates a representational space of the in between, of neither this nor that. In chapter 2, I will attempt to connect Conrad's complex and often perplexing mimesis with paradigmatic features of his own psychology, focusing on both the conclusion to the tale and the preface.

The Search for Coherence: Paradox in Secular Theodicy, Organic Culture, and Ritual Refigurations of the Other

In order to describe Conrad's perspective on society and social identity, I want to situate his views with respect to those of his forebears (Carlyle and Eliot) and his contemporaries (Nietzsche, Weber, Durkheim), though not in an effort to trace influence or simply to establish similarities and differences. Though other scholars (particularly Watt) have also attempted to place Conrad definitively in the late nineteenth century, their efforts have proven partial, since influence and similarity, however subtly understood in terms of conscious structures of belief, have failed to examine Victorian discursive forms in terms of conflicts operating at half-conscious or unconscious levels. I will also explore how the whole texture of Conrad's mind reflects conflicts predicated on contradictions that could not be incorporated into any one ideological system. Conrad has been seen as reinforcing the organicist values of work and discipline (the ethics of conservative regulation) because these were for him strongholds against anarchic freedom/egotism;[11] but I do not believe a careful genealogy of organicism has been undertaken in order to see how Conrad fits, or fails to fit, into this ideological frame. Nor has anyone discussed how the tale depicts "work" in rigid yet brittle terms, or how its lack of a new politics butts up against

disillusioned representations of capital. In fact, Conrad's intellectual instabilities actually lead him toward a more subtle, and more weirdly self-
contradictory, position than has been generally recognized.

Probing the more philosophical implications of Conrad's belief in
work and duty, Watt has observed that Conrad possessed a "fairly conscious
dualism of attitude, a dualism in which, very roughly, ontology is opposed
to ethics" (CN, p.149). Separating moral belief (in God) from empirical evidence of divine indifference, Conrad, like other late Victorians, adopted
Carlyle's gospel of work—that is, Carlyle's stoicism and Hebraism[12]—but as
a form of willed fidelity, without the benefit of supernatural sanction (tran-
scendentalism). This typical response to the unprecedented technological
and ideological transformations of mid-nineteenth-century England privileged, as James Clifford has noted, "order and system over disorder and conflict."[13] Duty meant subordination of the self to the needs of one's fellow
human beings rather than subordination to the will of God. It also meant
realizing oneself through one's function within the organic order of the
social totality, according to the dictates of a patriarchal hegemony. And it
was the watchword of nineteenth-century "secular theodicy."

George Eliot addresses herself to "God, "immortality," and "duty" by
earnestly pronouncing "how inconceivable was the first, how unbelievable
was the second, and yet how peremptory and absolute the third."[14] For
Eliot, the "absolute" quality of duty was intimately connected to the notion
of society-as-organism. In a didactic essay that continues the themes of
Felix Holt, Eliot refers to society using the organic metaphor, and, of course,
derives from this a reconciliationist political message:

> But taking the world as it is—and this is one way we must take it when
> we want to find out how it can be improved—no society is made up
> of a single class: society stands before us like that wonderful piece of
> life the body, with all its various parts depending on one another, and
> with a terrible liability to get wrong because of that delicate depen-
> dence. . . . Now the only safe way by which society can be steadily
> improved and our worst evils reduced, is not by any attempt to do
> away with actually existing class distinctions and advantages, as if
> everybody could have the same sort of work, or lead the same sort of
> life (which no one of my hearers are stupid enough to suppose), but
> by the turning of Class Interests into Class Functions or duties.[15]

Eliot describes a secular theodicy, a social narrative that suggests a necessary relation between conformity to hierarchy and the teleological pro-

gressivism of natural law. She tells us that we glimpse the order of nature (the social body as a "wonderful piece of life") in the harmonious pursuit of "class functions" (as opposed to "class interests"), and that, in thus realizing our natural functions (as parts of the body "depending on one another"), society itself conforms to nature's order, its law of steady improvement. Organicism leads, as the historian of science Robert Young says, "to the reduction of social change to the uniform action of natural law."(*DM*, p. 194) On the one hand, Eliot belongs in the company of early Victorians, such as Carlyle, who made duty their religion; on the other hand, she anticipates late Victorians, such as Spencer and Spengler, who articulated a secular theodicy premised on the theme of evolutionary struggle. Both claims (absolute duty and society as a natural order) were operative, though unevenly so, during the period.

Organicism became integral to the British imperialist program. Throughout the nineteenth century, the notion of organic totality provided a reconciliationist political agenda; however, when Disraeli directed the British nation to become self-consciously "imperial," the ideology was elaborated as a naturalizing explanation for English superiority, a superiority gained through evolution. English cultural identity (white, male, upper-class) sat atop the evolutionary ladder, and it designated positions on the lower rungs for the working classes of England, as well as for other cultures under English influence or control. For example, the threat of workers hostile to capital was displaced in upper-class understanding by representations that equated the working class with the "evolutionary function" of manual labor. The valorization of archaic images of the wage earner—of peasant or of soldier-citizen—conveyed the message to the working class that their contribution to the national culture depended on exemplifying the virtues of the yeoman—that, in effect, such virtues were constitutive of the worker's "true" place in the evolutionary scheme.[16] A historical identity became an immutable one, or as arch-organicist F. H. Bradley put it, a "station" and a set of "duties" to be performed.[17] Such prescribed identity determined what evolutionary part had been played in the past by a person, class, or colony in the teleological creation of ideal Englishness, and hence delimited the conditions for partaking in or paying tribute to present glory.

Organicism is thus one of the indispensible forms of nineteenth-century bourgeois ideology, projecting, as Claude Lefort says, the illusion of "imaginary community." As a discourse it dissimulates actual social divisions, recasting them in the form of a totalizing intellectual dichotomy between "the subject," who speaks and whose mandate is established according to the rules of "Humanity" or "Science" or "Progress," and "the other" who either conforms to a prescribed position in the process of social evolution, or is denied visibility and membership for failing to conform. Moreover, there were several variations of organicist discourse—for example, anthropology (and folklore), the history of the English language, and Oxfordian ethics and the theory of the state (Bradley and Bosanquet)—that together gave shape to the scientific and moral rectitude of the nineteenth-century English bourgeoisie. However, as Lefort observes, an "intellectual hegemony" that commands only by unproveable assumptions of homogeneity, continuity, and essence, is implicitly vulnerable to ideas and social practices (such as those of capitalism itself) that reveal the socially contingent nature of this very appeal to immutability. In nineteenth-century bourgeois culture in general and English culture in particular, class antagonism (and other cultural tensions organicism sought to cover over) could not be entirely avoided; and in certain respects Conrad was the perplexed recipient of these discrepancies.

In contrast to secular theodicy as voiced by Eliot, and to the imperialist ideals and suppositions that followed from the effort to endow society with the binding power of transcendental sanctions, Conrad made work the only consolation (a sort of negative reward). He does not integrate willed fidelity to duty into a narrative about its larger, essential human and cosmological meaning. As we know from his private letters, and as we can infer from *The Nigger of the "Narcissus"*, Conrad had little patience with traditional theodicial aims. He clearly approached "the obstinate clamour of sages, demanding bliss and empty heaven"[18] with a large dose of agnostic suspicion, because he saw neither heavenly rewards nor social improvements being gained through human suffering. Several years before writing the tale, Conrad noted in a letter to his aunt, Marguerite Poradowska, that the doctrine of expiation through suffering was a "product of superior but savage minds" and "quite simply an infamous abomination when preached by civilized people. It is a doctrine that on [the] one hand leads straight to the inquisition and on the other discloses the possibilities of bargaining with the Almighty."[19] While Eliot could assimilate pain and suffering into the narrative of organic unity and higher harmony, Conrad's ethic had no absolute base. "Each act of life is final," he told his aunt, implying that existential finality cannot be the means to transcendent ends, whether divine or social.

Thus it is not surprising to find Conrad's "proto-existentialism" (Jameson's term) giving birth to an alternative vision that sees Nature as perfectly indifferent to humanity. In a letter written to his friend

Cunninghame Graham a few months after completing the novel, Conrad subverts the ideology of natural and social fulfillment through his own version of evolution: pessimistic naturalism. He offers Graham a powerful image, the "blind" knitting machine of fate, in explaining his materialist vision of human tragedy:

> It evolved itself (I am severely scientific) out of a chaos of scraps of iron and behold!—it knits. I am horrified at the horrible work and stand appalled. I feel it ought to embroider—but it goes on knitting. You come and say: "this is all right; it's only a question of the right kind of oil. Let us use this—for instance—celestial oil and the machine shall embroider a most beautiful design in purple and gold." Will it? Alas no. You cannot by any special lubrication make embroidery with a knitting machine. And the most withering thought is that the infamous thing has made itself; made itself without thought, without conscience, without foresight, without eyes, without heart. It is a tragic accident—and it has happened. You can't interfere with it. The last drop of bitterness is in the suspicion that you can't even smash it. In virtue of that truth one and immortal which lurks in the force that made it spring into existence it is what it is—and it is indestructible! . . . It knits us in and it knits us out. It has knitted time [sic] space, pain, death, corruption, despair and all the illusions—and nothing matters.[20]

Though this passage has often been cited in Conrad studies, it bears reconsideration in the context of organicist discourse. Descriptions of nature, history, and persons as parts in a great unthinking machine predates the organicist metaphor, of course, since their provenance is the sixteenth and seventeenth centuries when, with Galileo, Newton, and Descartes, "life went out of nature and physical imagery began to replace the imagery of the organism."[21] The metaphor of the machine, of dead blind physical movement, is at the very root of empiricism. Conrad is being more "severely scientific" than he slyly lets on, since empiricism has always been the best available means for critiquing teleology and its presupposition of directionality. But Conrad's mechanical view of process also betrays the weakness of this mode of explanation: without a narrative of development, it is difficult to establish what counts as an event, because the simple noting of inexorable regularities of occurrence cannot determine a beginning, middle, and end. Hence, Conrad describes process as essentially anarchical. Indeed, he uses the mechanical metaphor to express a nihilistic position, which simultaneously borrows its language from contemporary, scientistic socio-evolutionary thought (Social Darwinism) and subverts any idea of progress.

Conrad's vision of cosmic and organic process as blindly mechanical can be interpreted as a social metaphor not only because its vehicle is an industrial image (that of a "machine"), but also because the tenor is overdetermined by the late nineteenth century's common understanding of the origin of evolutionary theory. That is, Darwin could not have elaborated his ideas about natural selection without Malthus and English laissez-faire capitalism. Spengler, for one, thought that the work of Darwin and his sociologically minded followers was derived from "the application of economics to biology," observing that "it reeked of the atmosphere of the English factory."[22] Thus, implicit in Conrad's trope (as we shall see in the novel) is the idea that society runs by the same mechanical laws that drive nature, and that man is victimized by impersonal forces of domination that determine both nature and society, processes that are without beginning, middle, and end, and that are therefore meaningless.

Conrad's pessimistic naturalism is also strongly influenced by Schopenhauer's recognition of the illusory and ultimately meaningless nature of human existence. Like Schopenhauer, Conrad views consciousness as an auxiliary function of a deficient (natural) process: in place of the absent order of instinctual regulation, humanity is reduced to consciousness—what Nietzsche called the "weakest and most fallible organ."[23] Conrad puts it this way: "We can't return to nature, since we can't change our place in it. . . . there is only the consciousness of ourselves which drives us about a world that whether seen in a convex or a concave mirror is always but a vain and fleeting appearance."[24] "There is only consciousness of ourselves" (and of ourselves desiring), namely, the recognition of our own contingency. Thus, like Nietzsche, Conrad adjures us to give up hope of "metaphysical comfort," the idea of process made purposeful by ultimate ends. But unlike Nietzsche, Conrad's pessimistic naturalism does not lead him to a renewed sense of human potential, to a view of humanity as creating institutions that enhance human life. On the one hand, Conrad does not follow Schopenhauer's quietism; but on the other, he shrinks from the ultimate consequences of Nietzsche's nihilistic willing. If, for Conrad, there are logically speaking no valid criteria of right and wrong beyond the momentary requirements of the struggle, then the perception of contingency, the darkness itself, compels him to absolutize traditional loyalty.

Duty is a true belief, paradoxically as absolute for Conrad as for Carlyle or Eliot, and is so despite the fact that it cannot be justified by social or physical realities, nor by the ways of an indifferent or (as Conrad

often sees him) imbecilic creator. Thus, while Eliot reformulates and repairs
the cosmological net on the basis of ethical naturalism and elaborates a self-
consistent secular theodicy, Conrad produces a genuinely paradoxical secular theodicy that embraces fully neither nihilistic uncertainty nor a
reparative belief in essential truths. Duty is necessary to the maintenance of
the collective essence, but the ontotheological foundations for the absolute
nature of duty have definitively receded. Conrad defers the question of
ground or groundlessness, and makes the theology of traditional forms *both*
cultural context and fragment.

Conrad's nostalgia for an unthinking belonging to tradition is
uneasily represented in the figure of Singleton. He is the novella's
mythopoeic sailor, epitomizing those "voiceless men" who "scorn in their
hearts the sentimental voices that bewailed the hardness of their fate," and
who bear the devotions of seafaring as "the privilege of the chosen!" (*NN*,
p.15).When asked by Graham, the Scottish aristocrat and labor activist,
why he had not given Singleton "an education," Conrad responded:

> Would you seriously, of malice prepense cultivate in that unconscious
> man the power to think. Then he would become conscious—and
> much smaller—and very unhappy. Now he is simple and great like an
> elemental force. . . .Would you seriously wish to tell such a man:
> "Know thyself". Understand that thou art nothing, less than a shadow,
> more insignificant than a drop of water in the ocean, more fleeting
> than the illusion of a dream. Would you?[25]

If Singleton is noble, it is because he never questions authority and hierarchy. Here one might say that Conrad is guided by organicist ideology: not
only is Conrad's view elitist and conservative, but Singleton's dignity
derives from his being in essence an uncomplicated, unconscious manual
laborer. Yet Conrad's desire to spare Singleton awareness of his position
also derives from the belief that with consciousness comes pain and little
compensation for the loss of brute instinct. Conrad's sensitivity to human
suffering makes it difficult for him to imagine a weaker form of social devotion, such as that envisioned by Max Weber. Like Conrad, Weber was convinced that the contemporary significance of "vocation" could effectively
model itself after the Puritan sense of calling; but unlike Conrad, Weber
saw that worldly asceticism had to be a much more limited project. For
Weber, the individual's obedience and fidelity are given only under circumstances that are consciously interpreted as requiring this ethical commitment, and as such, only *individually* realizable.[26] Conrad's mistrust of

autonomy, which is based on his equating autonomy with consciousness of insignificance and suffering, causes him to rely that much more on community—that is, on a nostalgic idea of traditional wholism or "solidarity" that he cannot thoroughly critique.

But Conrad's faith in solidarity does not ease his disquietude. He recognizes that few will spontaneously work for the good of each and all, since modern institutions do not provide the individual with meaning or reward him fairly. In "Autocracy and War," for example, he deplores the fact that "democracy has pinned its faith on the supremacy of material interests," and that in the laissez-faire system, it is "the bizarre fate of humanity to produce for the benefit of a few employers." [27] Like Durkheim, the first to apply the solidarity doctrine to sociology, Conrad is very much aware that material relations of power and production do not satisfy our need to participate in just institutions; but, unlike Durkheim, Conrad does not call for a new social ethics. In his conclusion to *The Division of Labor*, Durkheim writes:

> The functions which have been disrupted in the course of the upheaval [of modern technological society] have not had time to adjust themselves to one another; the new way of life which has emerged so suddenly . . . has not been organized in a way that satisfies the need for justice in our hearts. If this is so, the remedy for evil is not to seek the revival of traditions and practices which, no longer corresponding to the present conditions of society, can live only an artificial and false life. What we must do is bring this anomie to an end. . . . In a word our first duty is to create a morality.[28]

Durkheim's view of alienation resulting from the division of labor implied, as Dominic La Capra says, "the necessity of basic structural reforms before solidarity could be created in modern society."(*ED*, p. 143) In contrast, Conrad does not go forward to advocate structural reforms and political justice. Instead he would prefer to withdraw into a defensive conservatism, returning to the traditions and practices that Durkheim regards as constituting an "artificial and false life."

Conrad's use of Singleton to recuperate tradition, in fact, resembles nothing so much as Carlyle's *Past and Present*, his literary reinvention of medieval moral coherence for a Victorian society for whom "religion is gone." Carlyle writes of the simple, unquestioning devotion of Abbot Sampson: "this comparative silence of Abbot Samson, as to his religion, [was] precisely the healthiest sign of him and of it. The Unconscious is alone complete.' "[29] Similarly, Conrad's eulogy for Singleton is a form of nostalgic redemption, a desire to recover a quasi-feudalism, because only the traditional order can endow Singleton's devotions with meaning. But for Conrad, more so than for Carlyle, this fantasy is utopian—it exists only in the no-place of a local, traditional community, which Conrad identifies with seafaring, even as he acknowledges (in the form of eulogy) that this way of life is passed and irrecoverable.

For example, Conrad's third-person narrator attempts to transform expressions of emptiness—silence, oblivion, muteness—into positive rhetorical values. As the narrator says of the ship's crew: "They must without pause justify their life to the eternal pity that commands toil to be hard and unceasing, from sunrise to sunset, from sunset to sunrise; till the weary succession of nights and days . . . is redeemed at last by the vast silence of pain and labour, by the dumb fear and the dumb courage of men obscure, forgetful, and enduring" (NN, p.55). Only because pain and labor are a vast silence and because fear and courage are dumb (and obscure men, in their endurance, forgetful) can Conrad's third-person narrator replace a traumatizing emptiness (the absence of ethical relatedness and the ontotheological ground) with archaic religious signifiers and suggest that these can actually persist with their original force. With this passage in particular, I think we can see Conrad striving to replicate Carlyle's "naked" religiosity. That is to say, he rediscovers in a fragmented way the moral viewpoint of Carlyle's later theism. This theism appeals to a "Calvinist taskmaster God" and insists that in the moral sphere not only is self-contemplation a diseased form of "self-seeking," but also that "unconsciousness" is evidence of "wholeness."("CA", p. 145) The difference (and this is decisive) is that Carlyle is possessed of (the hope for) an inarticulate faith that stretches beyond understanding and will, whereas Conrad's sailors are *kept* dumb and forgetful by the novel's ideological constraints in order to remain blind to their victimization.

Insofar as Carlyle tells us that society ought to go back, and Durkheim tells us that it must go forward, Conrad's rejoinder is that society can go neither forward nor back. Conrad's England, made coherent to itself by virtue of organicist ideology, is hopelessly constrained by the impossible project of finding a moral telos in capitalist regulation—a materialist pragmatics—that is intrinsically amoral. It is in light of the conditions of the modern world, which witholds the ethical construction of the social claim upon the individual, that Singleton's lack of reflectiveness becomes a social necessity, if not a metaphysical virtue. Only the ideology of duty can offset the fatalistic view that, in a mechanistic world, humans stand defenseless against an absolute loss of the social self.

Conrad's paradoxical narrative of grace-through-labor is above all else a disavowal of suffering that splits the discourse into two forms of knowledge about the world. His pessimistic naturalism is an attempt to confront a difficult reality, while his vision of secular grace simply replaces reality with an impossible wish. Thus, Singleton and Allistoun become metaphors for the text's central contradiction, its representation of work in terms of both salvation and emptiness.

On the one hand, Singleton is "like an elemental force" who, according to the terms of Conrad's secular theodicy, is an "oracle" and an "idol." On the other hand (and despite Conrad's extratextual comment to Cunninghame Graham that the old sailor is without consciousness), Singleton ostensibly sees like no one else into the dark of life's empty core. We are told: "he looked upon the immortal sea with the awakened and groping perception of its heartless might; . . . and he saw an immensity tormented and blind, moaning and furious, that claimed all the days of his tenacious life, and, when life was over, would claim the worn-out body of its slave" (*NN*, pp. 60–61). His devotion to duty saves the old sailor even as it wearies him literally to death.[30] Work redeems Singleton, since as the narrator says, "for many years he had heard himself called 'Old Singleton,' and had serenely accepted the qualification, taking it as a tribute of respect . . ." (p.60). When Singleton becomes simply "broken at last," the narrator ironically transforms the honor of age into a form of gilded impotence (p.60). Singleton as votary and priest of Conrad's ethic of labor intersects with Singleton as wretched sufferer who sees "thou art nothing, less than a shadow." He embodies Conrad's double vision: the self-canceling oppositions of secular grace and intellectual nihilism that threaten to render him incomprehensible. Singleton, who has lived "no more than forty months ashore" and who, when ashore, drinks himself into a state in which he cannot "distinguish daylight," *must be* forgetful of life apart from working the sea. In this he is symptomatic of larger patterns of reification. Though an icon of the great seafaring peasant, he is also a mindless moving part in the great knitting machine of the world, and hence alienated much like the "inexperienced, oafish" and transient fellows who sail with him. For Conrad thus to assert Singleton's unreflectiveness as a moral good over and above meditating on "the complicated and acrid savour of existence" (p.55) is to preserve a tenuous social order at the price of an obvious self-deception.[31]

As with his rendering of work and devotion to the craft of seafaring, Conrad's portrait of authority is presented doubly. On the one hand, Captain Allistoun is made to appear archetypally Olympian. By employing quasi-religious rhetoric, Conrad characterizes Allistoun in ways similar to

Singleton. Allistoun is an icon and an idol, "a stone image [that] shed a miraculous tear of compassion over the incertitudes of life and death" (*NN*, p.78). On the other hand, Allistoun becomes only a more elevated supporting player in the dominant order, beholden to it for the image of honor and responsibility he conveys, and dependent upon it for the shape and substance of his dreams. He is a bureaucrat, and his basic relation to the crew is that of an impersonal and efficient manager. "I am here," he says, "to drive this ship and keep every man-jack aboard of her up to the mark" (p.82). Allistoun sees his men as no more than tools, and wants them to have uncomplicated desires—to be, in short, subordinate functionaries and characterological copies of Allistoun himself. Focused primarily on efficient administration (and the administration of efficiency), Allistoun invests his hope of personal reward in an impoverished dream of public acclamation. His secret ambition is to "accomplish a brilliantly quick passage," thus advertising his personal worth through mention in the national papers.

Allistoun has little critical intelligence, and his few acts of kindness are both misguided and ultimately ineffectual. Reflecting with his first mate on the tangle of oppressed feelings that finally provokes the crew toward mutiny, feelings that he only dimly perceives, Allistoun is at a loss: "I suppose it's all right now. Can never tell tho', nowadays, with such a . . . Years ago—I was a young master then—one China voyage I had a mutiny; real mutiny, Baker. Different men, tho'. I knew what they wanted: they wanted to broach the cargo and get at the liquor. Very simple. . . ." (*NN*, p.84). The disparity between Allistoun's simplistic understanding and his elevated position as "ruler of that minute world, [who] seldom descended from the Olympian heights of his poop," and who seldom looked "below him" at "common mortals [leading] their busy and insignificant lives" (p.19), suggests how his mythic demeanor actually conceals a systemic discrepancy between merit and power, and how his lack of sympathy for the crew's real needs serves his merchant employers. As the crew learns, it is the integrity of the vessel and its cargo, not the lives of the men who sail the *Narcissus*, that matters most to Allistoun. During the storm, Allistoun refuses to cut the mast lines, even though cutting the lines is, or so the crew believes, the only way to save lives. " 'The Old Man wouldn't have it,' " we are told by one of the crew, " 'much he cares for us' " (p.49). Allistoun is both deity and bureaucrat, father and oppressor to his men. This is not simply an ironic juxtaposition, since irony would move the reader to see the narrative's critical intentions as uncomplicated and clear. But such a reading is disqualified by the third-person narrator, who time and again legitimates Allistoun. In Conrad's text, there is at once the wish to deify Allistoun and the reality of the captain's cold and narrow heart, and each view of Allistoun undercuts the other. Authority can no longer convey a unified image, grounded in the personal rule that characterizes patriarchal forms of administration, since the old values are being unevenly subsumed into exchange value, and authority itself is becoming a direct function of the market economy.

In these ways, then, Conrad expresses a fundamental and textually unconscious ambivalence toward the ideology of an organic social order under a free-market system. The alienating social structure prompts him to invoke the regressive fantasy of traditional community, for society seems to him neither to acknowledge nor to meet human desires for self-realization. We see this failure in Singleton's empty and broken condition. We also see it in the crew's vague feelings of oppression, their untutored neediness as expressed "in an interminable and conscientious analysis of their unappreciated worth," and in dreams of "the time when every lonely ship would travel over a serene sea, manned by a wealthy and well-fed crew of satisfied skippers" (*NN*, p.63). As Georg Lukács has said, consciousness is emptied of everything save greed for fame and possessions, when men themselves lose the possibility of finding satisfaction and of living out their personalities in their work.[32] Though the novel does not explicitly link the crew's embittered, covetous desires to capitalism, it does condemn such amoral individualism, which is the patent result of laissez-faire.

In an "organic" social regimen that determines the subject by the duties of its station, in this "imaginary community" that covers over hegemonic economic interests in a moral telos, the desolation and desire of those who serve cannot be alleviated or gratified, only fitfully managed or, to use Jameson's word, "contained." The individual can neither find himself in the factitious social order nor in asocial desire, which is its alienated mirror image. Instead of a regime of obedience from which self-realization might eventually (and unproblematically) be won, there is only a joyless instability that can never safely be lost.

According to one thoughtful reader of modernism, Perry Meisel, it is this type of figurative complex—that is, one identifying "codes in conflict"—that interrogates society and sends modernist texts "into a chaos of oscillating possibilities of meaning."[33] The critique implied by the semiotic doubleness of Conrad's tale, however, is much more a result of unselfconscious disorder within the text itself than an attempt to undermine social surfaces through an explicit understanding of their false unities. Even when read solely at the level of social understanding, the novella is perpetually at odds with itself. I argue that the textual discontinuities in the story strongly suggest a dialectic between psychological ambivalence and ideological contradiction (or "codes in conflict"), betokening British fears for their turn-of-the-century society.

In his collection of review articles entitled *In Peril of Change*, the liberal politician and widely read journalist Charles Masterman voiced the typical anxiety of the 1880s and 90s. He notes that beneath the surface tranquility, where "outwardly things seem settled and unchanged," England stood on "the verge of some vast disquietude, [and] our ears might well be deafened by the noise of the crash of elements, of *growing and dying* worlds" (my emphasis). Where Conrad envisions an England that can go neither forward nor back, Masterman equates impasse with anarchic change and decline. In fact the instability characteristic of impasse offends the principles of order and progress that continue to structure Masterman's worldview. Masterman observes that even while men attempt to confirm bourgeois industriousness and national greatness with "their minds turned toward other horizons: expansion 'beyond the skyline,'" nevertheless "the buoyancy of impetuous life" is steadily being eroded "by a poverty which it can *neither ameliorate nor destroy,* and an organized discontent which may yet prove the end of civilization" (my emphasis).³⁴ Here social goods represented by "expansion beyond the skyline" and "the buoyancy of impetuous life" are seen to be insidiously undermined by the lower-class sins of "poverty" and an "organized discontent." While Masterman acknowledges impasse ("neither ameliorate nor destroy"), his reflexive inclination to blame the lower classes betrays his inability to tolerate a clear view of the ineradicable destructiveness of industrial processes, and the uncertainties that follow from it. Masterman observes social decline from a position fixed by his belief in the Collective Ideal of the English Bourgeois Self as ruler and exemplar, whereas Conrad is encrypted in the problematics of impasse, and has no alternative to the ideological myths of organicism and teleology, stories that he neither believes nor disbelieves. What Conrad teaches us is that the "change" Masterman envisions—either progress toward the ideal or regress away from it—actually describes a conflict between the desire to incarnate an imperiled ideal and enslavement to its tenuousness, the possibility of its loss. What Masterman sees as decline is actually a type of repetition: an impasse reflective of social contradiction, and characterized by the inability either to relinquish the ideal of England as the apex of civilization, or make it true.

Middle-class entrepreneurs frightened everyone with fantasies of proletarian and native colonial rapacity and revenge, even as they themselves eroded or destroyed the traditional foundations of life by turning all corners of the globe into emerging markets.³⁵ In 1895, fearing the capacity of the urban working class to attack English security, Cecil Rhodes rearticulated the imperialist "solution" to England's pervasive anxiety. "If you want to avoid civil war, you must become imperialists."(Rhodes in "EPC", p. 46) If the solid citizens of the bourgeoisie could not bear looking into the very darkness their own entrepreneurial activity had created, then the mystifications of imperialism—this massive remythologization of culture according to rungs (or stations) of the evolutionary ladder—became almost inevitable. When faced with the disparity between fact and value, those operating within this teleological framework responded by asserting that the gap between the projected ideals of strength and rectitude and their achievement had to be closed. And thus it seemed, especially to those who had envisioned the world only in terms of absolutes, that a failure to maintain Britain at the top of the ladder of cultures would almost certainly result in its ruinous collapse.

The perceived incompatibility between English ideals and English practice led to a pattern of exaggerated, hostile, often dehumanizing striving, all in the interest of self-preservation. Discontinuity raises the specter of social disorganization, which generates anxiety, which is in turn defensively dampened by a projection outward of what is already inwardly dangerous. Yet there could be no successful resolution or even effective repression of the conflict. Imperialist expansion was a parochial contraction of the world, since the hierarchical view of the world re-assembled all classes and all peoples as but prior moments in the evolution of Englishness. The globe itself became a conjury of autotelic reflections. As Price Collier said, "England knows no world but England."(Collier in "EPC," p. 58) The conflict between England's desire for a seamless nationalistic dream and her enslavement to capitalist hegemony (as the means of realizing the dream) fueled the hostile ambition that defined English imperialist society's imaginary relation to the colonial or domestic "other." Colonial aggression was, in part, an expression of fear of domestic social disorganization. Discussing industrial processes in England and their relation to colonial rule, cultural historian Robert Colls observes: "The English state grandiloquently exported its fear in the form of power and reimported its power in the form of fear."("EPC," p. 47) Such anxiety took different forms. Eugenicist and fascist C. H. Pearson projected not the salvation of English superiority through an ever-expanding imperialism, but rather the inexorable destruction of the white man's delicate culture by yellow and black hordes, the proletariat of the world. Thus Pearson identified Englishness not with the ideal of national greatness but with its opposite.[36]

Pearson is but one example of the anxiety and urgency that characterized England's response to the inherent destructiveness of industrial society. Indeed, organicism was itself an ideological attempt to efface the ravages left in the wake of bourgeois progress with the atemporality of essences (as Lefort says). But it was the *interrelation* between social change and psychic self-preservation in late-Victorian England that underpinned and intensified the effort to freeze change and replace it with a static, taxonomizing system. As Cornelius Castoriadis explains, ideology cannot be fully understood without considering the desires of the individuals who support it, individuals whose personal identities are built on the social significances that define collective identity. A circle of interdependency therefore linked the out-of-time quality of ideology to defensive psychological repetition. Thus, the basic psychodynamic of late-Victorian England increasingly depended on the proposition that *our* goodness depends on *their* defectiveness or, in effect, the degenerate or atrophied traces of "our" evolution. The colonized other (internal or external) must serve as the projected and misrecognized image of England's vulnerability to its own destructive course, and England must protect the ideal of a wholistic world by making the other the only obstacle to its realization. Projecting their own insufficiency into an unraveling social world, those who defined themselves according to totalizing cultural ideas either became more vehemently chauvinistic, or lapsed into a self-serving fatalism. In either case, they saw themselves in the distorted and defensive reflection of ideology, and thereby continued to repeat and to defer their perception of the mass of workers and sufferers that they created, a vision of alterity they could "neither ameliorate nor destroy."

In *The Nigger of the "Narcissus"*, cultural impasse leads to just this sort of social projection. The problem of the factitious (but necessary) order's inability to avow its own desire is played out in relation to the reified image of the black man, James Wait. As the other par excellence, Wait is presented as the objectification of the crew's desires and anxieties, and as a container for the crew's defensive projection of hostile impulses. Wait thus becomes the instrument by which the crew preserves needed constituents of identity and self-regard. As we shall see, the crew's "imaginary" use of James Wait lies at the heart of the complex psychological life of the ship.

Conrad establishes the black man as an object in (and not of) desire. In other words, Wait's personal identity is unimportant (white men cannot see it) as long as he serves "the ship" by embodying the crew's desire and fending off their unconscious conflict. But in the tale, collective desire assumes a much more complex and primitive shape than any of England's social apologists could possibly have imagined. The crew's desire is limned in Conrad's tale by a potential for brutal egotism and a fear of absolute emptiness, and it is shaped by two contrary forces: the impossibility of finding self-realization and an unmoderated need to do so. Wait is an object, accessible to magical thinking, that allows the crew to cope with oppression, sickness, and death—with being used up and spat out by the modern industrial process of seafaring. During the first part of the text Wait is thought to sham illness, and during the second, when he is truly dying, to pretend health. Indeed, that Wait is experienced by the crew as both a figure of death and disavowal allows them to project and disclaim what they find most intolerable in their own lives.

The crew knows Wait only according to narcissistic fear and need, that is, as absolutely empty (degenerating toward death) and absolutely full (eternally vital, powerful). Conrad's depiction of the process of projective fantasy therefore relates to and is supported by two superficially opposed, but fundamentally complementary, social representations of the black other. These myths, which developed out of the teleological grid of organicist ideology, depict the other as both an attractive "exotic" and as a repulsive "ignoble savage"—as superhuman or inhuman, but never as human. Though seen as a member of the "lower race," Wait is credited by the crew "with mysterious demonical powers" that derive from their perception of him as a kind of shaman, a vestige of magical "primitive" life.[37] He is endowed with an inexplicable charisma and at the same time viewed as a degenerate wastrel, using his illness as a means of furthering his idleness. As Sandor Gilman explains, illness was a stereotypical sign of physical and moral degeneracy. It was also the central justification for slavery, one that continued to inform the background of late-Victorian preconceptions, precisely because blacks were thought to degenerate in a condition of full freedom.[38] Wait is not only reified and held captive by the crew's desires; he is made into a simulacrum of power, of a "fullness" that conceals prior emptiness as its most essential quality.

The crew transforms Wait into a ritualistic, even quasi-religious, fetish, and hence Wait becomes (as Derrida might put it) "the supplement" to Conrad's secular ethic of labor-as-grace. Like Singleton and Allistoun, Wait is an idol and an icon; unlike them, however, he is a "*black* idol, reclining stiffly under a blanket, [that] blinked its weary eyes and received our homage" (*NN*, p.64, my emphasis). Conrad's workers, rather than acting according to their ideological prescription as simple, emotionally inert drones, act out how organic society has insufficiently allowed for their complicated and potentially transgressive wants. They do so by building a cult of fantasy around Wait in order to acknowledge and serve needs that are nowhere else met by the social order. In this, Wait both supplements what is lacking in the original (and ostensibly) complete order, and also provides a counter to the original order. He is able to perform this quasi-religious and transgressive function because as other he is not regarded by the crew as a separate individual (an ego), but rather as their charismatic emissary or agent.[39] By conjoining Wait's refusal to work with his seemingly diabolical control over natural processes, including death, the crew seduces itself. Moreover, by the crew's having cast even their own mutiny in the language of charity—their "philanthropy" or their "sentimental" care for Wait in his illness—the novella transfers the quasi-religious signifiers of Victorian self-understanding to the crew's perception and use of Wait. At once a figure soliciting charity and bestowing immortality, a phantasmatic savior and a group pathogen, Wait functions to supplement the dominant order by becoming the figurehead for a dangerous cult or "religion."

Wait is thus a compromise formation between an untenable status quo and a subversive expression of desire. He is made necessary to the original order by serving the crew's desire; but because their asocial aggression and self-absorption threatens the ship's society, Wait can also be identified as the disease that plagues the *Narcissus*. As part of the projective logic of "organicism," where everything good is the ego's, and everything bad and evil is the alter's, Wait can also serve social "solidarity" by being cast as the scapegoat, as the racially defined, malignant member of the group-body who must be expelled for the good of the organic whole. On the one hand, the novella shows the pathogenic sentimentalism of the crew and condemns the basic dynamic of social projection. Yet still on the other, the tales shows that within its own terms, there is no escape for the crew from the dilemma posed by the need for meaningful service to the group, and the equally insistent need to rebel against and master a social order that robs them of meaning. The problem is refigured in the complicated process by which Wait is sacrificed. But this ritual offering reenacts the problem without working through it, and hence repetition only defers any meaningful awareness of these defining contradictions.

"A Wilderness of Babies": Psychosocial Dynamics Onboard the *Narcissus*

The preceding discussion of late-Victorian culture highlights how the gaps or discrepancies between the languages of cultural justification (revisionist organicism) and capitalist practice might evoke the social self's "need for

justice" (in the words of Durkheim). However, such gaps might just as easily lead to a type of "social madness" in which the subject fears the loss of
"the social body," and psychological defenses falsely reconstitute the sense
of power and protection that comes with belonging to what is "good" and
"whole." This proliferation of fantasy helps us to see that it isn't entirely the
case that ideology *constructs* the subject's "imaginary" relation to the social,
as Jameson would have it. Rather, the latent fantasy life or, in Castoriadis's
terms, the "unifying madness" of social individuals attempts to fill the gaps
that lie "in between" ideology and practice. In this respect, fantasy serves
to reconstitute an imperiled sense of "wholeness"; and while fantasy uses
the terms and patterns laid down by ideology, this is not to say that it is in
any simple sense *produced* by ideology.

I begin by examining how Conrad opens up or exploits the discrepancies and contradictions in British culture by revealing the structures of
fantasy that work to repair these holes in the social fabric. In the interest
of gaining some redress for their own afflictions, the crew uses Wait as a
fetish, an empty object that can be invested with different meanings at different moments, including their deepest anxieties and longings, or alternatively vacated of meaning, in order to defer living in historical time and in
capitalism's desacralized world. Moreover, the crew uses Wait to create an
alternative group identity, even though this "counter-culture," while mutinous and noisy, never seriously challenges Allistoun's authority. Wait-as-
fetish is a vehicle for enactment or repetition rather than for symbolic
mediation. He is the inanimate thing that, when ruthlessly used, substitutes
for and forecloses on what the psychoanalyst D. W. Winnicott calls "transitional experience." The crew in this respect simply appropriates the dominant order's terms of power-to-control and power-to-save, categories of
experience that, as lumpen-proletariat, they learned firsthand from their
masters. Their appropriation of Wait, offering as it does the benefits of
wearing the oppressor's boots, proves to be a useful but not transformative
instrumentalism—it salves the crew's dis-ease without ever becoming a politics. Finally, I want to argue that Conrad not only anatomizes the psychological life of the crew, but also shows how Allistoun keeps his power by
relying on the unconscious fantasies that Wait evokes. On the one hand,
Conrad opens up possibilities for an important critique of British culture;
but on the other, his sympathies lie with authority, and thus we see him
enacting the very structures of fantasy which he lays open to critical view.

The tale opens with Wait's enigmatic arrival. Though critics have
often located the metaphorical significance of Wait's name in its homonym
"weight," signifying, as the narrator says, "an unfair burden" (*NN*, p.99), this

is misleading insofar as it merely accedes to the racist commonplace that the negro is the white man's burden. Though the crew plainly perceives him in this way, his onerousness really follows from the role he is given— that of the target of projective identifications, by which he is both idealized and invested with the crew's own unacceptable malignancies and fears. This defense makes an "object" out of a process, that of being waylaid; and the literal significance of the verb "wait" is of course deferral or suspension.

The initial scene encodes Wait as delayed expression and explicitly connects him to the crew's unconscious thoughts. Wait is encountered almost immediately as a temporal deferral and a verbal absence: he has not reported for duty on time, and his name on the roster is "all a smudge" (*NN*, p.10). When he arrives it is as a voice: " 'Wait!' cried a deep, ringing voice" (p.10). Baker, the First Mate, is stymied by the audacity and ambiguity, and blurts out: "What's this? Who said 'Wait'? What . . ."(*NN*, p.10). From the first, Wait's name signals the dilatory, the gap in knowledge. Baker wants to know "who is talking?," "what is he saying?"; but he shifts rapidly from questions of information to questions about Wait's "meaning." " 'Ah! Your name is Wait. What of that? What do you want? What do you mean, coming shouting here?' " (p.10). By moving from fact to meaning, Baker initiates the interpretive process, but in such a way that the absent signified eludes determination yet continues to pose itself as the successively repeated signifier (Wait). Without telling the reader anything about Wait, Conrad deploys "Wait" to describe the structure and movement of psychic expression itself. He gives the signifying chain, where the signified is a nonpresence, a content that is and is not there; and as absent cause, the signified generates the differential replication of the subject's (Baker's) speech. Deferral thus initiates repetition, and this repetitive posing of questions produces an oblique but perfectly appropriate response from Wait. He says, " 'I belong to the ship' " (p.10). But this simple assertion affirms nothing simple. In effect, Wait is saying: "I am neither this nor that, but I belong to you." At the moment of his arrival, Wait is encoded as a collective object of ambiguity, which has neither individual existence nor univocal meaning. For, always at the point of arriving, Wait, the absent signified, never quite arrives and is always deferred.

Wait's name suggests stoppage of the temporal flux, and seems allied with what Kierkegaard called the stagnant "recurrence of our errors" as opposed to "recollection forwards," that is, the insightful acknowledgment of repetition as a source of despair from which a progressive maturity might be wrested. The kind of regressive repetition associated with Wait is also contrasted with Singleton's connection to natural cycles. The transposition of unthinking, natural existence to the human realm is, as Kierkegaard says, living life's "fractions without remainder," namely, without any room left over for unscheduled contemplation, which is the task of consciousness and freedom.[40] This is how the "elemental" Singleton lives, and the way sailors ought to live, according to the dictates of Conrad's theodicy—"he had never given a thought to his mortal self" (*NN*, p.60). Contrastingly, the novella connects Wait to the crew's despair of spiritual freedom, to the repetition in Wait of their own fears experienced as imposed malignity. The first-person narrator informs the reader that after the storm "we had died and had been resuscitated" (p.61); but later we are told that, in the confused current of the crew's impotent thoughts about Wait's obstinate nonrecognition and their own misrecognition of his death, "Jimmy bobbed upon the surface, compelling attention like a black buoy chained to the bottom of a muddy stream." Again, "Falsehood triumphed. . . . through doubt, through stupidity, through pity, through sentimentalism" (p.85). The crew repeats their need to believe in Wait and thereby exorcise their fears. In this image, figuration of the unconscious is insistent, with Wait bobbing on "the surface" of the crew members' collective awareness, because he is tethered to the "bottom" of their experience, which can go neither forward nor back. If consciousness is said to flow like a stream, then James Wait is the marker of the suspended "in between" around which the "confused currents of impotent thought" toil. Yet the choice Conrad offers the reader between Singleton and Wait is really no choice at all: the reader must choose between being unconscious in two different ways, neither of which is tenable for the thinking individual. Both, however, point to the psychosocial impasse delineated by the novella, which is foregrounded (in the comparison between Singleton and Wait) as the crew's inability either to return to a "life without remainder" or go forward through insight, beyond the stagnant "recurrence of our errors."

Singleton participates in an unthinking natural existence, and Wait is also aligned by the first- person narrator with nature, specifically with perilous changes in the weather. During the first half of the narrative, the confusion aroused in the crew by Wait's feigned illness coincides with the perplexing "fair monsoon" (a violent downpour coming out of sunlit skies). After Wait is rescued from the sea, he denies that he is becoming progressively weaker, yet his influence, as Bonney notes, is still confusing. Wait is now, according to Singleton, the cause of calm weather, of head winds, and a high barometer, all of which spell impending death for the crew. In the face of nature's dangers—the fair rain, the violent storm, and the deadly calm—the universe is perceived as conspiring with James Wait (*NN*, pp.

87–88). It is this projection of cosmological conspiracy that permits the first-person narrator to forget that Wait is merely human, and to align him through the power of his exotic blackness with "the immense and hazy ocean." The reader is told that Wait "seemed to hasten the retreat of departing light by his very presence; the setting sun dipped sharply, as though fleeing before our nigger; a black mist emanated from him; a subtle and dismal influence; a something cold and gloomy that floated out and settled on all the faces like a mourning veil" (p.21). As Bonney says, Wait "appears capable of extinguishing the sun as does the sea at sunset" (*TA*, p.166).

Wait is invested with the power of death precisely because he seems to suspend or defer it ("his presence" or power hastens the sun's retreat, yet Wait himself does not die). He is made to seem invulnerable by virtue of his "promise of speedy corruption" (of imminent death); and while the crew is made wretched by his power, it is a power they allow him to wield.[41]

> In his promise of speedy corruption he trampled on our self-respect;
> he demonstrated to us daily our want of moral courage; he tainted our
> lives. Had we been a miserable gang of wretched immortals, unhal-
> lowed alike by hope and fear, he could not have lorded it over us with
> a more pitiless assertion of his sublime privilege. (*NN*, p.29)

Though motivated by "hope" and "fear," the crew seems to openly indulge their fear of death so that they might secretly flirt with the hope for immortality—hence the paradoxical image of the crew as "a miserable gang of wretched immortals." Having externalized their own fear and frailty in Wait, in hopes of attaining the narcissistic fantasy of invulnerability, they are controlled by the wretchedness that returns from without in the form of Wait's "sublime privilege," making him master of the crew. Thus, they participate in Wait's presiding influence, or the power that is in fact the group's own. Wait is made a thing whose autonomy is but an illusion necessitated by his social function, which includes the crew's need to disavow those parts of themselves—their unmasterable fear of death, their grandiose conviction of privilege in relation to him—that they have given to Wait on loan. Podmore, the ship's cook, is exemplary of the crew in this respect. He makes it his mission to redeem Wait's black soul, but Podmore's ministrations only mask a murderous desire to dominate Wait and become himself godlike, with "the pride of possessed eternity, with the feeling of might" (*NN*, p.71).

Thus, the novella presents Wait as a double threat: the danger of being waylaid and the lure of the simulacrum. Indeed, if the crew is

condemned to the stagnant in-between of their recurring errors, it is
because they take Wait as a fetish, thus "taking some substitute for the
thing itself,"[42] and in the process disclaiming their own burden of "impotent
thought." This egress into fetishism depends on Wait being perceived not
just as the white man's burden but as his means of salvation, the reification
being produced by the myths of seductive power and degeneracy associated with the black other. On the one hand, for the crew Wait is an empty
thing for them to fill up. During his resurrection from the sea, Wait "emit-
ted no sound; he looked as ridiculously lamentable as a doll that had lost
half its sawdust" (*NN*, p.44); and during the second half of the voyage,
Belfast says, " 'I've put him to bed . . . an' he ain't no heavier than an *empty*
beef-cask' " (p. 81, my emphasis). But on the other, Wait is regarded by the
men as what psychoanalyst Roy Schafer has called "an autonomous happening."[43] That is, Wait is something that the crew believes it experiences
passively—for example, his having "lorded" death over them from a position of "sublime privilege." This action of the crew, this filling Wait up with
their autoerotic and asocial fantasies of omnipotence, but then experiencing him passively (as his being inhumanly "pitiless" with them), aptly
defines the paradoxical defense of projective identification. The projective
fantasy, or fetish, depends on the subject's unconscious ties to the other, for
it is by means of the other that the subject not only vicariously enjoys its
own pleasurable and willful fixations, but also disavows whatever it finds
unacceptable about those fixations. By remaining unconsciously tied to
Wait and thus actively impeding change, the crew can be seen as able to
resist, in Schafer's words, "the loss of secret gratifications" as well as exposure to its more dangerous thoughts (*NL*, p. 136).

Conradians have often discussed the crew's pity for Wait. Yet none,
at least to my knowledge, has tied the circular, projective relation of Wait's
"pitiless" regard for the crew to their sentimental "pity" for him, or has
shown how the late-Victorian discourse of "degeneracy" is at once implicated in Conrad's description of the crew's pity and complicated by their
projective identification with Wait. The reader is told that Wait "influenced the moral tone of [the crew's] world as though he had it in his power
to distribute honours, treasures, or pain; and he could give us nothing but
his contempt. It was immense; it seemed to grow larger, as his body day by
day shrank a little more, while we looked" (*NN*, p.86). We have already
been told that the crew's treatment of Wait is governed by their attributing
to him as his simplest meaning their own fear of death ("we lovingly called
him Jimmy, to conceal our hate of his accomplice")—that their affection
for him is in fact a reactive disavowal. Since the crew fears death and Wait

signifies it, they hate Wait without at the same time avowing the murderous wish to dominate. Thus, Wait's contempt is seen to grow in proportion to his proximity to death, and his power is felt to expand along with his contempt. The crew's complicity in this image of Wait follows the logic of a sadomasochistic projective identification. In other words, the crew's solution is to project onto Wait the feelings of hatred they cannot tolerate in themselves, perhaps in hopes that these feelings will die with him. During the interim they submit to the power of their own disavowed hatred and fear, for passive submission reinforces the subterfuge of their disavowal, makes pristine the assertion that murderous contempt is not theirs but Wait's, that they are not killers but victims. In this way, the crew's own will to dominate is disclaimed in favor of being dominated. Schafer describes the fantasy underlying such process as "the embodiment of one action that the analysand is disclaiming, as such action can neither be integrated nor rejected by him in a basic way" (*NL*, p. 70). The crew disclaims acting destructively toward Wait by both acting protectively (sentimentally pitying him) and endowing him with supernatural power. They are caught in the basic double-bind of being able neither to integrate nor reject their social aggression. As a result their disclaimed hatred of Wait becomes masochistic idealization, or idolization, of him.

The crew's false pity is part and parcel of this sadomasochistic economy. The reader is told that "Through him we were becoming highly humanized, tender, complex, excessively decadent: we understood the subtlety of his fear, sympathized with all his repulsions, shrinkings, evasions, delusions—as though we had been over-civilized, and rotten, and without any knowledge of the meaning of life" (*NN*, p.85). The crew identifies with Wait's "degeneracy"—they must become masochistically passive, soft, receptive—in order to feel they have the right to appropriate his life substance. The crew's ministrations are actually passive acts of appropriation: "[A]nd each, going out, seemed to leave behind a little of his own vitality, surrender some of his own strength, *renew the assurance of life*—the indestructible thing! " (p.91, my emphasis). Though degeneracy, as I have indicated, was used to establish the difference between the white subject and the black other, the novel demonstrates keenly how the interaction between projection and identification, expulsion and merger, other and self, is a relation of endless inversion (one into the other, other into the one) that asserts only a fantasied difference or separation. Difference is maintained in fantasy—Wait's inhumanity, the crew's excessive humanity—because both self and other act out the stereotypical positions of degeneracy. However, merger between self and other is actually reinforced when the crew

passively seduces Wait, identifying with his illness in a way that denies the
reality of his pain by exploiting it, and hence secretly renewing their assurance of life, "the indestructible thing," by means of Wait's own loss.

The masochistic idealization of Wait, a death-denying idealization,
is the outlet society provides the crew in the face of frustrating necessity.
Since the prescription of blind duty cannot hope to mollify the asocial
impulses of aggression and omnipotence that society itself promotes in the
crew, their devotion to Wait substitutes for authentic redress and remedy.
After the storm Wait is given his own cabin and becomes a religious leader:
"The little place, repainted white, had, in the night, the brilliance of a silver shrine where a black idol, reclining stiffly under a blanket, blinked its
weary eyes and received our homage" (NN, p.64). Though the narrator sees
through the crew's construction of the false totem by imagistically aligning
Wait's blackness with the light of a mendacious salvation, the crew's sense
of political and social oppression, as well as their disclaimed hatred toward
Wait as a psychological response to this oppression, is the basis for their
ritualized faith in him.

> We lied to him with gravity, with emotion, with unction, as if per-
> forming some moral trick with *a view to an eternal reward*. We made a
> chorus of affirmation to his wildest assertions, as though he had been
> *a millionaire, a politician, or a reformer*—and we a crowd of ambitious lub-
> bers. When we ventured to question his statements we did it after the
> manner of obsequious sychophants, to the end that his glory should
> be augmented by the flattery of our dissent. (NN, p.86, my emphasis)

Thus, Wait influences "the moral tone" of the crew's world, becomes the
fantasied donor of "honours" and "pain." This passage describes several key
elements of the tale: masochistic idealization, parody of traditionalism, and
the overdetermined conflict of religious and political meanings that is generated when religious devotion is confusedly observed as a means to gain
social ends. Conrad's crew does not know whether they are talking about
death or political power, eternal rewards or sublunary reforms. The crew's
disclaimed aggression against Wait places him in the position of the arbiter
of their fate: disavowing their own transgression, they nevertheless identify
with his. His illness becomes their political cause celebre; his refusal to
work or to die is the very image of their own desire. As long as Wait can
be what psychoanalyst André Green has called "the master of signification,"[44] he possesses power over first and last things, and therefore provides
a charismatic legitimation for the crew's struggle—the near-mutiny under-

taken in "weird servitude" to the black idol who seems to promise both heavenly and earthly rewards.

Born out of masochistic idolization, Wait's quasi-religious function reflects what Wilfred Bion, an analyst of group behavior, would call the descent from sublimated homoerotic connections between individuals in a group into dependency, or "the basic attitude of dependency"—a condition of relative subjugation to unmediated wishes for merger with the powerful other (the group leader). Bion also speculates about the odd phenomenon of reliance on the most ill member of the group: "perhaps it is an unconscious [belief] that the baby is . . . insane, and in the basic attitude of dependency it is [as] necessary to have someone who is dependent as to have someone on whom to depend."[45] The epithet ("insane baby") is appropriate when adults act like infants, or rather, like narcissistic monsters who engage everything in the world as an extension of their need. In the tale's context of dependency and merger, Wait is the "baby" who permits the crew to look after him like a parent, and also a parent-deity who encourages the crew to approach him in the manner of a needy infant. Projective identification allows for a pattern of increasingly rudimentary fantasies of merger on the part of the crew, and thus Wait permits such primitive desire by virtue of the role they have given him.

* * * * *

In Conrad's serial plot the middle-passage of the storm interrupts the Wait story of the first and later sections. Guerard argues that, with the storm sequence, the novel is primarily concerned with positively depicting the courageous and unified action of the crew, but that the positive story is then subverted with the negative Wait story, slowly changing bright heroism to a murkier shade with ever darker implications. By reading such a large dose of nobility into the storm sequence, Guerard effaces the troublesome ambiguity of the scene and fails to account sufficiently for the crew's enduring attachment to Wait and their palpable ambivalence throughout. He also marks a trail for later criticism to follow.[46]

As I read it, the storm sequence is not a story of virtue so much as a demonstration of the struggle to repress psychological conflict. There is a real psychological drama in the storm that belongs not to Singleton, who only endures, but to the rest of the crew. They suffer terror and perplexity at being suspended between the cold sea and an obligation to a fixed standard that makes them less than their cargo. The storm is in fact underwritten by a latent narrative about basic issues of integrity and loss, about the crew's deepest fears of self-fragmentation. Only by virtue of this trauma, which underlies the danger of the adventure narrative, is it possible to appreciate Conrad's emphatic stress on the radical discontinuity between the storm and Wait's resurrection—a discontinuity that is itself articulated as a massive repression. "[A]ll the first part of the voyage, the Indian Ocean on the other side of the Cape, all that was lost in a haze, like an ineradicable suspicion of some previous existence. It had ended—then there were blank hours: a livid blurr—and again we lived!" (NN, p.61). "A livid blurr" of "blank hours" suggests something inadmissible. Repression accompanies trauma, is levied against what is unbearable even in remembrance. Given this, the projection of psychic conflict onto Wait seems that much more inevitable. The crew carries forward a dialectic of ambivalence based on repression and projection, and Wait's role as receptacle becomes essential to keeping the dialectic alive. The storm sequence simply raises the stakes of eventual "resolution."

Bonney has observed that the storm sequence is rife with the vocabulary of both childbirth and mortality (TA, p.170). Wait's "rebirth" is likened to grave-robbing. As the men extricate the half-drowned Wait, trapped below the deck of the capsized ship, they totter "on the very brink of eternity . . . with concealing and absurd gestures, like a lot of drunken men embarrassed with a stolen corpse" (NN, p.44). In addition, the imagery (expressing dependency between Wait and the crew) increasingly blurs the distinction between parent and child. Wait is described not only as a new-born infant, but also as "a tortured woman" giving birth. "He screamed piercingly, without drawing a breath, like a tortured woman. . . . Every movement of the ship was pain . . . Then Jimmy . . . began again, distressingly loud, as if invigorated by the ghost of fear" (NN, p.41). Each of these figures—the first conflating Wait's birth with death, the second condensing the identities of birthing mother and newborn child—describes aspects of the crew's dependency on Wait. On the one hand, he is imaged as a just-born corpse stolen from the ground and concealed. It is a kind of nightmare image wherein Wait becomes the vessel for their fear of death. On the other hand, Wait is seen as both a helpless fetus and the mother giving it birth, as a figure of self-creation that embodies together the want of succor and the power to gratify. Wait's second meaning (self-creation, self-gratification, immortality) seems a response to the first (fear of death). The crew depends on him to contain both.

Of course, their fear is based on real circumstance; it comes from the sea's "avenging terror," as when "the wind flattened them against the rat-lines," pinning them "all up the shrouds, the whole crawling line, in attitudes of crucifixion" (NN, p.33–4). But the crew's response to this danger follows from the psychological patterns we see throughout the tale. These patterns are intensified during the storm and lead to a meltdown of sorts, a threat of "conscious exposure," as Schafer puts it, to "the loss or fragmentation of the self and . . . to narcissistic and persecutory fantasies."[47] Hence, awareness of imminent death or self-dissolution intensifies the already existing perception that Wait is at once an incarnation of loss (the living corpse) and a magical fetish with the power to save himself and others from the threat of self-absence (the mother). In their passion, oscillating between hatred of Jimmy and a wish to be one with him, the crew is like an infant unable to find a sustaining balance between connection and differentiation, between self-in-other and self apart.

Indeed, throughout the storm sequence the crew is represented in actions and descriptions that fit with patterns of conflict and quiescence associated with separation-individuation in early childhood. Psychoanalysis tells us that as the early self gradually accomplishes the task of becoming relatively autonomous, it also faces the developmentally related task of integrating two absolute and contradictory images of the object—the one all "good," untouched by constraint or scarcity of nourishment, the other all "bad," a source of loveless persecution. In the early stages, the child is not only possessed of these two opposed fantasies of maternal power, but keeps them apart in order to preserve the image of the "good" mother. This condition is then transformed by what Winnicott calls "the good enough" or the adequate involvement of caretakers. By means of this, the child gains the sense that those who meet its needs are simply human (neither all good, nor all bad), and hence is able to negotiate relationships without overlaying its perceptions of the world with the ambivalence of the primal maternal legacy.[48] When, however, separation from the (m)other is experienced as a loss of a vital part of the self, the subject continues to cling defensively to the object, has difficulty developing its own identity, and is impeded in its maturation toward genuine relatedness. As psychoanalyst W. R. D. Fairbairn says, the entanglement with the unempathic yet necessary parent leads to a conflict between "the regressive lure of identification [with the object] and the progressive urge to separate."[49] This conflict describes a psychic paralysis in which the subject is able to do neither one nor the other. When separation is felt to pose a threat to the basic survival of the self, it becomes difficult to transfer the emotional investment in the (m)other to a parallel investment in the self, leaving the psychologically separating self to struggle with an intolerable sense of insubstantiality. As Green says, "the lack of differentiation between self and object" leads to "the blurring of boundaries to the point of narcissistic fusion."[50] The failure to differentiate adequately stems from the subject's own disabled narcissism, from the fact that the self continues to project the omnipotent fantasy of the all-nurturing and all-depriving aspects of the early object onto the external world, and from the fact that severe self-depletion mobilizes the desire to partition off the unwanted elements from those that gratify. The defensive strategies used to ward off what has become a crisis in the creation of one's separateness are projection and splitting. Projection externalizes what is unwanted in the self; and splitting keeps contradictory ideas (about the self and others) apart, thereby separating good from bad, and positioning what is unwanted or disowned in such a way that it can be safely controlled, devalued, or persecuted. All infants similarly repudiate what is unwanted according to these defenses, since these strategies are basic to rudimentary mental organization; but a continued dominant tendency to control difficult feelings through projection and splitting reinforces developmental failure and the sense of a self always teetering on a steeple-point.

Before the storm, the crew's sick parent (Wait) asks for and is given paregoric, and we are told, "they sent him a big bottle; enough to poison a wilderness of babies" (*NN*, p. 28). Now, this is an odd description by any account, but in fact it is an unusually apt one when applied to the crew, who are "poisoned" by the narcotizing effects of passive dependency upon Wait. The crew members, in fact, are not only babes psychologically ill-equipped to confront the wilderness of the storm, but also behave like a "wilderness of babies" when confronting the "pitiless vastness" of the sea, upon whose mercy they have been thrown.

During the height of the storm, from the crew's perspective, the sea seems to take the form of "waves [which] foamed viciously, and the lee side of the deck disappeared under a hissing whiteness as of boiling milk" (*NN*, p.48). It is an "unnatural" maternal image hostile even to micro-organisms, the sea as Anti-Breast. Fantasies of dismemberment follow, as when the crew glimpses the shapes of their own mortality in the sway of their empty rain gear: "Hung-up suits of oilskin swung out and in, lively and disquieting like reckless ghosts of decapitated seamen dancing in a tempest" (p.33); and more menacingly, "Archie's big coat passed with out-spread arms, resembling a drowned seaman floating with his head under water" (p.36). Fantasies of nurture have been dashed and replaced by morbid inversions. Indifferent to human want, the sea appears persecutory and invasive, threatening the crew with decapitation like "a madman with an axe" (p.35). Their distress gradually reaches toward relief in nothingness: "several, motionless on their backs . . . [were] immobilised in a great craving for peace" (p.33). Fearful of the sea's intrusive, annihilating power, almost all of the crew members seem to lose their sense of human self-cohesion, as if they were wounded at the core. In the "hopeless struggle" they seem to themselves like sick animals, at once inhuman, "like vermin fleeing before a flood" (p.35), and insane, "we all spoke at once in thin babble; we had the aspects of invalids and the gestures of maniacs" (p.54). As the crew lapses into simple dread, poised at the breast of the bad mother, they do in fact take on the likeness of a wilderness of babies in a loveless world, terrified and beyond the reach of meaningful utterance.

Pilloried by the sea, haunted by regressive fantasies of dissolution and lethal fragmentation, the sailors frantically try to recoup themselves: "The longing to be done with it all gnawed their breasts, and the wish to do things well was a burning pain. They cursed their fate, contemned their life, and wasted their breath in deadly imprecations upon one another" (NN, p.57). The will to survive by doing things well exists side by side with the crew's regressive inclination to experience everything external, including one another, as vicious and anarchical. That for the crew differentiation between inner and outer conditions is always tenuous (particularly in times of crisis) is suggested when the narrator describes the stars overhead as "remote in the eternal calm," and glittering "hard and cold above the uproar of the earth . . . more pitiless than the eyes of a triumphant mob, and as unapproachable as the hearts of men" (p.47). It is a small but signature Conradian moment. The unreadable interiority of the human heart corresponds to the world as a place absolutely threatening and empty. And issuing from regressive feelings of maternal impingement and abandonment, from a pitiless invasion by that which is unapproachable, is an inner terror that finds its object in the night sky: familiar but far away, enveloping yet distant, omnipresent yet detached and untouchable.

The crew defuses its ambivalences by continually projecting outward one or another aspect of itself. Its members "do things well" only by keeping contra-valent wires (their need to retaliate or withdraw, their blind passion for duty) from crossing. Moreover, we find evidence at the height of the storm that the sense of the narrative is complicated by unintegrated, ambivalent representations of the mother, either as the omnipotent and destructive sea, or as the sea's co-conspirator, "mother" Wait, to whom the crew clearly attributes the elemental power of a natural force.

For it is at this desperate juncture that the crew "rescues" (or rather reunites with) Wait, their surrogate parent. As has been said, Wait is described in language more evocative of a woman undergoing a difficult childbirth than of a merchant sailor. In fact, Conrad gives an extended description of the crew's midwifery. They reach through a hole in the deck with their hands—"Groaning, we dug our fingers in, and very much hurt, shook our hands, scattering nails and drops of blood"—and then attempt to widen the opening with a crowbar. When Mother Wait becomes his own half-born child, it is a miracle of dumb helpless fear and the work of men, not the saving resurrection of an idol out of darkness:

> The ship, as if overcome with despair, wallowed lifelessly, and our heads swam with that unnatural motion. Belfast clamoured . . . "Knock! Jimmy darlint! . . . Knock! You bloody black beast! Knock!". . . [Belfast] struck time after time in the joint of planks. They cracked. Suddenly the crowbar went half-way in through a splintered oblong hole. It must have missed Jimmy's head by less than an inch. Archie withdrew it quickly, and that infamous nigger rushed at the hole, put his lips to it, and whispered "Help" in an almost extinct voice; he pressed his head to it, trying madly to get out through that opening one inch wide and three inches long. In our disturbed state we were absolutely paralyzed by his incredible action. It seemed impossible to drive him away. . . . [But] he disappeared suddenly, and we set to prising and tearing at the planks with the eagerness of men trying to get at a mortal enemy, and spurred by the desire to tear him limb from limb. . . . [Belfast] sobbed despairingly:—"How can I hold on to 'is blooming short wool?" . . . He came away in our hands as though somebody had let go his legs. With the same movement, without a pause, we swung him up. His breath whistled, he kicked our upturned faces, he grasped two pairs of arms above his head, and he squirmed up with such precipitation that he seemed positively to escape from our hands like a bladder full of gas. (NN, pp. 42–43)

Their primitive, contradictory connection to Wait can be measured in their willingness to risk all, both themselves and him, to pull him from the hole in the ship's hold. This is a double need, since the desire to rescue Wait is as strong as the desire to "tear him limb from limb." Each need seems equally driven by a wish to survive, as if it were inconceivable to be without Wait, and equally unbearable to be with him. But each need also carries with it a threat of annihilation, evoked by the situation of either savagely wounding themselves, or of dismembering him. If we recall that the passage begins with a coalescence of self and object, of Wait becoming his own child, then the contradictory desires expressed in moving toward and away from Wait at the same time become clearer. When wanting carries with it the seeds of catastrophe, then the ambivalence of wanting multiplies and contradictorily becomes paralyzing. And such paralysis power-fully suggests that the crew experiences itself and its predicament in terms familiar to a small child suspended in the circumambience of a bad parent.

Moreover, as with such a child, there is a blurring of the boundary-line between self and other and victim and abuser; an oscillation between projection (of disavowed qualities) and identification (with those same qualities, now viewed as outside the self). Wait is described as "a bladder of gas," as though the crew had "inflated" him with their own life-breath. They seem to give him life, just as they imagine getting life from him; they are helpless without him, just as he seems helpless without them; and they imagine tearing him apart, just as they imagine "the black beast," the "mor-tal enemy" turning on them. Helplessness, love, and aggression are always implicated in one another. To the extent that the crew is caught in the iden-tificatory aspect of their projective identification, losing Wait carries the psychological seed of their own erasure, and so they want to keep him from death—"[It] had become a personal matter between us and the sea" (NN, p.44)—for he is their Jimmy.

Thus, the account of the crew's reunion with Wait, interwoven as it is with Conrad's description of their adherence to duty, problematizes the idea of the storm sequence as a unified representation of positive solidarity. First, it shows that the crew is capable of working within the ship's struc-ture only if its members split off their underlying feelings of narcissistic helplessness, persecution, and hostility. Splitting requires an amputation of self, and hence cannot be equated with the idea of merely suppressing "ego-tism" in the interests of "altruism." Since the crew members are (or always have the potential to feel) insubstantial, the tenuousness of their self-cohesion renders solidarity tenuous as well. Second, it shows that the crew is addicted to illusion. They are unable to acknowledge the other as psy-chically differentiated from the self, and hence are potentially threatened by what Green calls "the horrors of emptiness," the unconscious fear that the "good" fantasies on which one depends will be turned inside out. Thus, they are neither here nor there, are stranded in a "negative in-between" of two equally impossible alternatives: that of withdrawing from what is feared and losing the possibility of goodness, or that of merging with what is depended on, only to risk the threat of annihilation (OPM, pp. 74–83). They are caught by their connection to Wait precisely because they are dependent on the very social order they experience as injurious. If "solidar-ity" means autonomous persons working together, agentic yet interdepen-dent, then the crew falls short. The tale reduces "solidarity" to a version of group action born of social necessity (extracting fraudulent coherence from a shared oppression), rather than seeing it in terms of balanced interdependence.

It might be argued that such a reading merely lends psychoanalytic language to a strategy of conservative regulation—in effect, to a dressed-up endorsement of Conrad's "reactionary" tirades. But it is hard to imagine Conrad representing the crew in terms of the "negative in-between" if he himself knew how to mediate the claims of the community and its individuals. What he deals with in the tale is a condition in which two equally valid desires—belonging to a meaningful collective, and having one's own needs met—are also made equally invalid or unmeaningful, and contradictory. To the extent that "solidarity" is achieved, it serves no purpose that Conrad can support ("it is the bizarre fate of humanity to produce for a few employers"); and to the extent that Conrad knowingly depicts the primitive incandesence of his crew, he must at the same time be repelled by their insistence that a place in the hive means following the contours of prescribed illusions. Thus, Conrad himself is in between two equally impossible alternatives, and "solidarity" in the tale becomes an artificial ideal that only masks the failure of politics to resolve its own contradictions. On the one hand, Conrad sees what psychoanalysis has also described: in bourgeois society, where rationalized transactions are typical, individuals have increased difficulty negotiating separation and creating the potential space where relative autonomy has a chance.[51] But on the other, he understands this difficulty from the position of a traditionalist, and hence is no more capable than his crew of moving forward to what Durkheim called a "new morality."

Hawthorn's observation that Conrad's depiction of the working class and of "the social and political contours of England" is "highly tendentious, partial, and (arguably) inaccurate" (*NI*, p. 70) is itself partial, and partly wrong. Either we should say that Conrad offers no criticism of narcissism in his society, or else take seriously Conrad's "partial" view, his *preoccupation* with the crew's fetishizing of Wait. If Conrad is to be faulted for working this out in terms of the lumpen proletariat (not even the working class), it should be acknowledged how complexly he brings to light the dynamics of what is at once a human failure to negotiate transitional experience, and a specifically late-Victorian imperialist form of that failure.

Winnicott describes a necessary stage in the development of human relatedness that requires the use of illusion in creating an "intermediate" experience of self and other. In the transitional realm, subject and object, self and other, fantasy and reality are held in playful suspension. As Jessica Benjamin says, here "the child can play and create as if the outside were as malleable as his own fantasy." This "intermediate" space eventually leads to the capacity to experience the other as real and as existing apart from the self, to structure things according to an either/or understanding, and to bracket that understanding in play. It is "a means of passage toward the awareness of otherness."[52] Others have elaborated on Winnicott's idea of the transitional to suggest that cultural productions—politics, ritual, art— can serve a similar transitional function for groups, since through them individuals might establish intersubjective balance, a sense of belonging to the larger culture, and of the culture belonging, in a somewhat malleable fashion, to the self. Along these lines, for example, Jane Flax writes about "processes of justice" as an "intermediate area" in which "relief can be found from the strains of our individual inner worlds and regulation from the outer world . . . of being simultaneously public and private, alone and related to others, desiring and interdependent."[53]

Within this context, the crew's failure, like that of the larger society to which they belong, entails their tendency to translate fantasy into some form of concrete enactment, their underdeveloped capacity for symboliz- ing fantasy as fantasy or, in effect, mediating between the world and our construction of it.[54] Without such mediation, illusion is insisted upon with utter seriousness. Just as the crew cannot experience Wait as someone who is at once constructed (imbued with subjective meaning) and discovered (pre-existing, separate), so organicist and imperialist constructions of the world view reality as an order of self-confirming representations, where the transformative dimension that comes with symbolization has been lost. And just as the crew uses their illusions about Wait to defend against "the horror of emptiness," so the larger culture is not only enslaved to the illu- sion/ideal of its own hegemonic identity, but is possessed by the fear that the many forms of otherness on which such hegemony depends might lead to its annihilation, its being turned inside out. The parallels are clear and Conrad shows them to us. However, though the dynamics of the crew's relation to the social order is dissected and laid bare, Conrad merely appro- priates his own critique so as to *uphold* the existing social order. Wait becomes in the last third of the tale what might be called an object of unconscious social exchange between crew and captain.

After the reconstitution of Wait as a religious symbol, Allistoun attempts to curtail "the foolish noise of turbulent mankind" (*NN*, p.77) by insisting on the primacy of duty.[55] Though the mutinous posturing of the crew (following Allistoun's command) seems motivated by a wish to regain control over the fetish and liberate themselves from the improvident father that Allistoun represents, it is impotent and disorganized from the start.

The question then becomes, Why does mutiny fail, and why is its failure inevitable?

Attacking that which is for the crew indispensible suggests either a need for catharsis (without an intention to see the action through), or a need for a certain self-appearance, or a nihilistic self-disregard. Allistoun's immediate inferior, Mr. Creighton, says, as the crew teeters on the brink of mutiny, " 'they have started a row *amongst themselves* now' "(*NN*, p.75, my emphasis)—which recalls the crew's anarchical response to the storm, when they "wasted their breath in deadly imprecations" against one another and beat each other with their fists. Now, "in the shadows of the fore rigging a dark mass stamped, eddied, advanced, retreated. . . . The elder seamen, bewildered and angry, growled their determination to go through with *something or other;* but the younger school of advanced thought exposed their and Jimmy's wrongs with *confused shouts, arguing amongst themselves* " (p.75, my emphasis). The desire to see Jimmy righted always devolves into chaotic hostility. The crew is never able to direct their hatred in a meaningful way at the appropriate object, and in their angry confusion are destined to devolve into greater isolation and dissolution. Their experience of relatedness (however minimal) and their self-coherence (however meager) are structured according to the very social order they experience as injurious. They are unable to change things because their rage threatens to destroy what they need. The crew ultimately serves the status quo by asserting their mutinous impulses and failing. Allistoun and the crew serve one another, since he assumes the burden of their repressed hatred toward Wait, and the mutiny demonstrates the futility of their rebellious feelings and the need for Allistoun's rule.

In this way, Conrad demonstrates to his readers the rightness of the captain's actions. The crew is left to make mutinous cries that in the end signify little beyond their ambivalent but irrevocable tie to a reifying social order. Their struggle with their confused feelings of oppression and dependency are always destined to slide back into ambiguity. As long as Wait is available as the signifier of unconscious exchange between Allistoun and his crew, rebellion will never happen, and mutiny is an illusion destined to serve as surely as Wait is destined to die. Having focused and brought to the forefront this underlying hostility of each against all, Wait can now be made the destination for all the impotent rage and feelings of victimage that have no redress except in displacement.[56] In the modern context there are no socially effective rituals for dealing with sacrificial crisis, and so Conrad invokes the myth of intolerable otherness to perform the duties of this older, culturally sanctioned form of catharsis.[57]

Singleton follows his master's lead by developing a new myth: "He said that Jimmy was the cause of the head winds. 'Mortally sick men'—he maintained—'linger till the first sight of land, and then die' " (NN, p.87). Singleton's fiction offers the belief that land draws life away from Wait. The crew has learned from Singleton to see itself as existing apart from Wait, and to believe that what happens to him will *not* happen to them. His death will be their life. Singleton, like Allistoun, reincorporates Wait into the novella's secular theodicy, thus transforming the human parchment (on which the crew could scrawl its secessionist impulses) into a document that serves secular authority. The exploitation of cosmology/salvation is accomplished under the cover of an old seaman's superstition, and thus Conrad's conservative irony prevents these "children" of the sea from ever growing up.

Death becomes the site of quasi-religious visitations and quiet communion: "Archie [Belfast] was silent generally, but often spent an hour or so talking to Jimmy quietly with an air of proprietorship. At any time of the day and often through the night some man could be seen sitting on Jimmy's box. In the evening, between six and eight, the cabin was crowded, and there was an interested group at the door. Every one stared at the nigger" (NN, p.86). When the dissembling obsequies are unconsciously connected with Singleton's myth, magical rite becomes absolutely efficacious. Even though rations are virtually exhausted during the last seven perilously calm days of the voyage, and "hunger lived on board" the Narcissus (p.88), no other crew member becomes sick or dies—only Wait, and he only "within sight of Flores' [Island]" (p.96). Then the wind picks up. Physical facts, inclusive of hunger, correspond once again (as during the storm) to regressive psychological need and anxiety. Though the third-person narrator, as well as the outsider Donkin, knows that Wait dies from tuberculosis, for the crew he dies magically and without their seeing. Given the dominant terms of the crew's psychodrama, tuberculosis as cause of death is almost beside the point.

The novella's covert logic dictates that the more experientially real cause of death is the group's unconscious wish to see him dead. The ambivalent need of all to use Wait as a fetish and sacrifice him as the embodiment of malignant aspects of themselves is facilitated by the two myths being invoked. His role as black other, inherently degenerate and given to illness, aligns him with death and distances him from the crew's self-definition. The myth of sick men dying in sight of land further removes responsibility for Wait's death from the society of the Narcissus, making his fate something magical and necessary rather than something willed.

In Conrad's tale, then, social context, which is not open to meaningful negotiation, and in which asocial personal emotions slit the cord of fellow feeling, interacts in a pathological dialectic, the resolution of which is
contingent upon a universally disavowed destructiveness. The return to
"order" is a simplistic reduction of complex lateral cultural relations—affiliation, communication, interactive conflict—to what is effectively a cruel
and distorted dyadic relationship: the predatory pack and its victim. As
Freud said, "hypnosis is a group of two."[58]

When Wait dies, unity is enforced in a ritual expulsion of the corpse.
Here we see the fragile artifice of the "solidarity" Conrad has reconstituted.
First Mate Baker reads the burial service. The words "rolled out to wander
without a home upon the heartless sea; and James Wait, silenced for ever,
lay uncritical and passive under the hoarse murmur of despair and hopes"
(NN, p.98). Wait is "silenced" and the ocean appears eager to swallow him:
"the whole vast semicircle of steely waters visible on that side seemed to
come up with a rush to the edge of the port, as if impatient to get at our
Jimmy" (p.98). Men and officers are together, the ship about to be "relieved
of its unfair burden." But then the narrator tells us "James Wait gave no sign
of going. In death and swathed up for all eternity, he yet seemed to cling
to the ship with the grip of an undying fear" (p.99). The men are together,
yet Wait still clings to the ship. That "clinging" seems to be Conrad's re-
evocation of how Jimmy has belonged to the crew and has had no meaning apart from what they have given him. For this "undying fear" of
separation, of persecution by loss and emptiness, is entirely theirs. A car-
penter's nail, like the nails that ripped the men's hands as they pried Wait
from dark captivity in the bulkhead, catches Wait's corpse on the inclined
plank, holding the body up against gravity and the hungry sea. Wait is held
on that pivot: the interminable instantiation of the crew's psychic deferral,
the precarious balancing point of "solidarity" that is suspended between
Conrad's knowing and not knowing that Wait is a ritual sacrifice. The swal-
lowing action of the sea is the repression of collective dependency on the
social other and psychic "bad" object. The crew's "despair" follows from its
inability to acknowledge and mourn loss, while its "hope" follows from this
same inability, expressed finally in its willingness to excrete James Wait
outside the body of human meaning, casting the persecutor (for now) into
the sea of the unconscious, where he leaves no mark.

CHAPTER TWO

Saved from Separation:
The Tale's Sentimental
Conclusion and the "Preface"

Conrad's "Preface" to *The Nigger of the "Narcissus"*, written in August of 1897 (more than six months after he finished the tale) is, as Watt says, "the most voluntary, single statement of Conrad's general approach to writing."[1] It is intended to be a declaration on the role of artistic creation in forging the bonds that make possible human community, emotional solidarity, and shared meaning. The "Preface" is also, I would argue, a psychological document, which in both its placement (written well after the novella was finished, but intended as a frame and guide to the story) and in its content traces many of the underlying psychological patterns at work in the tale itself. The "Preface" ramifies in aesthetic terms the tale's conclusion, which presents a highly sentimental image of community restored, as when the *Narcissus* returns to England, and the country itself is called the great "ship mother of fleets and nations!" (*NN*, p.101). The palpably sentimental qualities of the "Preface" (which prepares us to understand the narrative in a particular way) and of the novella's conclusion (which wants to lend a specific meaning to what comes before) create a false sense of continuity and containment, as if the contradictions and ambivalences that permeate the bulk of the narrative might somehow be resolved or expunged.

Conrad's effort to move past the sacrificial quality of Wait's death, and to find a secure anchorage in a nostalgic vision of community, is disturbed by images of the "soulless" modern world. The meaning of these images, like that of Wait, must be deferred.

When the *Narcissus* returns to home port, she is overtaken.

> Brick walls rose high above the water—soulless walls, staring through hundreds of windows as troubled and dull as the eyes of over-fed brutes. At their base monstrous iron cranes crouched, with chains hanging from their long necks, balancing cruel-looking hooks over the decks of lifeless ships. A noise of wheels rolling over stones, the thump of heavy things falling, the racket of feverish winches, the grinding of strained chains, floated on the air. . . . The *Narcissus* came gently into her berth; the shadows of soulless walls fell upon her . . . and a swarm of strange men, clambering up her sides, took possession of her in the name of the sordid earth. She had ceased to live. (*NN*, p.102)

It is important to remember that these machines of modernity are not only a destination, but also signify the world that launched the ship, its point of origin. As I have argued, it is in various forms of social mechanization, including relationships of rational exchange, that we find the distortions and disruptions of traditional social coherence foundational to Conrad's experience of the modern world. It has been the main business of the tale to trace the psychosocial conflicts and contradictions, anxieties and defenses, that at once constitute and follow from modernity. Though James Wait is made to embody ambivalence and contradiction, and though his ritual sacrifice seems designed to eliminate that incoherence and conflict, Conrad returns his crew to an England of vacant mechanism and lifeless commerce. The cost of the effort to reconstitute a unified sense of self and society (by scapegoating) has included the loss of vital aspects of desire that had to be handed over to Wait and then split off and made unconscious, a kind of emptying out of subjectivity rather than an integration of ambivalence. No sooner is order resecured than it is once again unsettled or made unsettling, for there is always the world's latent emptiness, the original danger. Conrad's vision of the industrial soulless-ness of mother England is the tale's psychosocial birthplace.

What Conrad configures in the tale, but cannot entirely acknowledge, is a dialectical relation between a psychic and a social emptiness: the crew members' loss of vital parts of identity through disavowal and projection, and the social machinery that compels them to defend against it.

Conrad's story is most real when he shows the crew knotted up by their own illusions and fears, repeatedly projecting this tangle onto James Wait. Hence, Conrad's attempt to frame the tale with a sentimental mythology of social coherence shows the extent to which he shares the crew's ambivalence, need to defer, and reliance on routine social fictions. "Sentimental lies," whether these are the tall tales the crew tells itself about their Jimmy or the contrivances of Conrad's own secular theodicy, only underscore the hollowness that follows when losses cannot be mourned, and when autonomous selfhood cannot be tolerated. This understanding of the novella's overall structure—conflict and contradiction held in suspension between the false sentimentality of the tale's conclusion and the mythology of emotional solidarity asserted by the "Preface"—suggests how Conrad was finally able to rebottle the genii of modernity. This structure, itself largely unconscious, motivated by both psychic and social tensions and contradictions, necessarily reframes how one reads the "voluntary" aesthetic claims of the "Preface," and, indeed, countermands any purely formalist approach to this document. I want therefore to explore the latent dimensions of Conrad's writing the tale's conclusion and "Preface" in the way he did, and to investigate the aesthetics of the "Preface" as reflective of psychosocial processes, rather than as removed from them and existing in a purely literary space.[2]

As Conrad was nearing the conclusion of his manuscript, he wrote to his early literary confidant Edward Garnett about the audaciously fragmentary character of its meaning: "As to lack of incident well—it's life. The incomplete joy, the incomplete sorrow, the incomplete rascality or heroism—the incomplete suffering. Events crowd and push and nothing happens."[3] Here Conrad anticipates his Victorian reviewers' criticisms, for some were indeed to complain, "there is no plot, no villainy, no heroism, and, apart from a storm and the death and burial, no incident."[4] Conrad seemed to know that his story was "about" the stagnant middle and that, as Frederick Karl says, Wait's malingering "accommodated" Conrad's own depressive and even morbid "indolence and reverie."[5] As Conrad neared the end of his seemingly interminable story, he again wrote to Garnett: "Nigger died on the 7th at 6 p.m.; but the ship is not home yet. Expected to arrive tonight and be paid off tomorrow. And the End! I can't eat.—I dream—nightmares—and scare my wife."[6]

Though Conrad never transcribes these dreams and nightmares, his fantasies following the completion of the writing convey a sense of loneliness and unreality, feelings that are also palpable in the story. Conrad writes to Cunninghame Graham, another of his inner circle, "Most of my life has been spent between sky and water and now I live so alone that often I fancy myself clinging stupidly to a derelict planet abandoned by its precious crew. Your voice is not a voice in the wilderness—it seems to come through the clean emptiness of space. If—under the circumstances—I hail back lustily I know You won't count it to me for a crime."[7] Conrad's personal psychic space (figured as a derelict and abandoned planet) seems devoid of objects of love. His fantasy does not include direct contact with his friend, but talks instead of trying to bridge the vast emptiness between them with his voice, a voice that only half believes in its own goodness. Surely this sense of solitude contributed to Conrad's night terrors and feelings of artistic impotence. During Conrad's period of enervation after completing the tale, when he was "seriously stalled,"(JC, 404–12) he wrote again to Garnett: "Yes—I see. *I am unreal* even when I try for reality, so when I don't try I must be exasperating. I feel like a man who can't move, in a dream. To move is vital—it's salvation—and I can't! . . . It's like being bewitched; it's like being in a cataleptic trance. You hear people weeping over you, making ready to bury you—and you can't give a sign of life!" (my emphasis).[8] Though Conrad here equates his inability to write with a kind of life in death, he also concedes at the start of the passage that he is "unreal even when [he] [tries] for reality"—that is, unreal even when he is able to write. Writing represents a compulsion, the pursuit of vitality and the promise of personal identity (almost as if he did not exist apart from writing, as if it conferred the hope of being). Conrad often talked about his writing as a form of action, where words take the place of deeds. Word-as-action fills space and does not tolerate the suspension of experience that Conrad equates with inertia and resourceless dependence.[9] Without words, Conrad doubts his existence. He begins to feel like his character James Wait, neither alive nor dead; and like his fictional crew, he is paralyzed. That this paralytic passivity was related to Conrad's sense of depressive isolation is further suggested by his expression of personal worthlessness ("You," he says to Garnett, are wasting time "upon my unworthy person"), and by the quotation's strong suggestion that people who ought to know that he is alive are ready to bury him. Despite Garnett's friendship, one senses that for Conrad there is really no one in whom he can put his trust.

Though the reader cannot know if the nightmares Conrad experienced as he neared the end of the tale were similar to the feelings of emptiness and anxiety that followed its completion, it is nevertheless apparent that Conrad felt the perils of "life"—the radical, repetitious incompletion of its being neither this nor that—in terms of a basic and enduring sense of narcissistic depletion. Conrad was certainly sensitive to the stagnant mid-

dle of his tale. Indeed, he recapitulates in his own life, in his inability to
write an ending, the anxious stasis of life in suspension. To conclude the
narrative on a note of triumph and sentimentality was to try, in part, to
resolve its terrible inertia. As to its triumph, Guerard finds Conrad attempting "to distance the reader from human perils either outward or inward and
sò confer on the crew, by association, some of the ship's glamour."[10] Doesn't
such "glamour," however, have an almost maudlin cast? And isn't such sentimentality conspicuously defensive and misplaced coming as it does at the
end of a novella in which the world has been presented as a brutal place of
impossible contradictions?

Conrad was himself extremely sentimental about his completed
work. After permitting a slightly larger circle of friends to look at the manuscript, Conrad referred to the praise that Helen Watson (the fiancée of his
junior colleague and fellow colonialist Ted Sanderson) lavished on the text.
"Those eight pages of Her writing are to me like a high assurance of *being
accepted, admitted within*, the people and the land of my choice. . . . I feel horribly sentimental—no joking matter this, at my age, when one should be
grave, correct, slightly cynical—and secretly bored. . . . I want to rush into
print whereby my sentimentalism, my incorrect attitude to life—all I wish
to hide in the wilds of Essex—shall be disclosed to the public gaze!"[11] What
Conrad wanted to expose to the public, then, was his sentimentality (certainly not his experience of narcissistic deficiency). It is perhaps significant
that Conrad finds gratification of his desire for acceptance in a woman's
praise. Helen Watson seems to redeem him as a writer, to affirm his "horrible" sentimentality, and to alleviate feelings of unreality and isolation that,
though fundamental to Conrad's character, are here directly associated with
his being an outsider. In the significance of Helen Watson's words, then,
Conrad finds a temporary relief from his ongoing struggle against what
seems to have been for him the consequences of separation: his depression
and his sense of insubstantiality. For through her he gains entrance to "the
people and land of [his] choice." And in the conclusion to the tale, we
should remember, Conrad is at his most rhapsodic when describing
"mother" country.

The third-person narrator's figuration of England as "a ship mother of
nations," and the first-person narrator's representation of Charlie and his
mother, typify the sentimental mystifications of Victorian popular culture,
or what William Veeder has called the "safely ordered unrealities" of "idealized situations and happy endings."[12] Concerning England, the omniscient
narrator says: "A great ship! For ages had the ocean battered in vain her
enduring sides; she was there when the world was vaster and darker, when

the sea was great and mysterious, and ready to surrender the prize of fame to audacious men. A ship mother of fleets and nations! The great flagship of the race; stronger than the storms! and anchored in the open sea" (*NN*, p.101). And with respect to Charlie, the first-person narrator (now individualized) says incomprehensibly: "over the untidy head of the blubbering woman [Charlie's mother] he gave me a humorous smile and a glance ironic, courageous, and profound, that seemed to put all my knowledge of life to shame" (p.106). This incredible bit of enthusiastic extravagance transforms Charlie, previously anonymous (except as Singleton's young admirer) and now representative of the crew as a whole, from a participant in a process of brutal dehumanization into the blessed, wise son of a devoted parent—an odd transformation indeed. The discrepancy between his role in the social process onboard the *Narcissus* and his embodiment of English pieties is altogether repressed.

For Guerard, positive rhetoric (including the less than admirable sentimental descriptions that he does not discuss) is a form of distancing that enables Conrad to end on a note of "magnificent courage and endurance," thus allowing for the interruption of the serialized narrative form (the negative Wait story followed by the positive storm sequence and back again). I would argue, however, that the assertion of sentimental virtues at the end of the tale in fact assures that repetition (the movement from brutality to bravery and back) is inevitable as long as fundamental contradictions must be repressed or obscured. The resolution of conflict is impossible, and the terms of conflict can only be reenacted endlessly. The situation of the narrative as a whole is analogous to that of Allistoun's decision to allow the crew to continue in delusional communion with Wait so as to safeguard the established order through scapegoating. For like Allistoun, both of Conrad's narrators identify themselves with the crew's mystification in order to rescue (narrative) order out of cultural disorder, and so to coerce unity by means of mythic delusions bearing the stamp of authority—in this case, with images of mothers.

This is not to say that everything in the conclusion is lacquered with sentiment. A passage bidding tacit farewell to the crew suggests the perdurability of the novella's essential pessimism:

> From afar I saw them discoursing. . . . And swaying about there on the white stones, surrounded by the hurry and clamour of men, they appeared to be creatures of another kind—lost, alone, forgetful, and doomed; they were like castaways, like reckless and joyous castaways, like mad castaways making merry in the storm and upon an insecure

ledge of a treacherous rock. The roar of the town resembled the roar
of topping breakers, merciless and strong, with a loud voice and cruel
purpose. (*NN*, p.107)

The passage is ambiguous in several important respects. First, it attempts to
distinguish between sailors—"creatures of another kind"—and other men;
but this distinction breaks down when the town is metaphorically equated
with the sea, and all men are effectively subject to "cruel purpose" (death).
It also recalls the theodicial notion that "unconsciousness" is the sailors' gift
of grace, permitting them to be unaware that they are "lost, alone, doomed,"
and therefore to be merry. Such forgetfulness is given here as a necessary
and conscious act concealing what is beyond the treacherous ledge, not as
an organic part of the seaman's life. The men are "forgetful and doomed";
their merry-making blinds them to what the passage focuses on: the loom-
ing fact of annihilation. But what Conrad struggles against (by emphasizing
his affection for his merry shipwrecks and their neglect of death) is the sense
of abandonment they represent by being life's "castaways"—discarded fragments of humanity, insupportably desolate and insecure. The narrative focus
on death as an abstraction, as an absolute existential fact and the ultimate
meaning of life, has a clear defensive function. When the anguish that
accompanies Conrad's sense that being separate means being isolated is displaced onto an abstraction, it can be dramatized and managed; and the narcissistic grandiosity that was diminished by such feelings of isolation is given
new life in the form of existential courage in the face of nothingness. The
existential abstraction is used to obscure the more immediate experiential
reality of loss, which courage steps in to replace, not to confront.

If Conrad appropriates the crew's courage and sentimentality, he no
less strongly identifies with their loneliness and their wish to stave off
dread. Indeed, only when faced with the anxieties of an unredeemable isolation ("lost, alone, doomed") are forgetful merry-making or sentimentality
presented as solutions. Thus, the passage ultimately reveals Conrad's
ambivalence toward the crew. On the one hand, they are "joyous" and
courageously "reckless" in their willful obliviousness to the merciless sea,
while on the other they epitomize the human fear of emptiness that makes
men "mad." In order for Conrad to salvage his heroic crew, it is necessary
to separate them from their "bad" nihilism by emphasizing their joyous and
forgetful courage, a defensive action that makes them creatures of another
kind. Since all men are in fact like the crew (subject to cruel purpose), the
effort to erase through splitting does not work. That is to say, it invites the
repetition of conflict rather than resolution.

Conrad's ambivalence about our shared existential uncertainties shows itself not only in how the crew members' inner perils are blotted out by the narrative's lapse into sentimentality, but also in his identification with this central mystification. As ever, ambivalence leads to splitting; and in this instance, we find one split-off dimension of the ambivalent wish in Conrad's use of the maternal image (the emblem of reunion that negates loss) as the insistent signifier of his own struggle to submerge the realities of loss, of endings. Thus, the narrative conclusion repeats the same sort of defendedness the crew demonstrates in their retrieval of Wait. For it is their Jimmy who carries the secret of maternal goodness from the sea; and it is the trauma of the storm, the anti-breast of the sea, that is forgotten. Splitting, in both cases, draws out the compulsion to repeat delusion. Or, in the terms provided by the conclusion, the return to good mothers—a reunion with the idealized promise of care that the individual life denies— is sought as a healing of the original separation. But it is a resolution that the tale cannot uphold except through sentimental deceit. Though the text implicitly critiques the crew's sentimental lie, it ultimately endorses this fantasy, thereby suggesting a global incapacity—on the part of the crew, the narrative as a whole, and Conrad himself—to tolerate separation, and hence relative autonomy.

The Nigger of the "Narcissus" is also a tale of fear chronicling the destabilization and (false) recovery of an indispensible community. Conrad's assumption of preindustrial unity, however, is deconstructed by the tale's narrative logic: the *Narcissus* is both "a society adrift,"[13] as Mark Conroy has called it, and a body of individuals caught in a pathological subculture. As Conrad knew from his own experience onboard ship, the exigencies of capitalism too easily erode the traditional underpinnings of community and self. In order to recoup these losses Conrad adopts, as the "Preface" tells us, the "unofficial sentimentalism" of Britain, and he does so in part to be accepted by the English public (a readership whose first member is Helen Watson). But as Conroy also observes, Conrad did not merely want to be accepted by a readership, but also to "found an audience"; and it was in the "Preface" that he outlined the terms of a "rapport with them that he felt constrained to fashion" (*MA*, p.87). Conroy is right, but also largely missing, I think, the psychological constraints that inform the "Preface."

Insofar as the rhetoric of the "Preface" is about establishing "rapport" with the reader, it reveals Conrad's attempt to use his writing as a transitional act (in the Winnicottian sense), to make imaginative play the means for establishing a sense of belonging to England and thus to prove the merit of his own artistic individuality. Through writing he wishes to be at once blissfully dissolved into the social body, and made distinct from it through the force of individual expression. But his sense of homelessness, of loss and estrangement, is perhaps as deep as that of any major literary modernist. For this reason it is the incompletion of Conrad's effort to establish human connection—his longing, and his privately felt incapacity—that comes through most searchingly in his tale. Though Conrad's novella continually raises the specter of the incommunicable isolation of individual lives and the voiceless indifference of larger worlds, it also continually revises itself. The sentimental conclusion, with its extravagant fiction of shared community, leads neatly back to the "Preface," where the tale's ambivalences are overwritten ahead of time by the assertion of a shared intuition, an emotional communion between author and reader. The difficulties of both reading and writing this tale are obscured by the assertion in the "Preface" of the human bond. Yet the need to render tolerable the fragility of human relationships only makes ambivalence that much more palpable, even before the tale's beginning.

The artist, says Conrad, "speaks . . . to the latent feeling of fellowship with all creation; and to the subtle but invincible conviction of solidarity that knits together the loneliness of innumerable hearts: to that solidarity in dreams, in joy, in sorrow, in aspirations, in illusions, in hope, in fear, which binds men to each other, which binds together all humanity—the dead to the living, and the living to the unborn."[14] But there is a problem here, a "knitting" altogether different from the machine of fate that knits us into life and into death without distinction, one from the other. Not only is shared temperament a precarious basis upon which to build a cultural community, it also completely ignores the fact that the feelings shared most by Conrad's characters are injury, hatred, ambition, and fear in one another's presence—expressions of the asocial potential of any polity.

Conrad invests in the "invincible conviction of solidarity" without having any real belief in cultural support for it, since the tale itself recounts the erosion and destruction of "solidarity"; and this investment, in turn, places an enormous burden on literature. It asks language, which becomes the iconic reflection and interpretation of a divided society, to substitute for the nurturing environment that is wished for, and to obscure the fact that it is not there. Conrad in part uses the mediating function of art to consolidate relations with his readers, but he also uses art to take the place of relatedness—and in doing so, he encourages us to entertain old fantasies of completion and reward. Julia Kristeva speaks to the problem, saying that "there is language instead of the good breast. Discourse is being substituted for maternal care."[15] In other words, the process of artistic creation (quite apart from content) functions as the good, social mother. Conrad would revise the (patriarchal) Burkean idea about tradition (that it ties "the dead to the living and the living to the unborn") to read that only the security of an *idealized* emotional relation ensures human continuity. In this way, patriarchal symbolism is overdetermined by a desire for the inviolate entwining associated with the maternal embrace.

Under what conditions might art be asked to substitute for human relationship? Green tells us that some people hobbled by the unmourned losses of separation "are characterized by a failure to create functional byproducts of the potential [transitional] space" (*OPM*, p.80). Which is to say, in part, that they are unable to become individuated selves who know how to connect successfully to the world around them. Keep in mind that symbolizing is not intrinsically transitional. Symbol-making can occur apart from processes of differentiation and the forging of connections with others. It can in fact serve to define a private, insular reality, to protect a wish or self-ideal, to refuse transitional play with either/or distinctions, or even to portray an attempt at failed connection. (Exemplary in this respect is the effort of someone caught between the need to protect the self and the wish to find comfort in association with others.) As Green also claims, "it can only be said that, from the point of view of the psychic apparatus of such individuals, transitional objects or phenomena have no functional value, as they do for other people" (*OPM*, p.80). I would argue that the use of the transitional object as a means for creating a real, fully present relationship with others may in fact have been impaired for Conrad, though his artistic *symbol-making* powers were exceedingly developed. Indeed, Green implies that the urgency of artistic creation may at times derive precisely from a failure to achieve the hoped-for result of symbolization in general: true relatedness.

The failure "to create functional byproducts of the potential space" leads to an instability of identity and difference in relationship. This explains, as I have said, not only the merger of Wait and the crew during the voyage, but also Conrad's own sense of existential-cum-artistic unreality. He communicated this in a letter to Garnett during his depressive episode, when he was overwhelmed by feelings of resourceless dependence. It also accounts for the central contradiction of the "Preface." We are led to think that the function of art is to establish communal solidarity and surmount atomization, but are then told that the means for doing so depend, as Conrad says, on *"an appeal* [that], to be effective, must be *an impression* conveyed through the senses. . . . And it is only through complete, *unswerving devotion* to the perfect blending of form and substance . . .

that an approach can be made to *plasticity, to colour;* and the light of magic suggestiveness may be brought to play for *an evanescent instant* over the commonplace surface of words . . ." (*P,* p.146, my emphasis). Impressionism, with its emphasis on vibrant and ephemeral materials, ironically underscores the disintegrative individualism which must be overcome.[16] But based as it is on self-depletion, Conrad's impressionism is a far cry from the Paterian solipsism to which the "Preface" alludes. The Paterian subject conveys a surfeit of self and seems the epitome of narcissistic plenitude. The Conradian subject, however, is left only with the stranded archipelagoes of a short-lived (though vital) psychic reality: impressions. By the light of his own epistemology, his tenuous sense of reality survives only momentarily in the creation of a linguistic image that, once made, is left to drift. As Conrad said in a letter to Garnett, "every image floats vaguely in a sea of doubt—and the doubt itself is lost in an unexpected universe of incertitudes."[17] Yet it is a triumph that an image should survive at all.

Because language stands in for a dependable sense of nourishing connection, a subject—though not a cohesive self—survives in the anxious world of its images, without being able to go back to the archaic mother or forward to full separation, realistic relations with others, and a stable sense of self. Combining solidity and flexibility in this way implies not only a capacity to assimilate and enter into conflict with paternal norms and values, but to modify them as well. (New political thought, as Jane Flax says, begins in the "intermediate area" of transitional social space.) The link in the "Preface" between Conrad's over-emphatic assertion of community and his quiet insistence on our tenuous individuality exists, perhaps, because Conrad implicitly eschews the idea of the reader as a wholly separate other with whom one negotiates understanding, and needs to imagine the reader as a reliable and supportive alter ego.

In his description of the artist's relation to both average and ideal readers, one sees Conrad's desire to make the reader an extension of himself. "His [the artist's] answer to those who, in the fullness of a wisdom which looks for immediate profit, demand specifically to be edified, consoled, amused; who demand to be promptly improved, or encouraged, or frightened, or shocked, or charmed, must run thus: My task which I am trying to achieve is, by the power of the written word, to make you hear, to make you feel—it is, before all, to make you *see!*" (*P,* pp. 146–47). Conrad's perception of the reader as demanding, self-involved, and even needy gives way to the vision of an ideal audience that is somehow made more receptive to the author's shaping perspective. The ideal execution of artistic vocation is realized by bending the reader into accord with the author's

vision ("to make you see"). Conrad plainly feared and needed his prospec-
tive readers, denigrating them even while making them coextensive with
himself. They are represented in terms of absolute polarities, either altogether alien by virtue of their neediness, or remade as continuous with the
artist's desire for perfect empathy. What he seems to have been unable to
do was negotiate an image of them that was realistic and tolerable at the
same time.

Conrad keenly felt his dilemma. Under Garnett's directive, Conrad
deleted a paragraph ("the personal part," as he said) in which doubts about
subjective integrity were expressed:

> But a preface—if anything—is spoken in perfect good faith, as one
> speaks to friends, and in the hope that the unprovoked confidence
> shall be treated with scrupulous fairness. And after all, everyone
> desires to be understood; We all with mutual indulgence give way to
> the pressing need of explaining ourselves—the politician, the
> prophet, the fool, the bricklayer they all do it; and if so then why not
> the writer of tales who is, as far as I know, no greater criminal than any
> of these. It is true that the disclosure of the aim otherwise than by the
> effective effort towards it is a confession of doubt and so far a confes-
> sion of weakness. Yet in the region of art such an avowal is not so fatal
> as it would be elsewhere. For in art alone of all the enterprises of men
> there is meaning in endeavor disassociated from success and merit—
> if any merit there be—is not wholly centred in achievement but may
> be faintly discerned in the aim.[18]

There is a double irony in this frank avowal of illegitimacy. The aesthetic
that should make "you see" has to be apologized for, first by the fact of a
preface itself, and second by a preface that explains that in art the (perfect) aim is more important than the (imperfect) achievement. Because of
his rather acute need to realize perfection and his wish to escape deep
feelings of inadequacy, Conrad is particularly driven by the disparity he
feels between the limitations of mature identity (including partial self-
achievement) and an ideal self, as well as between himself, a fallible and
weak creature, and the reader, the source of completion. This disparity
causes him to doubt the very images in which he places all his faith. For
him, there is something transgressive and false about his image world,
making the writer like a criminal in need of confession. Conrad doesn't
just assert "his failure to connect," as Conroy explains (MA, p. 87), but also
tells us how he must anxiously survive in the consciously acknowledged

counterfeit space of his writing. The confession of criminality reflects at
once a desire to circumvent the harshness of the reader's sentence (an
expression of Conrad's masochistic feeling that condemnation is the price
the subject pays for longing after impossible ideals), and the means of
holding open the possibility of reward. Though Conrad calls upon the
reader as an empathic friend, he can no more trust in the reader than in literary friends such as Garnett or Graham. Ultimately, the gap, the emptiness of the transitional space between subject and object is experienced as
more real than any relationship that might bridge it. The self and the other
are projected as equally bad. Both are criminals who can only find absolu-
tion in confession, and yet confession makes both of them isolated and
alien to one another.

Conrad's solution hinges on the cleansing properties of self-disclo-
sure. The idealization of his desire, which has the effect of making the
reader over into what the author most needs (a duplicate self), works to disarm the reader's dangerous otherness. In his "Preface" Conrad virtually
appropriates our alterity and defines us by the light of his own fear and
desire, and in a sense effectively sacrifices us to his greater need. Thus,
Conrad's effort to seduce the reader resembles how the crew "colonizes"
James Wait according to the sentimental lie; and in this the writer shows
himself influenced by the same psychic processes and misdirections he so
skillfully anatomizes in his fiction.

Sending his work out into the world engendered in Conrad feelings
of melancholia—a symbolic death that resonated with earlier experiences
of loss. Thus toward the end of the "Preface" Conrad offers up restitutive
images. The first is that of the field laborer, like "the workman of art": "If we
know he is trying to lift a stone, to dig a ditch, to uproot a stump, we look
with a more real interest at his efforts; we are disposed to condone the jar
of his agitation upon the restfulness of the landscape; and even, if in
a brotherly frame of mind, we may bring ourselves to forgive his failure" (P, pp. 147–48). Conrad adopts for himself the role of cultivator (the
culture-maker). In this he invokes traditional and shared cultural assumptions, as if to seduce the reader into leaning with him upon this conjured
image of commonality—an action that (in the deleted paragraph quoted
above) he guiltily recognizes as a sort of transgressive appeal. He also relies
on traditional patriarchal affiliations to mask his inability to insert himself
into the actual social order, a failure that forces him to take on himself the
task of creating culture as if it were a pure extension of himself. Yet this
metaphor is doomed "to failure" because he fully believes neither in the reli-
ability of the common ground nor in his ability to constitute culture from

the bottom up. The failure of both the subject and his readers, as well as
that of the external world, leads Conrad to produce a familiar image of
death: Atropos, the mother.

> To arrest, for the space of a breath, the hands busy about the work of
> the earth, and compel men entranced by the sight of distant goals to
> glance for a moment at *the surrounding vision of form and color* . . . such is
> the aim, difficult and evanescent, and reserved only for a very few to
> achieve. But sometimes, by the deserving and fortunate, even that task
> is accomplished. And when it is accomplished—behold! all the *truth* of
> life is there: a moment of vision, a sigh, a smile—*and the return to an eter-*
> *nal rest.* (*P,* p.148, my emphasis)

Though virtually every word of this passage is overdetermined by the
meanings already described, I want to focus on the implications of Conrad's
syntax and its relation to unconscious emotional significance. As Watt
observes, Conrad's referent slips, for "there is no wholly acceptable gram-
matical subject for 'the return.' " In the first sentence, says Watt, "the person spoken of is the reader." He further observes that "the referent of 'it is
accomplished' can only be the successful work," but that "by the time we
get to the middle of Conrad's [third] sentence . . . we are back to the reader
again, since he must be the recipient of the 'moment of vision.' " Yet Watt
concludes that this won't do, because "we do not expect to find the reader's
contact with the text to be 'lethal.' "[19] Such syntactic confusion is compounded by the fact that the implied agent capable of arresting "busy
hands" in the first sentence is either the work, the author, or both. These
referents are again implied by the "there" of the final sentence, since "the
task" must be accomplished by the author.

The slippage produces a logical inconsistency, but the underlying
motive for this overdetermination of referents seems clear: the return is a
reunion bringing together author, work, and reader that puts an end to all
affronts to authorial insecurity in the perfect rest of death. That is to say,
mortality is conceived as an illusory desire for rest, a wish to bring back the
original paradise of narcissistic fusion between subject and object, child
and mother. To this end, Conrad not only unconsciously uses the first sentence to erase the reader's own aspirations (his fascination by "the sight of
distant goals") but also to conflate the reader's experience of the world with
the work's capacity to produce that experience. The reader, in other words,
does not see the world until the work generates "the surrounding vision."
Perhaps this can be regarded as idealist metaphysics, an engineering of the

world according to the work (an artistic creation that is prior, natural, and translucent); but the moment is also a moment of narcissistic expansion for the author, unifying himself with his reader, as both are allowed to "see" the same thing. Thus the author captures his other, but only for an evanescent instant—unless, of course, the union can be transformed into "the truth of life" and preserved forever as death. Through this deathwish-as-lovesong, the author's desire to avoid separation is fulfilled, and death becomes not an end of desire, but a strategy for deferring loss. Conrad and his tale resonate together. Both assert organic harmony between the subject (the crew, the author) and the larger culture to which "solidarity" must be pledged, despite the fact that any hope of true solidarity is disqualified at every turn and in innumerable ways. Between hope and hopelessness lie the dynamics of deferral.

PART TWO

Tales Told in the Matrix of Imperialism:
Heart of Darkness *and* Lord Jim

CHAPTER THREE

Imperialist Nation and Self-Fashioning

In part one, I discussed Conrad's depiction of the dynamics of disavowal in *The Nigger of the "Narcissus"*, and emphasized that these dynamics are important for two reasons. First, Conrad dramatizes how individuals manage cultural losses in psychological ways, especially losses experienced in the context of modern relations of production. This argument about the centrality of "loss" to general patterns of psychological entanglement with social institutions (which in the broadest Weberian terms follow a trajectory from the traditional to the rational) is not meant as a pessimistic rejection of modernity, nor as a nostalgic reconstruction of tradition as a locus of stability and cohesion. Such reconstruction is certainly something to which Conrad aspires, but my interest lies with his armature—how he defends himself against cultural change, and why—and with how these defenses, and other related preoccupations, show themselves in the patterns both of his fiction and his life.[1] Second, Conrad's novella is complex and telling in part because, by at once enacting and interpreting the psychological misdirections and half-measures that are needed when incoherence threatens identity, it shows that the "lowest" entry on the ship's social ledger can be made a sacrificial vessel when, and only when, his jailers strictly follow the strategies of disavowal operating in the wider culture.

In *Heart of Darkness* and *Lord Jim*, Conrad's Marlovian narratives about the imperialist mindset, we are presented with contradiction and disavowal as shaped in the discourse and institutions of British imperialism. We must go back to Murray Krieger's *Visions of Extremity* (1960) to find a critical reading that considers the clear congruity of the novels. As he says, Marlow's "very presence and the similarity of his role" in both stories suggests "something in common between the two men he tries to save and fears to judge."[2] Krieger of course never addresses the impact on each text of imperialist ideology and society. The new wave of political interpretation, represented for example in the work of Terry Eagleton, Fredric Jameson, Patrick Brantlinger, and Edward Said, clearly takes account of the imperialist context. However, while these readers have explored how Marlow's positionality wavers between critique and mystification, they have not sufficiently explained the terms and reasons for such vacillation or adequately situated Conrad in relation to Marlow.

Perhaps Eagleton provides the classic statement on the purported "hypocrisy"[3] of the novels: "Conrad neither believes in the cultural superiority of the colonialist nations, nor rejects them outright. . . . [His] viewpoint disturbs imperialist assumptions to the precise degree that it reinforces them."[4] If we take this pathway of criticism, it becomes easy to conflate author and narrator, and then to dismiss the novels through reductive, monodimensional social readings. For example, Jameson ends by summarily dismissing a work like *Lord Jim*, which in his view is little more than "mere ideological distraction, a way of displacing the reader's attention from society and history," and which, in its plain use of the melodramatic elements of imperialist romance to manage social contradiction, has "forfeited its status as a literary text."[5] I agree that *Lord Jim* uses melodrama in this way (at least in part), but I am not at all sure that the blurring of generic categories (popular/high literature) is sufficient grounds for casting the text aside as mere "distraction." Though Jameson is right in part, what he does not see is the import of Conrad's critique, even in this "mystified" novel.

My effort to see Conrad's texts in the matrix of imperialism is in some ways indebted to Brantlinger's *Rule of Darkness*, which situates Conrad as the inheritor of the assumptions and vocabulary of nineteenth-century adventure fiction, including, of course, the work of Kipling and Haggard.[6] In this chapter I borrow certain of Brantlinger's formulations; and in the next, I will show how my interpretation of *Heart of Darkness* departs from his more Jamesonian reading. However, whereas Brantlinger's primary focus is on the conventional (racist) tropes of imperialist culture, my interest is in the dialectic between the social language of imperialism and subjective structures of desire that at once lean on, reinforce, and resist it.

In contrast to much of the fiction of Empire, Conrad's texts, at their most critical, reveal the imperial vision as a self-aggrandizing delusion, and disclose how discrepancies within the culture create subjective incoherence and fragmentation, as well as cultural or group pathology. *Heart of Darkness* and *Lord Jim* invite the reader to see Kurtz and Jim as representative pathological types—Kurtz the *reductio ad absurdum* of domination and control, and Jim the self-styled omnipotent rescuer and desperate martyr to a schoolboy code of honor. The quality of Kurtz's malignancy helps us to see exactly how Jim's illusions are destructive rather than visionary, while Jim's archaic self-idealizations (his wish to be the hero of his own adventure romance) provide an important analogue to Kurtz's primitive chaos. A question posed in *Lord Jim* suggests just how strongly both characters are following paths mapped in advance by grandiose imperialist expectations. "Is not mankind itself, pushing its blind way, driven by a dream of its greatness and its power upon the dark paths of excessive cruelty and excessive devotion?"[7] Kurtz follows the path of "excessive cruelty" and Jim that of "excessive devotion," but both are the damaged freight of the same social world.

Conrad is a critical ironist of the first order. As Said puts it in *Culture and Imperialism*, "Conrad's realization is that if . . . imperialism has monopolized the entire system of representation—which in the case of *Heart of Darkness* allowed it to speak for Africans as well as for Kurtz and the other adventurers, including Marlow and his audience—your self-consciousness as an outsider can allow you actively to comprehend how the machine works, given that you and it are fundamentally not in perfect synchrony or correspondence." However, in the end, Conrad is not able to sustain this active, critical comprehension. Why not? According to Said, Conrad allows the imperialist "system of representation" to speak for the cultural other: "Marlow [is a] creature of his own time and cannot take the next step, which would be to recognize that . . . a non-European 'darkness' was in fact a non-European world *resisting* imperialism . . . , and not, as Conrad reductively says, [reestablishing] the darkness."[8] Said's brief but incisive argument about *Heart of Darkness* points up the general limitations of purely discursive, ideological readings of Conrad's imperialist texts. First, when it comes to analyzing the blindnesses of the novels, there is a too-easy elision of the narrator and the "author-in-the-text" (note how "Marlow" becomes "Conrad" in the above quotation); and second, the discursive formation of imperialism, à la Foucault, has swallowed up immanent critical positions, in that Conrad, while seemingly aware of how "the machine works," almost involuntarily recapitulates the binarism (civilization/darkness) of racism. He cannot but do so. As a creature of his own time, he is already in the belly of the whale. The explanation both defers explanation and reifies history as controlling agency. I introduce these problems via Said because they centrally plague Jameson's and Pecora's developed treatments of the novels, which I will discuss later at some length.

My own notion of the "author-in-the text" is partly derived from Kaja Silverman, whose interpretation of authorial subjectivity is not limited to a consciously ordered and organized set of representations and beliefs, but includes the inscribed regularities of unconscious fantasy. In her discussion of Henry James (in her book *Male Subjectivity at the Margins*), Silverman foregrounds the idea of "the author 'inside' James's work," and employs terms from the psychoanalysts Laplanche and Pontalis—for example, the "structuring action" of paradigmatic fantasy, or the dramatic "scene of desire"— to describe the psychological aspects of authorship. This is not for Silverman simply a matter of psychological themes being treated by the author, but of a patterned unconscious from which, in part, we derive our sense of the "author" as such. Further, like Silverman, I construe authorial subjectivity in dialectical terms: the author "outside" the text is the site of desire that "in some sense 'gives rise' to the author 'inside' the text." However, "interrogation of authorship" begins with an interpretive reconstruction of the author "inside" the text, and this according to both conscious and unconscious representations.[9]

My purpose, then, is to provide a more satisfactory answer to the question of Marlow's ambiguous narration, and of Conrad's relation to it. My discussion proceeds by steps. In this chapter, I will try to show how imperialism is not just an ideological formation or practice of domination, but also a psychological matrix—indeed, a culture built around narcissistic fantasy and maintained through the weird logic of misdirection, denial, and disavowal. Establishing this fantasy dimension of culture as a context for Conrad's fiction will then allow me to develop two further claims: first, that Marlow's "critical" and "loyal" positions involve ambivalent emotional commitments, and hence cannot be understood exclusively in terms of ideological contradiction and mystification; and second, that while Conrad is in some respects not as positionally implicated as Marlow, he too is reliant on archaic structures of defense, and so cannot carry off an integrated critique of imperialism.

My reading of critique and complicity in *Heart of Darkness* and *Lord Jim* argues, then, that Marlow's ambiguous narration is both the dialectical medium *for* and the outcome *of* his psychosocial interactions with imperialist culture. Moreover, while authorial awareness and blindness are in some ways distinct from Marlow, Conrad in other ways plainly shares in the constellation of fantasies that influence how Marlow sees and what he tells. My understanding of Marlow in both texts is itself premised on two prior common sense relational assumptions. First, the individual's ongoing connection to social meaning is essential to the process of self-constitution and the experience of self-coherence; and second, even when social relations involve manifestly irrational contradictions, the need to affirm one's attachment to an existing world of meaning (which confers the possibility of personal identity) often supersedes rationality. When selfhood and ontological security depend on the survival of both poles of an irreconcilable contradiction, strategies of disavowal become intrinsic aspects of subjectivity. My understanding of Conrad's vexed relationship to Marlow follows from a third relational premise (consistent with the first two), which is this. A fully self-aware critique of imperialism would indicate that the author had found new terms for negotiating the capacity to be relatively autonomous, while remaining relatively connected to the shared world. This would mean that he had mourned his disillusioning recognition of the narcissistic fantasies and anxieties of imperialist culture, and also that he had used this insight to restructure his personal cultural ethos. Conrad, I believe, could not undertake this psychological process of separating from and re-envisioning his culture. He is certainly alienated from the social (in some ways, as Said says, "an outsider"), an alienation that is reflected in his Marlovian novels, as well as in certain contemporaneous letters. However, what these texts show most plainly is that Conrad is divided between harsh repudiation of society and acceptance of the "criminal" nature of its organizing symbolic. It is in this intricately ambivalent, often melancholy attitude toward his own culture that Conrad's distinction as a turn-of-the-century chronicler of modernity resides.[10] Thus we begin to see, from a psychosocial perspective, how Marlow can condemn the brutality of imperialism and yet collude with its ruling ideology, and how the author, at times a penetrating ironist, can follow Marlow into this collusive relation with imperialism without any apparent critical distance or perspective.

I begin my argument (which extends over this and the next two chapters) with an investigation of the imperialist context. My discussion of the matrix of imperialism foregrounds contradictions within social norms (for example, humanitarian virtue and racial superiority), and between social norms and economic practices (for example, social equity and exploitation)—discrepancies that, in turn, require a mystified ideological resolution. However, my discussion also emphasizes that such "resolution" encourages a splitting of self and others into good and evil, of the world into us and them, and structures social relationships according to narcissistic principles. My emphasis on the Western "subject" as strategically disconnected from the colonial "other" resonates with Franz Fanon's claim that

"the Negro is needed, but only if he is made palatable in a certain way,"
namely as a deficiency in "whiteness" and hence "goodness."[11] However,
Fanon's main purpose is to show how the consciousness of the colonized
deals with imposed distortions. In contrast, I want to investigate the specific historical ways in which the imperialist self is fashioned; how, for
example, idealization and grandiosity are implicated in cultural representations or are evoked by authoritarian social structures.

The narcissism of the colonizer helps to explain how and why he
uses mystified and self-referential representations. This claim, in turn, bears
some resemblance to the ideas of postcolonial theorist Gayatri Spivak—for
example, that the subaltern's "truth" is "always already" disfigured by the
Western observer, who enacts "epistemic violence" by interpreting the cultural other, but without having real access to this experience.[12] Of course I
agree with Spivak that European imperialist representations have historically violated native cultures, but I disagree with the epistemic (categorical) nature of her assertion. Her generalization obscures two facts. First, as
Bhabha observes, while imperialist representations have the power to
define and, in extreme cases of oppression, to define absolutely, that defi-
nitional power most often depends on the "active consent" of the subjects
on both sides of the cultural divide. And second, such consent or complicity is predicated on specific psychosocial investments in particular cultures.
Spivak risks lapsing into a categorical discourse that merely mimics, in
inverted form, the colonialists' attempts to erase the specificity, which is to
say the truth, of those they ruled.

It is important, I think, to pay attention to how colonial narcissism,
taking the form of hostility toward the other and idealization of the self,
was promoted by the late-Victorian discourse of race and the bourgeois
ideology and institutions of "education"—namely, the autocratic management of the native via the colonial practice of stewardship, and the "shaping" of the male child in the British public school. In late-Victorian
England, social structure (normative expectations) came to influence
shared psychological patterns, so that the institutions of imperialism were
buttressed by deeply unconscious aspects of individual English men and
women.

Theorizing the Psychosocial Matrix of Imperialism

From 1890 to 1910, "imperialist ideology," as historian James Sturgis says,
"established something close to hegemony" over social and cultural life in

Britain.[13] Both Conservatives and Liberals ensured the sovereignty of the imperial idea. Historian Michael Doyle has explained that such sentiments reached their peak from 1886 to 1906, when the Conservatives controlled the government, and even Liberals became imperialists.[14] The germ for the new expansion can be traced back to Disraeli, who in 1872 put this rhetorical question to the ruling classes of Britain: "Will [you] be a great country, an imperial country, a country where your sons when they rise, rise to prominent positions, and obtain not merely the esteem of your countrymen but command the respect of the world?"[15] By century's end, the glamor of Empire seemed to have hardened into a necessity. In 1893, when Britain was experiencing its own industrial decline and heightened global competition, the "liberal imperialist" Lord Rosebery drew attention to the fact that Britain must stake its imperial claim or be surpassed by Germany and the United States. "Countries must be developed by ourselves or some other nation."[16] As Chris Bongie observes, Britain experienced the distinctly modern consciousness of the world's finitude, an awareness which justified in part the "scramble" for territory not yet annexed by a rival Western power (*EM*, p. 18). Its economic interests and social cohesion (both at home and abroad) seemed to depend on a permanent Empire.[17] The ideology was meant to solidify status quo social arrangements at a problematic time in Britain's history; but as we will see, the so-called new imperialism was itself deeply problematic.

In his effort to describe a general imperialist ideology, Brantlinger enumerates a comprehensive, if unsurprising, list of elements that, as he says, "may appear separately or in varying combinations, with various degrees of intensity." His list includes: territorial expansion by military force; chauvinism based on loyalty to the existing empire; glorification of the military and of war; the racial superiority of white Europeans; and the "civilizing mission" of Britain, the greatest nation in history (*RD*, pp. 7–8). Though I generally agree with Brantlinger's categories, I believe all these elements articulate two basic virtues—aristo-military virtues, i.e., "manliness"; and the enlightened character of British rule, i.e., the justice and morality of the British political system, which legitimated its position as first in the world and sanctioned its right to "civilize" the globe. These virtues, however, stand in implicit contradiction to one another. How could a modern nation like Britain be despotic as well as just?

Among historians who have ruminated on this central conflict in British colonialism, Eric Hobsbawm perhaps gives the best description of it: "Within the metropoles . . . the politics of democratic electorism were destined to prevail," but "within the colonial empire, autocracy ruled"—an

84 WRITING IN BETWEEN

autocracy "based on the combination of physical coercion and passive submission to a superiority so great as to appear unchallengeable."(E, p. 82)
Imperial and local interests, sanctioned government and liberty, had
become contradictory values.[18] Such contradictions entailed further discrepancies between norms, as well as discrepancies between norms and
economics: social expectations ran in the opposite directions of aristocratic
and democratic values; and the plain fact of exploitation violated the norms
(by accepted British standards) of *any* good government.

These incendiary contradictions might have been resolved in a couple of ways. First, Britishers could have forced the issue, exerting the power
of national institutions on imperialist methods abroad to make them conform to accepted ethical and democratic principles. This probably would
have led much more quickly to the historical conflicts of decolonization.
In the late nineteenth century, only a step or two was taken in the direction of curbing the worst excesses of autocracy, by means of the "benevolent paternalism" of colonial stewardship and the convention of indirect
rule. What was "new" about the new British imperialism, apart from the
highly intensified scramble for territory (especially in Africa), was that it
was guided by the ideology of a more enlightened (as opposed to an
unabashedly despotic) form of paternalism. Indeed, the British Empire was
relatively humane as compared to the colonial rule of other European
states, such as Germany.[19] Nonetheless British rule did not mean the
democratization of colonial power. Were it loathe to relinquish the autocratic edge, then Britain might have pursued the alternative course of a
consistently ruthless domination, thereby affirming the principles of leadership and the cultural mythologies appropriate to tyranny.[20] Either
course—whether relinquishment of the colonies or frank exploitation—
would have been more unequivocal and self-coherent than British confusion about condoning contradictory ideals and policies, and the defensive
ignorance that allowed people to look the other way as colonial practices
trampled on the ethical foundations of British self-definition.

Habermas has remarked that bourgeois democracies often "require
supplementation by a political culture that screens participatory behavioral
expectations out of bourgeois ideologies and replaces them with authoritarian patterns remaining from pre-bourgeois traditions."[21] His point is well
taken, for it begins to explain how certain colonial practices could affect
social life within Britain itself. In assuming, however, that "authoritarian
patterns" are unproblematically accepted by a democracy, Habermas has
left himself no way of explaining the sometimes tumultuous resistances
generated by the contradictions of bourgeois society, or the fact that vir-

tually all societies experience culturally specific contradictions of their own.

Political theorist William Connolly takes a somewhat different tack from Habermas. "Every culture seems to contain some themes that are both indispensible to it and inherently problematic within it. The pressure of their indispensibility works to conceal their problematic character."[22] Connolly's dialectic between discrepant themes and their indispensibility invites us to think about both the unique and the problematic character of British colonialism. And while Connolly does not say so, the very fact that something problematic can at least in part be experienced as such, also generates the possibility of social critique. Indeed, some of the central contradictions and strategies of concealment were understood in late-Victorian Britain, even though the indispensibility of imperialism (and its contradictions) was not subverted. Connolly therefore allows us to see that differences between cultures can be vast, and that even as the themes and conflicts vary, so too can the shifting pressure of their necessity, not to mention the ideological and psychic strategies by which the problematic is disguised and deferred. Cultural difference is measured by the depth of existing contradictions, the extent to which opposing elements must each be preserved in some form, and the economic, political, and normative factors that predispose a culture to negotiate its own kinds of solutions. Britain was in the broadest sense *like* other imperialist nations, but quite distinctive in how specific social factors were interarticulated.

In the following pages, I want to outline a general view of British imperialist ideology and practice, which brings into relief some of its central contradictions (discrepancies between norms, and between norms and economics). I will do so by looking at three of its interrelated and problematic structures: benevolent paternalism, racial myths and hierarchies, and education (both as a model of power and as an institution). Each of these structures is examined in ways consistent with the principles of group and individual psychology. There are important differences in British approaches to the "development" of its various "dependents." However, there are also important (albeit implicit) similarities between the paternalistic management of cultural others and the "colonization" of the English working classes, and between colonial paternalism and the "cultivation" of boy children in the ruling-class institution of the public school.

This discussion is generally guided by the ideas of Lefort and Castoriadis, specifically by Lefort's view that much of nineteenth-century ideology is pedagogically motivated, and by Castoriadis's claim that there is a mutually informing relationship between social identity and psychological dynamics. Lefort tells us that nineteenth-century ideological discourse is based significantly on the pedagogical model of power, in which the distinction is enforced between the subject, who establishes himself with his articulation of the rule, and the other, who, not having access to the rule, does not have the status of subject. This distinction between rule-articulators (who have the status of subjects) and rule follow- ers (who do not) applies to the relation between the colonialist and the col- onized and, with some qualification, to that between the "masters" (educators, fathers, group leaders) of the ruling classes and their own male children, or between upper-class and working-class men. By casting the discussion in Lefort's terms, I hope to clarify the profoundly interactive relation between colonial and domestic conventions and contradictions— something that, incidently, was not lost on late-Victorian critics. Further, by following Castoriadis and bringing the psychological into play, I want to claim that the lived culture of imperialism and the cultural practice of lit- erature unavoidably "leaned on" the unconscious, that there is a cycle of mutual influence between the social significations of imperialist society and the constitution of the psyche.

Colonial "Estates Management": Paternal Trusteeship

In the notion of paternal stewardship (trusteeship) over the colonies, the British seemingly found a way to make their own economic needs congru- ent with their ethical sense of themselves. Paternalism was part of the dis- course at mid-century, but the notion had not yet become that of *benevolent* responsibility. Charles Kingsley wrote in 1853 that "a moral duty lies on any nation, who can produce far more than sufficient for its own wants to supply the wants of others with its surplus. . . . Each people should develop the capabilities of their own country or make room for those who can develop them"(Kingsley in *BIC*, 106). Kingsley's emphasis is clearly on obligations owed by the colonized to the colonizer; but as the century wore on, the British would also stress their "moral duty" to "the subject races." As historian Andrew Roberts says, a benevolent paternal mandate meant that Britain took charge "of territories whose peoples were not yet able to stand by themselves under the strenuous conditions of the modern world," and that Britain must protect "the well-being" and guide "the devel- opment" of such peoples as "a sacred trust of civilization."[23] British historian John Seely noted in the last quarter of the century that enlightened state intervention would "purify" the excesses of colonial opportunism generally, and even, perhaps, self-government to colonial peoples. Liberal politicians such as Joseph Chamberlain also praised the role of paternalistic colonialism, identifying it with "estates management."[24]

There is considerable slippage in this turn-of-the-century imperialist representation of the civilizing mission, however. On the one hand, colonial paternalism was understood as disinterested service and responsibility to the people who had been brought under its control; on the other, the British found ample justification in the idea of paternalism for "managing" the countries of those who were unable to turn them to account, and for "developing" the people of those countries as best suited imperialist policy. Benevolent stewardship was partly violated by, but partly congruent with, the autocratic forms of control that were actually being exercised. As historian Philip Darby has observed about British India, "increasingly towards the end of the nineteenth century, there was a tendency for British rule . . . to become more [and not less] authoritarian."[25] Chamberlain's phrase "estates management" is both ironic and apt. It undermines the enlightened rule it promises by recalling in the word "estates" both the lands of the aristocracy and the divisions of European monarchical rule, namely, the estates of the *ancien régime*.

Given this discrepancy between the paternalistic representation of colonial politics and their actuality, it is not surprising that the new imperialism would come under attack, most trenchantly perhaps by J. A. Hobson. In Hobson's view, this form of imperialism is inevitably autocratic because both colonial administration and British state policy serve the economic interests of the British ruling classes. While Hobson did not condemn any and all European interference in native cultures, he keenly saw that the new Imperialism "has established no single colony endowed with self-government"; it stands on "militarism," and it violates democracy at home, since "the public policy, the public purse, and the public force" are all used "to extend the field of [upper-class] private investments and improve their existing investments."[26]

In contrast to Hobson's close analysis of the contradiction between the rhetoric of benevolent paternalism and the facts of despotism and exploitation is Kipling's promotion of Empire on the basis of exactly the same self-canceling oppositions. Kipling's "The First Sailor" is an astonishingly unselfconscious myth of imperialist ethical purity. The narrator tells the sons of Albion: "You'll win the world without anyone caring how you did it; you'll keep the world without anyone seeing how you did it. But neither you nor your sons will get anything out of that job except four gifts— one for the sea, one for the wind, one for the sun, and one for the ship that

carries you."[27] The insistent question that this tale asks us to explain is how
one can participate in world domination and all that this entails, and nevertheless believe that nothing is gotten out of the job, except for the cultivation of manly virtues and pride in responsible service undertaken strictly
for its own sake. Is this innocence, hypocrisy, or something else?

Orwell, for example, excuses Kipling in part on the basis of naivete.
He writes that Kipling did not "seem to realize" that "an Empire is primarily a money-making concern."[28] But in order for this explanation to satisfy,
we need to look at the extent of Kipling's knowledge of imperialist economics; and on this point Kipling was anything but naive. He knew very
well that great sums were made—indeed, how could this close friend of
Cecil Rhodes not have realized this plain truth? In his travelogue *From Sea
to Sea*, Kipling writes about entrepreneurs such as Rhodes. "In this land God
first put gold and tin, after these the Englishman who floats the companies.
. . . That means mining rights; and that means a few thousand coolies and
a settled administration . . . where the heads of the mines are responsible
Kings."[29] As Kipling indicates, concession owners were the de facto autocrats of the colonies. (The new imperialism was an effort to reform such
opportunism, though during the "scramble" private companies continued
the work of expansion). Further, Kipling knew not only that men like
Rhodes were despots, but that the administration of India was autocratic
(something that Britain had no interest in reforming); and he sanctioned
this brand of monarchy and exploitation.

Kipling was hardly naive about the political and economic facts of
colonialism. And given the perfect seriousness with which he approaches
some of the central ideological mystifications of Empire, he cannot be
viewed as a hypocrite, since on some level he needs to believe in, and is not
entirely conscious of, the illusory status of these justifications. Once again,
how does one explain this contradiction between what Kipling knows and
what he seems not to know? How is it possible for him to know and not
know at once? Hobson observed this central problematic of the imperialist
mind, and explained it according to what he called "psychic departmentalism." "The genius of inconsistency, of hiding ideas or feelings in the mind
in water tight compartments is perhaps peculiarly British. It is, I repeat, not
hypocrisy: a consciousness of inconsistency would spoil the play: it is a
condition of this conduct that it should be unconscious. For such consis-
tency has its uses. Much of the brutality and injustice involved in
Imperialism would be impossible without this inconsistency" (*IM*, pp.
222–23). "Psychic departmentalism" is not of course "peculiarly British,"
but it is a significant defensive strategy that psychoanalysis understands as

splitting—the capacity to inhabit contradiction by bringing into view one aspect of the conflictual object relation and then the other, but without making connection between them. They exist as islands that can only be visited separately, each lying safely beyond the view of the other.

Splitting is, as Hobson says, an effort to defend against colonial injustices. But such a strategy is, I would argue, also a means of preserving an unconflicted or coherent sense of self when one is compelled to condone brutal policies that violate ethical self-definition. Through Kipling's example, we begin to understand the interaction between social contradiction and individual unconscious motivation—how the social, in Castoriadis's words, "leans on" certain patterns of unconscious response, which are then reinforced by social practice. There is a powerful cycle of mutual influence between the two, which is all the more powerful for being hard to see.

The Politics and Dynamics of Race

Appeals to the idea of "a lower race" that requires stewardship—"improvement and elevation"—did not pave the way for self-government for the colonized, but rather became the basis for perdurable regulation. This is described by zoologist Julian Huxley, who, after visiting East Africa in 1929, lists "various current assumptions" about "trusteeship."

> The chief assumption is that black men are in their nature different from and inferior to white men. The second is that since white men know how to do a great many things of which black men are ignorant, they therefore know what is best for black men and are entitled to lay down what they ought to do and how they ought to live. The third, continuing the second, is that natives should develop 'along their own lines'—their own lines being those on which there is the greatest possible taking on of European useful arts; the least possible . . . danger of their claiming or obtaining political, social, or intellectual equality with Europeans. . . . The fourth is economic: it is that production for export is virtuous, while production merely for your own consumption is not—and is, indeed, rather reprehensible.[30]

In 1929, Britishers "felt rather than thought through" (as Huxley says) what Charles Kingsley had clearly expressed in 1853—that it was "the moral duty" of the colonies to produce for export. Huxley's description is particularly important because it argues that the process of improving the

cultural other in ways that are "useful" to Europeans but restrictive to the
other, depends on a convenient ideological gulf between the races. The
mystified education of racial inferiors was merely a form of control with a
pedagogical cast. As such, it allowed white masters to play the role of
enlightened teachers—"to lay down" the rules for Africans—without the
worry that blacks would attain the status of subjects, and so claim their
rights. The ideal of self-government, as Darby has said, was put into "some
distant, unforeseeable future" (*TFI*, p. 43). Further, Lefort has explained that
the pedagogical model of power is effective because it institutes a gap
between the discourse of progressive enlightenment (which is based on following the rules) and the underlying threat of coercion that maintains the
dominance of white over black.

On one level this strategy of power is effective because the coer-
civeness of the "educator" remains latent; but on another level, the strategy
is dangerous because it ensures that exploitation of the "pupil" is a violation
of the pedagogical code. The racial paradigm, which resolves the problem
that "improvement" can in no way lead to authentic subjecthood for the
cultural other, reinstates the contradiction between morality and power. An
increase in rigid ethnocentricism—for example, the racist tenets of Social
Darwinism—becomes requisite for splitting off colonialist abuses. In *Prester
John*, a 1906 novel about the Natal Rebellion, John Buchan recounts how
an African king, John Laputa, attempted the desperate uprising against
Proconsul Milner in the Transvaal. Buchan portrays Laputa's revolt as a
social Darwinist backsliding from "civilization" to "savagery," and thus
teaches his readers the "difference between white and black, the gift of
responsibility."[31] The totalizing idea of racial "responsibility" functions in
Prester John to disclaim the exploitation that led to the rebellion, and to
legitimate the force that is subsequently used against the uneducable—that
is, unredeemably "irresponsible"—African.

Due to colonial uprisings like the Natal Rebellion or to the protracted conflict of the Boer War, the value of "responsibility" in the civilizing mission came into conflict with the value of race "efficiency." The high
priest of the jingoist press, Charles Steevens, counseled his readers to relinquish all pretenses of responsible comportment ("The naked principle of
our rule is the way that shall be walked in, cost what pain it may"). Steevens
openly glorified the hard clarity of ruthless power, exalting a military figure like Kitchener as an indomitable mechanism. "His precision is so inhumanly unerring, he is more like a machine than a man. . . . His officers and
men are wheels in the machine: he feeds them enough to make them *efficient*, and works them as mercilessly as he works himself" (my emphasis).[32]

Men like Steevens wanted to imperialize Britain as a whole, not just exert principles of racial efficiency/superiority in the colonies. Indeed, the nation took significant steps in this direction—for example, in its military spectacles and its efforts to breed "an imperial race." Democratic political institutions tended to keep more or less in check the tyranny advocated by imperialist interests. However, Britishers had to deal with their own highly contradictory amalgam of social arrogance and standards of social justice, and hence reduced others to the status of manipulable things, even while disguising such narcissistic appropriation from themselves.

During this period, as Hobsbawm and Cannadine have shown, tradition was invented for both domestic and colonial purposes.[33] Monarchical and military displays of "a superiority so great as to appear unchallengeable" projected the requisite image of power. Such displays seem to have commanded the passive allegiance and admiration of the masses, just as they had forced the submission of colonial peoples. Between 1877, when Disraeli made Victoria Empress of India, and 1897, when Chamberlain brought the colonial premiers to London to parade in the Diamond Jubilee procession, every great event of the British monarchy was also an occasion for colonialist mythography.

In Ryder Haggard's *She*, the white African Queen, Ayesha, is actually "He," having adopted something like Steeven's masculinist "naked principle" of rule, as well as the imperialist spectacle of power. Ayesha is, first of all, a Social Darwinist, who subordinates all relations to the marketplace. She explains that "Those who are weak must perish; the earth is to the strong and the fruits thereof," and that "The world is a great mart . . . where all things are for sale to him who bids the highest in the currency of our desires."[34] Ayesha's consumerism makes pleasure—defined by a plainly narcissistic economy of desire—life's only business. What is more, Ayesha exerts control by means of an extraordinary image of beauty and invulnerability ("My empire is of the imagination"). Like so many imperial Proconsuls, she relies on image to augment the substance of power, and on her subjects' need to affiliate with her power.

The mythology of race superiority, as cultural historians J. A. Mangan and James Walvin have shown, fostered in all citizens a sense that they were members of an "Imperial race," encouraged them to identify with the ideal of their nation's world role, and allowed them to accept the otherwise disquieting hegemony that their society exercised over pre-industrialized cultures.[35] However, comparisons inevitably arose between racially "inferior" peoples abroad and the "barbarians" and "pygmies" of "darkest England." Ironically enough, this identification tended to undermine imperial claims—either those to rectitude or to efficiency—because representations of the British lower classes as "a population sodden in drink, steeped in vice, [and] eaten up by every social and physical malady" could hardly encourage the British to think of themselves as belonging to a superior nation.[36] Eugenicists, Fabians, criminologists, and the medical establishment in general took it upon themselves to breed "efficiency" into lower-class Britons, and in the process identified the poor with their physical deformities and with their bodies rather than their persons.[37] Such reifying identification corresponds to the commodification of African labor (their improved performance of "the useful European arts," as Huxley said), and to the action of making "riflemen from mud,"[38] as Kipling had described the British training of Indians. The poor and the working class had to be saved *from* themselves and *for* the ruling-class interests of Empire.

This extended use of racial categories did not end with their application to the domestic "other," however. The Boer War (1899–1901) was regarded by many Britishers as a war between *races*. Hobson relates how his countrymen regarded the conflict as "a conflict of races, in which the race of lower social efficiency must yield place to the race of higher efficiency. . . . Such is the jargon which 'sociologists' offer as a screen for the naked inequities of aggressive war."[39] Under the strain of the Boer War, the country seems to have entirely acceded to the social Darwinist equation between racial "superiority" and "efficiency." Perhaps because it was not an everyday affair of imperialism, this war provides a remarkably naked illustration of the culture's narcissism.

The Boers were especially infuriating to the British, Hobson says, because they wouldn't "stand on the skyline and let us shoot at them, or come out and mass in the open within range of our guns" (*PJ*, p.74). The British fantasy of cultural omnipotence had led them to expect that the Boers, intimidated by British military might, would simply give up without a struggle. When they didn't, many different social groups at home and in South Africa (the jingoist press, churches, private investment firms, and so forth) became enraged. Hobson considered the British incapacity to understand their own folly an "eclipse of humour" by "dull ferocity." Psychoanalytic historian Peter Gay takes Hobson's term "dull ferocity" and makes it diagnostic of narcissistic impairment. "Dullness and ferocity," Gay writes, "are characteristic responses of the child in the body of the man; they suggest impaired reality testing and infantile self-absorption."[40] Psychoanalyst Heinz Kohut notes that the narcissistically enraged individual experiences the enemy as "a recalcitrant part of an expanded self over which the . . . vulnerable person had expected to exercise full control. The mere fact, in other words, that the other person is independent . . . is experienced as offensive."[41] The Boers, who had violently (and for a time successfully) opposed British forces, inflicted a grave injury to British self-esteem. While political and economic factors were certainly at work in the British action against the Boers, the extremity of British reaction has the character of childish rage at a frustrated fantasy of omnipotence. Of course, the racial ideal was inherently vulnerable: a grandiose illusion maintained only by the elimination of a realistic relation to a foreign culture. Unable to get (as Hobson says) "outside of self," or to recognize the impartial spectator in others, the British imperialist too often redressed his mortification with cold fury.

We have seen how the masters of colonialism denied (while professing to encourage) the subjecthood of their "inferiors," and how the other, whether native or working-class, assumed the function of either mirroring imperialist self-perfection, or obstructing the self's "responsible" or "efficient" conduct. The question now becomes, given the pedagogic/racial paradigm of ideology that confers true subjecthood only to those with power, how did ruling class men *learn* to constitute themselves, to recreate and sustain identities that tended to include profoundly childlike characteristics?

Breeding Masculinity: The Training of Ruling Class "Subjects"

In the humanist view, education is *Bildung* (self-formation). Such formation depends to no small extent on standardized methods of training; but what the notion particularly stresses is the cultivated expression of *self*, the freedom to "remake" ourselves through reading, talking, writing, and so forth. British imperialists of course actively discouraged self-expression in native subalterns. One would think that the stable and prosperous parts of English society would permit humanistic freedoms of education to their own male children, the very "flowers" of the culture. Yet the development of British adolescents into relatively autonomous subjects was not the primary aim of the public school. Whatever else the educational process meant to the privileged, the "total institution" of the public school was designed to instill loyalty and conformity to the ideals and demands of Empire. Lefort's view of ideology therefore applies nicely to the British public schools, in which the adult (who enjoys subject status) is divided from the child (who does not), and authoritarian principles inculcate obedience in the child in ways suggestively parallel to the governance of natives.

Certain authoritarian patterns—strict organizational hierarchy,

obsession with competitive games, and hero worship—worked to transform the freedoms of a humanistically conceived model of self-formation
into subjection. Such patterns were conveyed to the culture at large by
means of the cult of "manliness," of values taken from "reinvented" aristocratic codes of honor and from the Social Darwinist scheme of world competition. Even more ominously, this type of pedagogical control
encouraged narcissistic personality structures in the public school men who
embodied the prevailing idiom of masculinity, and who gave it voice in the
larger society. Thus, it is not overstating the case to say that the public
school character, and hence very largely the "ideal" of British manhood,
was actually a cult of narcissism. That is, a cult based on impossible, rudimentary and unmodifiable wishes for perfection, illusory needs derived
from grave injuries to self-esteem (the injuries of training), leading to over-
dependence on external sources of support and authority.

The public school ethos was transported to the larger culture because
it was thought to inspire the production of fit and proper men from all stations of life who could assist in the work of Empire. "Manliness" brought
together the theme of national prestige and responsibility with that of
physical and mental readiness for the challenge of international competition. The cult not only reasserted masculinity, but also seemed to provide
an antidote to masculine fears. In 1904, L. T. Hobhouse wrote about central aspects of "manliness," what he ironically termed "the preparation
game" and "the pleasures of national posing," which at once revealed and
deferred the narcissistic anxieties of the imperialist patriarchy.

> Here was England with drained resources and a damaged military rep-
> utation in charge of a magnificent imperial domain which rivals were
> eyeing enviously. It was then that the subtle pleasures of national pos-
> ing began to be cultivated. Our ancient pride in England's greatness
> gave place to brooding self-consciousness. . . . The English must agree
> to 'believe' in the reality of the plotting enemy against whose das-
> tardly attack they are preparing, they must 'believe' in the 'world of
> blood and iron' and all the rest of the preparation game.[42]

Since the fears of elite males were identified with anxieties of the
nation as a whole, all segments of the public were to be enlisted into "the
preparation game." Hobhouse (like Hobson) was a keen observer of imperial narcissism at the time of the Boer War. In fact, Hobhouse recapitulates
many of Hobson's categories—self-assertiveness, underlying vulnerability,
paranoid over-reaction—but adds the dangerous insinuation of athleticism

into conceptualizations of world struggle. Granted, this insinuation was nearly a century old ("The battle at Waterloo was won on the playing fields of Eton"), but Hobhouse points out its relevance in the new context of global expansion, the "world of blood and iron" governed by the limitlessly destructive process of capital and power accumulation.

The "games" of the public schools and the new boys' clubs that sprang up in lower-class neighborhoods brought most British adolescents into the competitive arenas of an accumulating society. The cult of manliness linked elite to proletarian culture. According to Mangan and Walvin, through adventure literature, school textbooks, youth movements, and philanthropic organizations, "both the image and associated symbolic activities of both Christian and Darwinian 'manliness' filtered down to the proletariat through an unrelenting and self-assured process of social osmosis" (MM, pp.6–7). As Micheal Kimmel points out, a clear example of popularized masculine virtue was the Boy Scouts, which was organized by Imperial proconsul Anthony Baden-Powell to counteract the shame of the Boer War.[43] Thus, in a condition of mind framed by the strategies and rewards of boyhood "play," the nation was well prepared to mystify economic warfare into a type of adolescent game.

During the 1860s the public school system began to move away from educator Thomas Arnold's ideal of "godliness and good learning." Heroic masculinity of the Christian type became more or less a respectable facade for competition, and by the 1880s and 1890s competitive athletic ideals displaced religious ones at the core of the educational process. As Mangan points out, the acceptable muscular Christianity of mid-century now worked primarily to disguise the atheistic and stoic reality of public school life, which "made bland use of Christian phraseology with the same purpose and deceit as the fifteenth-century chevalier!" (MM, p.145). Games were cast in the social Darwinist mold of "efficiency" and "competition," and at the same time masked by Christianity and chivalry. Mangan observes that the whole process of public-school education was designed to ensure a winning edge in the contests of a materialistic world (MM, p.147).

From his earliest social experience, then, the upper- and middle-class identity of the British boy was built upon contradiction. He was to be, as George Santayana puts it, "the sweet, just, boyish master of the world"[44]—which is to say, not just "sweet and boyish," but also an efficient "master," a robo-cop like Kitchener. Boys were asked to construct a social identity by somehow weaving these discrepant cultural significances into a workable accommodation. They thus became practiced at splitting their experience into opposite trends, worshipping either spotless virtue or relentless tyranny (depending on which aspect of their experience they brought into view). Boys were disciplined into splitting their experience between rectitude and ruthlessness, if only because conformity to the corporate cause was brutally enforced. H. B. Gray, who served as headmaster at Westminster and wrote an important critique of the schools, puts his criticism of the system this way: "A code in which coercive measures predominate does not form an ideal plan of government for the evolution of the adolescent. On the contrary, it suggests the atmosphere of a barrack-room or of a prison or asylum."[45]

Just as the norms and ideals of personal conduct could be "osmotically" transferred to the larger culture by elite writers of social propaganda and adventure fiction, and by various philanthropic efforts to organize boys' activities, so the basic structure of the public school house system could itself be adopted from the domain of the upper classes and deployed as a method of discipline at home and in the colonies. A famous boys' reformatory—the Borstal Institution—was modeled after this structure. In 1930, the Commissioner of Borstal, Alexander Paterson, reviewed widespread assumptions on training:

> Once upon a time the method employed to deal with [boys] simply consisted in the use of force. The lad was regarded as a lump of hard material, yielding only to the hammer, and was, with every good intention beaten into shape. . . . There ensues a second method which has flourished in many schools and places where boys are trained and might be termed the method of pressure. The lad is treated as though he were *a lump of putty*, and an effort is made to reduce him to a certain uniform shape by the gentle and continuous pressure of authority from without. . . . In course of time, by perpetual repetition, he forms the habit of moving smartly, keeping himself clean, obeying orders and behaving with all decorum in the presence of his betters.[46] (my emphasis)

According to Paterson, the lump-of-putty theory was held by pedagogical experts from the late nineteenth well into the twentieth century. Training was a matter of both reducing to uniformity and instilling the internalized watchdog of habitual submission. Like Paterson, Gray notes that when the adolescent character is thought of as "wax to receive and marble to retain," then the system promotes "imitation" rather than "self-evolution." The grandiose ambition suggested by the public school house system is the desire (on the part of educators) to fabricate and manipulate a pliable human product.

Interestingly, Paterson almost reflexively uses the adjective "gentle" and the noun "decorum" when referring to the method. Though by "gentle" he undoubtedly means continuous, the subversion of his meaning is implied by the alternative association of the word "gentle": polite society (genti-lesse). Though it often went under cover of good breeding, educational authority was anything but "gentle"—namely, marked by the influence of women. Indeed, the cult of the hard-muscled frame was designed in part to counter the forces of feminization. As Kimmel has observed, the manly ethos worshipped strength and feared impotence; it displaced fears of cul-tural castration (Oedipal dread) by removing boys from their mothers, seg-regating them from heterosexual society, and reorganizing them into bands of brothers ("CC", p. 149). The primal horde was recreated in various forms—in football "mauls" on the playing fields, in group adoration of the athletic "bloods," or (as in the case of scouting) in masculine preserves that reinserted boys into nature, away from the urban world of enfeeblement, refinement, civility, and women.

The fear of the sexual body, the attempt to efface the personality of the child, the endeavor to eradicate "inefficient" (indigenous) cultural influ-ences in order to colonize the adolescent, the proletariat, and the native, all of these elements ultimately betray a hatred for basic psychological and social realities. Late-nineteenth-century education, a significant part of this program, shows contempt for human beings, while glorifying what man can be made into, the Human Thing. The colonizers' fantasy of a com-pletely pliable, suppliant being was thus rooted to a significant degree in a narcissistically constructed reality.

The pedagogical effort to create "docile bodies" might be understood in Foucauldian terms as a "microtechnology" of power. Yet a Foucauldian analysis of imperialist pedagogy is problematic here for at least two rea-sons. In identifying social agents with their bodies and with the coercive manipulation of these bodies, Foucauldian principles lead to the same elim-ination of subjectivity that the colonizers themselves sought to effect, even if Foucault's own "leftist" sympathies are clearly with the victims of power.[47] Further, inasmuch as Foucault sees psychoanalytic inquiry as itself a form of coercive power, he prevents any consideration of the fantasies at work in the process of controlling or being controlled. Foucault should be resisted to the extent that he refuses to look into the complicated (psychological) dynamics of the person as these relate to and influence "technologies" of power.

From a dialectical, psychosocial perspective, the central irony is that pedagogical exercises of discipline, which so effectively serve narcissism at the level of cultural practice and institutional structure, do not necessarily curb (and in fact often promote) the narcissism of individuals, especially with regard to feelings of privilege, flights of grandiosity, and impaired empathy. Flawed in so many respects, public school tutelage could not even create a predictable product, and more than anything cultivated what Winnicott calls a "false self."

Alexander Paterson wrote that "it happens, therefore, sadly often that the lad who has been merely subjected to the pressures of authority from outside will, when exposed to different influences of free life, assume quite another shape."(Paterson in *BR*, p.105) Paterson is right to emphasize the false, compliant self—the constrained and arid facade—that merely conforms to external demands. What Paterson neglects, however, is the psychological dynamic that underlies this artificial self. If the individual's central pedagogical experience is one of being bullied, he may end up depressed, terrified, or enraged. For example, a graduate of Uppingham, C. R. Nevison, wrote eloquently of injuries inflicted in the dormitories. "Apathy settled on me, I withered. I learned nothing . . . I was kicked, hounded, caned, flogged, hairbrushed morning, noon, and night. The more I suffered, the less I cared. The longer I stayed the harder I grew."[48] The result is not just conformity, insensitivity, or both, for the student might well leave school without positive, stable memories of a caring adult world to which he can always refer. He will leave therefore without the positive relational images ("self-objects") that are the basic elements of stable self-regulation, and that, once internalized as self-regulatory functions, allow him to maintain a balanced sense of self-worth. As a consequence, he may never learn to moderate archaic longings for omnipotence. Not only are these archaic longings encouraged by reigning ideological formations, they are also made necessary as defenses against the effects of the child's emotional battering. Powerless children cannot help but fantasize either rescue by a powerful other, or magical realization of their own power, because helplessness by itself is intolerable. Self-regulation becomes in everyday life *compliance with* or *appropriation of* what is outside the self, and finds its compensations, both in action and in popular fantasy, in entitled and appropriative exercises of power.

There is the example of Milner's staff, his "kindergarten" (as it was called at the time), demonstrating the ways in which relational patterns internalized in childhood influence standard ways of functioning in the imperialist (adult) world. In Northeastern Rhodesia young British men, explicitly recruited because of their public school education, were locally known as "bum switchers." Viscount Milner, the Administrative Head of the Transvaal, was so casual about flogging Chinese "coolies" that when the Foreign Office investigated the irregularities of his rule, Milner remembered nothing of this practice—not in order to protect himself, but because the beatings themselves had made no impression on him. Milner's self-absorbed and calloused view of his role as top administrator demonstrates a very high order of what Hobson had called the "dull ferocity" of the British. But the practice of flogging was an everyday insensitivity and cruelty which, as Hyam says, "can hardly have been unrelated to the traumas many [Britishers] endured at the hands of sadistic school masters" (BIC, p.147–48).

Similar patterns and themes emerge in Kipling's "The Slaves of the Lamp" stories about public school and Empire. Kipling makes of his hero "Stalky" an idealized protagonist who not only gratifies fantasies of despotic power by becoming a legend in his own right, but also satisfies national ideals by converting entire Indian tribal territories to British domination. Though the Viceroy attempts to knock Stalky down a peg, Kipling makes it clear that the field generals and Stalky's military peers admire him unreservedly. Stalky is in fact worshipped as an ideal masculine type: "Stalky is the great man of our century"; or "Stalky was goin' strong then— about seven feet high and four feet thick"; or "Stalky was an invulnerable Guru"; or "Stalky, out in his snows, began corresponding direct with the Government . . . after the manner of a king."[49] Coming after Kipling's account of Stalky's mistreatment in school, however, such descriptions of Stalky's triumphant masculinity provide a kind of compensatory fantasy. Such heroics in themselves unintentionally betray unresolved conflicts with institutional "fathers," which mark them as vulnerabilties rather than strengths.

Stalky's efforts to make himself King lead to reprimands by the Viceroy and his second-in-command, General Von Lennaert ("he must be slain officially"). While censure should by design enforce a constructive disillusionment with absolute desire (a symbolic castration), censure in Kipling is more often seen as an empty formality, the appearance of obedience that leaves untouched the "criminal" desire to refuse prohibition and affirm uncompromising self-assertiveness. Stalky's response to being "horrid disgraced" also suggests an underlying rage at and disappointment with the Viceroy. " 'If I thought that basket hanger . . . governed India, I swear I'd become a naturalized Muscovite tomorrow. I'm a *femme incompromise*. This thing's broke my heart' " (SAC, p. 270). The comedic style of the remark does not obscure how Stalky associates his social humiliation by the Viceroy—this failure to achieve narcissistic affirmation from the institutional "father"—to genital castration, to being feminized by patriarchal authority.

The unconscious worry is of not being truly masculine, or that male identity may be lost. This anxiety is the result of the enfeebled sense of a self whose subjective definitions of masculine and feminine have not been sufficiently differentiated or detached from early object ties, from the meaning those ties have for fathers, personal and cultural, and for sons. Stalky cannot identify in an abstract and positive way with female traits—for example, with maternal nurturance—because patriarchy regards the feminine as only a source of enervation and weakness. His unconscious association between the woman as "castrated" and the effeminate submissive self is therefore the consequence of social and familial expectations, and not, as Freud would have it, the result of innate drives and anatomical difference. Further, the need for omnipotent fantasy, for hyper-masculinity as a defense against a (sexualized) narcissistic injury, is exacerbated by patriarchy's anxiety about passivity. The male's passive longings, first experienced in the mother-child bond, remain potentially unresolvable when transferred to the father, since patriarchal authority only excites worshipful submission to heroic but cruel idols. To the extent that the adolescent continues to live according to these archaic attitudes and object attachments, the sense of self and of (male) embodiment cannot be satisfactorily consolidated, and mature capacities remain uncertain of accomplishment. Stalky cannot love a partner of either the opposite or the same sex; he cannot work according to reality-oriented ideals rather than grandiose ones; and thus he is best understood as a perpetual adolescent.[50]

The manifest claim Kipling wants the story to illustrate, however, is that, given a certain kind of training, an adolescent can move easily from public school into a position of imperial command. The story's demonstration of this transition is positively ludicrous, since Stalky divides and conquers Indian subjects by means of the same practical joke he used with great success as a 14-year-old in turning a servant against the House Sergeant. Stalky appropriates his piece of Empire in the same way he survived and flourished in the public school environment, where those who learn their lessons well develop a habitual vigilance about enemies dressed up as friends, enemies whom one must submit to or conquer. The Empire is in fact to be protected and extended by cruelty and cunning. In the fantasied colonial playground, adolescent ruthlessness wins the game of primitive self-completion by quite literally killing the opponent. Lionel Trilling talks of the book's "callousness, arrogance, and brutality."[51] I would add that attention must be paid to how Kipling renders callousness so callously,

without feeling the need to call it what it is. His equation of imperialist violence with Stalky's practical jokes derealizes both the natives and their subjugation. Brutality assumes in the story the quality of comic-strip or
television violence; indeed, the representation itself has the crudeness of
the archaic. Above all else, Kipling's unselfconsciously chauvinistic tale
shows not just the assumptions but the fantasies that underlie such adolescent, grandiose militarism, and illustrates how imperialist culture is drawn
to the compensatory fantasy represented by Kipling's hero.

In Kipling, then, we see how the autocratic and patriarchal aspect of
imperialist culture obtrudes into the mother-child preoedipal bond with
the requirement that the male child live up to the standards and masculine
imperatives of the "parent" with the most external, socially sanctioned
power (the father, who wields both personal and cultural power). There is
in this an unwelcome appropriation of the child's identity—in the words
of psychoanalyst Peter Shabad, "a premature 'phallic' intrusion by the
father into the private 'womb'" of the mother-child relationship.[52] The
removal of boys from mothers, and their carefully managed absorption
into the male horde, constitutes a process of separation that is imposed
from without, and for reasons which have nothing to do with the child's
needs, thus inhibiting a more spontaneous and gradual maturation. If the
primary parent (the mother) has been herself unable to provide the child
with a full complement of recognition and approval (with appropriate mirroring), or if that recognition is radically devalued and substituted for by
submission to "taskmaster" fathers, then the child has no option but to fit
himself to narcissistic paternal expectations of achievement and institutional demands of conformity. Moreover, to be "evicted prematurely from
unconsciousness," Shabad tells us, can have serious ethical consequences;
for in such a situation "the 'ethical' function of understanding—and of
being compassionately responsible for what one knows—may become
confused with the moralistic duty" of obligatory conformity. The pressures
of being responsible for what one knows can in turn lead to a desire to
sever the ties of compassion that bind one to such knowledge. Knowing
can become so laden with the burden to be accountable for, or to take care
of, what one knows, Shabad says, "that a person may impulsively escape
into the id-like carefreeness of unconscious action" ("TI" p. 346). For the
child of imperialism, however, unconscious repetition is regulated, not
carefree. The cultural structures are patrolled avenues of escape that permit specific forms of unconscious repetition (and rationalization), and also
substitute this unconsciousness for action grounded in compassionate, ethical accountability.

Under the auspices of imperial institutions, the world of "others" serves the colonizer as a fantasy-space in which to recuperate regressive satisfactions and to disarm deeply held anxieties. We have seen how contradictions in British imperialism (such as that between responsibility and exploitation) required the ideological mystifications of benevolent paternalism, of monarchy and ceremony, and of various "pedagogical" dichotomies (civilized/savage, bourgeois/worker, adult/child) in order to sustain authoritarian domination. Both the ideology and the practice of colonialism influenced individual psychological adaptation and the formation of social identity. First, they promoted various defensive strategies (splitting, denial, projection) in order to protect the illusion of a coherent ethical self; and second, they nurtured a more general cultural narcissism, along with accompanying forms of grandiosity and idealization, subtle and otherwise. Those who participated in this matrix of social language and practice, of wish and defense, did so in part because conformity provided safety from the abuses suffered when learning the rules for achievement, group loyalty, and efficiency; in part because the moralistic obligations of a false social self had eclipsed compassionate fellow-feeling; and in part because bearing the truth about oneself, and one's cultural fathers, required a willingness to give up the narcissistic fantasies and imperialist prerogatives of one's cultural capital.

CHAPTER FOUR

Marlovian Narration and Unreconstructed Ideology Critique

We have seen that imperialism, as an ideology and a psychological formation, sanctions racist domination, and that while the myths that accompany empire-building feed on narcissistic fantasy, they are not free of fear and trembling. If, as Marshall Berman has observed, modern society is epitomized by its excesses of individualism and corporateness—by "the sort of individualism that scorns and fears other people as threats," and by "the sort of collectivism that seeks to submerge the self in a social role"—then imperialist culture epitomizes that modernity.[1] And Conrad is its critic. His portrayal of Kurtz's monomaniacal individualism, and of Jim as one who is defined by a paralyzing fear yet fashions his loyalties and his claims to power on the storybook fictions of an idealized patriarchy, are crucial testimonies to Conrad's disenchantment. However, Conrad's position in this matrix is also paradoxical. He is caught between his sense of community/solidarity as a moral and social requisite, and his awareness of how imperial narcissism makes a mockery of noble deeds, self-sacrifice, and heroism. And while Conrad is appalled by the excesses of this "collectivism," he also appeals to its group-think and is even fascinated by its narcissistic passions—as if the confrontation with excess, its endemic irony and ambiguity, could only lead him to an ambivalent enforcement of colonial "solidarity," and not to a transcendence of it.

Conrad's texts are permeated by a sensibility that resists but continues to live within the confines of imperialism. More is at stake in them than in the work of Kipling or Haggard because Conrad's work is more destabilized by recognition, and more implicated in the play of desire and defensive indirection. On the one hand, Conrad portrays Kurtz and Jim as individuals profoundly damaged by their culture, making each in his own way, representative of characterological deficits and ideological subterfuge. But on the other hand, through Marlow, Conrad is carried along by the same ideals he would scuttle. As we have seen in the discussion on the preface of *The Nigger of the "Narcissus"*, Conrad needed to sustain and protect his emotional investment in Britain, and could only carry cultural criticism so far.

Conrad's position is difficult to demonstrate, of course, in part because *Heart of Darkness* and *Lord Jim* are narratives-within-narratives, or nested forms of telling. Patrick Brantlinger raises important questions about both tales. First, there is the difficulty of interpreting "the frame narration that filters everything that is said." Ultimately, I think, the question is one of how Marlow wants his tales to be received. Conrad identifies the listeners of both tales as supporters of the imperialist project. Therefore even if Marlow were entirely critical of imperialism (which he is not), he must measure his words against what his listeners are prepared to hear. As he says in *Lord Jim*, "it is not my words I mistrust, but your minds."[2] Even if we could adequately assess Marlow's audience, there remains the more fundamental issue of Marlow's relation to Conrad. Can we suppose that Marlow speaks for Conrad? Or, as Brantlinger puts it, "At what point is it safe to assume that Conrad/Marlow expresses a single point of view?"[3]

In much of the recent criticism, the issue is precisely at what point Conrad is to be identified with Marlow, and on what grounds that identification is to be made. It seems clear, however, that while Conrad has a wider and more ironic awareness than does Marlow, the author "inside" the text(s) is to a significant extent aligned with the narrator, if only because in the end Conrad cannot surmount his psychological need to belong to the colonial world. At once belonging to and estranged from the imperialist collective, Conrad in certain respects shares his narrator's ambivalence. By focusing on this in-between position, I am putting forward a perspective that attempts to move beyond strictly ideological readings of the texts.

Thus, to argue that narratorial complication and ambivalence is motivated by something other than ideology is to counter Jameson's strictly Marxist reading of *Lord Jim*, in which there is from the beginning an ideo-

logically motivated refusal to consider the complications of Marlow's perspective, and from which it follows that neither the limits of Conrad's irony
nor the psychic factor of ambivalence can be entertained.[4] And it departs
from Brantlinger's and Vincent Pecora's readings of *Heart of Darkness*. On the
one hand, these critics (unlike Jameson) appreciate the complicating factor
of Conrad's distance from Marlow. Indeed, Pecora foregrounds Conrad's
irony.[5] And Brantlinger's focus on the ambiguous nature of Conrad's telling
allows him to claim that labeling the novel as critical of imperialism is as
unsatisfactory as condemning it for endorsing racism. But on the other, both
of these more nuanced positions end with the idea that Conrad as authorial
subject is only the sum of the social/literary discourses that speak him.
Hence, for both critics Conrad and Marlow converge at the point where
ideological mystification itself subsumes (rather than shapes) the writer.
This emptying out of Conrad as an authorial subject is but the logical consequence of Brantlinger's theoretical indebtedness to Jameson, and of
Pecora's allegiance to Foucault. Their theoretical commitments require it.

However, the novels' commitments and ironies cannot be subsumed
by purely discursive readings. An interpretive space must be cleared so that
Conrad, the author in the text, can be read psychosocially through Marlow,
the voice and witness.

Rereading Jameson's "Romance and Reification"

For Jameson, the central conflict of *Lord Jim* is, not surprisingly, the double-
bind of universal instrumentalization. Capitalist "activity" produces the
"antivalue" of pragmatic ends-means rationality, and hence evokes an opposite longing for spiritual "value" that the very logic of capitalist social organization excludes. This conflict between "activity" and "value" is at once
revealed and masked through Jim. On the one hand, there is the "antihero"
of the first part of the novel, who exposes the fact that value and activity
cannot be unified. But on the other, there is "the ideal Jim, the Lord Jim of
the second half" who actualizes "an unimaginable and impossible resolution," or who in effect provides an imaginary "containment" of capitalist
social contradiction by realizing his heroic destiny on Patusan (*TPU*,
p.254–55). I want to critique each of these points—the economic theme,
the idea of an antiheroic Jim, and the pseudo-resolution of imperialist
romance—in order to restore the novel's richly vexed nature.

It is hard to argue with his claim that one of the central contradictions of the novel is produced by the capitalist transformation of social

values into economic ones. (Indeed, we have seen Conrad's awareness of
this process in *The Nigger of the "Narcissus"*). However, the antinomy of "activity" and "value," derived from a structuralist Marxist reading of the text, is
meant effectively to eliminate the rhetorical device of Conrad's narrator.
Jameson's justification for not considering how Marlow's standpoint shapes
the narrative is that point of view as such is "a powerful ideological instrument in the perpetuation of an increasingly subjectivized and psycholo-
gized world," a world that programs individuals to the "freedom and
equality of sheer market equivalence" (*TPU*, p.221). For Jameson, interest
in psychology has the power to blind us to the economic rationalization of
society because (psychological) subjectivity is itself an ideological relation
to the world. Thus, what allows Jameson to deconstruct Marlow, to dissolve point of view into an antinomy of class ideology, is the Althusserian
notion that "ideology interpellates individuals." One is hardly taking a
reactionary position, however, to argue that while class myths may shape
the individual's perception of the world, Marlow himself is only ever partly
interpellated. To see both sides only means reading with both eyes, that is,
with depth perception.

   In the matrix of colonial culture, and of the novel in specific, the economic reduction of social values produces a normative contradiction , a
contradiction that is embodied by Conrad in "the fixed standard of conduct." On the one hand, fidelity to duty endlessly perpetuates the triumph
of trade and administration, but on the other, the standard allows the individual, as Marlow puts it, "to save from the fire his idea of what his moral
identity should be" (*LJ*, p. 50). Marlow as a servant of Empire has to build
his identity across the fault lines of the fixed standard. And the scandal of
the *Patna*—Jim's censure for having deserted the apparently sinking ship—
reveals to Marlow that his ideal of allegiance is overdetermined by being
itself a regulatory rule of power, that the ethical axiom guarantees the
social imperatives of an inequitable system.

   To Marlow, the indictment leveled by the official court is chilling. It
is a pronouncement "uttered in the passionless and definite phraseology a
machine would use if machines could speak" (*LJ*, p.97). "These proceed-
ings," he says, "had all the cold vengefulness of a death-sentence, had all
the cruelty of a sentence of exile" (p.96–97). Marlow understands that Jim
is regarded simply as a faulty cog in the imperial machinery, and that he
has been conveniently tossed away in the interests of the system's "efficiency." The verdict was "so much in accordance with the wisdom of life,
which consists in putting out of sight . . . all that makes against our efficiency—the memory of our failures, the hints of our undying fears, the

bodies of our dead friends" (p.106). Further, Jim's formal exclusion serves to
obscure two facts. First, Jim's failure of nerve in the face of outward and
inward terrors is a fear shared by many others, all equally vulnerable.[6] As
Marlow puts it, he was "a lost youngster," but "his situation got hold of me
as though he had been an individual in the forefront of his kind, as if the
obscure truth involved were enough to affect mankind's conception of
itself" (p.57). Second, in abandoning ship Jim has breached more than a
professional standard. "Its real significance," Marlow explains, "is in its
being a breach of faith with the community of mankind" (p.95). That is to
say, Jim's crime is not just against the official code, but also against the
Malaysian lascars who stood at the wheel instead of jumping ship, and
against the ship's passengers, the 800 Moslem pilgrims. Thus, the values
that are fundamental to Marlow's sense of social status and morality are the
same values he must bring into question in confronting the economic
agenda of colonialism. Jim leads him to the possibility that there is "a doubt
enthroned in the fixed standard of conduct" (p.31).[7]

What Jameson's economic thematization of the novel in part leaves
out is the psychological consequences of commodification. Jameson does
not consider—in fact, has precluded from consideration—Marlow's disillusionment with, and his intense ambivalence toward, the system. Marlow's
need to question, and his sense of loss in relation to his social world, makes
his perspective on the self-justifications of colonial culture quite ambiguous. What have been disrupted are the ideals and occupational ethos normally internalized by the individual, the ties to culture that bestow purpose
and self-worth. According to social psychologists Fred Weinstein and
Gerald Platt, the individual typically copes with loss of such crucial connections either by treating it as "deprivation" or by "accepting it as an
opportunity for enhanced autonomy."[8] Marlow clearly treats his experience
of Jim as a deprivation of the meaningfulness of their "common life." Jim,
he says, "had *robbed our common life* of the last spark of its glamour" (*LJ*, p.80,
my emphasis). Marlow himself appears to be hung-up, as on a hook,
between acceptance and non-acceptance of that loss, and hence between
cultural critique and loyalty. His ambivalence toward his culture is manifested in his ambivalence toward Jim. Thus, Jim's inspired imaginative existence becomes for Marlow both an invitation to question the world in
order to gain a truer sense of it, and "a faculty of swift and forestalling
vision" that allows Marlow himself to inhabit illusion, and thus to defer critique.

By failing to consider the intrinsic limits of Marlow's perspective,
Jameson's interpretation of Jim, the very heart of Marlow's tale, becomes

itself myopic. Jameson gives two different descriptions of Jim. First, he tells us that Conrad stresses the caricature of "Jim's bovaryisme" (Jim's having modeled his life on adventure fiction), but "in the second half of the novel goes on to write precisely the romance (earlier) caricatured" (*TPU*, p. 211, p. 213). Second, Jameson explains that Jim's experience of the sea in the *Patna* affair is coded in an "existentializing metaphysics" that marks nature as Jim's insurmountable "adversary." Once Conrad has set up this code of "good" and "evil," he uses it to melodramatic effect in the Patusan story, in which the "ideal Jim" enjoys a sustained triumph that culminates in the final victory over his "natural" foe Gentleman Brown. These descriptions are in some respects right. However, each is monochromatic, dependent on the proposition that a text (and hence a character) is only ever an enactment of ideology, or a denunciation of it by way of reversal. Further, Jameson's two characterizations of Jim are brought together only to enforce the idea that the second half of the novel presents a pseudo-resolution of imperial-ist propaganda. By viewing character as a series of ideological containment strategies, Jameson is blind to how scrupulously Conrad portrays Jim as an exemplar of colonial narcissism. By keeping Jim's narcissism always out of view (because he fears collusion with the mystifying potential of any psy-chological reading), Jameson actually denies himself access to a crucial aspect of this always ideologically ambiguous text.

Jameson identifies "Conrad" with the frame narrator of the opening pages of the novel, and asserts that from the outset the novel offers a cari-catured description of Jim as "adventure hero," a description that over the course of the tale serves to denounce imperialist ideology by reversing it. This characterization is right enough but inadequate to the novel as a whole, since it develops neither the problematic of Jim's psychology, nor how the frame narrator's commitments lead him to pass the problem of ide-ological ambivalence on to Marlow.

As the frame narrator presents it, Jim is the clean-living son of a cler-gyman, raised in both the eternal truths of Christianity and the governing myths of contemporary imperialist faith. But this is just to say that Jim is sheltered by nothing more than a fantasied prowess: "He saw himself sav-ing people from sinking ships, cutting away masts in a hurricane, swimming through a surf with a line . . . He confronted savages on tropical shores, quelled mutinies on the high seas, and in a small boat upon the ocean kept up the hearts of despairing men—always an example of devotion to duty, and as unflinching as a hero in a book" (*LJ*, p.5). In the frame narrator's view, the tradition of God-fearing manliness and derring-do has become hypocritical, derelict, and unreal. The piety of Jim's clergyman father comfortably coexists with social inequity, since the parson "possessed certain knowledge of the unknowable as made for the righteousness of people in cottages without disturbing the ease of those whom an unerring Providence enables to live in mansions" (p.4). Such convenient negligence would seem to extend even to his son. The parson simply assents to Jim's romantic valorization of youthful ambition, as if a father's role were fulfilled in offering a few sternly pronounced rules. Jim's father, like imperialist patriarchy itself, seems most concerned with Jim's potential to conform to socially authorized illusion and cultural clichés. The narrator describes Jim's early segregation from his family, and his absorption in adventurous aspirations, in this way: "The living [parsonage] belonged to the family for generations; but Jim was one of five sons, and when after a course of light holiday literature his vocation for the sea *had declared itself,* he was sent at once to a 'training-ship' for officers of the mercantile marine" (p.4, my emphasis). The "vocation" somehow materializes for both son and father. However, the reader is allowed to see that the fantasy of heroism, generated by filial innocence and light reading, is coupled with a patriarchal failure to draw a line between youthful enthusiasm and consequential action. The opening portrait of Jim is more than a simple caricature, for it deftly sketches how narcissistic fantasy becomes the vehicle for patriarchal ideology, the illusion of a reclaiming power that at once masks and carries forward the parson's complacency. Jim's destiny, it seems, will be to outstrip the mundane by realizing his dream of invulnerability. And he is never to be disabused of this belief in the "knights of Empire."

The narrator's descriptions introduce the imperialist problematic and its shaping effect on Jim. We are given to understand that what is true of the man is true of the culture. In this respect, Jameson is right that Conrad's view provides a kind of critical analogue for Britain's outward thrust: imperialist society is deeply rooted in empty pieties and self-referential ideals (fantasies of heroic perfection) to legitimate a world view rather than examine inherent contradictions. Such insight is mitigated, however, by the narrator's straitened dedication to the subject of "work," for the early clues that lie in Jim's upbringing slip quietly away when he focuses on Jim's failure to gain "a perfect love of the work" in officer's training school (*LJ*, p.7).

In claiming work as its own reward, the frame narrator of *Lord Jim* resembles the third-person narrative voice of *The Nigger of the "Narcissus,"* which also counsels that only love-of-work rescues humans from their darkest fears. And in that novella as well, Conrad upholds the value of hard labor while still managing to interrogate it by showing how even an icon such as Singleton can be laid low by what is supposed to raise up and lend meaning. Similarly, in *Lord Jim*, work (as advocated by the frame narrator) is less a solution than it is Conrad's means to defer reckoning with a missing element in the social compact. To valorize Jim's work for Empire is also to give tacit approval to how this absence of what Winnicott might call "good enough" relations between rule-giving fathers and imperialist sons creates a reliance on illusion, on fantasies that, because they are opposed by reality, can only be maintained by deadening misrecognitions. The shift from the frame narrator to Marlow is therefore a passing on of the problem of Jim's narcissism, which itself embodies the insufficiencies of the culture.

In the novel's first part, Marlow is made privy to Jim's account of what happened the night onboard the *Patna*, when he thought the ship would stave in. Jameson observes that Conrad shrouds this unheroic version of Jim in existentialist metaphysics. But the situation is in fact far more complicated and equivocal. Conrad positions Marlow to see things through the lens of Jim's paranoid self-involvement. As a result, Marlow is also inclined to see that Jim's "idealized selfishness" is at the root of the *Patna* scandal, and that this selfishness is what has robbed their "common life" of meaning. Though Jim is often, in his willful innocence, his own (and Marlow's) worst enemy, Marlow's relation to him is multiple.

At one point, for example, Marlow does create the existential alternative (that Jameson points out) to Jim's irrational handling of the *Patna* affair by imagining what he himself might do as a sailor were his ship to go down. Marlow tells us how he fell under "the suggestive truth of [Jim's] words," which also have to do with falling under "the shadow of madness" that comes in a small boat on the open sea, where nothing any longer matters. "When your ship fails you, your whole world seems to fail you; the world that made you, restrained you, took care of you." Thus ruminating on the abyssal consequences that "you"—himself or any one of us—might face, Marlow comes finally to avow that the Dark Powers that "lurk at the bottom of every thought," and that emerge to our sight especially in situations of extreme duress, "are perpetually foiled by the steadfastness of men" (*LJ*, p.74). Marlow identifies with Jim, but does he do so because there is in fact existential clarity in Jim, or because this is what Marlow needs to find there? The attribution of suggestive "truth" might only be the result of Marlow's having placed himself under "the shadow of madness." While Marlow's identification leads to a characteristic Conradian affirmation of the verities that stave off meaninglessness, and while this apolitical, existentialist moment partly obscures the real issue of Jim's subversive significance for the colonial world, Conrad has left it entirely up to the reader to decide whether or not Marlow has read Jim rightly. The scene shows

Marlow reinstating Jim as "one of us," but doing so on the basis of a possible fiction.[9] Marlow perhaps invites us to settle here, but in fact the issue is still quite unsettled for him. Consider how Marlow also regards Jim as the absent center of colonial desire.

During the night-long conversation with Marlow at the Malabar Hotel, Jim shows that for him engagement with others is not a challenge to be negotiated, but rather a potential source of either self-completion or injury. Jim protests that he had been in a "perfect state of preparation," a readiness braced against every danger except the "inconceivable" one of a collapsing bulkhead, but that "He had been taken unawares," and "Everything had betrayed him!" (LJ, p.59) He would therefore show his heroism by remaining completely passive, without "lifting as much as his little finger," as if the external world were either to conform magically to his wishes or to deny him utterly. Marlow also learns from Jim that he hadn't wanted to jump, but that the derelict crew members of the Patna had forced him to do so (p.76). After leaving the still floating ship, Jim had an irresistible urge to swim back to it; and Marlow can only suppose that Jim needed to make certain that all lives were lost ("as if his imagination had to be soothed by the assurance that all was over"). Without this assurance of the death of every passenger onboard, self-dissolution seems to have been Jim's only option. Marlow explains that Jim viewed his "saved life [as] over for want of ground under his feet, for want of sights for his eyes, for want of voices in his ears. Annihilation—hey! And all the time it was only a clouded sky, a sea that did not break, the air that did not stir. Only a night; only a silence" (p.70).

Marlow thus traces for us Jim's tendency to move in imagination from one radical extreme to another, from perfect preparedness to abject self-loss and ruthlessness. Here we see Kipling's Stalky turned inside out and exposed as a compensatory fantasy. Conrad's Jim cannot find the middle ground on which to come to grips with his own humanity and accept the world as it is ("Only a night; only a silence"). Jim, as Marlow sees, is neither able to renounce grandiose wishes, nor cope with the underlying helplessness that makes illusion necessary. Jim's response to the demands placed on him by experience is at first a passive surrender to agony, and then withdrawal into the thought that the world has not treated him fairly, that it has not lived up to the ideal of "playing up the game."

Jim sorts both the imaginative and practical aspects of his experience into clear categories of "good" and "bad." If Jameson is right that the unheroic Jim cannot unify "value" and "activity," this is not because Conrad pictures Jim as a failed existentialist in combat with nature. Rather, it is due to the fact that, once Jim projects his own failings onto the world, he imagines that he has been "betrayed by everything." In his case, the fundamental fracturing in imperialist culture, its inability to negotiate between the otherness of the world and the emotional (defensive and wishful) requirements of the self, encourages a splitting of experience into archaic absolutes: fullness and emptiness, perfection and powerlessness, purity and taint. Though Marlow sees the malignancy of Jim's fantasied existence, he also identifies with the trials and potentialities of his "pure exercises of the imagination" (*LJ*, p.172), and in this way, remains both critical of and loyal to this astonishing narcissist, whose ambition to master fate is never more than a pale promise.

Jameson sees the Patusan sections as examples of degraded romance depicting "an imagined wholeness that is part of reality only insofar as it is dreamed there, and projected by this particular world, but has no other substance" (*TPU*, p.253, my emphasis). In contrast to Jameson, I believe that these parts of the novel in many ways signal the incongruity between Jim's dream of heroic responsibility and his ruinous behavior.

Though much of what Jim does appears to be constructive, his greatest need is always to confirm his sense of power. Hence, even his accomplishments turn out to be manifestations of a magical wish to appropriate others as adjuncts to himself, a wish for personal "wholeness" that actually denies others their reality. John McClure has observed how Jim's performance of the role of benevolent patriarch means that he "must rob the Patusan community of some of its most precious resources . . . an appropriation, supported by the Malays themselves as the price of security, [that] weakens the community and renders it vulnerable."[10] As Jim's power grows, the elders of Patusan counsel submission to Jim's authority, and feel forsaken in his absence, thus losing confidence in their own rulers (such as Dain Waris). Though Cornelius, the stepfather of Jim's lover (Jewel), is irrationally resentful of Jim, his observation that Jim orders people about "like a little child" (*LJ*, p.230) is incisive indeed, for Jim often seems like a little boy trying on Father's trousers before a mirror, exhilarated by the largeness of fit, the trappings of paternal power. The novel therefore describes how Jim enforces dependency on his governance and thereby damages the complex and fragile bonds of community, whose preservation would require that he act in the interests of others. But Jim invariably proceeds in infantile ways, seeing others according to his own desires or disavowals.

Conrad's text allows the reader to see the hidden violence of Jim's need, his "projection" of Patusan as a dream-world confirming an illusion of personal, autocratic invulnerability. Moreover, all of Jim's putative achievements are ultimately laid waste by his manifest destructiveness—his decision to send Dain Waris to his death, his suicide, and his abandonment of Patusan to Gentleman Brown's depredation. Certain descriptive and situational ironies convey the disastrous career that follows from Jim's essential self-mis-understanding, his isolated and unrelated pursuit of the fantasy of self-com-pletion. In this way, the text encourages a reading of Jim's self-idealizations, and of his idealizations of patriarchal authority, as at once requiring imperi-alist autocratic rule and preventing him from performing the necessary duties of the colonial father. The institution seems to undermine itself by allowing Jim to abuse communal trust and by encouraging him to under-stand his accomplishments and failures simply as measures of self-worth.

Though Jim wins great admiration and affection, these prove evanes-cent: the desire that shapes his relations with others is too insensible to the differentiated reality of the other as another subject. Conrad has Marlow admit that "I can't with mere words convey to you the impression of his total and utter isolation," the solitude of his achievement (*LJ*, p.166). Conrad thus calls attention to Patusan as a dream-world, and hence would contrast dreaming and reality. That Jim's dream leads him to death, that it kills Dain Waris and does irreparable damage to Doramin's people and to Jewel, only leads Marlow back to his habitual ambiguousness and ambiva-lence. On the one hand, Marlow resolves the disparity through a romantic synthesis of Jim's suicide-cum-redemption; but on the other, Marlow knows that Jim is "pitiless," and that his lack of remorse for (or empathic compre-hension of) the damage he has done *matters*. Conrad has constructed the text to show that Jim's career, from beginning to end, is but one "breach of faith with the community of mankind." While this vision is certainly wider than what Marlow can provide, the question remains whether or not the author "inside" the text shares Marlow's ambivalent investment in Jim—in his need to redeem, but also in his anxiety over Jim's guilt. If the entire Patusan episode is not just an unproblematic projection of wholeness, then the meaning that such a wish might have for Conrad's narrator—indeed, for the author himself—is unfathomable unless one looks at how Marlow is positioned psychologically in the text.

Heart of Darkness in Brantlinger's *Rule of Darkness* and Pecora's *Self and Form*

Lord Jim both debunks and propagates imperialist romantic myth. Similarly, *Heart of Darkness* at once offers an ironic view of colonial cultural assumptions, and affirms their value. Brantlinger rightly characterizes the novella when he points out how its "contradictions lie between Marlow and Kurtz" and "between Conrad and his ambiguous characters" (RD, p. 265). Of course, Heart of Darkness is in many ways a critical exposé of imperialist rapacity.[11] As Benita Parry and many others have shown, the goings-on at the central station provoke Marlow to dismantle virtually all colonialist pretensions, including the putative justice of the civilizing mission, as well as Western efficiency and enlightenment.[12] However, Marlow also reverts to racist myths, especially when feebly rationalizing how Kurtz, as a self-anointed power, has become one of "the high devils" of the land. Marlow lapses into the mentality that, in Brantlinger's words, "painted an entire continent dark"—talking as he does of "rudimentary souls" and devil worship, of the colonist's atavistic regression, and of the sinister seductiveness of Africa. He demonizes otherness and sees it as the external agent of Kurtz's fall, or at least the externalization of ugly impulses repressed by civilization but here unleashed. Just as Marlow in Lord Jim makes the salvaging of his familiar colonial world contingent on the salvaging of Jim, so in Heart of Darkness imperialism is affirmed to the extent that Kurtz can be rehabilitated and even redeemed.

Where Jameson rejects the idea that Lord Jim might have a serious critical purpose, both Brantlinger and Pecora acknowledge the critical dimensions of Heart of Darkness, if only to question the constancy and moral hygiene of these critical elements. Moreover, for both Brantlinger and Pecora the issue of Conrad's relation to the novella's ambiguities is to be explained exclusively in ideological terms. In my view, however, Brantlinger and Pecora fail in similar ways to accomplish precisely what they see as the main purpose of their style of reading.

Brantlinger argues that ideological ambiguity is the result of what Jameson terms Conrad's "will-to-style." The idea, as Jameson explains it, is that Conrad's literary modernism, or impressionism, is a veritable "sensorium" of visual and aural detail, but that it is essentially empty of political content. Brantlinger develops this notion much further: on the one hand, the will-to-style in Conrad is an appropriation and remaking of imperialist adventure fiction for the purposes of high art, and presumably critique; while on the other hand, the romance conventions that Conrad reshapes are themselves racist, and bear within them the projections and hierarchies of imperialist ideology. Thus, according to Brantlinger, it seems to follow that "on some level the impressionism of Conrad's novels and their romance features are identical—Conrad constructs a sophisticated version of the imperialist romance—and in any case both threaten to submerge or 'derealize' the critique of Empire" (*RD*, p.265).

For Pecora, the doubleness of *Heart of Darkness* is the result of Conrad's irony. On the one hand, in Pecora's view, Conrad is something of a Foucauldian ironist because he shows how Marlow's discourse replicates the discourse of the culture. "Conrad . . . demonstrates that Marlow's 'counsel' cannot escape the imperial ironies that determine it. He is, and must be, a product of that culture" (*SF*, p.161). But on the other hand, Pecora reads Conrad's irony as being itself an effect of the same rationalized order of meaning that determines Marlow. "The efficacy of Conrad's formal irony lies in its decentering of [Marlow's] reified narrative subjectivity, [but] irony itself has become a rationalized tool" (p.152). In Pecora's view, Conrad is consistently distanced from Marlow, and knows that Marlow has the same ideological blindspots as the culture. But that same authorial distance replicates at a higher level imperialism's endless capacity to dislocate, defer, and empty out meaning. For all intents and purposes, Pecora's notion of authorial irony is equivalent to Brantlinger's "will-to-style"—which is to say, modernist style and modernist irony are seen as manifestations of cultural reification, and, like imperialism itself, as empty and dark. Hence, for both critics, Conrad's critique founders on an interconnection between imperialist ideology and modernism.

While Brantlinger and Pecora seem to take authorial agency into account—Conrad has a will-to-style or an ironic distance from the culture—this gesture is more apparent than real since, for both, ideology is predeterminative. Consider Brantlinger's use of Jameson. Though Jameson himself believes that the will-to-style is the last retreat of emancipatory desire, Brantlinger reformulates this "will" in ways closely resembling the Althusserian notion of ideology as the individual's "imaginary" relation to society. The modernist seems to be reshaping culture through art, but that reshaping is already managed—or as Jameson says, "contained"—by the distorted languages of society. This is true because, in Brantlinger's view, modernism in and of itself either has no content (represents "a refusal of moral and political judgement") or has only bad political content ("is readily aligned with imperialism and facism"), and hence is "identical" to the patterns of mass discourse, the racism of popular romance. Yet, modernist style is not intrinsically irresponsible or fascistic. While it is certainly the case that specific practitioners of this style were social conservatives and reactionaries (Eliot and Pound), others were feminists and Marxists (Woolf and Benjamin). Brantlinger answers the question of why ambiguity prevails in Conrad's texts or why his judgement is blocked by making Conrad's "will" a function of "style," namely, a function of the preprogrammed equivalency between modernism and romance. In effect, Brantlinger begs the question of why Conrad as a specific authorial subject remains unresolved, maintains contradictory values, and cannot entirely follow through on the project of transforming a popular art into a serious one.

Pecora's Foucauldian and deconstructive moves create an interpretive machine that, in the excess of its determinism, outdoes even Althusserian Marxism (Jameson and Brantlinger). For Pecora, modernist irony is always a "failure of irony" (*SF*, p.99), and hence *Heart of Darkness* is a political tool for producing "a more effectively administered subject" (p.153). While Pecora, unlike Brantlinger, gives an interpretation of Conrad's relation to Marlow, the reading compels us to see Marlow as an entirely "administered" subject and to see Conrad's "irony" as all the more surely inscribing Marlow in the imperialist regime.[13] In Pecora's view, Conrad continually demonstrates that imperialism has always already usurped Marlow's "autonomous being," and that, moreover, such "autonomy" is only an illusion of discourse. The author continuously deconstructs Marlow's impression of coherence into its constitutive social discrepancies and, as a result, dissolves the discursive ground on which Marlow would take his stand against the culture.

Despite Pecora's theoretical complexity and often astute insights into the social dimensions of the novel, his analysis simplifies too much. It presents, for example, an absurdly one-sided view of power. By making imperialist discourse all-powerful, both in its falsehoods and its infinite capacity to defer and render the "truth" undecidable, Pecora has eliminated the possibility of understanding how social discourse might be something the subject invests in, and thus how it *becomes* a mechanism for control. For Pecora, social discourse always already *is* such a mechanism.[14] And while he claims that Conrad is a consistent ironist, the claim is empty: ironic enlightenment means the undoing of the subject, and hence irony, rather than being a device for illuminating, is only a futile conceit. Like Brantlinger, Pecora factors out the subject as a psychological, agentic presence. Both critics miss the point that the individual (decentered by a particular configuration of conscious and unconscious processes), and the subjectivity allocated to the individual by social languages, are not coextensive.[15] Ultimately, Pecora gets no closer to answering the question of Conrad's authorial subjectivity and its patterns of irresolution than does Jameson or Brantlinger.

To illustrate the extent to which ideology constricts Brantlinger's and Pecora's arguments, I want to consider how each critic treats Marlow's claim about ideals. At the beginning of the text, Marlow tells us that what redeems imperialism is "the idea only." "Not a sentimental pretence but an idea, and an unselfish belief in the idea—something you can set up, and bow down before, and offer a sacrifice to. . . ."(HD, p.10). The claim certainly seems to be ironic for Conrad. As the narrative progresses, it reveals a succession of worshippers—the pilgrims of the central station, the Intended, Kurtz, and even in certain respects Marlow himself—each of whom bows to some aspect of imperialism, and hence bows to false ideals or idols.

On this basis, Brantlinger asserts that for Conrad "all ideals transform into idols," and that the author's "ingenious inversion" (which universalizes fetishism) depends on the proposition that "European motives and actions [are] no better than African fetishism and savagery" (RD, p. 262). Brantlinger seems to have accounted for the novella's central contradiction—that it is a critique of imperialism that is also racist, that the text is both an inversion and a replication of its racist sources. However, he does so only if we also believe that the imperialist idea represents all ideals for Conrad, and that authorial irony mimics the moral judgements that imperialism makes about its own injustices (that is, either "we" are superior to "them," or we revert to their barbarism). Brantlinger does not figure into the equation that Conrad holds to traditional ideals—for example, loyalty, solidarity, duty, love of work—that are actually rendered problematic for him by the reified conditions of imperialism. This need to protect problematic values fractures political discourse in The Nigger of the "Narcissus" and Lord Jim. Conrad doesn't suddenly relinquish these values in favor of a ubiquitous nihilism in Heart of Darkness, even though the text is fractured by the nihilistic strains of Conrad's thought. In any case, if racism is to be considered systematic in Heart of Darkness, then the assumption that "all ideals transform into idols" needs to be proved. And lacking this, the claim that Conrad's modernism has no content other than through imperialist ideology tends only to be a self-confirming one.

If Brantlinger's analysis depends on the formula that inversion is recapitulation, Pecora's claim is that negation from within is reinscription—or, in effect, double negation (Marlow's negation followed by Conrad's negation of him). He points to how Marlow invokes "the saving idea" to measure imperialism's best intentions against its crass commercialism. On the one hand, this type of opposition permits Marlow to stand at the edge of his culture, but on the other, it is "always already managed" by the facts of hegemonic control (SF, pp. 144, 143). Since Pecora focuses on Marlow as "a product" of culture, all of Marlow's protests are only "the fictions of self and other that come into existence as differential negations and validations of the privileged center of authority" (p. 143), and hence always presuppose that center. Thus, while Brantlinger sees Conrad himself as always presupposing the center, Pecora reads this as the basis for Conrad's ironic treatment of Marlow and the means by which Conrad reveals Marlow as an "administered subject." The problem, however, is that Conrad systematically negates all of Marlow's protests, and in the process dissolves even "the fiction" of his relative autonomy. Pecora's argument depends on Conrad's not only having anticipated a late-twentieth century understanding of imperialism in the manner of Foucault, but on this same keen understanding going completely haywire, and using corrosive political irony to subvert the very possibility of politics. As he puts it, "Such irony only reinscribes the remainder in an even more efficient version of the imperialist dream" (SF, p. 145).

I don't see Marlow and Conrad as locked together in an endless spiral of negation, but following Pecora, I do see Conrad's nihilism as part of a failed critical dialectic. In effect, Conrad's nihilistic irony blocks Marlow's tale from becoming a full-fledged critical utterance, but does not subvert it entirely. The critical dimension of the text is obvious, and yet also obviously and untenably "de-realized" by ideological readings. The issue, as I have said, is not to resolve ambiguity, but to account for it.

It is necessary therefore to rehabilitate the critical dimensions of Conrad's modernism, on the one hand, and to pose from a different perspective the central issue of Marlow's ambiguous relation to Kurtz, on the other. I want to bring out the novella's contradictions by showing how certain critical elements outstrip the explanatory power of the monodimensional critical paradigms we have looked at, and how the novella's irresolution is overdetermined by being both ideological and psychological.

Brantlinger believes that *Heart of Darkness* founders on its modernist impressionism, that the text's black and white imagery, whether in subversion or corroboration, recapitulates racist romance. However, like Jameson, he misses the fact that much of this imagery is psychological in nature, and that Conrad at least in part de-mystifies the psychology of imperialism. Pecora might retort that Conrad's modernist irony is always critical, but that it problematically dissolves subjectivity. Of course, the problem with Pecora's claim is that it collapses subjectivity into its cultural fictions, and obscures how Conrad's psychological ironies allow us to see why and how Marlow consents to those fictions.

Marlow assumes his steamboat command due to the death of the vessel's former headsman, Captain Fresleven. And so Marlow is brought his

appointment in the Congo before he "had fairly begun to hope for it." Prior
to recounting his own visit to the trading company offices, Marlow tells us
that Fresleven was killed in a scuffle with natives over "two black hens."
Marlow's predecessor attempted to assert his sovereignty by whacking "the
old nigger [the Chief] mercilessly," until the chief's son "made a tentative
jab with a spear at the white man—and of course it went quite easy
between the shoulder-blades" (*HD*, pp. 12–13). After Fresleven has fallen,
both sides clear out, with the blacks expecting "all kinds of calamities," the
whites in "a bad panic." Marlow continues:

> Afterwards nobody seemed to trouble much about Fresleven's remains
> till I got out and stepped into his shoes. I couldn't let it rest, though,
> but when an opportunity offered at last to meet my predecessor, the
> grass growing through his ribs was tall enough to hide his bones. They
> were all there. The supernatural being had not been touched after he
> fell. And the village was deserted, the huts gaped black, rotting, all
> askew within the fallen enclosures. A calamity had come to it, sure
> enough. The people had vanished. Mad terror had scattered them,
> men, women, and children, through the bush and they had never
> returned. What became of the hens I don't know either. I should think
> the cause of progress got them, anyhow. However, through this glori-
> ous affair I got my appointment before I had fairly begun to hope for
> it. (*HD*, p.13)

Marlow first tells how an African nobleman came to kill a white colonial servant, then disclaims or rationalizes Fresleven's role in what happened.
Agency is oddly erased in Marlow's account: rather than say that whites sav-
aged the African tribe in reprisal for Fresleven's murder, he remarks that "a
calamity came to it"; and rather than explaining that he got his post because
Fresleven lost control, he implies that his appointment befell him, that he
passively accepted in surprise and perhaps even gratitude, as though it were
an act of fate. But it is precisely this strategy of disavowal that leads to the
destruction, the emptying out that follows—the whited bones, and the huts
gaping black, ruined, and rotting (perhaps set ablaze by the colonialists in
their "bad panic"). He is being advanced through a system that requires that
the split between white and black races be maintained and guilt alleviated.
Marlow becomes complicitous precisely by absenting himself from the reality of imperialist atrocities except as a passive second-hand witness.
    The account of Fresleven's remains raises a key question: Why is he
simply left to rot where he fell? Even diseased remains are normally made

safe through burial, and Fresleven was, as far as we know, a perfectly healthy corpse. The answer, I would suggest, has to do with the uncanny resonances evoked in Fresleven's colonial compatriots by his petty cruelty, his vulnerability to retaliation, and the moral legitimacy of his attacker's response. Marlow's account of Fresleven's death and its aftermath focuses us on the ambivalence that runs through both. Fresleven might have been made into a martyred hero, or into a catalyst for a recognition of the illegitimacy of imperialist tactics and motives. Neither option is taken up, and yet neither is directly contradicted. Instead his cruelty, his death, and the destruction of the villagers are presented as happenstance, and Fresleven is made into an untouchable, "supernatural" being. His body is untouched because to acknowledge it at all requires that domination be recognized (and either applauded or condemned). As the site of unconscious cultural ambivalence, Fresleven's body is left to the natural process of decay and eventual disappearance, rather than to memory.

Yet, clearly Fresleven's bones threaten Marlow with what they might mean because he is troubled by the story, and directly benefits from the death. In the very next paragraph he recounts traveling to the trading company's offices in Brussels to receive his formal appointment.

> In a very few hours I arrived in a city that always makes me think of a whited sepulchre. Prejudice no doubt. I had no difficulty in finding the Company's offices. It was the biggest thing in the town, and everybody I met was full of it. They were going to run an oversea empire and make no end of coin by trade.
>
> A narrow and deserted street in deep shadow, high houses, innumerable windows with venetian blinds, a dead silence, grass sprouting between the stones, imposing carriage archways right and left, immense double doors standing ponderously ajar. I slipped through one of these cracks, went up a swept and ungarnished staircase, as arid as a desert, and opened the first door I came to. Two women . . . sat on straw-bottomed chairs, knitting black wool. (*HD*, p.13)

Conrad's repetition of key images is too plain to miss: grass sprouting amidst the sepulchral bones of a terrible emptiness and aridity; the black-clad women and black hens carefully placed as putative reasons, symbolic alibis, for the death culture of imperialism.[16] These parallel sets of figures strongly suggest what Conrad seems to know and what Marlow only enacts—that the contradictions within imperialism are successfully mystified, first by being projected onto a scene of cultural otherness, and second by being disclaimed (in the form of skeletal remains left in the open, unsanctified). Through its ironic juxtapositions, then, the novel highlights a strategic psychic gap in the imperialist imagination that Fresleven's unburied and unmourned corpse at once protects and reveals.

Marlow's consent to benefit is the means by which Conrad reveals the scene of colonial violence and the trading company as the source of it, and how the culture splits off that "calamity" by leaving untouched Fresleven's uncanny remains. The incident is at least a corrective to Brantlinger's reductive claim that Conrad's imagistic rendering of European darkness plays strictly within the hierarchical dualisms of racist ideology. For here black Africans are part of Conrad's demonstration of symptomatic psychological splitting within imperialist culture, which is more complicated than a simple ideological dualism. Thus, we are confronted in a real way with the novella's ambiguity, and not so predisposed to resolve it. The Fresleven incident also provides something of a corrective to Pecora, or at least to the idea that Marlow's subjectivity is the sum of its cultural fictions. For we see Marlow managing what disturbs him by absenting himself from recognition. This psychology of tacit consent cannot be equated with Marlow's social fictions, in that it allows such fictions to operate, and hence is larger than the fictions themselves. However, this is not the only example of Conrad constructing Marlow as a defended imperialist self.

Marlow feels an ethnocentric dread of otherness when he begins to travel upriver toward Kurtz's inner station, but Conrad's rendering does not sanction Marlow's unconscious effort to locate (project) its cause outside the self. Marlow tell us that he could have fancied himself "taking possession of an accursed inheritance," but that this imperialist dream of being an originator of meaning in a cursed land fails when the fantasy is challenged. "Prehistoric man was cursing us, praying to us, welcoming us—who could tell? We were cut off from the comprehension of our surroundings; *we glided past like phantoms*, wondering and secretly appalled, as sane men would be before an enthusiastic outbreak in a madhouse" (*HD*, p.37, my emphasis). Suddenly human, the landscape sees him, responds to his presence, awakens his anxiety (he becomes "phantom"-like), and he defensively sees himself as a sane man surprised by primitive madness. His place in the world, a constellation of protected meanings, becomes less real the farther upriver he travels. And in parallel fashion, the farther he goes the more phantasmatic he seems to himself. Community and selfhood decline together. Marlow's perception of the world momentarily becomes an hallucination of it; and his recourse to conventional racist polarizations is the direct consequence of that fearful solipsism, that awareness only of self, with no pathway for mutual comprehension.

In the original manuscript, this encounter on the river is directly followed by an unusual appeal on Marlow's part to an imagined audience. He uses the second-person pronoun to refer to the decorous reader, the Victorian bourgeois "pacific father, mild guardian of a domestic heartstone [sic]," and says of him, "[did you never] suddenly find yourself thinking of carnage. The joy of killing—hey? Or did you never, when listening to another kind of music, did you never dream yourself capable of becoming a saint—if—if. Aha! Another noise, another appeal, another response. All true. All there—*in you* " (*HD*, fn, pp. 37–38, my emphasis). Here Marlow shakes free of his hallucination through the recognition that "the enthusiastic outbreak" of madness is in himself and not outside in Africans. Marlow's moderation of racist dualism (the split between the "sane" colonialist and the "mad" African), and his ownership of an imperialist passion for carnage, might not be all that late - twentieth century readers like, since what is owned, in taking back the projection, is an atavistic or "prehistoric" passion. But notice that Marlow sees this "joy of killing" not in terms of imitating savagery, as in Brantlinger's reading. On the contrary, Marlow doesn't need African role models because his "joy" is intrinsic: "all there— in you." He therefore distinguishes civilized barbarism from untamed life in the jungle. Additionally, imperialism's two ruling desires—to kill and to act in a saintly manner—are both insinuated into the consciousness of the "mild guardian of the heartstone," thereby making it impossible for this consciousness to accept one without accepting the other. Why, then, did Conrad excise these lines? Perhaps he regarded the evocation of an imagined listener as out of synch with the fact that Marlow tells the story to a set of British colonialists onboard the *Nellie.*

Conrad's ironic, modernist imagery and psychology clearly demonstrate a willingness to interrogate the manichean values and defensive splits through which imperialism operates. But irony in the modernist mode is susceptible to slippage, and not necessarily because technique becomes its own raison d'être (Brantlinger), or because irony fails to know its own limits (Pecora). The impressionism of *Heart of Darkness* is in many ways designed, as anthropologist Michael Taussig puts it, "to make us feel . . . the madness of the [imperialist] passion."[17] But to do so, Conrad cannot avoid positioning himself *affectively* within the intricacies of the imperialist problematic; and to the extent that he is unable to work through this passion, his ironic relation to his own text becomes destabilized. The paradox of irony viewed psychologically is that it can cut both ways: given certain

unconscious imperatives, what has been problematized can also be rein-
stated. The critical force of the above examples, then, serves to bring into
even greater relief the central problematic of the novella as a fiction of contradictory motives—particularly as these contradictions are organized
around Marlow as at once forcing his listeners to question their complicity
with ideological illusion and yet attempting to resolidify this illusion, and
around Conrad's self-implication in Marlow's wavering and unstable narration. Though the focal point of the narrative's ambiguity lies in Marlow's
relation to Kurtz, their connection is overdetermined. It is not only an issue
of Marlow's taking contradictory ideological positions, but also an issue of
his psychological ambivalence, an ambidextrous effort to be both Kurtz's
critic and redeemer.

As critic, Marlow is conscious of Kurtz's civilized barbarism, and
grasps the dark irony in Kurtz's idealism, in how "right motives" (benevo-
lence and efficiency) mask the ugliness of self glorification. There is of
course Kurtz's pamphlet, which ends with the post-scriptum "Exterminate
all the brutes!" (HD, pp. 50–51); and there are the severed heads positioned
on stakes around Kurtz's compound. They face inward, as if in blind tribute; and Kurtz becomes a law and idol unto himself, the very embodiment
of genocidal tyranny. This is "efficiency" with a vengeance. This is also the
tragedy of Western modernity, which, as Marshall Berman observes, resides
in the paradox that the limitless power to develop civilization entails the
limitless power to devastate whatever stands in the way (ATIS, p.75).
Hence, what Marlow is forced to confront in Kurtz is very much a Western
and European "joy of killing."[18]

Marlow is also rattled by what he sees, and his anger and fear is raw,
visceral, and unthematized. Kurtz necessarily disrupts Marlow's basic identity, his commitments, his relationship to his social world, and thus experientially positions him in a situation of social loss. And so Marlow discovers
the need to rescue Kurtz's nobility, to transform his traumatic experience of
Kurtz and somehow quarantine Kurtz's most dangerous meanings. Part of
this salvaging mission is that Marlow reinstates racist projection when he
strategically blames the sinister otherness of Africa for Kurtz's malignancy,
telling us that the wilderness and Africans, its satanic agents, devour Kurtz,
and not his own will-to-power (HD, p.49). Brantlinger is perfectly right
that, at certain moments in the text, "Conrad paints Kurtz and Africa with
the same tar brush" (RD, p. 262). But Brantlinger is not attuned to how
Conrad can at other times critique racist projection. Just as importantly,
Brantlinger doesn't factor in the psychosocial context in which Marlow—
or Conrad via his affective link with Marlow—is compelled to cope with

being a partisan of the project that Kurtz defines (*HD*, p.62). And given both of these textual elements, one can see an overdetermined, defensive use of racist ideology, rather than a preprogrammed reproduction of it.

Upon reaching Kurtz's outpost, Marlow realizes suddenly that he has all along identified Kurtz's "genius" with his "voice." In fact, Marlow tells us that Kurtz's trangressions hardly matter when measured against the powerful eloquence of his voice. "The point was in his being a gifted creature and that of all his gifts the one that stood out preeminently, that carried with it a sense of real presence, was his ability to talk, his words—the gift of expression, the bewildering, the illuminating, the most exalted and the most contemptible, the pulsating stream of light or the deceitful flow from the heart of an impenetrable darkness" (*HD*, p.48). This second phase of Marlow's recuperation goes beyond negative defense (blaming the other) to positive illusion (a reunion with the ideal). Marlow never becomes disabused of his faith in Kurtz's greatness, and never gives up associating Kurtz's greatness with his voice.

Yet how do we explain a faith not in what is said or made present by the voice, but in the fact of its non-verbal "presence" being its essential reality? Is this, as Brantlinger suggests, the utter vacuousness of Conrad's modernist will-to-style? Is it, as Pecora asserts, Conrad's ironic negation of all that is left to Marlow, and thus a final emptying out of Marlow's own voice together with his belief in the fullness of the voice? As we have seen, Brantlinger's explanation presupposes that Conrad has no real "will" except the will to reproduce socially reified (empty) language. Pecora's relies on a non-contingent bond between power and Conrad's failed irony, for only when irony is equivalent to social constraint can *Heart of Darkness* be seen as extruding carefully administered subjects. However, to accept either explanation is not just to accept that ideology, in one way or another, has foretold all. It is also to miss the weirdness of this desire itself, this wish for Kurtz's voice to be de-signified and to achieve in some way the status of an ideal. In order to preserve the essential ambiguity of Marlow's utterance, and avoid the reductive view of subjectivity as a conduit for imperialist mystification, I would put forward a psychoanalytic thesis that addresses Marlow's and Conrad's need for irresolution. For to acknowledge a need invokes an experiencing subject, and discursively goes beyond the mere description (however accurate) of an effect.

Marlow's formulation of an "ideal" Kurtz occurs in the context of Marlow's own losses, which come in the form of traumatic events or realizations whose quotient of despair remain largely unthematized. When the abstract ideal cannot be maintained, its loss is partly deferred by this archaic belief in the "voice," in an essential goodness that survives Marlow's intellectual awareness of imperialist "sham and reality." His attachment to the culture is preserved only by leaving unresolved what cannot be mourned, and hence by balancing a fragile social identity between the losses that come with knowing too much and the illusions that come with disavowal, or between seeing into the horror of Kurtz's empty heart and the desperate pretense of finding redemption in a nullity. And if Conrad is distanced from Marlow's investment in the saving "idea" or "voice," still the unconscious patterns of the author "inside" the text demonstrate a need for irresolution similar to the narrator's. In the next chapter, then, we will investigate patterns of ambivalent fantasy in both *Heart of Darkness* and *Lord Jim* for how they inscribe Conrad's inability to mourn, and the reversion of authorial subjectivity to a position of suspension between contradictory valences and opposed desires.

CHAPTER FIVE

Positioning Conrad:
Reading for Affect in
Heart of Darkness **and** *Lord Jim*

In *Heart of Darkness*, Marlow tells us that the ordeal of looking into Kurtz's soul is "withering to [his] belief in mankind" (*HD*, p. 66). In *Lord Jim*, he interprets Jim's criminal "weakness" (his fear) as "a thing of mystery and terror," and also notes that the obscure truth involved in that fear is "momentous enough to affect mankind's conception of itself" (*LJ*, pp. 32, 57). If it is Kurtz and Jim who act out the primitive narcissistic urges and anxieties of the imperialist psyche, then their breach of communal principles represents for Marlow a crisis of faith, a withering and terrifying loss of his cultural ideals. In losing these cherished "social objects," these commonalities of value and belief that make the world meaningful, Marlow is given the psychological task of mourning the meaning(s) of Kurtz and Jim, and of acknowledging what was lost in him when they perished.

The idea of social loss and the mourning of cultural objects is crucial to how one reads Marlow. But what is cultural mourning? Freud saw mourning primarily as a process of reality testing, in which the mourner must discover again and again that the loved object no longer exists, that what must be revised is "each single one of the memories and expectations in which the libido is bound to the object."[1] From the perspective of object relations theory, mourning is not just a matter of reality testing. As Kleinian analyst

Hanna Segal observes, it also involves a difficult process of reinstating and reconstructing internal object representations, whereby absence is mediated through substitute symbols or creative fantasies.[2] In a general sense, then, mourning is what we do with our dead—whether we are crippled by loss, or are able to generate, from loss and memory, new connections with the past for creative purposes in the present. And in healthy cultural mourning, as Peter Homans puts it, one "individuates" from an un-self-aware (sometimes an idealizing) relation to cultural symbols, and heals the breach by means of an introspective reinterpretation of one's cultural ethos. The products of culture are therefore returned to the subject to be used "as the raw material for the construction of new meanings and of a new relation to the past."[3]

However, Marlow is "stuck" between his experience of the loss of cultural meaning and a process of mourning/reinterpretation. Unable to reassess inherited cultural idealizations and to mourn their loss, he is more or less buffeted by the conflicting emotions and fantasies that Kurtz and Jim awaken in him. Unable to acknowledge and mourn certain aspects of his social reality, he risks a radical disordering of his relation to that reality; and it is in an effort to alleviate this risk that he employs defenses designed to suppress his unease and rescue his cultural identifications.

Close psychological readings of Kurtz and Jim, and of Marlow's "inability to mourn," suggest that Conrad shares Marlow's inclination to disavow loss and the need to mourn it. Conrad cannot seem to find the right psychological distance on Marlow's narration, always seeming either too close or too far. In *Heart of Darkness*, he is not just ironic but nihilistic and contemptuous toward Marlow's need to idealize Kurtz, and yet his rendering of Marlow's emotional life is dizzyingly impressionistic, not at all distanced. His scorn inverts Marlow's vulnerability without overcoming his inability to disentangle himself from it. In *Lord Jim*, Conrad seems too close, too ready with sympathy for Marlow's (and Jim's) defensive idealizations. Instead of affirming the gravity of the suffering he recounts, he seems to have relinquished in some important way an emotional connection to loss. Moreover, if the author "inside" the text seems unconsciously entangled in the vicissitudes of an unresolved, melancholy relation to culture, the author "outside" the text corroborates this supposition in letters to Cunninghame Graham, written during the same period of time as the novels.

Conrad cannot manage a dependably disenchanted, ironic, and dignified stance, because central aspects of his narrative are, from a psychological perspective, so chronically disordered. On the one hand, he has a disillusioning and afflicting vision of psychic primitivity in the social realm;

but on the other, he (like Marlow) seems unable to give up the structures of denial of the imperialist self, and hence is unable to mourn the losses entailed by his own recognition. This creates the narrative's irresolution, the doubleness of seeing but not affirming the vision, as lucidity is played off against ideational density. His texts seem to demand from the reader a subjective entanglement in psychological undecidability, a capacity to enter into certain compensatory alternatives to understanding. Reading Conrad, we are asked to try to make sense of the personal idiom through which he unconsciously communicates psychic unrest, and to do so from within the idiom itself.

In the following psychoanalytic readings, I will argue that Conrad is psychologically, and inordinately, unresolved as an author. I do so by reading Marlow's emotional entanglements with Kurtz and Jim for what these relationships reveal about authorial subjectivity, and by referring to extra-textual evidence from Conrad's letters to contextualize and shore up my claims.

Heart of Darkness: "The Dream-Sensation"

Marlow's experience, in both living and telling the tale, is affectively rich. After recounting the atrocities he has witnessed at the Central Station, Marlow tells his audience that to narrate successfully his experience he must somehow convey a "dream-sensation."

> "Do you see [Kurtz]? Do you see the story? Do you see anything? It seems to me I am trying to tell you a dream—making a vain attempt, because no relation of a dream can convey the dream-sensation, that commingling of absurdity, surprise, and bewilderment in a tremor of struggling revolt, that notion of being captured by the incredible which is the very essence of dreams. . . ."
>
> He was silent for a while.
>
> ". . . No, it is impossible; it is impossible to convey the life-sensation of any given epoch of one's existence—that which makes its truth, its meaning—its subtle and penetrating essence. It is impossible. We live, as we dream—alone. . . ." (HD, p.30)

Marlow attempts to remember and represent "the dream-sensation," but this sensation, which precedes yet is somehow integral to making "meaning," seems not to be memory in the usual sense of a cognitive recollection thematically available to the subject.

So what *is* a "dream-sensation"? How do we get at Marlow's dream-feeling and its uncanny quality, at once awful and familiar? And what does it mean for Marlow to tell his experience as if it were a dream, a strange drama in which the subject has been cast to perform (what seems to him) an unintelligible part? This is not to say that Marlow "dreams" Kurtz or his own story, but that the nature of what he is trying to convey might be clarified by considering it in light of psychoanalytic notions of dreaming.

Freud's account of the dream as a structure comprised of a manifest text and latent thoughts does not really explain what Marlow might mean by "dream-sensation," or the experience of a dream. Psychoanalyst Christopher Bollas has persuasively argued that Freud's emphasis on the dream as an unconscious message or psychic theme leads to Freud's relative neglect of his own discovery about dreaming, "the notion of the dream space as a night theatre involving the subject in a vivid re-acquaintance with the Other," or with an infantile part of the self.[4] For Bollas, the dream is an aesthetic event, a space in which the dreaming self (a character in the dream setting) is managed by the unconscious ego. "When the subject experiences the dream setting," Bollas writes, "he is being handled by the dream aesthetic, . . . [and] the ego (an unconscious organizing process) arranges the place where the Other speaks" (*TSO*, p.71). In Bollas's terms, the self is "the thought known," the subject who puts the dramatic experience of the dream into narrative form, and thus reverses the dream experience in order to manage it as text. In contrast, the unconscious ego, the unconscious dimensions of subjecthood responsible for directing the dream experience, is "the unthought known," the mode of being and relating—the existential grammar, as it were, learned from early relations with the maternal environment that have been internalized into the structures or patterns of character. Or again, the "unthought known" is the affective memory of the preverbal subject, "a remembering by being . . . that is manifested in the [dramatic experience] of the dream" (*TSO*, p.77).

The notion that unthematized or pre-representational affective states constitute primary subjectivity is a valuable corrective to theories of the subject that radically foreground language. Subjective experience is in a fundamental way a "remembering by being" (the unthought known), a wordless recollection of self, that might never take thematic form as unconscious fantasy or as cognitive memory. These unrepresented self-states, the moods and affects that become woven into permanent features of character, can inflect waking life just as they do dreaming activity. Thus, when Marlow struggles with how to speak the uncanny, we might say Marlow feels he needs to convey through representation a deeply existential mood, a pre-representational feeling-state set vibrating or brought to life by his experience of Kurtz. Narration cannot relate this mood, this "life-sensation," but Marlow needs to be inside of it in order to be in contact with "true" self-experience. Marlow's dis-ease with the dream sensation—his feeling of "being captured by the incredible which is the very essence of dreams," his sense of being held by what has been processed in being but not in thought—leads to his dis-ease with his audience. They do not feel what is unthought in Marlow, and hence cannot understand the "dream" he is telling. Thus it follows for Marlow that to know how Kurtz has affected him and to make sense of this, Marlow must resonate with what is felt but unseen in Kurtz, and Marlow's audience must resonate with his subjective experience of this same darkness. As the tale is told, importantly enough, darkness falls, and the telling ends in darkness. The narrator and his audience experience but cannot see what lies at the heart of the talk; it is existential, but unrepresentable except as darkness.

Of course, Marlow's search for the meaning of Kurtz is partly a cognitive one. He explains, "I am trying to account to myself for . . . Mr. Kurtz" (*HD*, p. 50). However, Marlow's attempt to see into Kurtz is guided by his feeling about Kurtz, and his affective bond with Kurtz does not fit neatly into conceptual or moral frames of reference. Reconsider for a moment the passage in which Marlow remembers his powerful attraction to Kurtz's voice. Approaching Kurtz's outpost, desperately worried that Kurtz's followers had turned on and killed him, Marlow suddenly recognized that for him Kurtz "presented himself as a voice." "The point was in his being a gifted creature and that of all his gifts the one that stood out pre-eminently, that carried with it a sense of real presence, was his ability to talk . . ." (p.48). Only later does Marlow's recognition of the atrocities committed by Kurtz have any hope of becoming "the point" of his discourse; and even then the point is in some measure lost on Marlow because "recognition" is rooted in the imagery of his "dream-sensation," his uncomprehended—or, in effect, his untranslated—"nightmare" of imperialism (pp. 30, 64, 65). For Marlow, whether Kurtz's voice speaks of evil or light, the voice itself conveys in speaking an experience of ontic fullness ("a sense of real presence").

Homi Bhabha, too, in his essay "Articulating the Archaic," sees a certain failure of "translation" in Marlow's colonial experience, and points to Kurtz's "voice" as just such an instance of this hiatus. Bhabha, it may be recalled, defines cultural difference in terms of the deconstructive principle of *differance*, namely, the idea that colonial authority can only be articulated by means of the other, and hence the boundedness of the center is at once constituted and subverted by the inclusion of the periphery. Thus, certain

acts of "colonial enunciation"—such as the self-canceling oppositions
Marlow uses to describe Kurtz's voice—are exemplary of the failure to
establish the hierarchical difference between colonizer and colonized, and
hence are emblematic of how colonialist discourse is fretted between its
transcendental claim to authority (closure) and its self-subverting practice
of de-authorization. In this sense, for Bhabha, the assertive authority of
colonial utterance is in principle confounded by its own "incoherence" or
"ambivalence."[5]

Marlow's appeal to Kurtz is indirectly an appeal to the unknown
other, as Bhabha says. However, Bhabha is altogether too abstract to
account for the layered complexity of Marlow's relation to "the voice."
First, Marlow's appeal is not the site of the disruption of imperialist sense,
because the loss of authoritative sense inheres in the discrepancy between
imperialist values and practice, which is everywhere explicit in Africa.
Second, while Marlow's confusion indirectly refers to the cultural other
(since colonial speech *always* refers to the unknown other), Marlow's
encounter with Kurtz is not ideological or discursive in any simple sense,
because his appeal to Kurtz's voice has an immediate subjective force and
meaning that exceeds explanations based on de-authorization, or self-
deconstructing discourse. Though Bhabha invokes the psychological term
of "ambivalence," he does not develop a subjective context in which to
make the term meaningful. Marlow is unconsciously motivated—that is,
forced back onto the non-verbal dimension of experience—to maintain an
inviolable connection with Kurtz that is somehow (perhaps magically)
impervious to the destabilizing incoherence of what the voice says.

Hence, what Marlow wants in being with Kurtz, in seeing into
Kurtz, is to establish a wordless rapport with a sacred, absolutely "good"
object. The illusion of such a rapport represents Marlow's longing for an
affectively full "aesthetic" moment, an experience that holds self and other
in synchrony, and that expresses, as Bollas puts it, "that part of us where . . .
rapport with the other was the essence of life before words existed" (*TSO*,
p. 32), when the other was an affectively inflected voice uttering the
sounds the experience of which was meaningful at the level of warmth,
hunger, or safety, for example, rather than at the level of language. We can
infer from Marlow's longing for affective synchrony with Kurtz (a communion transcending words) that Marlow's sense of self has been deeply rup-
tured—that what he knows about imperialism has radically undermined
him, though he cannot make conscious sense of what the nightmare subjectively means to him. And Kurtz, Marlow hopes, might have the power
to lift the intolerable spell of the "dream," to redemptively restore Marlow's

"own reality" (*HD*, p.31). For Marlow, Kurtz is akin to the primary object of infancy, at once the source of traumatic loss and the hoped-for redemption.

Marlow's narrative is given to us as a confusing nightmare, and as an experience of his deep need for redemptive communion, each of which suggests that to understand Marlow, his listeners must feel and tolerate what *he* feels. However, Marlow's descriptions of Kurtz's magical "voice" and of the "dream-sensation" are contextualized in a way that shows how the audience lacks attunement to the emotional experience Marlow is attempting to convey. When Marlow wonders if the others "see" his dream, he turns to them for reassurance. "Of course in this you fellows see more than I could then. You see me, whom you know. . . ." (*HD*, p.30). Marlow looks to his audience to affirm his subjective experience, to "see" him so that he can begin to interpret his experience, and in this way once again become meaningful to himself. But he seems to solicit only incomprehension. The principal listener comments on how Marlow, sitting in darkness and alone, "had been no more to us than a voice," and on how the listener himself "listened, I listened on the watch for the sentence, for the word that would give me the clue to the faint uneasiness inspired by this narrative that seemed to shape itself without human lips in the heavy night-air of the river" (*HD*, p.30). Like Marlow, the listener wants a clue to understand and thereby dispel the uneasiness. However, what the listener offers is only a "faint" mirror for Marlow's turmoil. The listener's affective involvement is insufficient either to overcome Marlow's sense of aloneness or shed light on his darkness.

Once we have appreciated the extent to which Marlow is riveted by perceptual and affective memories of his jungle experience, and seen how difficult it is for him to make his experience coherent, we can begin to read Marlow's narrative situation onboard the *Nellie* as a kind of re-creation of what in psychoanalysis is sometimes called a holding environment. This is interlocutionary space in which the analysand (Marlow) presents his own prereflective patterns of being to the analyst (the listener). In effect, Marlow asks his audience to recognize him as a subject who can be understood and to do for him what he cannot do for himself—to assist him, that is, in finding meaning for these unthematized feelings. The listener must discover symbolic equivalents for Marlow's sensations, but he can only do so if he can "be with" Marlow in the existentially specific way required by the dream-sensation or mood-state. Rather than seeing Marlow and resonating with him, however, the listener responds only to Marlow's sense of tragic isolation. And Marlow returns to his conviction that "we live, as we dream—alone."

Similarly, when Marlow thinks he might have missed his chance to experience the "real presence" of Kurtz's voice, and starts to articulate his disappointment ("I couldn't have felt more of lonely desolation somehow had I been robbed of a belief or had missed my destiny in life"[HD, p.48]), the audience becomes restless and sighs with impatience. Marlow infers that someone has called him "absurd." Marlow retorts: "Why do you sigh in this beastly way, somebody? Absurd? Well, absurd. Good lord! mustn't a man ever . . ." (p.48). The failure to empathize with his desolation makes him agitated and anxious. Resuming his narrative, his hope of fellowship turning again to a cynical awareness of his isolation, Marlow provides a culminating memory: "I was cut to the quick at the idea of having lost the inestimable privilege of listening to the gifted Kurtz. Of course I was wrong. . . . A voice. He was very little more than a voice. And I heard—him—it—this voice—other voices—all of them were so little more than voices—and the memory of that time itself lingers around me, impalpable, like a dying vibration of one immense jabber, silly, atrocious, sordid, savage, or simply mean without any kind of sense" (p.48–49). The audience finds no clue to unlock the absurdity in Marlow's expression of longing and disillusionment, and this calls forth a memory of voices that are empty and offer neither comfort nor sense. One acutely feels Marlow's sense of being alone with the jabber of his own voice.

The phrase, "the memory of that time lingers around me . . . mean without any kind of sense," expresses the disillusioning loss of Kurtz's "real presence." However, one also senses anger with "this voice—other voices—all of them were so little more than voices," a corollary of Marlow's sense of betrayal at being "robbed of a belief." Marlow wanted Kurtz to mirror back to him an idealized image of their shared beliefs. But Marlow now experiences the crumbling of that ideal ("I was wrong") in terms of betrayal and desolation, for, by subverting the symbolic values of imperialism, Kurtz has failed him. In this terrible deceleration from an illusion of perfect rapport to a conviction of utter senselessness, Marlow substitutes anger and despair for mourning and a gradual acceptance of loss. The "sadder but wiser" tonalities that are, as Peter Homans says, part of working through disillusionment, are not part of Marlow's experience (and reexperience in the narrative dream) of Kurtz (ATM, p. 25). For him, anger and senselessness follow each other in a futile round: the absurdity of Marlow's experience of Kurtz (and of all the other imperialist voices) incense him; but this impedes his ability to make meaning, to move on, to know himself and the world in new ways. And if his angry devaluation of the clamoring voices gets in the way of sense, then desolation becomes a position of protest, including a refusal to avow what has been lost—which is to say, to avow the very thing that has triggered his desolation. He does this by holding in separate hands two different versions of Kurtz: the redemptive Kurtz who held the promise of light in darkness, and the despair-laden Kurtz who spoke no sense and razed all value. Thus, in a place thick with pain, the promise and the hope of Kurtz is never lost or grieved. If, as Bollas says, affective synchrony, the generative illusion of fitting with the object, constitutes the psychological aesthetic, Kurtz becomes for Marlow a "frustrating aesthetic," a subjective experience of unresolved emptiness. And Marlow's frustration is intolerable to both him and his audience because neither he nor they are able to make sense of the loss of any redemptive meaning in imperialism. Marlow can only convey to his listeners his own disorganized feelings, the longing and frustration of the private self, which paradoxically uses despair to avoid loss, and deploys emptiness to fend off the death of a needed ideal promise.

While my full argument about Conrad's positioning in the text can only be given after we have explored Marlow's economy of despair more fully, I want to step back for a moment to suggest that in these passages, which offer a preliminary view of Marlow's relation to Kurtz and to the listeners of the tale, the text seems designed to affect how its readers feel— an obvious point that gets ignored in the analysis of discursive formations. Conrad would have us attend closely to the multiform quality of Marlow's "sensation(s)"—to Marlow's involvement in imperialism as a confusing and formidable nightmare; to his need for generative (mirroring) and redemptive (idealizing) illusions about "the voice"; to his anger at the disillusioning meanness of "the immense jabber." Just as Marlow must struggle with affect, so too must the reader. And the reader's experience of Marlow's emotions casts doubt on the notion that Conrad is entirely ironic toward his narrator. For example, while it is true that Conrad undermines the reader's belief in the plenitude of Kurtz's voice (for example, with Marlow's self-subverting statement that the voice is empty and senseless), affect changes irony and modifies it with the reader's textual experience of unironic anger and frustration. What is left cannot be irony in the usual sense of a distanced recognition of a reality different from a masking appearance, because here unironic affect compels the reader to identify with the reality of Marlow's struggle, and to do so even as the reader criticizes Marlow for not learning from the reality of Kurtz's emptiness. If the "affective aesthetic" traps the reader in too narrow a frame of reference, and if it is not circumscribed by the moral and political reasoning that makes *Heart of Darkness* a critique of imperialism, perhaps this is so because the signification of Kurtz cannot be reduced to *non-sense*, but must be mourned as *a lost value*. Conrad's irony seems to depend on a nihilistic interpretation of Kurtz, on the lack of meaning articulated by the notion of the "voice" as "simply mean without any kind of sense"—which is also to say that Conrad's nihilism in the novella blocks Marlow's negative affective states from unfolding into sense, and might be itself the function of a context-specific need to defend against working through the experience of loss. And if irony, like emptiness, does stand in for mourning, it follows that Conrad is at once merged with and distanced from the narrator. However, we need to look more closely at the text to see if this idea bears fruit.

I have said that Marlow, compelled by the nightmare of imperialism run amok, looks to Kurtz, and to the transformative and redemptive experience of affective synchrony, to gain release from the unintelligibility of what he sees. Marlow's affective aesthetic is at once positive and negative: he idealizes and de-idealizes Kurtz, and he seems captured between the two poles of the split. Even before Marlow's journey upriver, he was drawn to Kurtz as both an ideal and debased figure, and his confrontation with Kurtz only made that ambivalence more acute. This ambivalence is at the center of what Marlow repeatedly refers to as his "fascination" with Kurtz. In its essence, fascination is the dual feeling of being attracted and repulsed, which at once seeks to merge with and to repudiate the object of fascination, and hence eschews loss and substitutes the arousal that comes with watching and hoping to see . It is primarily through the lens of fascinated vision that Marlow interprets his experience of the Congo, imperialism, and Kurtz.

There are two passages on fascination. The first, a crucial part of Marlow's introduction to his story, images a soldier of imperial Rome wading through the water and bushes of the Thames—though, of course, Marlow has in view modern colonialists like himself and Kurtz. Of the Roman soldier Marlow says:

> The utter savagery had closed round him ["the decent young citizen"]—all that mysterious life of the wilderness that stirs in the forest, in the jungles, in the hearts of wild men. There's no initiation either into such mysteries. He has to live in the midst of the incomprehensible which is also detestable. And it has a fascination too, that goes to work upon him. The fascination of the abomination—you know. Imagine the growing regrets, the longing to escape, the powerless disgust, the surrender—the hate. (*HD*, p.10)

In a second passage, Marlow describes how he shared with Kurtz the "ordeal of looking" into Kurtz's dying soul. As Peter Brooks has observed, this passage confirms Marlow's need for a parental figure whose last words impart "all the wisdom" (*HD*, pp, 65, 69).[6] Marlow says:

> Oh, I wasn't touched. I was fascinated. It was as though a veil had been rent. I saw on that ivory face the expression of sombre pride, of ruth-less power, of craven terror—of an intense and hopeless despair. Did he live his life again in every detail of desire, temptation, and surren-der during that supreme moment of complete knowledge? He cried in a whisper at some image, at some vision—he cried out twice, a cry that was no more than a breath.
> 'The horror! The horror!" (*HD*, p.68)

Let's consider first "the fascination of the abomination." On the one hand, Marlow's discourse conforms to imperialist binarisms (civilized/savage, human/inhuman) and to the imagery of the Fall (wildness is the diabolical agent compelling the colonialist's surrender). But on the other, simple con-formity to imperialist discourse is complicated by Marlow's fascination with wildness, by his captivation by the "abomination" he detests. We are most fascinated by what we feel variably or conflicted about; and we feel most conflicted about that which seems other ("incomprehensible"), and espe-cially when this other is a disavowed part of ourselves. Marlow is no dif-ferent. Since he is a participant in imperialism, Marlow's fascination is stirred by the sentiments that fill the colonial heart with savagery, the nar-cissistic disorder figured by Kurtz's face, by "the expression of sombre pride, of ruthless power, of craven terror—of an intense and hopeless despair."

Marlow is bound to Kurtz by his own disavowed participation in colonial surfeit and brutality. Marlow is what Kurtz is, but hopes that by seeing into the dark heart of Kurtz he will not himself have to *be* Kurtz, that by seeing he can make this aspect of himself other to himself. Hence, he is fascinated by Kurtz ("Oh, I wasn't touched. I was fascinated.") And balanc-ing the fascinated dread of what is disavowed is Marlow's fascinated hope that he might either merge with an idealized Kurtz, or have the great man reflect back to him Marlow's self-ideal. In this Marlow turns to Kurtz as a small child turns to a parent.

Similar to the affective synchrony he imagines flowing from Kurtz's "real presence," Marlow looks into the depths of Kurtz ("Being alone in the wilderness, it [Kurtz's soul] had looked within itself. . . . I had—for my sins, I suppose—to go through the ordeal of looking into it myself" [*HD*, p.65]), in the hope that Kurtz will look back at Marlow in a mirroring recognition. He hopes, in other words, that Kurtz will transmit to him "complete knowledge," and teach him how to feel and what meaning his feelings should have. Fascinated vision therefore promises to provide Kurtz with the meaning that Kurtz by himself lacks or has destroyed. It is as if by struggling to see into Kurtz, Marlow can also create on Kurtz's behalf the meaning both need. But Marlow cannot give content to Kurtz without Kurtz first providing it to Marlow. It is the wish for a parental mirror that sets up the fascinated relation between Marlow's question ("Did he live his life again in every detail of desire, temptation, surrender during the moment of complete knowledge?") and Kurtz's response ("The horror! The horror!"). Marlow transforms "the horror" of narcissistic power, terror, and despair into something like Kurtz's assumption of collective imperialist "sins" ("desire, temptation, surrender"). He discovers in Kurtz's final words the expression of a quasi-divine omniscience, of "complete knowledge," rather than, as Brooks puts it, a simple "cry" of indecipherable pain (*RFTP*, p. 250). Marlow's fascination provides the hope that Kurtz can be resurrected, that the mystery of grace in evil can be looked into and found true.

Fascination can entail a huge distortion of perception; but Conrad seems to have ironic distance on Marlow's image of Kurtz as a great man. Marlow's rhetorical affirmation, "Did he live his life again in every detail?," asks to be read as a literal question; and Kurtz's utterance, "the horror," suggests only emptiness and unintelligibility. Kurtz's ultimate expression exemplifies, ironically enough, how "the voice" is "simply mean without any kind of sense." However, irony is continually butting up against the complicated psychology of the text. In Kurtz, Marlow feels the pathos of a denied promise on which his psychic life depends. He pursues a hope of redemption in order to undo his disillusioning experience of imperialism. What he finds upriver, however, is not redemption but trauma, a rupture in the world and in the self that throws him back on pre-representational ways of being. Trauma arouses Marlow's need for Kurtz to be a kind of mythic parent, one whose "grammar of being" structures for the self the immediacy of percept and affect, even while Kurtz is also the instigator of Marlow's trauma. Kurtz is the all-in-all, and so Marlow's relation to him can only have this quality of being captivated or in a bind. At once rhapsodically idealized and hopelessly cruel, Kurtz becomes for Marlow a narcissistic parent—in fact, the epitome of imperialist culture's indifference to "decent young citizens" like Marlow. We are not letting Marlow off the hook to recognize that he is

bound to Kurtz much the same way that grown children of abusive or malig-
nantly selfish parents maintain tormented loyalty and love for those who
hurt them. In fact, we have already seen how the training of Empire's servants begins with such social parenting, and Marlow turns to Kurtz for the
same sort of (redemptive) instruction.

Marlow bears witness to the ideals and the chaos that reside in Kurtz.
But in the end, all collapses into the chaos, where the expansion of self
(based on an exorbitant fantasy of appropriation) becomes a diffusion of
self. Marlow repeats Kurtz's litany of ownership. " 'My intended, my ivory,
my station, my river, my . . .' everything belonged to him. It made me hold
my breath in expectation of hearing the wilderness burst into a prodigious
peal of laughter that would shake the fixed stars in their places" (HD, p.49).
Marlow then traces the fantasy of narcissistic assumption back to a chronic
hunger, as he recounts how Kurtz opened his mouth wide as if to devour
all the earth with all of its mankind. But Kurtz's voraciousness leads only to
starvation: "I could see the cage of his ribs all astir, the bones of his arms
waving. It was as though an animated image of death carved out of old
ivory had been shaking its hand with menaces . . ." (HD, p.59). His impossible wish ends in despair. At the very bottom, beneath the pride and
power, Marlow sees Kurtz's hungry, vengeful, empty self, full of impotent
anger and fear, unceremoniously reduced by a world that, in its derisive
contempt, seems as cruel as Kurtz himself.

To say that Kurtz constitutes himself by appropriating others is also
to acknowledge that he is dependent on those he controls. Indeed, his fantasied omnipotence defends against an insurmountable dependency, and
suggests an original, inordinate frustration or wound (symbolized by the
blurted, incomprehensible cry "the horror"). This injury has left him caught
between two equally unrealizable desires. One is to submit by merging
with the omnipotent other (lose himself in the African darkness). The other
is to enter the fecund body of the wilderness and dismantle and appropriate it from within, to steal its power and refuse absolutely his dependency
(lose the basic relatedness on which selfhood relies). Positioned between
absolute submission and absolute hegemony, merger and isolation, Kurtz
becomes the perfect embodiment of a radical, unresolvable, malignant
ambivalence. He has nowhere to go but to death. Marlow sees that Kurtz
lives his narcissistic dilemma, his split between grandiosity and vulnerability, to the end. For with death he is racked by both "the diabolic love and
the unearthly hate of the mysteries [his soul] had penetrated" (HD, p.67).
Kurtz must always try to assure himself of his control (his "diabolic love"),
expand his dominion, and crowd out the stubborn realities of the world

through either sadistic expansion or rage ("his unearthly hate"), lest he experience his own vulnerability. Kurtz operates on a survival footing: either he consumes the world or it consumes him. The irony, of course, is that in imagining that he consumes the world, he voids it and makes it into the inhuman place he fears, the very image of his own hunger and emptiness. Since Kurtz can neither fulfill desire nor accept limit (engage others and receive what provisions they have to give), he is unable to nourish himself. The image of Kurtz's devouring mouth and wasted body (the "pitiful and appalling" skeleton, with its wide gaping mouth) crystallizes his inability to metabolize psychically what he takes in, and in this he suffers from a kind of existential bulimia.[7]

Marlow stands mute before the enormity of Kurtz's degradation. There are no words in Marlow's belief system to make sense of either Kurtz's self-worship or of his own complicity in imperialist atrocity, his "unforeseen partnership" with Kurtz (HD, p.67). The collapse of Marlow's illusion of moral integrity correlates with Kurtz's disintegration. What can Marlow do to keep himself from sliding into the same oblivion? The answer, I think, lies precisely in his ambivalence, for in his frustration and fascination with Kurtz, Marlow manages to disavow his own losses. To say that Marlow is ambivalent is also to suggest that he holds himself in suspension, in between two conflicting aspects of his relation to Kurtz, neither of which he can pursue without grave consequences. To the extent that Kurtz is experienced as other, he demands resolution into conceptual and moral clarity. However, to the extent that Marlow identifies with Kurtz, speaking or clarifying what Kurtz means would threaten Marlow with self-collapse, with following Kurtz into "a muddy hole" (HD, p.69). For Marlow, ambivalence is a balancing act that must be maintained in the interest of survival.

Marlow's narrative is informed at every turn by this ambivalence, the impossible task of being in between wanting to speak and not speak a truth that demands equally that it be spoken and hidden, seen and obscured. For Marlow to emerge from the in-between—to speak of the "unspeakable" connection/disconnection he feels in relation to Kurtz—would be to tell the story of his trauma. Our adaptations to trauma—how we express or defend against traumatic rupture—tend to follow characteristic patterns (reactive hyper-vigilance, or dissociative torpor, for example). Similarly, healing entails certain stringent requirements. As Judith Herman explains, in order for survivors of crisis to successfully re-immerse themselves in the traumatic past (in an effort to master it), they must first have a "protected anchorage in the present," a safe relationship or holding space.[8] In addition, the retelling, which is itself a painstaking exploration of "context, fact, emotion, and meaning" (*TR*, p. 182), requires making connections between emotions and perceptual/cognitive memory, and thus finding the subjective meaning of the traumatic event. In time, this meaning must be mourned. As Herman says, "trauma inevitably brings loss . . . and plunges the survivor into profound grief" (*TR*, p.188). Finally, the subject must reconnect with the world. Herman explains: "Not only must she restore her own sense of worth, but she must be prepared to sustain it in the face of the critical judgments of others" (*TR*, p.178). In a general sense, Marlow tells the tale in the hope that by re-experiencing the "nightmare" and "sensation" of the dream, he will find in Kurtz, or in his audience's response to Kurtz, the meaning of his own experience—not affect and not percept, but the subjective sense that integrates the two and allows for the mourning of what has been lost in accepting what the story means.

What creates discontinuity in the telling process, and keeps meaning in suspension, is Kurtz's negative presence, recreated in the audience's unresponsiveness. In this respect, what is most real for Marlow is the gap between himself and Kurtz, between himself and his audience, between himself and his own experience. As André Green describes it, the non-object has become the object, which in this context "means not the representation of the object but the non-existence of the object."[9] For someone lodged in this position by traumatic discontinuities in relation to primary others, the life-motto becomes, as Green says, "All I have got is what I have not got" (*OPM*, p. 291). It is the gap that occludes mourning, the paradox that Marlow's telling is intended either to dispel (with the felt presence of the other) or reaffirm (protecting the object's non-existence).

More specifically, we can say that what is decisive for a successful narrative retelling, one that opens itself to mourning, is the task of connecting Marlow's feelings of moral betrayal and despair with his cognitive recognition of the brutal emptiness of Kurtz's narcissism, "so withering to one's belief in mankind" (*HD*, pp. 65–66). For only by creating this interpretive link can Marlow name his shameful collusion in imperialism, begin to mourn the lost illusions of ethical selfhood, and eventually find a way to take responsibility for what cannot be undone. To speak the unspeakable is thus to discover the subjective meaning of the trauma story. Yet what Edward Said calls the "contingent situation" of Marlow's telling his tale for British listeners, who believe in "the sovereign historical force of imperialism," places Marlow in a difficult if not untenable position, since his audience (the Director of Companies, the lawyer, the accountant) must be able to bear what Marlow has to say.[10] But wouldn't he be asking those listeners to undo the established necessity and rectitude of imperialist hegemony, and peel away the skins of their collective identity? Should Marlow, then, expect fellowship and anchorage for the meaning of his complicity with Kurtz, or should he accept, along with his audience, the injunction to repudiate the rupture in colonial myth-making that Kurtz signifies?

Recall how, in the passage about Marlow's frustrated longing for Kurtz's "voice," the audience defensively shuns Marlow's need for fellowship (to be listened to), which leaves him feeling "absurd" in their presence. Though his immediate response is equally defensive ("Absurd? Well, absurd."), he goes on to reveal something of his disappointment and disenchantment ("I was cut to the quick at the idea of having lost the inestimable privilege of listening to the gifted Kurtz. . . . [But] he was little more than a voice. . . . simply mean without any kind of sense" [*HD*, pp. 48–49]). Marlow's fascination with Kurtz ultimately allows him to bracket his sense of moral incoherence. Moreover, Conrad's irony toward Marlow bears a strong family resemblance to the audience's refusal to struggle along with Marlow in making sense of what he tells. This refusal to find significance, and Conrad's ironic insistence on Kurtz's meanness and meaninglessness, both allow absurdity to block the expression of loss, and hence to counter the process of working through that disillusionment. Thus, when Marlow aligns his fascinated reading of "the horror" with his hope that "my summing-up would not have been a word of careless contempt" (pp. 69–70), what Conrad would have the reader infer is that Kurtz's cry is merely a word of contempt. The meaning of Kurtz is unspeakable for Marlow and his listeners because it destroys their shared assumptions about order and truth; and though Conrad's irony mocks this order, translating as it does the loss of value into contempt for that value, it cannot (any more than Marlow) bring the burden of traumatic dislocation into the healing realm of speech.

Since the meaning of the trauma story cannot be represented, the losses it entails cannot be mourned. Marlow remains out of sight when Kurtz's body is committed to a muddy hole:

> I went no more near the remarkable man who had pronounced judgment upon the adventures of his soul on this earth. The voice was gone. What else had been there? But I am of course aware that next day the pilgrims buried something in a muddy hole.
> And then they very nearly buried me. (*HD*, p.69)

Marlow veers between dissociation from and identification with the reality of Kurtz's corpse. Were Marlow entirely separate from Kurtz, he would neither turn away from the finality of Kurtz's death, nor imagine being "very nearly buried" with him. Marlow's dilemma—that he must withdraw his investment in Kurtz as a need-gratifying object ("The *voice* was gone. What else had been there?" [my emphasis]), or incur death himself—once again reveals that he struggles with the loss of Kurtz in the way that a small child struggles with the loss of an irreplaceable parent. Like the child, Marlow cannot move through death, cannot think productively about it or reach beyond it emotionally. Mourning requires not just painful recollection, but also the testing of fantasy against the reality of the loss, and a sense of one's distinctness from the lost object, even while it feels psychologically present. Instead of mourning, Marlow resorts to defensive splitting. He can superficially acknowledge that the object is lost, but at a deeper level he denies this loss, both by avoiding the corpse and by identifying with it. Marlow cannot confront the finality of Kurtz's moral emptiness (death in a muddy hole) without losing hope that hidden in emptiness is the promise of ontic fullness. He is compelled instead to conserve loss without clarifying or accepting its reality and significance. Because he cannot grieve Kurtz, cannot find a way to tolerate his meaning and overcome it, Marlow is stuck in the ambivalent dualism of narcissistic identification. He can neither accept the promise of Kurtz's "voice" without merging with Kurtz in death, nor acquiesce to the unprocessed trauma of Kurtz's loss without surrendering to a death-in-life, isolated in Kurtz-like darkness. And because Marlow is in between the absolute hope-in-despair of restitutive narcissistic fantasy, on one side, and a potentially unbearable emptying out, on the other, his capacity to critique imperialism is at best severely compromised, at worst entirely undone.

But what is Conrad's psychological relation to Marlow's inability to mourn? After telling how he avoided Kurtz's burial, Marlow contrasts his own futile struggle with death and Kurtz's remarkable end.

Destiny. My destiny! Droll thing life is—that mysterious arrangement of merciless logic for a futile purpose. The most you can hope from it is some knowledge of yourself—that comes too late—a crop of unextinguishable regrets. I have wrestled with death. It is the most unexciting contest you can imagine. It takes place in an impalpable greyness with nothing underfoot, with nothing around, without spectators, without clamour, without glory, without the great desire of victory, without the great fear of defeat, in a sickly atmosphere of tepid scepticism, without much belief in your own right, and still less in that of your adversary. . . . I was within a hair's-breadth of the last oppor-

tunity for pronouncement, and I found with humiliation that probably I would have nothing to say. This is the reason why I affirm that
Kurtz was a remarkable man. He had something to say. He said it. . . .
And it is not my own extremity I remember best—a vision of greyness
without form filled with physical pain and a careless contempt for the
evanescence of all things—even of this pain itself. (HD, p.69)

If authorial irony dictates that Kurtz's final pronouncement is more akin
to a word of "careless contempt" than it is to "complete knowledge," then
one would expect Conrad's attitude toward death to resemble the anti-
climactic skepticism voiced by Marlow. However, such skepticism (which
aligns the subjectivities of author and narrator) is underwritten by emotional numbness, a kind of inner deadness that comes when the circulation
of unconscious desire is cut off, when psychic pain is miscast, and the subjective meaning of loss is left unresolved. The psychological "unsaid" of the
novel, the unconscious element that the author "inside" the text shares with
the narrator, is the inability to mourn.

Like Marlow, Conrad is subjectively undermined by a traumatizing
disillusionment. With the withering of belief he becomes indistinct, static,
helpless. But unlike Marlow, he eschews the magical compensation of
Kurtz, the mystery of grace in evil. Conrad seems to know that the imperialist system is false, and he seems to suffer that falseness as a loss. But for
Conrad the pain of loss is simply *determinative* of the tragic self, rather than
a provocation to construct a new system of belief—one that rebuilds personal worth, adjudicates moral and political responsibility, and hence
makes suffering meaningful. Paralyzed by melancholy and stained by
knowledge, he is stuck in the subjective realm of "contempt," "pain," and
"greyness," and cannot move to a sadder but wiser engagement with others, and to a dialectical reconstruction of new terms of relatedness from the
ruins of the old.[11] Positioned between the nothingness of loss and the sham
of imperialism, Conrad is in effect connected to the "bad" social object (the
imperialist system), and can neither disguise its badness nor relinquish the
attachment. Hence, implicit in *Heart of Darkness* is an unconscious authorial
need to sustain the social object relation, a need that might be formulated
as: "the object is bad but it is good that the object exists."

This textual attachment to something diseased finds a kind of counterpart in Conrad's political pessimism. In an 1899 letter written to
Cunninghame Graham, when Graham was reading *Heart of Darkness*,
Conrad explains that, despite the ways in which the novel's critique of
imperialism coincides with Graham's liberationist convictions ("So far the

note struck chimes in with your convictions—mais après? There is an après"), Conrad himself does not believe that critique can transform the intrinsic badness of society. He writes: "L'homme est un animal méchant. Sa mechanceté doit être organisée. Le crime est une condition nécéssaire de l'existence organisée. La société est essentielment criminelle—ou elle n'existerait pas" (Man is a wicked animal. His wickedness must be organized. Crime is a necessary condition of organized existence. Society is fundamentally criminal—or it would not exist).[12]

If we assume that a connection to the social is essential to the survival of the self, then Conrad's framing of the problem as a choice between organized criminality and the dissolution of society is tantamount to suggesting that survival of the self depends on the existence in some form of dominant criminal forces, codes, and institutions. By describing his choice in this way he is effectively saying that, in the realm of moral and political critique, he has little choice. There is loyal acceptance; there is critical irony; and there is ironic acceptance. Conrad's choice is to choose all three, and to create from their intrinsic tensions a textured richness, a feeling of depth, that often obscures an agonizing lack of freedom. He is bound to a social order he loves and despises, something he needs and yet cannot bear. The need for the "bad" social object relation produces the equivocal text of *Heart of Darkness*, allows for the novel's irony toward imperialist criminality, and for its deferral of what Conrad must see as the annihilating consequences of a fully realized critique. Conrad reinforces imperialist assumptions by leaving his subversion of them unresolved—by leaving the reader with untenable options. The reader must either accept that society is a lie, that it cannot exist otherwise, or else complete the critique, but still be left with—and unable to get out from under—the criminal nature of society. The defensive negativity of the letter corresponds to the ironic emptying out of a meaningful encounter with loss by the author in *Heart of Darkness*, and both find their psychological home in subjective impasse—the failure to work through and mourn the meaning of traumatic experience, and the consequent incapacity to articulate new terms for reconnecting with the world.

Inasmuch as Marlow and Conrad share the burden of the trauma story, each in his own way must conserve the relation to the bad social object. Marlow does so by means of his fascination and fear toward Kurtz, and Conrad does so by deploying nihilistic/pessimistic irony to foreclose and counter the idea that values important to the self have been lost. Thus, both the narrator and the author in the text are situated between self-loss (the fear of self-encryption within terms of traumatic experience) and object-loss (fear of the world's contempt for the critic, and fear of the malign power of critique to make the social world worse, or even destroy it). The tale's conclusion brings into relief the pathos of the inability to mourn, of being in between self- and object-loss. For the burden of trauma leads not only to Marlow's need to protect the Intended and himself with the lie, but to the inconclusive narrative act that ends the text. Here, Conrad hands over to the listener "the darkness" of Marlow's story of Kurtz, in order for the listener (the reader) either to find a resolution to the darkness, or else to feel the impasse and irresolution, and hence be led by affect to understand the twilight realm of being in between.

Marlow returns to the sepulchral city. Everything about Kurtz has passed from him, except for his bad dreams and the prospect of seeing Kurtz's fiancée face to face. "My imagination," he says, "wanted soothing" (HD, p.70). Marlow does not visit the Intended simply to perform a social obligation. Instead, he approaches her (who "apparently knew Kurtz best") with a demonstrable need for understanding. Marlow at first imagines her as a serene and concerned motherly figure. "She had a mature capacity for fidelity, for belief, for suffering" (p.73). This woman might well ease his troubled loneliness. He soon discovers, however, that far from being able to help him, the Intended is desperate for *him* to bear witness to "the lie" that only Marlow can vouchsafe.

He says that the Intended looked as if she would "mourn forever," and then describes his impressions of her while they are still shaking hands:

> [S]uch a look of awful desolation came upon her face that I perceived she was one of those creatures that are not the playthings of Time. For her he had died only yesterday. And by Jove, the impression was so powerful that for me too he seemed to have died only yesterday— nay, this very minute. I saw her and him in the same instant of time— his death and her sorrow—I saw her sorrow in the very moment of his death. Do you understand? I saw them together—I heard them together. She had said with a deep catch of breath, "I have survived"— while my strained ears seemed to hear distinctly, mingled with her tone of despairing regret, the summing-up whisper of his eternal con- demnation. I asked myself what I was doing there, with a sensation of panic in my heart as though I had blundered into a place of cruel and absurd mysteries not fit for a human being to behold. (HD, p.73)

The question of course is how Marlow travels in such a brief time from the safety felt in her trustful glance to panic in the face of despair. First, the ironic convergence of the Intended's survival and Kurtz's death shows him the manifest discrepancy between the man who died (as Marlow sees it) condemning himself and all else besides, and the loftiness of Kurtz's original "intention" as embodied in the woman who lives now only in the sanctuary of an ideal remembrance. Though Marlow does not see it, Conrad's ironic superimposition also suggests the way imperialism cloaks (Kurtz's) destructiveness in moral illusions. Second, Marlow panics because he intuits that her emotion is not sadness, but rather "desolation" and "despairing regret." The Intended is emotionally frozen at the instant of Kurtz's death, and made desperate by her inability to move beyond her loss. Her emotions seem to transport Marlow to the turmoil of his own nightmare. Whereas Conrad ironically compels Marlow "to behold" Kurtz and the Intended "in the same instant of time" in order to undercut Marlow's eventual obedience "before the faith that was in her, before that great and saving illusion" (HD, p.74), the author seems unconscious of what Marlow shares in common with the Intended. There is an undeniable correspondence between his "lonely desolation" (p.48) and "unextinguishable regrets" (p.69), on the one hand, and her "awful desolation" and "despairing regret," on the other. Like the Intended, Marlow has been unable to mourn the loss of Kurtz. One of the "mysteries" that neither narrator nor author seem fully capable of beholding is life after the rupture, the cruel aftermath of helplessness afflicting not just Kurtz's deluded fiancée, but Marlow's own colonial self.

The Intended grasps tenaciously at her ideal image of Kurtz, and Marlow reaffirms it. In a series of exchanges, she tells Marlow how she had all of Kurtz's "noble confidence," that she "knew him best," that "we shall always remember," and Marlow can do nothing but echo the Intended's words and agree. She leads him by the nose to his appropriate response, the last of which is his lie, the prize she covets. Marlow responds shakily, "I heard his very last words," and then (with "the horror" ringing in his head), pulls himself together to add, "The last word he pronounced was—your name" (HD, p.75). But why does he do it? His overt rationale is that "we must help them [the women] to stay in that beautiful world of their own lest ours get worse" (p.49). Conrad's ironic view of Marlow as putatively appealing to the human care of a corrupt system subverts Marlow's belief in the power of illusion to save. The irony empties out Marlow's rationale, but without explaining the psychological constituents of the lie, namely, the deep-seated anxieties in Marlow to which the Intended's manipulations appeal. Since the irony does not entirely comprehend Marlow's motivation, we must return to the affective dynamics of the scene.

Marlow no longer refers to Kurtz's fiancée as a mature and empathic woman. "And *the girl* talked," he says, "easing her pain in the certitude of my sympathy she talked, as thirsty men drank" (p.74, my emphasis). Her neediness has made her young. She is *certain* that he senses what she needs, that he wants only what she wants. The Intended recreates Marlow as an extension of herself, and toward the end of the conversation her narcissistic use of him becomes overwhelming. " 'I believed in him [Kurtz] more than any one on earth . . . more than—himself. He needed me. Me! I would have treasured every sigh, every word, every sign, every glance.' " At this, Marlow feels "a chill" grip his chest, and he says simply: "Don't" (p.750). The Intended is an empty house, inhabited only by the idealized ghost of Kurtz. She asserts her illusion of perfect ascension by affirming Kurtz's absolute need of her, thereby maintaining the idealizing thrust of her discourse with herself. Marlow does not understand the Intended's narcissism; rather, he experiences *in his body* her narcissistic use of him, the chill of her gripping at his chest.

The weight of an appropriative hand: this wordless affective state is something that Kurtz has also made Marlow feel. When narrating how the dying Kurtz was taken onboard the steamer, and how the General Manager's hypocritical verdict on Kurtz's methods as "unsound" had forced Marlow himself to declare that Kurtz had gone beyond "any methods at all," Marlow also recalls for his audience that "It seemed to me as if I also were buried in a vast grave full of unspeakable secrets. *I felt an intolerable weight oppressing my breast*, the smell of the damp earth, the unseen presence of victorious corruption, the darkness of an impenetrable night" (p. 62, my emphasis). The repetition suggests how Marlow (in the presence of the Intended) re-experiences his bond with Kurtz. The chill grip, the weight of secrets heavy on his breast—these unthematized sensations convey what it feels like for Marlow to have the light sucked out of him, to be robbed of personal agency.

Marlow hears the Intended's words as being akin to the cries of the jungle and Kurtz's incomprehensible talk. He tells us that "she went on and the sound of her low voice seemed to have the accompaniment of all the other sounds full of mystery, desolation, and sorrow I had ever heard—the ripple of the river, the soughing of the trees swayed by the wind, the murmers of the crowds, the faint ring of incomprehensible words cried from afar . . . from beyond the threshold of an eternal darkness" (*HD*, p.74). The sounds recall for Marlow his isolation in the wilderness—that moment when he hears Kurtz's followers, who seem now, as then, to echo his own melancholy: "a cry . . . as of infinite desolation, soared slowly in the opaque air" (p.41). And when the Intended extends her arms as if in supplication to

Kurtz, Marlow connects her with another shade, namely, that of the jungle lover "stretching bare brown arms over the glitter of the infernal stream, the stream of darkness" (p.75). The two women are brought together in Marlow's mind's eye by their "dumb pain," the mute prayer first proffered by Kurtz's jungle lover at the time of Kurtz's death (*HD*, p.69). These are wordless—that is, acoustic and visual—memories of desolation. Had Marlow the words, perhaps he would say that the Intended's despair and narcissistic emptiness recall Kurtz, and thus recall Marlow to his own pain. Again, Marlow cannot make the translation, but only feels lost in the echoing darkness.

We can see how Marlow's scene with the Intended generates a re-experiencing of his internal bond to Kurtz, but in the form of sensation. That is to say, his memories—the grip of death, the cries of desolation, the sight of suffering and longing—are all in the idiom of prereflective perception. Psychoanalytic researcher Robert Emde has observed that the self is a process, constituted in the first instance by "affective core" experiences.[13] Christopher Bollas extends this notion of the self as a structured, affective process with the idea of the "unthought known," which (as we have already seen) designates the emotional and existential states that shape the unconscious ego or internal Other. Synthesizing Emde and Bollas, we begin to see self/other interaction as grounded in the subject's relation to the internal Other, and the internal Other as having its origins in pre-representational affective experience. It follows that Marlow is unconsciously gripped by the Intended's demand that he confirm Kurtz's value and devotion (and in this way fill her incomplete and empty self), and that he is utterly vulnerable to this demand, both because his own being is structured by his internal relation to Kurtz as the source of absolute meaning and non-meaning, and because that relation itself exists for Marlow at the level of the pre-reflective "unthought known." Bollas explains that "seeing is not knowing and hearing is not understanding"—that sense discourse cannot "substitute for mental representation and thinking" because the idiom of sensation is not available to awareness (*TSO*, p.193).

For Marlow, no new object relation can replace the indispensible attachment to Kurtz ("It was ordered I should never betray him. . . . [A]nd to this day I don't know why I was so jealous of sharing with any one the peculiar blackness of that experience" [*HD*, p.64]). This attachment was configured by the coexistence of the unmediated polarities of goodness and deprivation. And if no object can replace the absent Kurtz, if Marlow cannot lose or mourn, then his idiom of sensation cannot be translated into communicative language. Unable adequately to *signify* affect, or the object

to which feeling binds him, Marlow is in danger of becoming the loss he
cannot express. Or as André Green has said, he is in danger of being wedded to the non-object, "not the representation of the [absent] object but
the non-existence of the object" (*OPM*, p. 291). When Marlow soothes the
Intended's vacant depression with "the lie," he does so because refusing her
would only leave him isolated within the "sensation(s)" of the nightmare,
the gap in being. Thus, the lie is spoken without choice; and the distortion
that stands in for (without providing Marlow with) the subjective meaning
of what has happened to him, is an enforcement of ideology as psych-
opathy.

Can we say, then, that Conrad (the author "inside" the text) gives a
conscious depiction of the dynamics Marlow can only unconsciously feel?
Does the scene with the Intended allow the reader a dispassionate and
detached view of Marlow's experience? Conrad seems sufficiently distanced from Marlow to show us that his effort to recuperate something
noble from Kurtz's last words is an act of false consciousness. In this
respect, Conrad seems quite ready to unmask the emptiness behind
Marlow's and the Intended's social and personal fictions. Indeed, the scene
leaves the reader with no illusion that the Intended's "love" can save anything, since Kurtz and the imperialist "home" culture are in the end connected by their shared hollowness. However, to the extent that Marlow's
telling is guided by felt experience and carries the reader along by the
power of affective resonances (the unthought waves upon which language
rides), then authorial irony vanishes. For this reason, Marlow's depressive
tie to Kurtz as a dark, insolent, and senseless power, the omnipotent "bad"
object, is essentially untouched by irony. Conrad's artistic style, his impressionism, is the verbal equivalent of Marlow's unconscious sensory memory.
It describes and is continuous with Marlow's depressive economy, and is
dominated by affectively imbued sensation, a verbal equivalent to unver-
balized meaning, ironic or otherwise. On the one hand, irony tells us that
Conrad "knows" Marlow's defense to be inadequate and false, that only a
lie can ward off "the triumphant darkness" from which, as Marlow says, "I
could not have defended her [the Intended]—from which I could not even
defend myself" (*HD*, p.74). But on the other, Conrad plunges the reader
into the affective dimension of Marlow's conflict, and as a result narrative
representation intensifies and preserves Marlow's vulnerability without
explaining it.

If it is true that Marlow is so confounded by loss that he can only
deny its reality, and that this failure to work through Kurtz's darkness is
what endows it with uncanny and impenetrable force, then it follows that

Conrad unknowingly trades on Marlow's vulnerability. That is to say, the ironic stance that the author-in-the-text takes on Kurtz's emptiness does not in the least abrogate or resolve his relation to trauma's supercession and rupture of meaning. Hence this stance does not undo the affective charge of Kurtz's mystery, of Marlow's fascination with him, of the ambivalence that is the heart of the tale. The text is therefore split. The scene with the Intended alternates between the author's overly near, uninterpreted relation to Marlow's *felt* experience and his too-distant irony; between his depiction of the finality of death and his depiction of its endless psychological repetition; between the repulsive non-sense of darkness and its unsanctioned attraction.

When Marlow tells of leaving the Intended's house, he comments on how his lie is arrayed against her "unspeakable pain," and how, once more, Kurtz seems to demand "that justice which was his due." But for Marlow and his listeners, no less than for the Intended, "It would have been too dark—too dark altogether. . . ." The frame narrator then intercedes with the line, "Marlow ceased and sat apart, indistinct and silent, in the pose of a meditating Buddha" (*HD*, p.76). As Brooks says, Marlow's narrative does not end with a summing up; it simply "ceases" or breaks off. He also claims that this method of telling places us as listeners "fully within the dynamics of the transference" in which we are "tainted" with "what [we] may not want to see or hear " (*RFP*, p.260–61). Brooks is right that Conrad places us at the end of the tale "fully within the dynamics of the transference," but he is wrong to think that Conrad has an unequivocal message that is located behind Marlow's indistinctness and silence. We need to look at Marlow first.

Marlow breaks off his telling because for him Kurtz's "justice" is frighteningly and irrevocably inhuman. There is no intrinsic limit to Kurtz's crime, and so there is no way for Marlow to describe his confrontation with the inhuman aspects of himself and of his culture without collapsing his sense of himself as a person embedded in a social world. And if we are positioned as "listeners" by Marlow's inconclusive narrative transaction to receive and describe his as-yet unthematized feelings and perceptions, we are also situated by the tale's matrix of imperialism as historically specific receivers who forbid "the unthought known" to emerge from the transference. And so we are situated to ratify Marlow's sense that his experience has to be foreclosed from human history, community, and speech. Marlow "ceases" or defers his telling because he is unable to go forward to a renewal of the intersubjective bond, and unable to go back to Kurtz and the annihilating muddy hole into which "something" was put. Marlow holds himself in suspension: the impenetrability of darkness at once expresses his condition of existential futility and preserves some hope that he can go on with being. With an exquisitely contradictory sense of both terror and relief, Marlow says, "it was too dark—too dark altogether. . . ."

Darkness then becomes the tale's psychological field. The frame narrator raises his head and observes that "the offing was barred by a black bank of clouds, and the tranquil waterway leading to the uttermost ends of the earth flowed sombre under an overcast sky—seemed to lead into the heart of an immense darkness" (HD, p.76). The Thames provides no passage out of the darkness that is at once the all-encompassing medium of narrative transaction and its visible yet unknown content. Insofar as darkness is the medium of the transference between Marlow and the principal listener, Brooks is mistaken, it seems to me, in thinking that Marlow's narrative act, which defers and transfers the burden of telling, is consciously structured by Conrad for the express purpose of "tainting" the receiver of the tale with an unwanted truth about imperialism. And Brantlinger and Pecora are also off the mark to conclude that Conrad, as modernist ironist, empties his text of the political knowledge that Brooks sees implicit there. The view of *Heart of Darkness* as successful critique and the view of it as "derealizing" such content both assume that there is an unacceptable but stable referent, a presence or an absence that the author "knows," and hence a meaning that readers may not want to see, but which Conrad himself has seen. In other words, both types of readings resolve (respectively as political knowledge, or as the futility of such knowledge) what Conrad projects, in indistinctness and silence, as a *felt* environment, a surrounding climate containing and intensifying the tale's motivational core, while simultaneously denying it or rendering it inaccessible. By situating the listener (and the reader) to feel the tension of what cannot be spoken directly, Conrad does not just avoid recognition of what lies on the other side of what he writes, but conveys his essential ambivalence toward the relational matrix of imperialism. He implicitly asks the receiver of the tale to use her own felt experience of herself in relation to the tale to bear witness to authorial subjectivity—to Conrad's unconscious aim of preserving being in a state of deferral, as well as to his wish to move the reader forward, so that the unseen, subjective meaning of the darkness that is everywhere visible will eventually be known. What emerges in reflection on one's own felt relation to the text—on being "fully within the dynamics of the transference"—is not Conrad's message, but rather his dilemma of unmourned loss: his disillusioned dependency on a criminal social order, an internalized object relation as impossible to give up as it is to change and renew.

Lord Jim: "A Lie too Subtle to be Found on Earth"

For Conrad, *Heart of Darkness* was a contrasting companion piece to *Lord Jim*. In May of 1900 he wrote to *Blackwood* editor David Meldrum that "It [*Lord Jim*] has not been planned to stand alone. *HofD* was meant in my mind as a foil."[14] While this statement is certainly not much to go on, *Heart of Darkness* does seem to stand to *Lord Jim* as imperialist "darkness" stands to its ideology of "light," or as a disenchanted confrontation with the horror in ourselves and the world stands to the reenchantment of reality through idealism, the righteousness of the dream. Such broad contrasts in how the narratives are configured are complicated, of course, by how Conrad sees through his culture's deceptive idealizations, and at the same time by how he blocks, or even flees from, the process of truth-telling for the sake of established illusions. Indeed, both works describe a series of defensive flights inspired by Conrad's need to escape from what he knows.

Kurtz cultivates savagery in order to make a false reality that forestalls the not-real in himself, while Jim's flight into suicide, into his self-sacrifice to the ideal, shields him from his inner terrors, and from the moral consequences of evading how his own empty fear is incommensurate with heroism. For his part, Marlow avoids what is destabilizing and disintegrative in his identifications with Kurtz and Jim, trying as he does to redeem magically what can only be solved by grieving. And Conrad seems to fear that the despair Marlow at once witnesses and covers over is indeed irreducible, that it can only be disclaimed through scorn and indifference—in *Heart of Darkness* through a "contempt" for "the evanescence of all things," and in *Lord Jim* through a "melancholy illusion" or pretense of courage that would cast off in death the "grotesque miseries" of the human heart (*LJ*, p.196). What is brought into relief by such comparisons is Conrad's irresolution. He encounters and recognizes the disorder that shatters the false closure of imperialist consciousness; he is transfixed by the fear of what is disordering; and he is committed to the structures of disavowal that would deny the very disorder and anxiety that summon him to write.

The affective center of *Lord Jim* is the *Patna* crisis, and the emotion that controls Jim, both onboard ship and afterwards, is fear. The terrors associated with this "catastrophe" have in turn a direct impact on every other aspect of the novel. Fear and Conrad's complicated relation to it are therefore central to how one thinks psychoanalytically about the text.

To enter into the novel's malady of fear, we might want to begin with a letter, written in 1898 to Cunninghame Graham, in which Conrad offers some thoughts on fear and cruelty. He composed the letter just prior to writing *Heart of Darkness* and *Lord Jim,* and was responding to one of Graham's Marxist critiques of British capital, which had helped to make Graham's reputation as a political journalist. Conrad addresses his friend in this way.

> ...You with your ideals of sincerity, courage and truth are strangely out of place in this epoch of material preoccupations. What does it bring? What's the profit? What do we get by it? These questions are at the root of every moral, intellectual or political movement. Into the noblest cause men manage to put something of their baseness; and sometimes when I think of You here, quietly You seem to me tragic with your courage, with your beliefs and your hopes. Every cause is tainted: and you reject this one, espouse that other one as if one were evil and the other good while the same evil you hate is in both, but disguised in different words. I am more in sympathy with you than words can express yet if I had a grain of belief left in me I would believe you misguided. You are misguided by the desire of the impossible—and I envy you. Alas! What you want to reform are not institutions—it is human nature. Your faith will never move that mountain. Not that I think mankind intrinsically bad. It is only silly and cowardly. Now You know that in cowardice is every evil—especially that cruelty so characteristic of our civilization. But without it mankind would vanish. No great matter truly. But will you persuade humanity to throw away sword and the shield? Can you persuade even me— Who write these words in the fulness of an irresistible conviction? No. I belong to the wretched gang. We all belong to it. We are born initiated, and succeeding generations clutch the inheritance of fear and brutality without a thought, without a doubt without compunction— in the name of God.[15]

Dismissive of Graham's socialism, Conrad was nevertheless sympathetic to Graham's chivalry, and operated by much the same code of genteel honor. Both men were aristocratic by birth: Graham was born into the Scottish landed gentry, and Conrad was an uprooted member of one of the lower orders of Polish noblemen. Graham, the former liberal MP turned radical social critic, had a chivalric sympathy with the underdog. Conrad shared with Graham his characteristically aristocratic disdain for the bourgeoisie, but not his radical sympathies. To counter defensively such political radicalism, Conrad voiced a Schopenhauerian contempt for the "wretched gang" of humankind. Thus, against what he takes to be Graham's melodramatic Quixotism, Conrad argues two things. On the one hand, he voices appreciation of the interpenetration of good and bad in human experience ("you reject [one cause] . . . and espouse [the other cause] as if one were evil and the other good while the same evil you hate is in both"). But on the other, Conrad fends off the necessity of dealing with this moral and political complexity by means of the claim that striving for social goods of whatever kind is futile because of our shared inheritance of fear and cruelty.

Conrad presents himself as a man who has grieved and thereby come to terms with the primitivity that underlies adult mental and political life ("we . . . clutch the inheritance of fear and cruelty without a thought"). But his world-weariness rings hollow, almost like an affectation, or a diversion. His response to the traumatic is too cold and contemptuous to suggest convincingly that he has surmounted loss and disillusionment. Conrad would deny the difficult questions of identity and social relations, questions that deserve to be posed in light of his unsettling feelings about the nature of things, rather than allow this discovery to act as a catalyst for change. For him, it would be "no great matter truly" if humankind were to vanish. Such bravado suggests not wizened acceptance so much as mourning gone awry, fraught as it is with the tensions Conrad carries forward in his confrontation with what is psychologically archaic in his age and in himself.

I introduce this letter early in the discussion because in it Conrad seems to anticipate some of the fractures we find in *Lord Jim*. In depicting Jim as a conservative idealist (rather than a Graham-like radical) who must, yet cannot, face the shameful consequences of his fear, Conrad sets himself the task of struggling with "the cowardice that is in every evil—especially that cruelty so characteristic of our civilization," and with Jim's fear of fear. Marlow puts the latter this way: "How does one kill fear, I wonder? How do you shoot a spectre through the heart, slash off its spectral head, take it by its spectral throat? . . . You require for such a desperate encounter an enchanted and poisoned shaft dipped in a lie too subtle to be found on earth. An enterprise for a dream. . . ." (*LJ*, p.192). Yet if Marlow would "kill fear" with illusion (the lie or dream of Jim's romantic tragedy on Patusan), then Conrad must either endorse such a cure or simply suffer the "encounter" in desperation. For what Conrad does not do in the novel is sustain a distanced and fully dialectical understanding of the relation between: first, feelings of abjection and terror in the face of imperialist crisis (the *Patna* affair), and second, the cultural need to evacuate anxiety through defensive grandiosity. As I have argued, Conrad is certainly aware of this structure of anxiety and defense in many of his descriptions and in his underlying emplotment of Jim's career. As in *Heart of Darkness*, however, irony is but one dimension of the text. In *Lord Jim*, Conrad is not ironic toward Marlow's need to distance himself from the immediacy of Jim's anxiety, which so rivets Jim to cultural ideals, nor toward Marlow's failure to mourn the loss of cultural- and self-idealizations. As a result, Conrad cannot adequately survey the psychosocial sponsors of Jim's dread.[16]

The novel's core confusion lies in how Conrad can begin by describing Jim as a narcissistically impaired individual whose sound appearance and weakness of character make him the exemplar "for all the parentage of his kind" (*LJ*, p.27), only to shift to an opposite but equally incomplete view of Jim as imperialism's tragic hero, "greater and more pitiful in the loneliness of his soul" (p.239). (This heroic dimension is at the heart of the "as if" construction of the novel's second part, and seems designed to supply the requisite catharsis, though what it leaves us with is an uninterpreted sense of malaise.) These contrasting versions of Jim, and the irresolution that destabilizes both views, invites reflection on what in him remains unfinished, on his failure to de-idealize cherished illusions and to mourn his losses, or, as Homans explains it, to undertake "the unwelcome but also liberating task of disillusionment" on the way to cultural and self-knowledge (*ATM*, p.203). In order for Jim to find his liberation in mourning, not only must he encounter the fears that follow in the wake of his idealizations, but he also must tolerate the disorganizing feelings that accompany loss and the gradual reconstruction of the self's relation to culture. And it is this double process of immersion in and reflection on the psychosocial self that Conrad (not just Marlow) can only approach obliquely, as it were, in the repeated shifts from meaning to disavowal. First I will clarify the deeper experiential basis of Jim's "idealized selfishness," and then show how that experience is disowned and brought back. I will show how the idealization culminates in the paradoxical image of imperialist heroic death, at once "the dream" that slays fear and "the lie" that smuggles away so much hidden suffering.

Motivated by Marlow's need for "an explanation" of Jim's weakness, and by Jim's sense that no one except Marlow "would understand" him (*LJ*, p.32, 49), the conversations between the two, both during and immediately after the trial, focus on how Jim felt on the night of the disaster, and on his complicated response to official censure for misconduct. Jim begins his story by describing to Marlow what it was like, that night on the *Patna*, to descend into the belly of the ship and come face-to-face with the rusted and bulging plates of the bulkhead. From the moment he looks at the ship's inner wall, he imagines himself a casualty of the waves pounding from without, a drowning man "floundering in a sea whitened awfully by the desperate struggles of human beings" (p.53). But it is not the ocean that rushes in to overwhelm him; instead he is overtaken by his own anxiety ("an overwhelming sense of his helplessness," [p.52]), as if his feelings were, like the sea, an uncontrollable external force. The description resembles what psychoanalyst Thomas Ogden calls "paranoid-schizoid" anxiety, which is experienced "not as a form of, or reaction to, [one's] feelings or fearful thoughts, but as a force sweeping over [one] that is frightening."[17] In such a state, there is a non-agentic, alienated relation between oneself and one's feelings, just as there is confusion in Jim's panic between what is inside and what is outside, between contending with one's own feelings and being subjected to forces coming from outside.

Marlow relates how, from the beginning of the crisis, Jim's "sensations . . . beat about him like the sea upon a rock." Marlow also explains that, while he uses this simile "advisedly," he is sure that Jim's "reality could not be half as . . . anguishing, appalling, and vengeful as the created terror of his imagination" (pp. 66, 69). Overtaken by fear, Jim turns his own passive immobility into the "strange illusion," grandiose in its way, of being the chosen victim of dark gods, "the infernal powers who had selected him for the victim of their practical joke" (p.66). His non-agentic relation to fear or to the thing feared (he can only "suffer" his helplessness) leads him to counteract this vulnerability with a self-inflating persecutory fantasy.

Jim's paranoid-schizoid anxiety is manifested in yet another way. Jim recalls how, just after eyeing the bulkhead and returning to the deck to inspect the lifeboats, his movement under the bridge is stopped by one of the Moslem passengers, apparently seeking a drink of water for his sick child. Jim narrates his memory of the incident:

> The beggar clung to me like a drowning man. . . . I hauled off with my free arm and slung the lamp in his face. The glass jingled, the light went out, but the blow made him let go . . . I had half throttled him before I made out what he wanted. He wanted some water—water to drink; they were on strict allowance, you know, and he had with him a young boy I had noticed several times. His child was sick—and thirsty. . . . He kept on snatching at my wrists; there was no getting rid of him. I dashed into my berth, grabbed my water-bottle, and thrust it into his hands. He vanished. I didn't find out till then how much I was in want of a drink myself. (*LJ*, pp. 55–6)

The man and boy are not so much persons as things for Jim, impediments to his survival. Again, we have evidence of reversion or impairment. Ogden explains, in this psychological position, "other people can be valued for what they can do for one, but one does not have *concern* for them—as one does not have concern for one's possessions, even the most important of them" (Ogden's emphasis, *TPE*, p.23). This helps us to make an important distinction, for while Jim identifies with the child, he lacks concern. Marlow notices the "peculiarity" of Jim's response (*LJ*, p.56). The child's feeling ("his child was sick—and thirsty") *becomes* Jim's feeling ("I was in want of a drink"). Jim does not enter into the child's experience or become *like* the child, but instead he *becomes* the thirsty child. He does not live in the realm of simile, where self and other can be similar and yet distinct. The identification is forged out of the immediacy and concreteness of Jim's fear, out of his need to alleviate his sickly anxiety. The identification is sensorily based because, as Ogden says, there is almost no subjective mediation "between the percept and one's thoughts and feelings about that which one is perceiving" (*TPE*, p.21). Trapped at the manifest level, unable to interpret his own feelings or those of the child, Jim cannot make the deeper empathic connection.

Jim is on a survival footing. He experiences the sick feeling of fear as an ontic given, as the immediate condition of his being that is absolute by virtue of its immediacy, and that triggers (as if without decision) his "throttling" of the Moslem beggar. Emotions seem to act upon Jim like the squall outside of him, which leads to Jim's eventual leap from the deck in a bid for safety.

The only options he seems to have in facing the *Patna* crisis are the contrary states of either "immobility," with his feet "glued to the planks of the deck," or "jumping"; yet he knows no more what caused him to clear out "than the uprooted tree knows of the wind that laid it low" (*LJ*, p.66–67). Anxiety overwhelms effective agency. Jim does not choose to jump; he is a vessel that is filled with what happens to him until experience overflows and spills out, and the squall within him and the sea outside him become the same.

As Jim's self-narrative unfolds, we come to see how loss of agency is inextricably linked to the unpredictable weather of Jim's internal emotional experience. After the Merchant Marine tribunal strips Jim of his certificate, Marlow provides him with a "place" (the private space of Marlow's rooms at the Malabar Hotel) to which he could "withdraw—be alone with his loneliness" (*LJ*, p.104). "Having a hard time," as Marlow puts it, Jim paces the bedroom, while Marlow, trying not to intrude, sits at a desk writing letters. The ensuing moments are a reprise of what happens to Jim when the rain falls on the *Patna*. At the time of the squall Jim was rooted like a tree to the deck, gasping and choking. Now we find him "rooted to the spot" in Marlow's bedroom, "convulsive shudders [running] down his back" and his shoulders suddenly heaving. It seemed to Marlow that "he was fighting, he was fighting—mostly for his breath" (p. 105). Jim goes out onto the patio, pushes "the glass door with such force that all the panes [ring]," and again stands still. A storm is coming up. Marlow hears the rumbling of distant thunder and sees a flash of lightning and then, in Marlow's words, "the darkness leaped back with a culminating crash, and [Jim] vanished . . . as utterly as though he had been blown to atoms" (p.108). Marlow's fantasy of Jim being *exploded* to atoms by the *imploding* darkness suggests a transfer, from Jim to Marlow, of the feelings revived in retelling the *Patna* trauma. Marlow says:

> I suffered from that profound disturbance and confusion of thought which is caused by a violent and menacing uproar—of a heavy gale at sea, for instance. Some of you may know what I mean: that mingled anxiety, distress, and irritation with a sort of craven feeling creeping in—not pleasant to acknowledge, but which gives a quite special merit to one's endurance. I don't claim any merit for standing the stress of Jim's emotions; I could take refuge in the letters; I could have written to strangers if necessary. (*LJ*, p.105)

Marlow taps into "the disturbance and confusion of thought" produced by Jim's panic, a "violent" storm that elicits Marlow's fantasy of Jim's disintegration, and evokes Marlow's own creeping fear (the "craven feeling" keeping him at his letter writing). Once again, Marlow's account is psychologically precise and consistent, for, according to Ogden, the paranoid-schizoid unraveling of thought and feeling into objects and forces generates in extremity "intense phantasies of the explosion of the subject (thus, dispersing the internal object world throughout the entirety of unbounded space)."(*SA*, p. 41) Yet, in spite of Jim's acute psychic tension (which seems at once to unleash and contain the "explosion"), he does not *himself* consciously experience the feelings he induces in Marlow. As he walks back into the bedroom, Jim addresses himself to Marlow in a way that suggests how oblivious he is to his own helplessness. " 'Jove! I feel as if nothing could ever touch me. . . . If this business couldn't knock me over, then there's no fear of there being not enough time to—climb out, and . . .' He looked upwards," seeming to catch sight of the high ground of invincibility (*LJ*, p.109).

The words "nothing could ever touch me" are bluntly grandiose, yet they constitute Jim's only conscious response to the pain of self-rupture and, indeed, to the very loss of his world. Moreover, he uses virtually the same phrase when he faces death on Patusan (" 'Nothing can touch me,' he said in a last flicker of superb egoism" [*LJ*, p.251]). This second loss, the sacrifice of his own life, is exacted because he decides, in a ruminative retreat into cowardice, not to lead Doramin's war party against Gentleman Brown. Instead Jim sends Dain Waris (Doramin's son) as his substitute; and when Dain Waris dies at Brown's hands, Jim's pact of honor with Doramin requires that Dain Waris's death be answered with Jim's own. It might seem that Jim's willing submission to punishment represents authentic guilt-taking. (I will talk about this "seeming" in some detail later in this section.) I would argue here, however, that when faced with both the crime of misconduct on the *Patna* and with the death of Dain Waris on Patusan (with the significant harm he has done to others), Jim does not in fact feel guilt for the victims he has left in the wake of his fear. His answer to the two "catastrophes" of his life is substantially the same. Even Marlow, who reads Jim's career on Patusan as an "extraordinary success," suspects that Jim never feels guilt. "[T]he idea obtrudes itself," Marlow remarks in retrospect, "that he made so much of his disgrace while it is the guilt alone that matters" (p.107). Jim's malady of fear precludes authentic guilt. In its place he installs omnipotent thinking, by which he denies archaic anxiety and forecloses on what might have become a sense of remorse for his failings. As he says, "nothing could ever touch me."

I have argued previously that Jim's narcissistic self-image as glamorous adventurer is wishful and defensive. I now want to claim that Jim's archaic vulnerability (the "explosion" and terror of self-negation) call into play defenses specific to the paranoid-schizoid realm of experience. Caught in a paranoid-schizoid state, the subject withdraws from psychic pain through the defensive use of "omnipotent thinking, denial, and the creation of discontinuities of experience," while "a feeling of guilt is dissipated through, for example, omnipotent reparation" (*TPE*, pp. 19, 23). The operation of splitting off and projecting fearful thoughts and feelings is what allows Jim to make his own experience magically discontinuous, in effect to rewrite his past. Marlow's arrangement for Jim to work on Patusan evokes this response from Jim: " 'I always thought that if a fellow could begin with a clean slate' " (*LJ*, pp. 112–13). To the degree ("measure") that the slate is clean, the harm one has done is expunged, and hence one need not have feelings of either loss or guilt. Marlow remarks that he "felt sad" as he listened to Jim. "A clean slate, did he say? As if the initial word of each our destiny were not graven in imperishable characters upon the face of a rock!" (p.113). Marlow can remember Jim's crime, and is suspicious of Jim's presumption of making a clean slate; yet he still misrecognizes Jim's defensive use of omnipotent reparation, and still leaves essentially unchallenged Jim's delusion that this evacuation of intolerable aspects of the self constitutes a mastery of personality (p.207). Jim short-circuits any experience of fear and guilt by replacing the old world of the *Patna* (where he "was going mad" and was "so lost" [pp. 77, 79]) with the new one of Patusan, where he is reincarnated as Tuan Jim. And we find Marlow increasingly setting aside his old view of Jim as untrustworthy. Instead he interprets Jim anew and sanctions the fiction of his new identity, magically repaired and good.

Marlow has a considerable investment in doing so. After all, Jim's "breach of faith with the community of mankind" has bitterly aggrieved Marlow, as though "he had cheated me—me! of a splendid opportunity to keep up the illusion of my beginnings, as though he had robbed our common life of the last spark of its glamour" (*LJ*, p.80). Instead of mourning the downfall of his cultural idols, Marlow defers any confrontation with loss by retreating into a useful confusion. On the one hand, Marlow says that Jim has robbed him; but on the other, he denies that he has any illusions for Jim to steal. As a seaman, Marlow tells us, his life began in illusion. The disenchantment that followed from these illusory beginnings was swift, "the subjugation [was] complete" (p.79). Marlow presents himself as invulnerable to the spell of illusion; yet, on the other side of this confused cynicism, he seems again ready to assume an enchanted view of the world. Jim's refusal of disillusionment, Marlow says, had "reached the secret sensibility of my egoism," for "he believed where I had already ceased to doubt" (p.93). Clearly, however, Marlow has not ceased either to wish or to doubt, since he does both splendidly and at the same time. And implicit in this doubleness is his effort to avoid recognition that Jim's example reflects not only on Jim's adolescent pipe-dreams, but also on "our common life" in the world of imperialism, where adolescent illusions stand in for cultural ideals and norms. The unbearable lightness of Jim's magical idealism seduces Marlow in part because the alternative would be to face the cultural meaning of Jim's malady of fear, and hence risk the disintegration of Marlow's own social world.

I have attempted to show, as plainly as possible, the disturbing psychological elements written into Jim's character. It follows from this that, in order for Conrad to have made Jim "a social example," he would have had to tell the full story of the disruption of "the culture within" (Jim's inner world) by "the culture without" (imperialist authority and ideals). That is to say, given the terms of the novel, Conrad would have had to show Jim

confronting the forces that tormented him. Were he to die truthfully, for
example, it would be a fragmenting fall into schizoid terror, not an act of
stoical tumescence. He also would have had to dramatize how imperialist
culture, having sent Jim to sea with only the flimsiest bark of a creed to
cling to, retreats behind the breakwater of ideology, and so masks from
itself the true meaning of the suicidal act. Conrad undertakes a narrative of
psychological loss and social disintegration, but then continually veers
away from it, and fails to maintain a consistent ironic distance from
Marlow's confusions, or from his retreat into ideology.

There are clues to understanding the relation between Marlow and
Conrad. Consider, for example, how Marlow formulates his rationale for
sending Jim to Patusan. When Marlow is exposed to "the strain of Jim's
emotions," he feels "the meaning of [Jim's] stillness," as if Jim's immobility
(this struggle to manage internal disaster) "sank to the bottom of my soul
like lead into the water." He wishes that "the only course left open for me
was to pay for [Jim's] funeral." Marlow also notes, "To bury him would have
been . . . so much in accordance with the wisdom of life, which consists in
putting out of sight all the reminders of our folly, of our weakness, and of
our mortality; all that makes against our efficiency . . ." (*LJ*, p.106). Then,
seeking Stein's assistance with Jim, Marlow voices this same desire to
" 'bury [Jim] in some sort [of way]. . . . It would be the best thing, seeing
what he is' " (p.134).

The locution "bury him . . . seeing what he is" is meaningful in its
ambiguousness. To bury Jim is at once to cover and to uncover him, or to
put "out of sight" and "to see" and remember. If Marlow is affected by Jim's
malady of fear, Conrad is not just affected, but has a thoughtful awareness
of the malady. However, the author "inside" the text disclaims the psychic
costs of Jim's funeral. "Seeing what [Jim] is," he still articulates the "what"
as a mystery, "the mystery of pain and distress" (p.85). He does not journey
to the end of Jim's "failure" and "undying fear," and hence does not integrate
or mourn what is lost there. For this reason, he struggles against the psychological and cultural core of his work, and cannot render Jim's rigid distortions with consistent irony. Paradoxically enough, Conrad uncovers
"what [Jim] is," and yet he does not affirm what he sees. He incorporates
the elements of a deeper vision, but does not integrate them purposefully
into the structure of the narrative perspective. The idealizing and romantic
components of the novel are therefore at once uncovered and used to
cover. What ultimately gets buried (covered up and yet revealed for what
it is covering up) is the story of Jim's fear as reflective of the fear of "our
civilization."

In the narration in the middle chapters of Jim's career on Patusan, Conrad takes up the theme of the imperialist self's desertion of the other (a revenant of the *Patna*). This theme is elaborated in part through what is for Jim a recurrent and polyvalent emblem (the moon); and this extended metaphor, in turn, bears the identifying marks of unconscious process, of inscription by revealing and at the same time disowning critical meaning.

Marlow visits Jim nearly two years after his rise to eminence on Patusan (he had become "the virtual ruler of the land" [*LJ*, p.166], and Marlow sees how Doramin's people attribute "supernatural powers" to Jim [*LJ*, p.162]). Conrad captures figurally Marlow's first impressions of Jim's new life when he describes a full moon rising from between two hills. Marlow and Jim survey the moonlit landscape, and "the moon, as seen from the open space in front of Jim's house . . . rose exactly behind these hills, its diffuse light at first throwing the two masses into intensely black relief, and then the nearly perfect disc, glowing ruddily, appeared, gliding upwards between the sides of the chasm, till it floated away above the summits, as if escaping from a yawning grave in gentle triumph" (p.135). To this, Jim says, " 'Wonderful effect. . . .Worth seeing. Is it not?' "; and Marlow thinks that "this question was put with a note of personal pride that made me smile, as though he had had a hand in regulating that unique spectacle. He had regulated so many things in Patusan—things that would have appeared as much beyond his control as the motions of the moon and the stars." At this point in the text, the straightforward metaphorical reading seems like the appropriate one: Jim is the moon on the rise, and, like the moon gliding out of the chasm of the "yawning grave," he has left his dark failings behind him. Because Conrad reinscribes this same figure several times, as we will see, the reader is implicitly asked to accept this unironic rendering of fullness as a necessary but provisional meaning—as that which will be confirmed, disputed, or in some other way given a more conclusive determination by the subsequent reinscriptions.

The emblem next appears in the context of Marlow's insight into how Jim's power creates communal relations of care and interdependency between him and the Malaysians. As Marlow puts it, "the conquests, the trust, the fame, the friendship, the love—all these things that made him master had made him a captive, too" (p.152). Then Conrad rewrites the figure this way:

> [Marlow and Jim] watched the moon float away above the chasm between the hills like an ascending spirit out of a grave; its sheen descended, cold and pale, like the ghost of dead sunlight. There is

something haunting in the light of the moon; it has all the dispas-
sionate-ness of a disembodied soul, and something of its inconceivable mystery. It is to our sunshine, which—say what you like—is all
we have to live by, what the echo is to the sound: misleading and confusing whether the note be mocking or sad. It robs all forms of matter—which, after all, is our domain—of their substance, and gives a
sinister reality to shadows alone. And the shadows were very real
around us, but Jim by my side looked very stalwart, as though nothing—not even the occult power of moonlight—could rob him of his
reality in my eyes. (*LJ*, pp. 150–51)

The issue, of course, is that of interpretive disjunction between the emblem
and Marlow's perspective. On the one hand, the figure conveys the idea
that, like the moon, Jim does not generate his own heat and light: all his
glory is reflected ("confusing and misleading," "cold and pale, like the ghost
of dead sunlight"); and there is to him as backdrop a sense of darkness and
void (the "sinister reality" of shadows) that is deeply unsettling. But on the
other, dead moonlight cannot rob Jim of his reality because (in Marlow's
view) he has pledged himself to his community, and so has authenticated
himself. Which is right: do Doramin's people invest their hopes for protection and illumination in a ghost that robs them of their substance, or has
Jim emerged from the darkness into something more self-generated? No
final determination of where Conrad stands can be made at this point. Yet
the incongruity between what the figure so powerfully suggests and what
Marlow says outlines the reader's interpretative options: first, that Conrad
is entirely ironic in his use of the emblem; or second, that Conrad's mastery over his own composition is at best tenuous. For in offering Marlow's
distorted view of Jim, authorial subjectivity seems to disown its own knowledge.

The emblem is submitted to a final inscription when Conrad turns
from the question of Jim's communal ties to that of his love for Jewel.
Marlow tells of Jewel's fear that men like Jim "always leave us—for your
own ends" (*LJ*, p.211). Just as Jim had pledged never to leave her, Jewel's
father had made the same vow. But Jewel's father had left Patusan altogether, abandoning both her and her mother. Thus, early in Jewel's relationship with Jim, she entreated him to leave her before she fell in love
with him. She explains later, "I didn't want to die weeping . . . like my
mother" (p.190). When at one point he attempts to assuage her anxiety,
Marlow is inevitably reminded of Jim's failure of nerve and betrayal of his
pledge to the *Patna* and its passengers. Jewel's persistent "craving for incer-

titude, this clinging to fear" (p.191) finally reduces Marlow to the absurd cruelty of telling her the reason for Jim's permanent exile on Patusan, as if knowledge of Jim's disgrace would do anything except breed further anxiety (p.194). Marlow's exchange with her lends to his view of the world "a vast and dismal aspect of disorder" (p.190). We are told that Marlow walks out into a field to get away from Jewel and Jim, and that there the moonlit sky casts shadows on the stumps of a few large trees that have been felled to make way for Jim's "experiment" with a coffee plantation. At this moment, all of Jim's activity seems to Marlow futile and empty. "Nothing on earth seemed less real now than his plans, his energy, and his enthusiasm" (p.195). What ensues from this thought is Marlow's imaginative vision of the landscape. The vision leads from Jim's field to the image of Jewel's mother's grave in the moonlight, and hence is something like an elaboration of Jim's field, or grave, of dreams.

> I saw part of the moon glittering through the bushes at the bottom of the chasm. For a moment it looked as though the smooth disc, falling from its place in the sky upon the earth, had rolled to the bottom of that precipice; its ascending movement was like a leisurely rebound; it disengaged itself from the tangle of twigs; the bare, contorted limb of some tree, growing on the slope, made a black crack right across its face. It threw its level rays afar as if from a cavern, and in this mournful eclipse-like light the stumps of felled trees uprose very dark, the heavy shadows fell at my feet on all sides, my own moving shadow, and across my path the shadow of the solitary grave perpetually garlanded with flowers. In the darkened moonlight the interlaced blossoms took on shapes foreign to one's memory and colours indefinable to the eye, as though they had been special flowers gathered by no man, grown not in this world, and destined for the use of the dead alone. Their powerful scent hung in the warm air, making it thick and heavy like the fumes of incense. The lumps of white coral shone round the dark mound like a chaplet of bleached skulls, and everything around was so quiet that when I stood still all sound and all movements in the world seemed to come to an end. (LJ, pp. 195–96)

The "black crack" in the moon's face, and the "cavern" from which the moon can no longer escape, both image Jim's inner darkness. The landscape is a mise-en-scène for what awaits Jim at the end of his life as Tuan Jim, his life of presumption and impossible heroics. The work of his hands comes to nothing, and the loss of meaning (imaged in this mournful eclipse) leads

abruptly to the shadow of a "solitary grave." Jim does not uphold the ideal
so much as he is absorbed into it, and the "special flowers" that garland this
grave commemorate that fatal assignation. And just as Jim, in his pursuit of
unreality, loses himself, he also abandons others in the process. Jewel's fear
that she will die like her mother, crushed by abandonment, is given cause
in this passage: already lost to himself, Jim can only be, in the end, lost to
Jewel as well. And this is, after all, a passage about endings. In the "dead
sunlight," what had once been living is now dead, what had been real is
now false. The fatal ideal, like the unearthly funeral wreath or "chaplet of
white skulls," interlaces Jim's losses, both those that are self-imposed and
those that he must inflict on Jewel and on his community; and hence the
grave of Jewel's mother comes to mark the resting place for all of Jim's casu-
alties, himself included. It is the final place where "everything around was
so quiet that when I stood still all sound and all movements in the world
seemed to come to an end." The chaplet of skulls also reminds one of the
staked heads encircling Kurtz's compound, and the parallel suggests that
Jim and Kurtz are brothers under the skin, dark and empty. Taken by itself,
the passage might all but convince one that Conrad is in fact the great
archeologist of imperialist narcissism. Marlow's subsequent commentary,
however, quickly brings that interpretation into question.

Directly following the passage, Marlow remarks:

> It was a great peace, as if the earth had been one grave, and for a
> time I stood there thinking mostly of the living who, buried in remote
> places out of the knowledge of mankind, still are fated to share in its
> tragic or grotesque miseries. In its noble struggles, too—who knows?
> The human heart is vast enough to contain all the world. It is valiant
> enough to bear the burden, but where is the courage that would cast
> it off? (*LJ*, p. 196)

It is worth recalling how Marlow's unwillingness to support the unreality of
Jim's project and promise ("nothing on earth seemed less real now") leads
him into the emblematic landscape of Jim's extinction. Marlow knows, or
at least has had a sighting of, the abjection underlying fantastic heroics.
One is therefore not surprised to read here of "the tragic and grotesque
miseries" of those buried in remote places. What is surprising is that
Marlow does not name who is thus afflicted, nor the ones "fated to share"
in that affliction, and that he does not affirm this "burden" of the human
heart. Instead he takes refuge in abstractions (the "human heart," the global
grave, the "noble struggle"), and suggests that true "courage" comes in cast-

ing off the tragedy of experience, rather than in bearing its burden and trying to master it in discourse. One can safely assume that there is little or no
ironic distance between author and narrator in the passage preceding the
commentary, because (in that passage) Marlow's perspective is saturated: he
has seen the misery and death behind the veil of idealism. Hence, authorial irony toward Marlow would serve no purpose. But the commentary
coming after the vision is an entirely different matter. One would expect
Conrad to distance himself from Marlow, but he does not. Effective irony,
I think, would be discursively shown by some dialogical indicator of
Marlow's insensibility to the pain he has seen and the losses he has felt.
There is no hint of this in what Marlow says, strongly underscoring that, in
this instance, Conrad's perspective coincides with Marlow's.

Conrad's vision of reality, represented in Jim's fatal abandonment to
the "special flowers" or "bleached skulls" of idealization, is given in close-
up. However, the author's hand strips this reality of its affective force
through the fantasy of the earth as one grave. Through the imposition of
an abstraction, Conrad defers the idea that it is the individual particulars of
life that must be mourned. In such a "great peace," loss gets erased, along
with the imperative that losses must be symbolized and affirmed. Conrad,
wanting to dull his own susceptibility to the "grotesque miseries" of Jim's
life, would have us imagine the perfection that comes when the world is no
longer a place of strife—when death is not death, but rather ascension by
way of "courageous" suicide. Conrad's phantasmatic, to borrow from Julia
Kristeva, is about death as a condition of "being beyond it all," a dream of
"completion" or "fictitious fullness" on the other side of despair.[18]

Marlow further develops this rhetoric of death in what follows. He
says, "I stood there long enough for the utter sense of solitude to get hold
of me so completely that all I had lately seen, all I had heard, and the very
human speech itself, seemed to have passed away out of existence, living
only for a while longer in my memory, as though I had been the last of
mankind. It was a strange and melancholy illusion . . . , which I suspect only
to be [a vision] of remote, unattainable truth, seen dimly" (*LJ*, p.196). He
hypostatizes the "remote truth" of death's being in order to deny the misery in front of his face, and so Jim's sad truth is allowed to pass "away out
of existence." The "melancholy illusion" allows Marlow then to assert that
"Nothing mattered, since I had made up my mind that Jim, for whom alone
I cared, had at last mastered his fate," and that "One could almost envy him
his catastrophe" (p.197). The artifice of such "melancholy illusion," this
phantasmatic staging of Jim's death as a kind of self-crucifixion that masters
death in its entirety, allows Marlow to dissociate Jim from the social other

(Doramin, Jewel, et al), to split him off because his death is a sacrifice, a theodicial excuse that permits lack of interest in others, who have already been redeemed by Jim's execution of an ideal. Such artifice allows Marlow to find in Jim's "catastrophic" and messy end some sign that Jim has in fact mastered his fate. Thus, Jim's agony is magically repaired by a fiction about death, fate, and mastery; non-being is transformed into fullness of being; and the suffering of others, which would impose an unbearable moral burden if allowed to stand, is rescued prematurely into a fantasy of quiescence.

The idiom of illusion in this passage is structured according to the specifications of denial, of *keeping out*. It is part of Conrad's narcissistic armor. We have two very good reasons for thinking that Conrad and Marlow are equally defended against touching Jim's fear, and equally unable to mourn what imperialist culture steals from those who follow its codes. First, we see Conrad's lack of distance from Marlow in the commentary on the dying, fractured moon, which helps us to discern Conrad's own unconscious desire to hypostatize death. Second, there is a parallel text, a commentary on the commentary, in the letter from Conrad to Cunninghame Graham.

Here, as I have noted, Conrad explores the theme of ruinous fear along lines similar to the novel ("in cowardice is every evil—especially that cruelty so characteristic of our civilization"). In the letter he remarks that "mankind would vanish" if any attempt were made to reform its dismal inheritance of fear and brutality, then adds that, after all, the extinction of humanity would be "No great matter truly." Perhaps Conrad needed to marshal this sort of negativism—the idea that no transformation is possible, or that there is no future, only the repetition of a dismal inheritance— because it offered relief from concern. The letter parallels the novel in that here too one finds fictions of death defensively coiled around the inevitable human experience of fear. However, the novel shows that what Conrad has always been talking about, most pointedly in his disavowals, is a fear (like Jim's fear) of his own potential for disintegration. The shadow cast by the author "inside" the text tells us that the conscious scorn that is voiced for political reform in the letter to Graham is overdetermined by Conrad's unconscious anxiety about losing himself, whether by death or psychic fracture. Because Conrad cannot himself pass through that anxiety intact, his compositional strategy reflects irresolution rather than acceptance of loss and change, or acknowledgement of what has been lost through mourning. His strategy consists of shifting back and forth between the *fact* of loss (death, cruelty, social values robbed of meaning) and the *fiction* of rehabilitation, between the reality that cannot be assimilated, and the constricting "illusions" (melancholy fantasies of completion) that cannot be given up. It is for these reasons that the complicated tensions of Conrad's language, his commitment to ambiguity as such, convey not just his wonder and perplexion, but also phantasms of anxiousness and self-concern.

It is at Stein's house that Marlow recounts the final episodes of Jim's story, when Jim confronts Gentleman Brown and then shows his readiness "to answer with his own life" for the death of Dain Waris (*LJ*, p.239). Here, Conrad juxtaposes Jewel's pain at Jim's death and Marlow's acceptance of it, which provides a context for the final episodes of the novel. First we see Jewel walking aimlessly through the house, struggling with the idea that Jim had been blind to her need, that "the curse of cruelty and madness" in Jim had thus made him blind (p.212). Marlow says, "there was no answer one could make her . . . no forgiveness for such a transgression," but then explains that Jewel cannot grasp "the real sense" of Jim's death. For Marlow, Jim was "a man torn [from his lover's] arms by the strength of a dream,"(p.212), or again, "He was romantic, but none the less true. Who could tell what forms, what visions, what faces, *what forgiveness* he could see in the glow of the west!" (*LJ*, p.203, my emphasis). Thus joined, Jewel and Marlow present a hybridized version of grief. In them, Conrad seems intent on structuring grief according to the terror (Jewel) and the pity (Marlow) of romantic tragedy, with Jewel's meaning (loss) apparently subordinated to Marlow's (redemption) because she does not understand "the real sense." But at a deeper level Conrad has made of Jim's death something impossible to unify. The final episodes, after all, are told in a way that lends considerable credibility to Jewel's suggestion that Jim's embrace of death is a flight from the world ("he fled driven by some accursed thing"). Conrad, it seems, cannot be entirely rid of the real sense of Jim's "madness." Redemptive tragedy shades toward a familiar ambiguity, as if Conrad were at once doubting and asserting his belief in forgiveness and resurrection, but needing to scatter Jim's underlying fear in the ambiguous tension between "the dream" and "the curse."

Gentleman Brown, a latter-day buccaneer, comes to Patusan for plunder, but Brown's real war is one of defensive self-assertion. His is "a lesson" and "a retribution" meant to legitimate vengeance against the "dishonest" aspects of a world he has repudiated but sees reflected in Jim's neatness, "from the white helmet to the canvas leggings and the pipe-clayed shoes, which . . . seemed to belong to things [Brown] had in the very shaping of his life contemned and flouted" (*LJ*, p.231). Though they appear as opposites, facing each other across the river, Brown asserts that he and Jim share

an underlying commonality—as Marlow puts it, "an assumption of common experience; a sickening suggestion of common guilt" (p.235). Thus,
we are invited to wonder whether Brown and Jim are, underneath the skin,
very nearly doubles, or whether, as Marlow asserts, Jim is a "spirit . . .
utterly out of [Brown's] reach" (p.234).

Conrad's portrait of Jim foregrounds his susceptibility to paralyzing
terror, and Conrad says the same about Brown, who has a harrowing dread
of prison, "an unreasoning cold-sweat, nerve-shaking, blood-to-water-turn-
ing sort of horror . . . —the sort of terror a superstitious man would feel at
the thought of being embraced by a spectre" (*LJ*, p.216). Both men know
the failure, censure, and privation that follow from the experience of "being
afraid once"—something that leaves them with an abiding sense of vulnerability. Further, each experiences himself as an abandoned son sent into
"exile" by imperialist patriarchy. Jim can never return home to seek forgiveness or accommodation, but instead flees into the cultural distortions
of an idealized righteousness, and pursues the "ideal" to the point of
becoming lost in it. The same vulnerability fuels Brown's criminal arrogance, his need to flout all paternalistic talk of "responsibility" and of "infernal duty," and to prove his own right to ruthless self-assertion. But Brown
escapes a prison cell only to become "an outcast" and a man without a
country (p.223); and in his reactive destructiveness, he is always already his
own victim.

Conrad's characterizations of Jim and Brown represent them as opposite sides of the same imperialist coin. Attempting to unmask Jim, Brown
reduces Jim's character and cultural values to what he takes to be their basic
features: the appropriative urge, the need to control, the unflagging protection of self at the expense of others. Brown believes in the urge to dominate and rejects the virtues that contradict it, whereas Jim embraces
imperialist visions of moral purity and boyish adventure. Jim reconstructs
his world as if it were a realm of magical, virtuous achievement that would
transcend and make ephemeral Brown's sordid realities. Both extract a narrow, inhuman, fragile equilibrium by incarnating one side of the imperialist divide, but always in reaction to the (unconsciously omnipresent)
obverse. Thus constituted, both Brown and Jim are compelled to confront
disavowed aspects of themselves and their cultural paternity *in* one another,
and this makes them dangerous *to* one another.

Because of who Brown is, he reawakens in Jim a panicky immobility.
First, Brown appeals to Jim by speaking in Jim's own idiom of honor, of
persistent readiness for the "clear fight" and squarely playing up the game

(*LJ*, pp. 235–36). Conrad thereby suggests that Brown promotes and exploits Jim's need to "manage" danger by coloring it with the tincture of necessary illusions. Second, Jim does not head up the reconnaissance party overseeing Brown's departure. Instead, Jim tells Doramin, the chief of the Bugis, to call in his son Dain Waris, " 'for in this business I shall not lead' " (p.239). Jim therefore elects to watch passively, leaving Waris to stare down the barrel of Brown's treachery and be killed. Conrad is able to show Jim's present situation of exile on Patusan as a repetition of the decisive moment of self-loss on the *Patna*. So the question is raised: Does Conrad see in this episode a fatal repetition of the past, or instead a repetition leading to a redemptive difference? Or are both of these alternatives some-how true?

On the one hand, Conrad seems to have envisioned Jim's intransigent passivity toward Brown according to the defining nature of the traumatic *Patna* experience (suggesting that trauma is not an event in life, but partly definitive of life itself). But on the other, Marlow defends Jim's innocence— "Jim did not know the almost inconceivable egotism of the man [Brown]," and Jim accepts "the morality and the consequences of his acts" (*LJ*, p.239)—and hence Marlow undercuts the potential irony of the repetition. Marlow's evaluation of Jim escapes authorial commentary. An ironic inter-vention would presumably suggest, first, that Jim's readiness to answer with his life does not mean he recognizes and accepts his acts, as Marlow thinks; and second, that death is the necessary consequence of Jim's inability to accept the core experiences of the imperialist inheritance he shares with Brown. To recognize Brown's malignancy is also for Jim to acknowledge resonance or resemblance, to confront the fear and guilt that exist in him, as in Brown, and in their shared patrimony. For Jim is actually faced with a terrible dilemma. If he acknowledges his kinship with Brown, he withers from the loss of the idealities by which he makes sense to himself; and if he repudiates kinship by clinging to his illusions, he extinguishes himself in their name. As Jewel puts it, Jim is lost because he has "the curse of cruelty and madness already within him."

Conrad offers us this vision of how Jim and Brown "secretly" share in the illusions that disguise or rationalize imperialist dereliction. But he doesn't affirm their similarity , and hence the ambiguous doubling rela-tion does not develop into an unmasking of shared dereliction. Instead of this, Conrad uses the self-idealizing cover-up of criminal passivity (when Jim shows himself "at last" ready to answer with his own death for the consequences of Brown's "inconceivable egotism") to underline the redemptive difference between Jim's virtue and Brown's perfidy. Thus Jim's history is revised and redeemed in the conviction that he is innocent—that it is not Jim's terror that makes him helpless and dangerous to others, but that Brown, the "inconceivable" external force, has victimized Jim. And both Marlow and Conrad hold defensively to the paradoxical conviction that, despite his fatal passivity, Jim is nonetheless heroic. That they do so is corroborated by certain descriptions of Patusan at the time of the execution.

Marlow interrupts his telling of Jim's death to offer this description of the evening sky. "The sky over Patusan was blood-red, immense, streaming like an open vein. An enormous sun nestled crimson amongst the treetops, and the forest below had a black and forbidding face" (LJ, p.251). He reports, "[Jim's servant] tells me that on that evening the aspect of the heavens was angry and frightful. I may well believe it, for I know that on that very day a cyclone passed within sixty miles of the coast, though there was hardly more than a languid stir of air in the place" (p.251). Though not present, Marlow once again imagines the landscape of Patusan as symbolic of Jim's spiritual condition. Pictured here in Marlow's vision of sun, heavens, and forest is the "immense" significance of Jim's moment of truth. The suicidal act by which Jim overcomes his ruin (the forest's "black and forbidding face") is figured in the sublimity of the blood-red sun "streaming like an open vein," and of the "angry and frightful" heavens. No longer vulnerable to terror, Jim himself becomes terrible, awe-inspiring, superb. Marlow resonates with Jim's dream of resurrection—the "superb egoism" located for Marlow in Jim's declaration that "nothing is lost" and "nothing can touch me" (pp. 250–51).

And Conrad seems to share Marlow's view of Jim's ascendancy in death. Consider first the passage's figurative elements in relation to earlier images in which natural phenomena also function as metaphors for Jim. The passage's sun and sky (symbolic in part of Jim's suicidal conquering of fate) stand in direct contrast to the earlier landscape in which the moon casts a "mournful eclipse-like light" over Jim's "solitary grave" (LJ, p.195–96). I have argued that this extended figure of the moon graphically suggests Jim's fatal abandonment of self to "the bleached skulls" of idealization. However, in the passages immediately following the extended descriptions of moon and moonlight, Conrad disavows the "burden" of misery, affirms the "courage" of suicide, and reifies the "great peace" of death. It might be said, then, that the celestial elements in the above passage (the sun, the frightful heavens) represent the final flower of Conrad's denial, the heliotrope that figures Jim's death as romantic (inso-

far as a bleeding sky is grand rather than sickening). This idea gains significance in the rather offhand mention that a cyclone raged unseen
beyond the horizon. Why does Conrad bother to add this distant storm
to his concluding metaphor? The storm, we are told, affects nothing on
Patusan ("hardly more than a languid stir of air"). It is certainly true that,
as figure, the storm amplifies Jim's reckoning with fate, giving the event an
"angry and frightful" aspect, in part because the menace originates from
something unseen and unfelt. But to the extent that there is something
cyclonic *inside of Jim* (his rage, terror, shame), why should it be figured by
a storm that only passes "within sixty miles of the coast," and that causes
"hardly more than a languid stir of air in the place"? Conrad seems to be
locating Jim's internal moral and emotional convulsion far offshore, projecting the internal not only outside of Jim, but at such a distance that it
is barely sensed, unthought and trembling only faintly in the atmosphere
of conscious experience. Or to put it another way, while the image seems
to endow Jim's act of reckoning with an ominous appearance, in fact the
vague menace of something far off is used to avoid the actuality of immediate experience—in this case, experience of Jim's paranoid-schizoid terror. The image relocates the storm described earlier in the tale when
Marlow and Jim are together in the hotel room on the evening of Jim's
censure. In the midst of the earlier storm, with the two of them shaken
directly by its force, Marlow could *feel* Jim's primitive anxieties over annihilation. The "violent and menacing uproar" inside of Jim expressed itself
through Marlow in the form of a hallucination: Jim vanishing into nothingness, being "blown into atoms." Nothing so stark or immediate survives
in the tale's final image of Jim. Instead, Conrad exiles Jim's underlying anxieties, making room for the fantasy that, in synthesizing a pseudo-courage
as a replacement for real terror, Jim creates significance.

The words that allow Jim to submit to execution ("Nothing is lost"
and "Nothing can touch me") reflect a narcissistic delusion. They anes-
thetize him to the sensation of falling and deaden him to the realization
that his faith in an ideal self is sustained by his utter faithlessness to others.
Hence, these words are the license by which an act of self-punishment
becomes a fantasy of magical reparation, one that extinguishes personal
anguish and undoes Jim's many sins. Ogden has described the way in which
self-punishment can become a manic defense for warding off feelings of
distress and worthlessness, especially when these begin to verge on primitive and uncompromising guilt. "In this case, one uses an omnipotent phan-
tasy that the self-punishment eradicates the present and past existence of
the crime and therefore there is no reason to feel guilty" (*TPE*, p.24). Jim

speaks to the father of his slain friend: " 'I am come in sorrow.' He waited
again. 'I am come ready and unarmed,' he repeated" (LJ, p.252); and when
the bullet pierces his chest we are told he "sent right and left at all those
faces a proud and unflinching glance" (p. 253). But for Jim, as for everyone,
real bravery is possible only when something can be lost, when something
in him can be touched. Denial of the basic preconditions for courage makes
him proud; and in the end it is a mere pretense of courage, born of denial
rather than mastery, that allows him to enact this omnipotent reparative
fantasy of self-disembarrassment.

Marlow's view is predictably double. On the one hand, he believes
that, in death, Jim achieves heroic stature, for "not in the wildest days of
his boyish visions could he have seen the alluring shape of such an extraordinary success!" (LJ, p.253). While on the other, he seems to have serious
doubts about Jim's prideful demise. Has Jim made good? Should he be for-
given? Marlow takes up these questions in the novel's final paragraphs, convinced that "we ought to know" how to resolve Jim's death, yet in the same
breath suggesting that the only possible answer to Jim's story might be
irresolution.

Marlow begins his interrogation of the problem in this way. "[Jim]
goes away from a living woman to celebrate his pitiless wedding with a
shadowy ideal of conduct. Is he satisfied—quite, now, I wonder? We ought
to know. He is one of us. . . ." (LJ, p.253). Here Marlow alludes to Jewel's
remark that Jim "was made blind and deaf and without pity" (p.212). When
Marlow came to Stein's house (just after Jim's death), he had to confront
Jewel's angry and inconsolate grief; and even though he could not help her,
Marlow could defend Jim to himself, and could do so because of his conviction that Jim died "in pursuit of the truth." Now, drawing on the memory of having thus affirmed Jim's tragic truth, Marlow says: "have I not
stood up once, like an evoked ghost, to answer for his eternal constancy?"
Marlow's use of the interrogative might be rhetorical, but then again it
might indicate that he only half-believes the substance of his earlier opinion. His questioning continues: "Was I so very wrong after all?" (p.253). If
Jim is true, then why is Marlow fretting about being wrong? Why does he
answer each question with another question, a process that further impli-
cates him in Jim's fate, but does not bring him closer to taking a stand? It
might be recalled how Marlow also "stood up once" to say "[Jim] made so
much of his disgrace while it is the guilt alone that matters" (p.107).
Perhaps Marlow feels guilty on Jim's behalf for Jim's pitilessness; and perhaps it is Marlow's perception of his own involvement in the harm Jim has

done to others that renders the triumph so self-canceling. Yet that very sense of guilt seems lost in even further interrogatories, as Marlow answers his own question, "Was I so very wrong?", with another question, "Who knows?", and then says Jim is "gone and inscrutable at heart." Marlow finds Jim's meaning indeterminate, and hence it follows that Marlow's own sense of blame can be deferred, since the moral judgement depends on Jim's reality or unreality, which is itself undecidable. Thus, Marlow forecloses on guilt and sorrow over the damage done to others, and for collective responsibility in that wrong. Ambiguity interrupts a more honest accounting, and refuses the resolution that might come with sorrow, empathy, and efforts at repair.

However, the novel's final lines describe terrible anguish in a way that seems designed to elicit our grief. "[T]he poor girl is leading a sort of soundless, inert life in Stein's house. Stein has aged greatly of late. He feels it himself, and says often that he is 'preparing to leave all this; preparing to leave . . .' while he waves his hand sadly at his butterflies" (*LJ*, p.253). Perhaps Stein's sense of romantic adventure, his pursuit of the dream, like his passion for pursuing butterflies, has been hollowed out because he must share Jewel's soundless, inert life, and hence must endure the sad consequences of Jim's boyish exploits. The logic of the sequence refers the reader from Marlow's self-interrogation ("Was I wrong?"), to his ambiguous answer (self-arresting guilt depends on the still unsettled question of Jim's reality or unreality), to a world of violated trust and dissolved dreams. Ironically, Jim's heroic death does not inspire those left behind, but instead drains the world—"all this"—of meaning. With the tale's final image, the sad wave of Stein's hand, Marlow, the evoked ghost, seems to end his tale by dismissing even himself. Jim has surrendered dishonestly to the shades of the shared world of imperialism, and in so doing leaves Jewel and Stein to an empty quotidian.

Is the hidden work of Conrad's conscious thought revealed in the logic of this sequence? It seems doubtful, if only because the reality of Jim's fear—the lit fuse leading to all of this destruction—is not named in any aspect of the tale's conclusion. Rather, it is the unspoken revenant of every enunciation: the myth of romantic heroism, the deflection of guilt by Marlow's ambiguousness, and the sad picture of Jewel and Stein fading from the world. And the imperative of burying that fear of disintegration, and hence of *not* destabilizing the self and its relation to culture, is what makes this last scene the epitome of Conrad's psychological problematic. The scene shows us the loss of "all this," but not the ability to grieve the loss, just as it raises the issue of the moral responsibility of imperialism, only to suspend any possible answer in doubt and duplicity. In the end, the grief "we ought to know" becomes unnamable and ungraspable by dint of the necessary and perpetual uncertainty of authorial naming.[19]

PART THREE

Disappearing Landmarks:
"Revolutionary" Social Change
and Psychobiography

CHAPTER SIX

The Political and Personal Cultures of *The Secret Agent*

Non-psychoanalytic critics have often observed that the process of inter-preting interrelations between the literary text and the unconscious trans-fers the study of literature to another field that is no longer literature. While this is partly correct, it is also true, as psychoanalyst André Green says, that "the role of literature is precisely to convert a sector of reality (whether psychic or external) into literary reality," and that, while the "neo-reality" of literature certainly has a significant claim to its own specificity, just as important is the study of "the reality from which [the literary] is derived."[1] In this section of the book, my psychoanalytic project situates Conrad's texts within the context or intertext of Edwardian prewar political culture, and attempts to retrieve both the social and the psychological real-ities Conrad has transformed and distorted in the process of producing his texts. What follows is psychobiographical, but not in any simplistic sense.

The familiar objection to psychoanalytic biographical study is that it is both reductionist, by basing itself on the "genetic fallacy" of finding all explanation in the uncovering of origins, and impossible, because it attempts to put a dead author "on the couch." Any effort to understand the effect of an author's personal history on his work is admittedly speculative. However, I think this objection to psychobiography can be countered in two ways. First, psychoanalytic interpretation is text-dependent. Any elu-cidation of the historical author evolves from the interpretation of the author as a quasi-presence in the text, and hence from the effect the work has on the reader. It is true that the interpreter constructs her own version of the author as a psychological subject, and does so by beginning with the work, illuminating consistencies between the work and the life, and in this way treating the two as comprising in certain respects mutually informing constructs. Thus, the most speculative aspect of psychoanalytic interpretation—namely, the exploration of the historical author's inner life—does not ground textual analysis. Rather, one starts with the text and reads backwards into the life, and only then offers illuminative suggestions *about* the life. Second, to overcome psychologically reductionist interpretation, I believe pyschoanalysis must treat the author as a context-dependent, "relational subject" who is constituted not just by social forces, but by psychic realities as well, and who translates these realities into literature. Thus, I am left with the complicated task of trying to sort out not just the psychological contours of the text and of the quasi-presence of the author in the text, but also relations between the text and aspects of the author's social world and psychological life.

Of course, I cannot simultaneously develop these multiple dimensions of psychosocial interpretation. Because I work under the assumption that these multiple interpretive narratives converge in the text, my task will be to anatomize and reassemble the dialectic, giving a sense of the whole but not recreating it in a single, blinding interpretive lightning-strike. My argument about the interrelations between Conrad's work and its social and psychological underpinnings will unfold in steps over the course of the next three chapters. In this chapter, I develop a historical account of Britain's political culture in the prewar years, and read *The Secret Agent* in relation to Conrad's social and personal (biographical) contexts. In the next chapter, I relocate the social world of the period within Conrad's matrix of personal relationships, the nexus of relations connecting Conrad to his world and to his traumatic Polish childhood. From this vantage point I will examine the extent to which contemporary, sociohistorical factors helped to shape the private character of Conrad's adult experience, and reconnected him in quite specific ways with his past. In the last chapter, I construct various interrelations between Conrad's psychosocial matrix and *Under Western Eyes*.

The novels *Nostromo* (1904), *The Secret Agent* (1907), and *Under Western Eyes* (1911) comprise the "major phase" of Conrad's career. *Nostromo* is by anyone's account a great but densely elusive text, and for me the very nature of its obliquity makes it continuous with Conrad's other novels on imperialism.[2] The work after *Nostromo* is different, still struggling with ambivalence about irredeemable ideals, but now in a darker, less balanced way. In these later texts Conrad is clearly responding to the modern political realities of revolutionary politics and nationalistic rivalries transforming European society in the years before World War I; and it is equally clear that these realities contribute to the darkening irony and hopelessness coloring his work. We find Conrad focusing in the novels on revolutionary intrigue, whether the scene is set in London (*The Secret Agent*) or in St. Petersburg and Geneva (*Under Western Eyes*). In "Autocracy and War," he confronts the volatile combination of class warfare and the machinations of *realpolitik* among the European democracies. There is a manifest deepening of Conrad's pessimism that seems to stem in part from his sense that the divisions and chaos of the period would put an end to the story of traditional Europe. In the introductory "note" to *The Secret Agent*, he expresses a dark conviction of "a mankind . . . tragically eager for self-destruction."[3]

For example, in "Autocracy and War" Conrad writes, "Il n'y a plus d'Europe [no longer is there a Europe]—there is only an armed and trading continent, the home of slowly maturing economical contests for life and death . . ."[4] Conrad writes this in 1905, well before World War I, suggesting his sensitivity to the dangers of the moment. During "la belle époque," and at a time when others were more hopeful about revolutionary change in Russia, Conrad was deeply apprehensive, and regularly took the role of Cassandra with his compatriots. But what Conrad could not do was think about these social changes in any progressive way. One important dimension of the moral predicament of the age lay in recognizing not just that the social environment was undergoing a total transformation, but that past political traditions and moralities were becoming increasingly obsolescent and unusable in any effort to reconstitute justice and tolerance in a climate of conflict. Given this, the challenge then was to search for new terms of social mediation, and for new collective values, that would promote equitable access to the social good (including social services and material goods), and that would permit a more democratic conversation in shaping what "the social good" meant. To reengage this historical moment in its full complexity would have required Conrad to grieve whatever losses came with the dissolution of the old Europe ("il n'y a plus d'Europe"). Conrad, I think, deferred the process of thinking through disillusioning recognition; and when he could no longer defer it, he was captured by it, since the only doorway out was mourning. Conrad's discouragement was now instigated, for example, by his understanding that modern revolution absolutely repudiates the old traditions (in "Autocracy and War," he says that class warfare is a protest *"en masse* against the monarchical principle," [p.135]). But as in his earlier texts, his struggle to mourn what was lost was largely unconscious and without resolution. He was not free to organize his perception of the new sociohistorical reality into a fresh vision, a newer and perhaps more radical perspective that could meet the changed meaning of existence.

The earlier work shows us that Conrad's capacity for tolerating irresolution (that is, for deferral) means that he has some hope of connectedness with an idealized version of group life, and some hope of achieving a sense of self-coherence through reliance on extant forms of cultural heroism. In order to sustain the illusion of solidarity, for example, Conrad relies on the conscious myth of the "good crew" of the *Narcissus*. And in order to recover the possibility of personal redemption, Conrad reifies the romance of Jim's death, and is compelled to limit Kurtz's traumatic significance—a strategy that allows him to hold forever in suspension the competing alternatives of Kurtz's emptiness and his authoritative self-presence. In contrast, Conrad's later work shows us that deferral (which requires balance between annihilation and ideality) has become untenable, or at least that deferral as the saving act that preserves hope in the ideal (the idealized resources of patriarchal tradition) cannot even be attempted without an unbalancing burden of anguish. During this part of his career, Conrad is consciously more contemptuous of what he sees in his cultural surroundings, and unconsciously more hopeless about the working through (the grieving) of aspects of his history and psychosocial condition that have wounded him—whether the injury comes in the present, or from the distant past, or in the act of casting a cold eye forward on an imagined future. His writings on the destructiveness latent within European culture, particularly his fictive vision of underground worlds of revolutionary conflict, are rigidly censorious and saturated with black irony. Such irony, deployed in order both to express and stave off bitterness and despair, is the surest trope of mourning's impossibility.[5] And when Conrad formulates reverence for the old patriarchal forms of order and heroism, these nostalgic fantasies seem more extreme and less credible, even to him. His later writing, then, is characterized by deepening hopelessness and polarization, where the ballast of needed idealities has leaked away without any available means of recovery.

These psychological aspects of the texts suggest how, in a general sense, Conrad "converts" sectors of reality into the "neo-reality" (as Green calls it) of literature. They tell us how Conrad's intensified literary re-envisionings transform and distort the underlying realities of social conflict and of those aspects of his psychic life, both present and past, having to do with such conflict. To defend this point of view is to embrace the idea that Conrad was a subject rooted in a complex personal history, and that the expression in Conrad's work of the political culture of the prewar years is influenced by aspects of "the child in the adult." Of particular influence is Conrad's early experience of sharing with his father the national identity of a Pole under Czarist rule, as well as the familial identity that came from their life as political exiles, and all the traumatic complications that this difficult life entailed.[6] To include Conrad's personal history is not to reduce his texts to the traumatic entailments of his father's revolutionary/nationalistic political activities, since what also has to be read against the past are the present configurations of Conrad's life, which include the tense political situations of Britain and of revolutionary Russia. What I want to do is to interpret the later texts both in terms of the social world in which Conrad writes, and in terms of the unchanging elements of his adult psychological organization, most centrally his inability to mourn lost objects. A clear picture of British culture is necessary in order to know "how to go on" with the psychosocial dialectic, to gauge how to interpret interrelations between the cultural and psychobiographical elements that underpin the texts.

British Society , Conrad, and *The Secret Agent*

As many contemporary historians have observed, the idea of militant social action was much on the minds of people in prewar Europe. The idea that history was a struggle between the "revolutionary" ardor of the dispossessed and the "counterrevolutionary" forces of beleaguered dominant orders (however superficial this idea might be) found general acceptance both in Britain and on the Continent. In fact, much of the politics of this period can be understood in terms of the notion that, as historian George L. Bernstein puts it, socialism was not, for mainstream society, "a theoretical evil which might emerge someday, but an immediate enemy to be fought and defeated."[7]

    The ignominy of the Boer War, that quagmire of Tory imperialist policy, was inevitably followed by a loss of confidence in the Conservative government and the election of a Liberal one (1906). Some social critics, such as the progressive liberals J. A. Hobson and L. T. Hobhouse, took the post–Boer War period as an opportunity to reflect on the inherent antagonism between imperialism and the democratic principles of British political culture. At this time, most influential liberals were liberal imperialists. In Hobson's words, they had "fled from the fight which was the truest test of liberalism in their generation," namely, the test of extending to the masses the substance of power so that they could use it to gain equality of opportunity.[8] Hobson well understood that the fight between imperialism and democracy was not going to go away simply by virtue of the election of a Liberal government. Indeed, both liberals and imperialists of the time recognized the need for economic and social reform, and both feared the prospect of "class war." Hence, the question was whether activist government would proceed according to the modernizing technologies of the jingoists or humanitarian, non-jingoist principles.

Some historians see the Edwardian years—even the political turmoil that rocked Britain between 1910 and 1914—as part of the process of Great Britain's ongoing constructive adjustment to the final demands of democratization, a constructive extension of personal and political freedoms and of equal justice.[9] However, other observers insist that despite the persistence of these typically British democratic values, the society was moving, as Robert Scally puts it, "in the direction of increasing class conflict and rigidity at the lower levels, . . .and perhaps most important, the ascendancy of a powerful aspiring 'successor elite' to traditional [politicians] which argued for a more disciplined and regimented society based on ideas of 'National Efficiency' and for whom the traditional democratic values were merely dangerous impediments to preparing the society for modern modes of production and modern warfare."[10] This "successor elite," comprised of technocrats from both the left and the right, might loosely be described as inheriting and amplifying the "Social Imperialism" of Joseph Chamberlain in the 1890s, and emerging as a quasi-fascist rival to both liberalism and socialism.

These different scholarly positions appear to be intrinsically opposed. The first argues for the natural evolution of native British institutions, an evolution in which conditions of conflict act as a stimulus to democratic development. The second stresses that some of the causes and symptoms of societal dislocation (for example, class conflict and the inefficacy of government) were systemic rather than passing, and that these problems made Britain similar to continental Europe, since British "counterrevolutionary" insurgents, like their European counterparts, arose hoping to save society from what they saw as the anarchical clash between traditional rulers and "revolutionary" socialists. In fact, there is truth in both of these positions, and they are not irreconcilable. British institutions did not evolve without to some extent departing from politics as usual, a shift that took the postwar form of a right-wing "prime ministerial government" under Lloyd George (ALG, p. 82). Before the war, however, traditional liberalism was evolving into a new progressivism; and yet the liberal party created unresolvable conflicts for itself in parliament and with its working-class constituency. Such conflicts in turn gave impetus to "counterrevolutionary" social elements—the National Efficiency ideologues who saw opportunity for their own advancement in destabilizing an already fragmented Liberal party, but who themselves remained only a vocal minority. Thus both Hobson, the Edwardian progressive, and Scally, the historian of quasi fascist elements in the British Establishment, tell us something true about the politics of the time.

While political instability threatened the internal landscape of Britain during the prewar years, Britain's dealings with the other European states were also becoming destabilized. Slowly maturing hostilities made Britain's conduct of foreign affairs a matter of *realpolitik*. Such adversarialism (carried on by means of negotiation), and such a sacrificing of the long-term goals of European cooperation to short-term imperialist gains, was true not just of Balfour's Conservative administration prior to 1906, but also of Asquith's Liberal government from 1906 to 1914. Because military ventures were too costly, both monetarily and in terms of public support, Britain protected its over-extended Empire by means of risky alliances with France (to play British interests in Africa off against those of both France and Germany) and with Russia (to insulate this country from its Prussian rival and to shield India). Such alliances, staking British imperial claims on the mutual mistrust of the European powers, and forged most especially at Germany's expense, contributed significantly to the events of 1914.

It followed from Britain's general aim to thwart the *Kaiserrealm* that, after the revolt in St. Petersburg (1905) was put down, the Liberal government forged its entente with Russia (1907). Contracting this alliance depended on the Liberal administration's determined denial of Czardom's massive political repressions. It was only natural for the public to reflect on the forces destabilizing the internal politics of both Russia and England, and on the imperialist/nationalist ambitions driving the two countries into an alliance of mutual convenience. What seems more strange is that the Russian novelists Tolstoy and Dostoevsky became such significant players in the court of English political opinion. Both Tolstoy and Dostoevsky had mystical visions of the social future. Tolstoy's spiritual ideal was informed by his leftist leanings, while Dostoevsky's ideal was based on reactionary, "Pan-slavic" nationalism. For Britishers, worried about their own society's present and future, the Russian novelists' utopian visions were heady and inspiring examples to either follow or revile, depending on one's point of view. So much was this the case that the contrasting spiritual philosophies of Tolstoy and Dostoevsky were used by English writers to legitimate their opposing views on English institutions and policies. For critics of the

Liberal administration, Tolstoy became a champion of democracy, and for English loyalists, Dostoevsky proved the wisdom of their own nationalistic agenda. For Conrad, however, the cachet of both writers among his contemporaries signified an abhorrent return of Russia and of Russianness into his life, and into his novelistic imagination.

Dostoevsky's mystic nationalism, in particular, seems to have called up for Conrad distressing memories of his father's Polish version of this same creed. Mystic nationalism had inspired Apollo Korzeniowski (Conrad's father) to fight against the Czar's oppression of Poland—a noble cause. But it also led the entire family into political exile, where hardship and disease claimed both of young Jozef's parents before he was 12 years old. I will return later to Dostoevsky's special significance to Conrad. I introduce the issue here only to note that the connection between England and Russia, between the political and the literary, and between Russian and Polish mystic nationalisms, were all at work for Conrad even before he wrote his "Russian" novel, *Under Western Eyes*. For Conrad, the political instabilities of prewar England always harbored the seeds for revivifying the instabilities of his past. This interaction between the social and the personal, the present and the past, further darkens the already twilit world of *The Secret Agent*.

In *The Secret Agent* Conrad elaborates his nightmare vision of history by focusing, consciously but also in ways that seem decidedly unconscious, on his prewar social environment. Here the distinctive players are liberalism and socialism, and the story is about how "revolution" from the underclasses provokes "reaction" from nationalist ideologues. Yet the way that Conrad reconfigures these elements is distinctive. Most important in this transformation is how "Russia" enters into the novel. Conrad does not see Russia as a source of inspiration for revolutionary struggle (the meaning St. Petersburg had for many of Conrad's British contemporaries), but rather as a goad to reactionary fervor, as that which would provoke the English authorities to clamp down on the revolutionary underworld. Thus, the Russian Ambassador Vladimir gives Adolf Verloc the mission of bombing the Greenwich Observatory, a terrorist plot that is designed to make English society itself more politically intolerant and repressive. Here, I think, Conrad is using otherness (the Russian Ambassador) as a dumpsite for what is ugly in the English soul, and also revealing something about his personal experience of Russian authoritarianism, about how the toxic world of contemporary politics represents for him a reinvigoration of early family experience. Above all else, what authoritarianism meant to young Konrad followed from the role it played in the suffering and death of his parents, and in his own early impoverishments. And in the novel, the only effect of the failed bombing plot is a titular father's utterly senseless destruction of self, family, and child. In this way, Conrad creates a situation in which political violence is visited on the family through the agency of the father, and in which the dependency of wife and child leads them to their ruin.

In this malignant family drama, Conrad seems to invoke and rework central dimensions of his psychobiography. When one reads this aspect of Conrad's novel against personal events in his childhood, as well as those surrounding the birth of his second son (which occurred at the time of *The Secret Agent's* composition), one sees that the Verloc-Stevie-Winnie relation is multiply determined. Most importantly, Conrad was re-envisioning himself in the novel according to deeply held but seemingly irresolvable feelings of both loss and attachment toward his father. Because he was compelled simultaneously to construct his own subjectivity in terms of the betrayed son (the victim of Apollo Korzeniowski's botched political plot) and the unreliable parent (who carries forward into fatherhood his own unmet need for nurture), Conrad marks his presence in his own text through a strong identification with the positions of both child and father. Hence, the point is to see unconscious interrelations between Conrad's ongoing experience of the parent-child bond and his perception of political violence in the social world, both present and past.

Political Tensions in England

During the prewar years, the dominant forces in English politics were the Liberal party, the new Labour movement, and the insurgents of the Social Imperialist bloc, which encompassed the Fabians (the efficiency ideologues among the English socialists), the Conservative Milnerites and Tariff Reformers, and (during and after 1910), the Lloyd George Radicals. The Liberal party, of course, attempted to hold "the center." On the one hand, they were looking for an ideological middle way between the "older individualism and the modern opportunist socialism"[11]—attempting, that is, to graft the "new liberalism" of social and economic reform onto the old stock of laissez-faire, private property, and individualism. But on the other hand, precisely because this middle position was rooted in traditional liberal principles and was meant to forge an alliance from different and increasingly conflicting interests, it offered no lasting basis for limiting the challenge of independent Labour. In the long term, the Liberal party gave way before the rival ranks of Capital and Labour. In the short term, the effort to satisfy the competing interests of the groups within the Liberal alliance—the moral and religious requirements of middle-class Nonconformists, Home Rule for the Irish, and state welfare for the working class—instigated some of the bitterest strife in parliament's history, and led to increasing both class enmity within Britain and the prospect of civil war with Ireland. In the eye of the storm, we find English liberalism.

The Liberals recognized that in the general election of 1905–06, they would not have gained the most massive majority in modern times without the support of working-class voters. Ever since the 1880s, the radicals within the party had endeavored to make it more sensitive to issues of poverty and unemployment. And mainstream Liberals understood very well that, with the departure of the wealthier classes from the party, political victory depended on forging common ground between liberal organizations and working-class national committees (for example, the Labour Representation Committee which, in 1900, became the new Independent Labour Party). The political necessity of a "Lib-Lab" alliance meant that liberal ideology had to become more progressive. The "new" Liberals attempted to move the party of Gladstone forward into the twentieth century—to join middle-class ideas of individual responsibility and a free-market economy with a commitment to equality of opportunity. This "new" stance acknowledged that, since poverty severely circumscribed individual liberty, the government had the right to impose its authority on the private sector in order to reduce or remove social and economic obstacles to individual development and independence.[12] However, the Liberals followed the "old liberal" principles of free trade, individualism, and war on unearned privilege, even as they adopted the "new liberal" language of state interventionism. As Bernstein puts it, the "new liberalism sought to justify, *within the context of traditional liberal values*, state intervention to improve [the] conditions [of life among the poor]" (*LLP*, p. 11, my emphasis). British liberal ideology in the first decade of the twentieth century was able to support a progressive alliance. But it was able to do so primarily because class politics had not yet fully taken hold.

Middle-class and radical priorities therefore dictated that the fight would be waged against the aristocratic landlords, not against the capitalists. The Liberals identified many of the priorities of Labour not just as instances of special pleading by a "class-bound interest," but as socialist attempts to change the system. Liberal bigwigs were certain that they knew what was best for the workers, because they knew what was best for society as a whole.[13] But an ideological gulf actually divided both "old" and "new" Liberals from the Independent Labour party. Socialism, not liberalism, was in fact the ideology that spoke to the concerns of the working poor. Thus, as Paul Thompson says, "Once Labour was separately organized, creating its own loyalties and interests, the ultimate outlook for Liberalism was bleak." The Liberal landslide of 1906 was the last great victory to which liberalism could ever lay claim; and by 1915, the progressive alliance was coming undone. In the interim, the Liberals were placed in the unenviable position of either challenging Labour, and thus accentuating working-class hostility, or of helping the growth of Labour as an ally, and thus, as Thompson puts it, "fostering the cuckoo in the nest."[14] The Liberals seem to have done both, at once helping Labour to grow by means of the progressive alliance, yet also limiting Labour's political and social clout within the alliance. The Liberal hope of holding the "middle ground" between socialism and toryism was undermined by the gradual but steady awakening of the working class to the intrinsic ideological limits of middle-class liberalism, and hence, as Bernstein says, the Liberal party was ultimately faced with extinction (*LLP,* p. 201).

The Liberal court's legalistic efforts (most notably the Osborne judgement) to limit Labour had the opposite effect of increasing trade-union militancy and revolutionary feeling in the rank and file. After 1907, and especially between 1910 and 1913, there was a dramatic increase in strike activity. Labour historian Walter Kendall writes, "1912 saw the greatest explosion of industrial discontent that Britain had ever seen." Much of this was wild-cat action. Kendall also observes that these waves of unauthorized strikes "seemed suddenly to let loose [a pent-up force], disregarding precedents and agreements, impatient of compromise, shaking the old complacent trade unionism by the ears, sometimes, as in the rail strike of 1911, forcing conservative leaders ahead of it like fallen leaves driven before the wind."[15] Thus, the incendiary rivalry between Labour and Capital was beginning to light up the British political landscape.

In the prewar years, the Liberals, though hardly dead, were very much embattled. It was left to Lloyd George, Chancellor of the Exchequer under Prime Minister Asquith, to take the initiative for the Liberals, and stress the urgency of an expanded welfare program. The result was his famous "people's budget" of 1909. The budget's constructive policies, which focused on temperance and education, on housing and reconstruction of the Poor Law, reflected the ideological bent of the old Radical and new Liberal combination. By taxing unearned income in a "land crusade" against aristocratic privilege and other forms of monopoly, the government would obtain the money to pay for a social welfare program for the workers, including old-age pensions and schemes of disability and unemployment insurance.

All of these measures were enacted, but not without inciting a massive crisis in parliament and in civil society that lasted from 1909–11. First, the House of Lords threw out the budget, and Asquith was compelled to dissolve the government and call for elections. The Lord's action, so extreme that one had to go back 200 years to find anything like it, had provoked the Commons to rescind the Lord's veto power. In turn, Conservative "last ditcher's" in the Lords sought revenge against the Liberal government, and in a dangerously seditious move openly backed the Protestant Ulsterites against the Irish Nationalists. Though the constitutional crisis was averted, and the question of Irish Home Rule put off into the distant future, the uncertainty and strain of the moment was not diminished. The British government was for a time completely destabilized, and the country was brought to the brink of civil war.

Lloyd George sought to steer the crisis to his advantage by aligning with the Social Imperialists, or at least by borrowing from their autocratic vocabulary and style of social reform. Ironically enough, in 1910, at the very time Lloyd George was agitating for a radical budget, he was also urging the leaders of both parties to adopt, as he put it in his Criccieth memo, "coalition against party government"—a commission of "both the great Parties in the state" that would work outside normal parliamentary channels to settle the "urgent problems" of the nation.[16] According to Kenneth Morgan, Lloyd George was proposing an anti-democratic "national synthesis that would soar above partisan strife," a national coalition that would allow him as its kingpin to realize "the kind of grandiose vision of leadership that attracted him [in 1910] to Milner's Prussian 'efficiency,' and in the 1930s to a false prophet like Hitler" (*ALG*, p. 47). Here we see the Liberal party's slow evolution toward humanitarian reform being derailed by imperialist ideas of modernization based on discipline and order. The imperialists' authoritarianism could not but influence Liberal leaders, for their party offered no pragmatic alternative to Lloyd George. And Lloyd George, who was very much in the vanguard of defining policy, and who never really had any enthusiasm for Liberal individualism (but who was ever-ready to rise to an autocratic position of power in collectivist crusades), had moved on to the industrial creed of the Social Imperialists, to the ethos of science and technology, of the professional manager and the businessmen's state.

Of course, Social Imperialism, whether of the left (the Fabians) or the right (the Milnerites), had been a dark thread in the fabric of English political culture since the 1890s and the Boer War. What in part had made fellow-travelers of these seemingly different groups was a Social Darwinist perspective on Empire, the idea that, as G. B. Shaw put it in the Fabian "Manifesto" of 1900, "the world is to the big and the powerful by necessity, . . . and the little ones must come within their borders or be crushed out of existence."[17] Following from this view was the programmatic combination of strong imperial defense and dynamic but illiberal social reform. An example of such reform was the Webbs' proposal for reconstructing the Poor Law, which gave various experts absolute and compulsory power of detention over anyone who fell below certain standards of mental and physical fitness.[18] Moreover, these political elites, on both the Left and Right, shared a common hatred for the "inefficiency" of the democratic process. H. G. Wells in *Anticipations* confidently predicted the failure of democratic ideas and of both the old and new liberalism: "The . . . optimistic Radicalism of the earlier nineteenth century, and the humanitarian philanthropic type of Liberalism, have bogged themselves beyond hope." There was a fierce anti-democratic streak in Wells's notion of a society operated by a cadre of experts: "There will be the suppression of the party machine in the purely democratic countries and of the official choice of the rich and privileged rulers in the more monarchical ones, by capable operative and administrative men inspired by a common belief in social order."[19] Similarly, the vanguard of the Conservative party hammered the Liberals with the logic of autocratic modernization. For Milner and others of his ilk, Asquith and company were "Cobdenite millionaires"—members of that "unpatriotic, anti-nationalist, down-with-the-army-up-with-the foreigner, take it lying down class of Little Englanders"—who conveniently focused on social discontent at election time, while continuing to lead lives of unbridled self-indulgence.[20]

According to J. L. Garvin, editor of the paper *The Observer* and member of the Tariff Reform League, the Unionist vanguard of the Conservative party ambitiously sought "a new age" in which government would fix the people, expertly order "the health and strength, the economic security and the vital efficiency of the mass of the nation."[21] In a 1909 memo written to influence Conservative leaders in the upcoming election, Garvin emphasized that their party, "like the other side," need "a dream" and "a bogey." The dream of "Imperial strength and security" must displace the Socialists' "earthly paradise," and the bogey must be "the foreigner" instead of the landlord. The average voter, Garvin says, dreads "an Imperial and Social catastrophe. That dread has got to be developed and defined in their minds. . . . The argument that the nation is prepared for is that the Radical-Socialist method means revolution, chaos, and peril, while the Unionist

Party stands for power, union, and security."[22] On both sides of the political spectrum, the intellectuals and politicians of "imperial strength and
security" advocated counterrevolutionary formulas to deal with the overwhelming problem of "national impoverishment," thereby hoping to pre-
empt Labour's appeal to the working classes.

The political and social forces at work in Edwardian England might
be analyzed in Marxist terms. Labour might be thought of as the revolutionary "negation" produced by the policies (and failures) of the traditional
political leadership, and National Efficiency as the counterrevolutionary
"negation of the negation." We have seen in previous discussions of imperialism how its despotic practices rebounded on society at home; but the
political process, which allowed imperialist ideology to assimilate collectivist reform strategies and then to become (under Lloyd George) a force
for excluding and silencing Labour in the name of "national order," is
undoubtedly the most reactionary development of the period. Still, this
description of the "revolutionary" and "counterrevolutionary" polarities of
prewar political culture in Britain is somewhat extreme. Britain's political
struggles pale beside those that led to European totalitarianism—namely,
the mobilization of fascism through a populist and demagogic movement
that united against an uncompromising socialism. More importantly, what
this Marxist description of "revolutionary" and "counterrevolutionary"
trends in Britain leaves out is the frustrating stagnation and inevitable fragmentation of liberalism, its inability to evolve sufficiently to mediate politically and socially from the "middle."

The Secret Agent: "Darkness Enough to Bury Five Millions of Lives"

Conrad's vision of the intersecting spheres of the political and the domestic in The Secret Agent is an ironic demonstration of the idea that the political, in the sense of the forces of change and of reaction, might shatter one's
deepest assumptions about the safety and security of one's world, one's relationships, one's life. His emphasis is everywhere placed on "human imbecility"—on the folly that appears in the current social establishment, in
aspirations toward societal progress, in acts or, rather, false pretenses of
love and commitment. As the great literary typologist Northrop Frye knew,
the type of irony that envisions all aspects of life in terms of "unrelieved
bondage" and beholds "a blasted world of repulsiveness and idiocy, a world
without pity or hope," is on the other side of tragedy—Sisyphean instead
of Promethean, bleak instead of tragic.[23] And according to Hayden White

(following Frye), irony of this extreme form often "arises in an atmosphere of social breakdown and cultural demise."[24] The political climate in English society in 1907 may not exactly have constituted an atmosphere of "breakdown" or "demise," but this was unquestionably Conrad's perception of it. The period's fierce partisanship, heading toward societal polarization and unrest—in Galsworthy's words, its "race of partisans feeding their pigeonholes with contradictory reports of life"[25]—aroused all of Conrad's political anxieties. For writers like Shaw and Wells, signs of trouble in British society provided an opportunity for their special intervention, a way of advancing their own careers as political crusaders. In contrast, Conrad eschewed even reasonable intervention into such a crisis, because in his long-held view reformist efforts invited only anarchy. For him, such efforts were the first and last steps into the abyss. In reading *The Secret Agent* one should strive to understand what motivates Conrad's excessive irony, to understand how the fictive presentation of social and personal conflict had become for the author a potential space filled by hopelessness and traumatization, and to inquire into why this was so.

The novel's ironic depiction of life as "unrelieved bondage" is a matter of Conrad's stripping us down to our "human, all too human" faults and daring us to feel pity for that which is constitutionally irremediable about ourselves. The reader's natural reaction when confronted with damaged and disfigured characters like Stevie and Winnie Verloc is to retreat into scorn and condescension (to think oneself better), but such retreat has the unhappy tendency of evoking recognition that one is simply too weak or too cruel to face the facts. Thus, whether one feels pity or scorn, one is faced with one's own irreducible faults and impotence.[26] Conrad holds the reader "in between" the positions of irony and pity, showing her the intrinsic deficiencies of either position, and denying any ethical means of extricating oneself from the impasse.

The bitter fruit of Conrad's prose took sustenance from both political and psychological experience. First, given England's malaise in the prewar period, Conrad had a strong intellectual motivation to pillory the current establishment and (what he saw as) the ferocious optimism and destructive modernism of imperialist-oriented reformers like H. G. Wells. *The Secret Agent* is dedicated to Wells, but as Martin Ray has observed, the novel harshly scrutinizes "many of Wells's most cherished beliefs." Ray continues: "It is possible that there is a touch of finality about this tribute to Wells, with Conrad paying old debts in the dedication while settling old scores in the text which follows."[27] I agree that in the novel Conrad set out to demolish the Wellsian view of the world, but I also think that, while Conrad might have been settling old scores, he was genuinely alarmed by Wells's growing influence in national politics. (For example, Scally points out that Lloyd George was greatly impressed by Wells's statement of Social Imperialist doctrine in the *New Machiavelli* [*OLGC*, p. 226].) I want to point out that the hellish quality of Conrad's social and political vision was motivated in part by his need to expose "the cheat" of Wellsian futurism, of the Fabian and Social Imperialist ideology that conceptualized society as a techno-pastoral, a utopia from which evil is engineered out of existence. Second, Conrad had a psychological need to swathe his experience in layers of hopelessness. Conrad's fear of political restiveness in Britain and his difficulties with his wife Jessie and his two small sons, both seem to have revived unsettling thoughts and feelings from his Polish childhood. If, as I believe, Conrad was feeling with special intensity the tidal pull of his childhood history at this time, and if these memories helped to shape and color the novel, then the novel's constricted, derisive voice can be viewed as overdetermined in several interesting ways.

Irony seems to have solidified Conrad's identity as a survivor, as the one specially authorized to survey the dark underside of human experience—the one to whom the darkness is known, but also who does not break under the strain of such knowledge. However, to the extent that Conrad sees only life's bleakness and has need of a narrator who is for the most part coldly distanced from all this "desolation, madness and despair," narrative irony is self-protective. Such black "lucidity" hinders critical insight into and feeling for the variegated colors and distinctions of life. Hence irony does commit (as the Note to the novel puts it) "a gratuitous outrage" on the reader (*SA*, p. 13), at least in the sense that Conrad's narrative posture is itself a pessimistic illusion about life and a narcissistic illusion about his own authority to bear it. Such lucidity does not move one to identify with Conrad's misery, but rather initiates a desire to understand his black and mistrustful sense of the world—to ask why this unrelieved pessimistic illusion is pressed into service.

The extremity of Conrad's skepticism and irony therefore motivates my investigation of the political and psychological dimensions of the text and the life. I substantially agree with Frederick Karl's observation that *"The Secret Agent* and the next novel, *Under Western Eyes,* are so ironical in terms of human relationships and social ties that the reader is encouraged to make some extraliterary associations."[28] Moreover, I am convinced by the specific relevance of Cedric Watts's view that "Conrad's pessimism was temperamental" (not philosophical and systematic), and that it was "implanted by his Polish upbringing and nurtured by his immediate domestic worries."[29]

I begin with one of the most remarkable letters Conrad ever drafted on the issue of political change, then move to the novel's social framework and attempt to map salient aspects of the prewar setting onto the text. After completing this social reading, I will investigate the Verloc-Winnie-Stevie triangle as a psychological structure, and as a literary analogue for the themes of parenting, of losing loved objects, and of grieving in both Conrad's childhood and adult life. My ultimate objective is to show that for Conrad the social and the personal intersect dialectically: that Conrad's perception of his cultural and personal surroundings, in and around 1907, returned him to his sufferings as a child, and that these two frames worked together to generate the melancholy vision and depressive fantasy structure of *The Secret Agent*.

In December of 1885, when Conrad was twenty-eight, already sailing on English ships for seven years and moving up in the ranks of the Merchant Marine, he wrote a letter on the politics of reform to Spiridion Klisczewski, another Polish émigré. In it we find evidence of Conrad's reactionary ideological leanings: as Karl says, it is not "the whole of [Conrad's] politics," but it is also not to be discounted as "simply the ravings of a youthful, unformed mind" (*JCTL*, p.227). Conrad had pretty much made up his mind on the issues of political idealism and progressivism, and his opinions were not to alter substantially in later life. The letter is important for two reasons. First, it is informed by Conrad's rejection of the politics of generations of Polish republicans, including Apollo's left-wing version of nationalism. And second, Conrad focuses on the British General Election of 1886 and on Liberal, Radical, and Socialist forces in British society—that is, on the very forces of change that, in the prewar years, were ready to boil over. Hence, the letter is directly relevant to *The Secret Agent*. To his friend Klisczewski in late 1885, when a Liberal and Radical majority had been elected to the House of Commons, Conrad wrote:

> Joy reigns in St. Petersburg, no doubt, and profound disgust in Berlin:
> the International Socialist Association are triumphant, and every dis-
> reputable ragamuffin in Europe feels that the day of universal brother-
> hood, despoliation and disorder is coming apace, and nurses
> day-dreams of well-plenished pockets amongst the ruin of all that is
> respectable, venerable and holy. The great British Empire went over
> the edge, and yet on to the inclined plain of social progress and radi-
> cal reform. . . . For the sun is set and the last barrier removed. England
> was the only barrier to the pressure of infernal doctrines born in con-
> tinental back-slums. Now there is nothing! The destiny of this nation

and of all nations is to be accomplished in darkness amidst much
weeping and gnashing of teeth, to pass through robbery, equality,
anarchy and misery under the iron rule of a militarism [sic] despotism!

Conrad then asserts his belief that "Socialism must inevitably end in
Caesarism." This view is echoed by the Note to *The Secret Agent*, wherein
Conrad scathingly dismisses humanitarianism and anarchist dreams (which
are but a degenerate extension of humanitarianism) as "a brazen cheat
exploiting the poignant miseries and passionate credulities of a mankind
always so tragically eager for self-destruction" (*SA*, p.9). Thus, Karl is right
to claim that the 1885 letter shows how Conrad had consolidated his
hatred for the political Left. Conrad concludes with bleak intemperance.

> I live mostly in the past and the future. The present has, you easily
> understand, but few charms for me. I look with the serenity of despair
> and the indifference of contempt upon the passing events.
> Disestablishment, Land Reform, Universal Brotherhood are but like
> milestones on the road to ruin. The end will be awful, no doubt!
> Neither you nor I shall live to see the final crash: although we both
> may turn in our graves when it comes, for we both feel deeply and sin-
> cerely. Still, there is no earthly remedy for those earthly misfortunes,
> and from above, I fear, we may obtain consolation, but no remedy.
> "All is vanity."[30]

Despite his bluster Conrad has, of course, a deep aversion to even the
mildest form of political conflict. His unreasoning reactionary gloominess
stems in part from Poland's special fate of having been crushed in the mill-
stone of Russia and Prussia, and more particularly from Apollo's ill-fated
involvement in the aborted 1863 Uprising of the "red" Polish Nationalists
against the Russian oppressor. Conrad's political anxiety, at once historical
and personal, overdetermines his 1885 view of British activism, his certainty that "social progress and radical reform" unleashes the inflexible
forces of revolution and reaction, and that historical change has no principles to guide it except anarchy on the one side, and tyranny on the other.
This is "the destiny" of Britain, as much as it is Europe's (or Poland's) destiny "to pass through robbery, equality, anarchy, and misery, under the rule
of . . . despotism." In 1885 at least, Conrad had hope for Britain's political
future, and was most likely counting on conservatism's return to power.
However, by the time of the General Election of 1906, after the British
Unionists had shown themselves rapacious imperialists in the Boer War,

after the bloody upheavals in St. Petersburg, and after British Labour ("Universal Brotherhood") began to derail the Liberal government ("Distestablishment and Land Reform"), Conrad faced the distinct possibility that his worst nightmare was being realized. Indeed, both "Autocracy and War" and *The Secret Agent* seem to convey a sense that for Conrad British Liberal society had traveled so far down "the road to ruin" that it was coming very near road's end. Both works seem to vibrate with an expectation of doom, like tuning forks held forward into the future toward the great humming apocalypse of 1914.

Conrad's disenchantment is reflected in "Autocracy and War": first, by his vision of the "beleaguered fortress" of peace at this time when the democratic nations of Europe were becoming embroiled in "slowly maturing economical contests for life and death" ("AW," pp. 143, 149); and second, by what seems to him the intractable British "hallucinations" about Russia— both the "folly" of the jingoists who project the mythic threat of the Czar's millions of soldiers descending onto the plains of India, and the misguided "hope" of the democrats who invest Russia's revolutionaries with the capacity "to initiate a rational scheme of reform" ("AW," pp. 127–129). For Conrad, Russia is "Le Néant," the political and moral abyss, and hence Britain only worsens its own problems by dealing with autocratic Russia, whether through expedient imperialist treaty or humanitarian aid. The Author's Note to *The Secret Agent* shows Conrad similarly bereft. The times, he says, were leaving him behind, "aimless amongst mere husks of sensations and lost in a world of other, of inferior, values" (*SA*, 8). The world was trampling on "all that is respectable, venerable and holy," turning against the ancient virtues (duty and loyalty) that Conrad prized; and Britain, in the tumultuous hustings of its prewar liberal democracy, seemed to forget its enduring allegiance to monarchy, the very principle that for Conrad made duty and loyalty meaningful. Thus, the London of *The Secret Agent* is "sunk in a hopeless night" and resting at the bottom of a black abyss (p. 222).

The political temperament of the novel is very close to that of the 1885 letter, not just because both are equally bleak, but also because both are suspended between fearful anticipation of catastrophe, on the one hand, and a conviction that the catastrophe has already occurred, on the other. In the letter, Conrad is clearly anxious about the unpredictability of the political future, and yet he gazes, he says, "with the serenity of despair and the indifference of contempt upon the passing events." In the novel, Conrad shows us imbecilic police and revolutionaries locked in an isometric and self-paralyzing embrace. As the Professor puts it to his leftist comrades: "You . . . are the slaves of the social convention, which is afraid of you; slaves of it as much as the very police that stands up in the defence of that convention. . . .You are not a bit better than the forces arrayed against you . . ." (*SA,* p.68). In a way, the world of the novel is so undermined by its own repulsive idiocy that chaos seems to be an accomplished fact. As Terry Eagleton observes, Conrad consecrates "a vast stalemated game which is society," but at the same time, and conversely, he "signifies an anarchic dissolution of social order." In Eagleton's view, however, the social paradox achieves resolution because the reactionary Conrad rejects revolutionary values, and "precisely because of this, everything seems to be left exactly as it was."[31]

Yet the novel does not achieve a status quo resolution in the way Eagleton suggests. On the one hand, any resolution comes in the violent dismembering of the Verloc family; and as I will argue, this domestic cataclysm is continuous with and illustrative of the potential for violence in the larger social world. On the other hand, Conrad needs the double frame of fear and of comfort—of expressing his anxieties about the slide into the abyss, and of imagining, as he puts it in the letter, no earthly remedy for these earthly misfortunes. There is something about the impossibility of changing the downward course that is extremely comforting to Conrad. There is something reassuring about witnessing the progress of chaos, and then envisioning its culmination, from a position of resigned "serenity." For then the world becomes predictable, like the trajectory of a man falling from a building once his feet have lost contact with the ledge: it becomes bleak but static because its course is known, and peaceful because change has been robbed of surprise or uncertainty. The doubleness of Conrad's position is that of melancholy impasse: he is hopeless about the trajectory of history; but he also imagines himself untouched by or indifferent to the forces of disorder, and hence is defensively and narcissistically hopeful.

The action of *The Secret Agent* takes place in 1886, and Conrad writes his disillusioned political letter in December of 1885 (in response to the upcoming General Election of 1886), a coincidence that can only lead one to wonder about its significance. Is Karl right that Conrad sets the novel at this time because "this was a period of considerable anarchist activity in England" (*JCTL,* p.605), and despite the fact that many of Conrad's contemporaries would certainly remember that the Greenwich bombing (the germ of the novel) occurred in 1894? The idea that there is a meaningful temporal coincidence between the letter and the novel seems more plausible when one considers how Conrad actually establishes the date, 1886, in the text. ·

When the narrator tells us that Winnie has been married to Adolf

Verloc for seven years it is already late in the tale. She has only just learned that her brother Stevie has been blown to bits in the bomb explosion, and that her husband Adolf is largely responsible for Stevie's death. "Seven years' security for Stevie loyally paid for on [Winnie's] part" (*SA*, p.201). Only later, at the end of the novel, does the narrator relate the date of the marriage—June 24, 1879—and allow the curious reader to do the arithmetic. Attention is drawn to the date. It is not given in a casual and offhand manner, but in the most pointed and dramatic way possible. Verloc's conspiracy has ignited a stunning sequence of events: Winnie has been deceived by Verloc, the man on whom she thought she could depend; her beloved brother is senselessly killed; she herself has become a murderer, having killed Verloc in a fit of vengeance; and she is betrayed by Comrade Ossipon, the man to whom she turns for help to escape the country. And finally, finding herself utterly alone on a cross-channel steamer, Winnie casts herself into a cold and lightless sea. The date of Winnie's marriage (the temporal frame of the novel) is only revealed here, on the occasion of her suicide, when Winnie leaves her wedding ring lying in the place where she had been sitting, with the date June 24, 1879 engraved inside, and one of the steamer's hands discovers it for us to see. Thus, the historical frame of Conrad's relation to his character, Winnie, is established in the most concrete of ways—the finding of an object, and an act of simple arithmetic (1879 plus seven). The dating of the action suggests that Conrad might be commemorating 1885–86 in a more personal way, as if he were memorializing the year of his definitive political disillusionment. In the novel, Winnie is driven to suicide in 1886, when the only path leading away from unbearable torment is down to darkness. She loses her domestic and personal security, "the supreme illusion of her life" (*SA*, p.201), and plunges away from the world, with Conrad's blessing.

Was Conrad telling his readers that, in 1907, with the writing of *The Secret Agent*, the social abyss he had so dreaded 20 years earlier had at last become for him an accomplished reality? There is no sure answer to this. Yet given the enduring nature of Conrad's dismal view of social reformism, and given the similarities between the 1885 letter and the novel in terms of psychological strategy and personal idiom, one can certainly infer that Conrad would respond with alarm to the General Election of 1906. It is hard to imagine that, in his text, he would not elaborate, in both conscious and unconscious ways, those aspects of contemporary historical reality that shook him to his depths. Too often the novel has been read as being simply about anarchist activity before the turn of the century. It is time that we see how this anarchist activity provided Conrad both with historical cover and with a means for elaborating his anxieties about the emerging forces of "revolution" and "counterrevolution" in the prewar period.

Conrad creates fictional versions of the agents of "revolution" in two ways. There is the friendship between a self-indulgent millionairess (the radical lady patroness) and an impoverished, parasitical Marxist (Michaelis), which caricatures the uneasy political relations between the Liberals and the subversives of Labour. And we are also given the anarchists Ossipon and the Professor, characters who represent a social Darwinist and Social Imperialist position similar to the one held by the Fabians and, more specifically, by H. G. Wells. True to the politics of the time, the novel offers up agents of "counterrevolution": Mr. Vladimir, the imperialist Russian Ambassador; and double agent Adolf Verloc, who is both agent provocateur and police spy. In the reactionary camp, Vladimir represents social "vigilance" while Verloc carries the banner of social "protection."

An ominous figure of state authority, Vladimir makes a backstage effort to move the British government and public opinion in the direction of "universal repressive legislation" (*SA*, p.38), and hence conceives of the Greenwich bombing conspiracy as an ingenious form of political manipulation. Verloc for his part is supposed to implement the plot in accordance with "the methods of the revolutionary world" (p.37). It is a plan that brings together elements from the Right (Vladimir and Verloc) with a co-conspirator from the Left (the Professor as technical expert on "revolutionary methods"). The Professor's utopian end, his anarchistic urge "to make a clean sweep of the whole social creation," justifies a special know-how in the art of dynamiting, but also requires an astute sense for choosing the right target: in this case, according to Vladimir, the "sacrosanct fetish" of science. (In Vladimir's view, bombing the National Gallery would be "like breaking a few back windows in a man's house," whereas "any imbecile that has got an income believes in [science]" [pp. 39–40].) What is Conrad up to in configuring the bombing conspiracy, and its contrivers and operatives, in this way?

Of course, there are numerous ways to expose revolutionary action as "a cheat." One way is to unmask its agents as "slaves of convention" who are too ineffectual to mastermind a conspiracy. To the extent that this is Conrad's way of deflating activism, however, he also must attribute the revolutionary threat to a counterrevolutionary source. Conrad's bombing plot conjoins the forces of imperialism (Vladimir) and social activism (the Professor). Its purpose is not to hurt anyone, but rather, in Vladimir's words, to awaken "the imbecile bourgeoisie of this country [who] make themselves the accomplices of the very people [the Socialists] whose aim is to drive them out of their houses to starve in ditches" (SA, p.37). The political alignments of Vladimir's plot (imperialism and social activism) and the aim of the plot (counterrevolutionary propaganda) bear a family resemblance to Social Imperialist political activity. We recall how the Social Imperialist J. L. Garvin undertook a press campaign to inculcate the populace with "dread," with the idea that "the Radical-Socialist method means revolution, chaos, and peril." Conrad entrusts counter-revolutionary propagandizing to a Russian imperialist. However, much the same kind of propagandizing was undertaken by the prewar British Social Imperialists, especially by fanatical ideologues such as Garvin and the Milnerites.

The British Social Imperialist claim (a claim made by groups both on the Left and the Right, by both Fabians and Milnerites) was that only a state with full compulsory powers and a stern approach to social reform would prevent British society from disintegrating in social unrest and chaos—or, as Scally puts it, "in a violent clash between revolution and reaction in which order and progress would dissolve" (OLGC, pp. 11–12). However, the Social Imperialist dream of social progress through compulsory order and discipline provides an inherently contradictory promise, because imperialist goals inevitably override humanitarian aspirations. Full dictatorial power cannot lead to social justice. In Vladimir's project, repressive aims leave no space for an alternative ideology or difference of perspective. Still, the Russian imperialist shares two premises with the British Social Imperialists: the preemptive manipulation of the Left, and state enforcement of order and discipline.

Was Conrad carefully parodying the British Social Imperialists in his rendering of the alignments and end-purpose of the bombing plot? Probably not. It is more likely that the social cachet of imperialist propaganda in Conrad's time worked to enflame his own preexisting dread of the "revolutionary methods" of social reform and "the peril" of the foreigner. Hence British Social Imperialism was, as a presence in Conrad's text, scrutinized sideways and at best incompletely. While Vladimir is the foreigner in the novel who embraces the credo of British imperialism, he is also conversely the one who attacks science as "the sacrosanct fetish" of British society (SA, p.38). Vladimir's tactic for scaring the bourgeoisie and stepping up "the vigilance of the police—the severity of the magistrates" (p.27–28) is to throw a bomb at the Observatory, and hence at "learning—science" (p.40). Had Conrad consciously meant for Vladimir to reflect a Social Imperialist agenda, the character would take a positivistic stance, and Conrad would pillory him for suffocating our humanity with tenets of scientific management.

Thus the novel peddles a significant ambiguity. On the one hand, Vladimir seems to enact the British Social Imperialist's call for fascistic social regulation. But on the other, he subverts their modernizing pretensions, namely, the social engineering of "damn professors" like Shaw and Wells. Vladimir says: "All the damned professors are radicals at heart. Let them know that their great panjandrum [of science] has got to go, too, to make room for the Future of the Proletariat" (*SA*, p.40), and then goes on to challenge the nonsense of scientific reform with his own "absurd ferocity," namely, the pure folly of blowing up astronomy.[32] The ambiguity of Vladimir's character arises in part from Conrad's having split off the "social" aspect of British Social Imperialism from its "imperialist" aspect, locating the latter in Vladimir, the foreigner, and the former in the character of the Professor, the harshly critical portrait of a Wellsian British radical.

The result is that Social Imperialism as it is represented in the novel is obscured in its role as a significant force in national politics. Conrad partly dispatches the internal danger posed by an imperialist ethos by locating it in a "Russian" figure of state authority. This strategic blindness toward the increased influence of home-grown fascists on the British government was very likely the by-product of Conrad's phobic preoccupation with Russia as "Le Néant," the black hole of blind despotism that he had already placed well outside of anything Western—or, indeed, human—in "Autocracy and War." We see this displacement in the novel when the Assistant Commissioner traces the bombing back to Verloc and Vladimir, and then tells Vladimir that he faces criminal prosecution. After this Vladimir is "not very often seen" (*SA*, pp. 189–90)—in fact, he all but disappears from the text. Disgorging imperialist oppression in the form of Vladimir, however, only eliminates half the problem. Conrad's strategy for dealing with the ruthlessness of Wells's social vision entails showing its ugliness, and then equating ugliness with insignificance. Wells's cold censoriousness is reflected in the Professor's passionate hatred of human weakness; but in the end the character of the Professor is reduced to an ugly little pest with absolutely no political voice, presence, or power. Conrad's strategy of critique seems to be to magnify what is grotesque, thereby shrinking it morally to the proportions of an insect.

In the last chapter of *The Secret Agent*, when Ossipon and the Professor have a conversation largely based on the Fabian credo that the world belongs "to the big and the powerful," Conrad is staging a version of Wellsian evil. The Professor tells Ossipon to contemplate how social progress will follow from an efficient program of extermination.

"Exterminate, exterminate! That is the only way of progress. It is!
Follow me, Ossipon? First the great multitude of the weak must go,
then the only relatively strong. You see? First the blind, then the deaf
and the dumb, then the halt and the lame—and so on. Every taint,
every vice, every prejudice, every convention must meet its doom."
(*SA*, p.246)

The Professor's statement echoes the postscript to Kurtz's pamphlet for the
"Suppression of Savage Customs": "Exterminate all the Brutes!" The
Professor merely follows to its logical end the kind of reasoning one sees in
Shaw's *Manifesto*, in the Webbs' reconstruction of the Poor Law, or in Wells's
futuristic monograph *Anticipations* and his novel *A Modern Utopia*.
    Anticipations tells us that the "inferior" cannot be accorded equal rights
under the law.

It has become apparent that whole masses of population are, as a
whole, inferior in their claim upon the future, to other masses, that
they cannot be given opportunities or be trusted with power as superior people are trusted, that their characteristic weaknesses are conta-
gious and detrimental to the civilizing fabric, and that their range of
incapacity tempts and demoralizes the strong. To give them equality
is to sink to their level, to protect and cherish them is to be swamped
in their fecundity. (*A*, pp. 250–51)

A Modern Utopia moves beyond mere discrimination to a program of "social
surgery," by means of which Wells excludes the incompetent, the weak of
character, the idiots and lunatics, the drunkards, and the otherwise tainted
from "the great body of the population."[33] In *Heart of Darkness*, Marlow—and
Conrad—cannot mourn what is lost in Kurtz's darkness, and hence his confession of evil becomes itself a kind of surrogate virtue, a substitute for
nobility. In *The Secret Agent*, the narrator has no idealizing illusions about the
imperialist evil the Professor represents, yet this danger is strategically
diminished in the portrayal of the Professor as "frail, insignificant, shabby,
miserable." His ideas are abominations, his essence a cancer, but he is
ignored by the multitude. "Nobody looked at him. He passed on unsus-
pected and deadly, like a pest in the street full of men" (*SA*, p.253). While
the autocrat of the left is made to loom large for the reader as a homegrown
social menace, he is in the novel's final phrase ironically served up as a pest.
    The diminishment raises complications, however, for the more

"insignificant" the Professor is made to appear, the more real or "deadly" the danger he represents actually becomes. The Professor's cruelty is treated with a narrative distancing, as if Conrad's only possible response to the Professor's "inspired" hatred were to cast him off hatefully in turn. And though the Professor is consigned to walk in the shadow of the crowd, that image also constitutes a human darkness, an ignominious mound of industrious ants thoughtlessly harboring a devourer of the world's light. One darkness (the Professor) is swallowed by another (the crowd), and in the process the "pest" of Social Imperialism becomes a kind of virus in the social body—which is to say, a virus that Conrad has not eliminated, but only defensively relocated. The forces of reaction are displaced away from the Observatory and Vladimir's "universal repressive legislation," but they nonetheless erupt domestically in the scenes of Stevie's death and of family extinction.

Vladimir, the arch-counterrevolutionary and imperialist ideologue, is the one who orders the bombing attack against the "overly-lenient" political culture of Britain, and by extension against establishment liberalism. And the Assistant Commissioner, Vladimir's nemesis, is the one who, in solving the mystery, protects elite Liberals from themselves, and protects their style of life, by safeguarding their assumptions and sensitivities. In Conrad's handling of the manhunt, Inspector Heat, the Commissioner's underling, wrongly accuses the shabby socialist Michaelis of the conspiracy; but the Commissioner's own effort to detect and apprehend Vladimir and Verloc is motivated more by self-interest than by a desire to see justice done. The Commissioner wants his own career advanced by the "great lady," who is also the radical patroness of Michaelis, the hopelessly infirm "apostle of humanitarian hopes" (SA, p.94). Were Michaelis wrongly to end up in prison, his lady protector would "never forgive" the Commissioner (p.100–101). The proper context within which to view the manhunt must include, therefore, the special relationship between the lady radical and Michaelis the Marxist, which more or less corresponds to the historical situation of the Edwardian Liberal elite styling itself as guardian to "revolutionary" labor. The text does not depict the specific historical failures of liberalism—its failure to mediate and hence its provocation of social unrest and aggravated factionalism—but does expose the class prejudices of the Liberal elite that led to the political restiveness of the prewar.

Michaelis optimistically predicts the downfall of Capital. He sees "the great capitalists devouring the little capitalists, concentrating the power and the tools of production in great masses, perfecting industrial processes, and in the madness of self-aggrandizement only preparing, orga-

nizing, enriching, making ready the lawful inheritance of the suffering proletariat" (*SA*, p.52). For her part, the lady patroness responds philanthropically toward Michaelis, but without understanding a word that he says. She
extols Michaelis as "a Saint"; she pities him as a "poor creature" who needs
"someone to look after him"; and above all she is firm in her faith that
Michaelis's socialism poses no threat to her own social status and wealth.
"She was not an exploiting capitalist herself; she was, as it were, above the
play of economic conditions. And she had a great capacity of pity for the
more obvious forms of human miseries, precisely because she was such a
complete stranger to them" (p.97–98). The historical failure of Liberalism
to move beyond "a great pity" for the material grievances of the working
class becomes in Conrad's handling a contradiction endemic to the ideology of the bleeding heart, a position at once self-congratulatory and manifestly, egregiously blind.

In this way Conrad focuses the reader on the misunderstandings and
miscommunications between elite Liberals and an increasingly Marxist
working class, an urgent contemporary political problem. The novel's
ironic perspective on this situation is premised, first, on introducing the
illusory idea that Michaelis and his lady patroness in fact share "a deep,
calm, convinced infatuation" with each other, or "a certain simplicity of
thought . . . common to serene souls at both ends of the social scale" (*SA*,
p.99, p.97); and second on our recognition that what they actually share
together is a mutually created disconnectedness. But any serious claim that
might follow from this irony is vitiated by Conrad's insistence that this is a
relation (or misrelation) between two social parasites, the harmless
Michaelis and an old woman no longer concerned with "a close view of
great affairs" (p.94). What Conrad shows is folly, to be sure, but folly made
small and drained of political urgency, a contemptible game of radical chic
that never leaves the drawing room. This constriction of ironic insight
leaves the larger political arrangement singed but on the whole under-
cooked, while drawing-room liberals and their radical benefactors have
been burned to ashes and fanned for the last traces of heat and smoke.

The well springs for the novel's social action, the bombing conspiracy and the hunt for the conspirators, seem to have their origins in the
social forces familiar to Conrad in 1907. First, the Vladimir-Verloc-
Professor configuration is roughly parallel to the propaganda activity and
disciplinary aims of the Social Imperialist "counterrevolution." Second, the
lady patroness - Michaelis relation parallels the "Lib-Lab" alliance, and
reflects something of the historical role that the Liberals played as guardian
to Labour reformers and their socialist "revolution." While the social text of

prewar Britain is implicit but present in the novel, Conrad's elisions and narrow constructions render it virtually illegible. It becomes readable only when one supplies the links that Conrad displaces (for example, the continuity between Vladimir's dictatorial view of the state and the Professor's dictatorial view of social reform), and when one gives due weight to that which Conrad diminishes and reduces (for example, when one corrects for the "impotence" of the Professor, or the "silliness" of Michaelis and his patroness). The social text as it appears in the novel is like a half-lucid dream, vexing thought without entirely awakening it.

However, in spite of these distortions, the polarizing forces that were alive in prewar Britain are also at work in the novel's social body, and the narrative provides a stage for the violent clash between "revolution" and "reaction." Police spy Adolf Verloc, as the Assistant Commissioner explains, "will spread the double evil of emulation [of revolutionary action] in one direction, and of panic, hasty legislation, unreflecting hate, on the other" (SA, p. 121)—and in so doing, he will set revolution and reaction against one another. In his role as double agent, Verloc acts as a conduit for the release of this "double evil" into the family. As Vladimir's pawn, Verloc "emulates" revolution, pretending to commit the bombing in the name of the revolutionary group "The Future of the Proletariat" (of which he is the vice-president). He also enlists his half-wit brother-in-law in the bombing plot, thereby giving political form to Stevie's decidedly unpolitical and unreasoning rage at the wretchedness he sees in the world, and teaching Stevie how to simulate revolution. It is this counterfeit copy of revolution that lights the bomb, then incites reactionary fervor from Inspector Heat. Needing to assert authority in the wake of the bombing, Heat warns the Professor that "it may yet be necessary to make people believe that some of you [anarchists] ought to be shot at sight like mad dogs" (p. 87). On the most arbitrary of legal pretenses Heat does all he can to pin the bombing on Michaelis, even to the point of going to Verloc's home on Brett Street to inform the police spy that he had best slip out of the country (p.176), thus hoping to clear the field of rival suspects. When Winnie overhears this conversation she learns the terrible truth that Stevie is dead, that Verloc is behind the "violent disintegration" of her brother, and that he is now conniving to escape criminal prosecution. Acting the authoritarian part, Winnie targets her husband for summary execution: he becomes "the mark for desperate and bloodthirsty indignations," though not from his public enemies, as he expects (pp. 195, 205). The narrator comments dryly on how Vladimir's botched propaganda ploy leads to Winnie's "bloodthirst." "The knocking down of a wall was not the aim of Mr. Vladimir's menaces, but the production of a moral effect. With much trouble and distress on Mr. Verloc's part the effect might be said to have been produced. . . . [H]owever, most unexpectedly, it came home to roost in Brett Street . . ." (p. 195).

Vladimir's intention, of course, was simply to scare the good citizens of Britain in order to awaken them to the wisdom of a social order based on authoritarian control and discipline. But if, as the narrator suggests, Winnie's response to the bombing—namely, to kill Verloc and then herself—foreshadows the form that Vladimir's "production of a moral effect" might take for the masses, then it follows that the wider counterrevolutionary intention of the bombing must lead to chaos and self-destruction. Like her unwitting brother, Winnie has become a part of the public terror. Just as Stevie, oblivious and good, publicly emulates violent revolution, so Winnie's reactive vengeance, fueled by the love she has for her brother, is the example of Vladimir's "moral effect." The manipulation is almost alchemical in the way it changes decency into destruction. The novel moves systematically from the conception of the bombing plot to the Verloc clan's enactment of the "double evil" of revolution and reaction. Hence, if Conrad relocates society's violent potential to the story of the self-immolation of the Verloc family, and if such displacement is shown as a possible strategy for "saving" society from itself, he also emphatically makes the familial continuous with the social, and in this sense makes it illustrative of the social and political peril of polarization and violence. Conrad employs the displacement while simultaneously tracing its course; and thus he undoes the strategy of misrecognition in the very act of creating it, doing and undoing at the same time.

This shows clearly that, to the extent that Conrad abandons the critical task of making sense of his prewar social environment, he abandons the opportunity for effective social commentary and hope. He is left with a reactionary fear that Britain's destiny "is to be accomplished in darkness amidst much wailing and gnashing of teeth"—a dread elaborated in the Verlocs' terrible fate. Hence, in the novel the author puts himself in a position of melancholy impasse: on the one hand, he is hopeless about the dark cataclysm ticking ominously in the belly of British society, often acting as if he were already living in the rubble at ground zero; but on the other hand, distortion and ironic overkill allow him to remain upright, observant, and engaged, with some hope that the progress of domestic entropy can be arrested, and that ironic dismissal of the general disorder can postpone detonation indefinitely. It is a melancholy that at once aches from what is already lost and anticipates the inevitable loss yet to come, and treats what

has been and what is to come as one continuous, timeless calamity—one
that has always already happened, but that is always on the verge of happening again for the first time. It is an authorial position predicated on
melancholy repetition, on impasse, as a substitute for remembrance, grieving, and living in the flow of time where losses cannot be magically
undone.

All of which strongly supports the idea that one mustn't neglect the
novel's bleak demonstration that "the personal is the political" and vice
versa. The "unintended consequence" of Vladmir's propaganda stunt is the
destruction of the Verloc family, but only because the forces at work in
society are able to enter into and irrevocably alter people's lives at the most
personal level. We also know, of course, that the patterns and forces of our
individual histories can influence those around us as well as larger societal
and political trends. Might it be, then, that Conrad uses the domestic scene
of the novel not just as a defensive means of dealing with societal violence,
but also as a Winncottian "potential space"—a phantasmatic container—
for the elaboration of personal traumatic experience? We recall how history
dovetails with biography in Conrad's 1885 letter. Conrad's unreasoning,
gloomy response to the British General Election of 1886 was overdetermined by his sense of Polish national politics, which was itself predicated
on how social forces of revolution and reaction subjected his own parents
to suffering and death. It seems likely that Conrad would use the fictional
scene of domestic dissolution in order to elaborate the deprivations of his
childhood in Poland; but to see this we first must understand how the personal and the social converge in Conrad's life in 1907. With this in mind, I
return to the novel itself to look more closely at the Verloc's domestic
scene as a psychological formation that brings into play realities from
Conrad's life, both present and past.

Verloc is "the far-famed secret agent Δ" (*SA*, p.152), a particularly apt
code name ("delta"), with its mathematical meaning as a sign for "change,"
and its familial suggestion of oedipal triangulation. Though Verloc is not
Stevie's father by birth, he is, as Winnie sadly observes, "as much of a father
as poor Stevie ever had in his life" (p.157); and she longs for her husband
Adolf to assume the role of Stevie's loving parent. The oedipal father is
generally understood as "the third" who potentially transforms and lends
differentiation to the nature of the child's intimacy with its mother (Winnie
is for all intents and purposes Stevie's mother), and who in this sense can
open the child to the abundance of the wider world. But Verloc, acting in
the father's name or representing his symbolic law, does not lovingly bring
Stevie into the social world. Instead he carelessly uses the boy, stealing him

from the safety of his relationship with Winnie to be a lackey serving someone else's grandiose design. Of course, Stevie blows himself to bits. Conrad's depiction of Verloc as wallowing in moral indolence, which allows him selfishly to enlist Stevie in the bombing plot, soaks "the far-famed secret agent" in ironic scorn. However, the more terrible irony is that Conrad has imbued his portrayal of Verloc-as-father with aspects of himself, and in this way lends to the portrait shades of self-hatred.

Stevie's "violent disintegration" resonates with episodes in Conrad's personal history, most immediately with events related to the birth of his second son, John, on August 2, 1906. At this time Conrad was in the midst of the final chapters of the novel, and hence was focused on the Verloc domestic drama. Four months later, when tasked with correcting proofs, Conrad decided to take his family, including his new son, on a working vacation in France. While riding the train to Montpellier, Conrad impulsively opened a window and threw out a bundle holding all of John's baby clothes. This gesture amazed and disturbed Conrad's wife Jessie. She remarked to him, "Well, I'm sure the man who finds that bundle will be looking for the baby's corpse."[34] Here, in an act so concrete and close to the unconscious intention that it qualifies as "symbolic" by a hair's breadth at best, Conrad could be seen to enact a wish to do away with his baby son John. Moreover, it is an action that seems to correspond to Verloc's having, in Winnie's words, taken "the boy away from [her] to murder him" (SA, p.202). Certainly Jessie understood the discarded bundle in this way, with her commonsensical association to "the baby's corpse." Conrad is careful in the novel to absolve Verloc of criminal intent (Mr.Verloc "did not mean [Stevie] to perish at all" [p.190]); however, that the boy dies, that Conrad portrays Verloc in scathing terms, and that Winnie murders Verloc for his crime, all are highly suggestive that Conrad felt a close affiliation with the novel's infanticidal wish, as well as a need to punish himself for this wish.

Many of Conrad's biographers have noted this correspondence between the novel's bomb- explosion and Conrad's response in life to the birth of his son. For example, Frederick Karl calls the bombing Conrad's "wish fulfillment for his entire clan" (JCTL, p.621); and Jeffrey Meyers tells us that the Verlocs' " 'domestic drama' expresses Conrad's considerable hostility toward his wife and jealousy toward his children."[35] Both Karl and Meyers look to the circumstances before and during Jessie's pregnancy as precipitating Conrad's hostile wish. The pregnancy had been preceded by a period of protracted illness in the Conrad family. Jessie was afflicted by worsening obesity, symptoms of a bad heart, and weakening joints in her knees (for which she had undergone major surgery in 1904). And the

Conrads' first son, nine-year-old Borys, came down in the fall of 1905 with scarlet fever. Jessie, during the time of her pregnancy, had to continue to nurse her young invalid back to health, and was more than likely preoccupied with her sick child and her pregnancy, with little time left over for her husband. The family at this time, as Meyer explains, "sorely tried Conrad's patience and drained his money" (*JCB*, p.236).

However, Conrad had felt similarly hostile about Jessie's first pregnancy. His psychoanalytic biographer, Bernard Meyer, is the only reader to have identified a pattern of infanticidal fantasy in the author's adult life. Conrad always regarded the male infant as a competitor for the care and love of the wife/mother. When Jessie was pregnant with Borys, she noticed how Conrad forced her to choose between him and the expected child. Jessie wrote that "it seemed to me I had played him false. . . . Could I continue to fill my post as guardian of my husband's peace and do my duty to my child? I saw quite plainly that my allegiance must be somewhat divided" (*JCC*, p.50). Jessie also remembered that Conrad often "indulged in a fit of gout," and that he had become rageful, almost paranoid, during an incident that ended with his threatening to shoot some children for stealing fruit from his orchard (p.53). According to Meyer, "this murderous anger was displaced upon the anonymous school children from the real thief of his 'fruit'—the expected baby." And about Conrad's pattern of infanticidal resentment Meyer says: "If during his wife's first pregnancy his infanticidal impulses were expressed by means of displacement upon the fruit-stealing children, during the second pregnancy he appears to have dealt with them through . . . *The Secret Agent*, a story in which a 'father' causes a small child to be blown to bits."[36]

Conrad's Childhood Losses and the Verloc Family Drama

The architecture of the Verloc drama seems, then, to be overdetermined both by Conrad's political anxieties and by his domestic conflicts, enacting as it does "the double evil" of revolution and reaction, the father's rage (toward mother and child) masked as indolent selfishness, and the swift discharge of (self)punishment. When one considers the highly overdetermined nature of the novel, and then the force and repetitiveness of Conrad's response to maternal preoccupation, it is reasonable to think that, during the period of his writing *The Secret Agent*, Conrad was feeling the pull of old and painful feelings rooted in the loss of his mother in childhood, and in the political martyrdom and pathetic death of his self-absorbed father. In order to find warrant for this backward pull, I want briefly to tell the story of Conrad's childhood, from age four to age eleven. I will also interpret those aspects of childhood history that seem most pertinent psychologically to *The Secret Agent* (later, in following chapters, I will return to some of this material for its relevance to *Under Western Eyes*).

On an October night in Warsaw in 1861, just before little Konrad's fourth birthday, the Korzeniowski's home was raided by the Russian police, and Apollo, the Polish nationalist, was arrested for planning the Uprising of 1863. Pending the disposition of his case, he remained at the Warsaw Citadel. One of Conrad's lasting memories is of standing as a child in the prison courtyard looking at his father's face behind a barred window. Conrad's Polish biographer Zdzislaw Najder explains that Ewa Korzeniowski, Conrad's mother, was an enthusiastic participant in her husband's conspiratorial activities; however, Jeffrey Meyer has more recently discovered that Ewa was forced into exile with Apollo, simply because her letters to her husband had incriminated him (*JCB*, p.114). In 1862, roughly seven months after Apollo's arrest, all three (father, mother, child) were led by police on their journey into exile to Vologda in northern Russia.

Outside of Moscow the four-year-old child became seriously ill with pneumonia, but local authorities ruled that, "as children are born to die," the journey should go on.[37] Ewa nursed her son back to health, and then almost immediately contracted pneumonia herself. Her condition worsened in Vologda, so that after a year in the colony of exiles the family was resettled in the somewhat milder climate of Chernikov, north of Kiev, where they spent the next four years. Only during the summer of 1863 were Ewa and her son allowed to see relatives. They were permitted to go to the estate of Tadeusz Bobrowski (Ewa's brother), where for a period of three months little Konrad enjoyed at least some semblance of a stable home life. Conrad recalled this brief respite as providing some of the happiest moments of his childhood, but it was also the beginning of the darkest event in his young life. During this interval doctors detected signs of tuberculosis in Ewa's lungs, and concluded that without medical attention she would most likely die.[38] Despite Ewa's worsening health, she and her son were forced to return to Chernikov. She was confined to her bed for several months during 1865, and eventually died at the age of 32. The tragedy of Conrad's being allowed but a few short months of happiness with his mother was compounded by the fact that he might very well have blamed himself and his father (in addition to the Russian authorities) for his mother's death.

The protracted period of his wife's illness allowed Apollo to become

absorbed by his grief, his guilt, and his sense of inadequacy. He wrote a letter in 1865 that describes his state of mind.

> My poor wife, who these last two years has been destroyed by despair
> and by the repeated blows that fall on members of our joined families,
> for the last four months terribly—gravely ill, has barely the strength
> to look at me, to speak with a hollow voice. This state has been caused
> by the lack of everything for the body and the soul—no doctors, no
> medicines. . . . I am unable to satisfy, help or console my poor patient.
> Konradek is of course neglected.[39]

Apollo had always viewed Ewa as a saintly figure; and now, at the time of
her agonizing decline, he was tormented by the guilty thought that his
arrest and exile had destroyed her. After Ewa's death, Apollo idealized her
in memory—turning his wife into what Karl calls "a mystical, holy
Madonna" (*JCTL*, p.60)—and did penance for his role in her death.
Another of Conrad's biographers, Gustav Morf, relates how Apollo would
sit with little Konrad "for hours, if not days, at Ewa's grave," and then
observes trenchantly that "here was a father who was obviously too narcissistic to understand the monstrosity of denying all happiness to the child,
a father who just wanted his son to feel like himself and to be a reflection
of himself."[40]

Apollo was never a resourceful or strong father and husband. Now,
after Ewa's death, chronic mourning made him utterly neglectful of his son's
emotional needs. Although Apollo took pains to supply little Konrad with
schoolbooks, and attempted to shield him from (what Apollo saw as) the
baneful Russian influence, the father knew that his son was too isolated and
too withdrawn into books. For a year and a half, from May of 1866 to the
autumn of 1867, little Konrad manifested various signs of ill health (the
nature of these illnesses remains highly speculative); and so, while receiving medical care, he was separated from this regime of isolation, grief, and
repeated lessons about the Muscovite oppressor. In November of 1866
Apollo wrote with characteristic self-pity: "I am lonely. Konradek is with
his granny. . . . We both suffer equally: just imagine, the boy is so stupid
that he misses his loneliness where all he saw was my clouded face and
where the only diversions of his nine-year-old life were arduous lessons.
. . . The boy pines away—he must be stupid and, I fear, will remain so all
his life."[41] Little wonder that Konrad retreated into books, and even into illness, in order to escape his father's melancholy, which misrecognized a
boy's love as "stupidity." In fact, his relationship to books in childhood

might have given him some of the emotional provisions he desperately needed (what the psychoanalyst Heinz Kohut calls self-objects or self-functions), whereas illness emerged at this time as a lifelong strategy of retreat, an effort to fulfill either a fantasy of self-care (a return to when his beloved mother nursed him back to health) or self-punishment, or both. As Bernard Meyer observes, illness for Conrad bears "a heavy imprint of psychogenicity" (*JCPB*, p.29) It is heartbreaking to imagine young Konrad, already psychosomatic and withdrawn, "pining away" for his absent father, as if anticipating the greater loss to come. For Apollo too had fallen ill with tuberculosis. Like most children in similar circumstances, little Konrad probably felt that even the neglectful presence of a sick and despairing parent, especially a parent so loved and feared, was preferable to absence.

In December of 1867, Russian authorities determined that Apollo was no longer a political threat and lifted his sentence of exile. After six months of travel with little Konrad, Apollo settled in the Polish city of Lwow, and once again the boy received home-tutoring. In the winter of 1869 they moved to Cracow. Apollo, near death, was now completely immersed in his cultish mourning for his wife, who had been dead for nearly four years. Conrad later wrote of how, had he not had the salvation of being "a reading boy," he "would have had nothing to do but sit and watch the awful stillness of the sick room flow out through the closed door and coldly enfold my scared heart," and of how, when his father's death came at last, he found not "a single tear to shed." Conrad continues: "I have a suspicion that the Canon's housekeeper looked on me as the most callous little wretch on earth."[42] The image of stillness and coldness enfolding a son's heart is stunning not just in the way it evokes death's embrace, but also in the way it tells of how distant Apollo had become. In May of 1869, after two years of living virtually in isolation with Apollo, the eleven-year-old boy lost his needed father forever. He walked at the head of the funeral cortege, and the occasion became a fervent patriotic tribute to Apollo Korzeniowski, the Polish martyr. What feelings might the eleven-year-old Konrad have experienced or suppressed watching his father be buried? And what influence did this event have in shaping Conrad's lifelong disposition to accommodate contrary passions and negotiate between them?

To use Apollo's words, "repeated blows" fell on Conrad as a child. He lost both parents in less than four years, and the catastrophe of Ewa's death threw the boy into what Jeffrey Meyers calls "a morbid conjunction" with Apollo. Though present in Konrad's life, Apollo was not alive to his son's needs, showing little capacity to feel with his son and to know how best to help him with his mother's death. Apollo's lack of empathic reach was only aggravated by his narcissistic self-absorption in his own martyrdom, in wearing the hairshirt of atonement so as to be worthy of reunion with the Ewa of hagiography. From the time of Ewa's death until Apollo himself fell into prolonged disabling illness, he made every effort to keep his child by his side. However, proximity to narcissistic melancholy often has the paradoxical effect of increasing one's sense of aloneness; and in this sense, Apollo left little Konrad to shift emotionally for himself, as if the boy were but an appendage to the father's struggle with unending guilt, shame, and lack.

It is reasonable to suppose that Konradeck needed his father's strength and guidance to properly grieve for his dead mother, to make sense of her death, and eventually to accept her absence in the world even as he deepened his sense of her survival as a felt presence in him, anchored in memory. Psychoanalysis teaches us that usually a child's grief and longing for a dead parent remains silent and unconscious. Moreover, from age two until late adolescence (or whenever a more-or-less definitive separation from parents occurs), a child responds to the loss of a parent with intense ambivalence. John Bowlby explains that the child not only possesses a deep "yearning" for the lost parent, but also deeply blames or "reproaches" both the lost parent and the self.[43] Sadness and yearning for the parent become inflected with anxiety and anger, with the sense of having been rejected or deserted.[44] The child fantasizes that the parent left because the child was somehow bad and unworthy of their continued presence. This fantasy turns a passively incurred injury into an active sense of responsibility for the desertion, and transforms anger against the loved parent into self-depreciation. Hence, the child's unexpressed and perhaps disavowed rage and anxiety over the lost beloved is the wellspring of abandonment depression.[45]

A further step in this primitive logic of magical restoration comes when a bereft child seeks to graft the self to an imagined ideal self (for example, to a version requiring that he be clean, good, strong, etc.) that is partly inherited, partly constructed, from the child's experience of the lost parent. The hope is that this reformation of character will bring the dead parent back. This defensive move affords the child a measure of control over the loss, but also leaves the child continually vulnerable to feelings of failure (she has not returned to rescue me) and reversion to self-recrimination, even suicidal despair. The pursuit of perfection as a means of protecting the hope for love, care, and presence is perpetually subverted by reality—by the fact that one's longing for the return of the lost object is always frustrated. The result can be a devastating insult to the child's fragile self-esteem. If the surviving parent can help the child to distinguish fantasy from reality in explaining the loss, and help in finding ways for the child to be more self-forgiving, then abandonment depression and defense against it need not, in Bowlby's words, "stabilize and persist." But what of the child whose father turns him into a twin of the father's melancholy, who substitutes a grotesquely idealized maternal presence for a real presence that might be authentically grieved, who projects onto the child a condition of melancholy impasse rather than helping the child discover a livable sadness?

Bowlby tells us that depressive self-reproach and self-depreciation are readily set in motion when a child contracts an infectious illness that in turn seems to lead to the parent's illness and death. "There are certain circumstances which can easily lead to a child reaching the conclusion that he himself is to blame at least in part. [An] example [is] when a child . . . has been suffering from an infectious illness which infects a parent" (LSD, p.286). Little Konrad had sufficient reason to blame Apollo for Ewa's death (and later in life Conrad did so). However, it might have been easier for Konrad to suppress his rage toward his father and to assume the major portion of the blame, because criticizing Apollo almost certainly carried the risk of emotional estrangement, and hence of losing the surviving parent. (We remember how Konrad "pined away" for his father.) Further, Meyers explains how, during the Cracow years, little Konrad based his sense of self-worth on his parents' ideals—that he recited from memory long passages from Mickiewicz's *Pan Tadeusz* (an epic poem of Polish nationalism), and wrote a play in which the Nationalists defeat the Russian enemy (*JCB*, p.27). Common sense suggests that Konrad did what children in similar circumstances have invariably done, unconsciously collaborating with his dead mother's and dying father's unmet ideals, making affiliation with them by making their ideals present in him in order to protect himself from deeper feelings of self-hate, powerlessness, and abandonment.

These few pieces of evidence by themselves, however, are sufficient only for making speculative inference. What one knows with more certainty is that Conrad later in life saw himself as losing out to his infant sons in the "rivalry" for his wife's attentions, as if the adult man were all along expecting a mother's "rejection." What one also knows is that Conrad's symbolic act of "throwing away" baby John (on the train to Montpellier) repeats Apollo's neglect of little Konrad, as if Conrad as a parent secretly wanted to do to his son what Apollo had done to him. Further, in *The Secret Agent*, Conrad's infanticidal wish—his rivalrous anger at "sons"—is accompanied by self-recrimination. To the extent that he identified himself with the thoughtless father Verloc, he also needed to turn the destructive wish back on himself, making his portrait of Verloc a representation of self-loathing and self-punishment. What is more, we have seen that failed mourning is in many ways the central psychosocial dilemma of the novels *The Nigger of the "Narcissus", Heart of Darkness,* and *Lord Jim.* In his fiction Conrad invariably gravitates to historical situations of loss; and in elaborating his critical disenchantment with modernity, he invariably shows himself to be stuck between reconciliation with the reality of loss and its disavowal or deferral—hence his reliance on idealizing or narcissistic defenses (some sort of nostalgic distortion, or some deferral of lost heroism) in order to maintain psychic stability.

In *The Nigger of the "Narcissus",* the traditional patriarchal order of labor is being subverted by industrial Capital. In *Heart of Darkness* and *Lord Jim,* the heroic ideal of imperialist adventure is breaking under the weight of its own contradictions, most notably the conflict between its rapacity (Kurtz) and its pasteboard heroism (Jim). Conrad cannot return to the security of an unproblematic emotional investment in some past social object (status, role, or ideal); and he cannot go forward and work through the loss in order to consummate his critical insight, and hence risk change. He is in between: he responds to the loss of the past with depression (anger, cynicism, chronic discontent), and defends against the loss with a distorting substitute, a "saving" illusion. In *The Secret Agent,* Conrad seems threatened not just by the loss of a cultural role or abstraction, but by the cataclysmic transformation of both social and personal worlds. That is to say, the political restiveness of the prewar and the birth of his second son led Conrad to envision reality in terms of disorder and chaos—to see only turmoil and loss where others. for example, might see challenge and risk, opportunity and growth. For Conrad, the prewar was about having nothing left to transfigure defensively into a substitute ideal. Hence, ironic pessimism itself became in *The Secret Agent* the last refuge of illusion.

If one reads the texts against the adult life, and measures both of these against (what is known of) childhood experience, it becomes much more plausible to say that young Konrad responded to the loss of his parents with abandonment depression and set in place idealizing and narcissistic strategies to guard against underlying emotional devastation. Bowlby writes that "those who have lost a parent by death during childhood or adolescence are at greater risk than others of developing psychiatric disorders and, more especially, of becoming seriously depressed should they do so" (*LSD,* p.310). And Bowlby also explains that this relatively high correlation between adult depression (the "scar tissue" of the psyche) and the child's having lost a parent or parents tends to be the result of failing to mourn the original loss (p.22).

What Konradek needed at the time of Ewa's death was a father who was alive to his son's grief. However, Apollo could not cope with his own grief, much less that of his son. It therefore seems likely that the mother's death established in little Konrad a pattern of failed mourning. When it came time to grieve the loss of his father, the boy could not find "a single tear to shed."

More specifically, Apollo failed to supply little Konrad with what Winnicott calls "a holding relationship" and what Roy Schafer (following Winnicott) calls "the developmentally necessary experience of distress-in-safety."[46] To say this is just common sense: Apollo, a narcissistic man absorbed in his own martyrdom, was not a father who could step into the breach and give his son the safety of a holding relationship. The "good enough parent" sustains a readiness to contain the child's negative emotions—for little Konrad, the angry and guilty attributions of blame for the mother's "desertion" and the hopeless and helpless feeling of being incapable of changing things for the better, or of being intrinsically unlovable. By tolerating the child's expressions of anger and dread, and especially the child's projective assaults on the parent, the "good enough" parent helps the child to rebuild a sense of the relative durability of love and trust, of needed other and self.

Massive loss in childhood supplies the psychic gravity, or in T. S. Eliot's words, "the dark embryo," of Conrad's novels. However, *The Secret Agent* (and the next novel, *Under Western Eyes*) reconfigure this dark embryo in particularly dramatic and disturbing condensations, perhaps because Conrad was predisposed to search his present moment for damaging experiences in an effort to repeat and displace (rather than repeat and work through) the traumatic gestalt of the past. Remaking the trauma is an important dimension of Conrad's fundamental aloneness. Psycho-analyst Peter Shabad explains this kind of repetition, saying that "in the absence of another person to validate the 'event' of his suffering," the child of trauma becomes himself an involuted witness to it, and "must continually re-create or 'make' the trauma over and over again."[47] When we are snared by the repetition, the present comes to meet us in the shape of the past.

The Secret Agent would seem to argue that, for Conrad at least, there could be no imaginative re-envisioning of relations to intimate personal objects, or to the internalized objects of social life, which has not first been scarred by experiences of childhood loss. If Conrad's representation of the Verloc household is shaped by the author's anxious and sometimes angry perception of present political and personal realities, this is to a significant extent true because the representation is overdetermined by the ways in which the political and the personal coincided in Conrad's early life. Hence, the character of Adolf Verloc serves to elaborate not just the author's fantasied assault against his family (and his subsequent self-punishment), but also Conrad's rage against Apollo as political father—that is, the father who unintentionally turned conspiracy into a source of familial oppression and destruction, not the father whom Conrad admired for his strength of principle. In one more turn of the psychological screw, Stevie's senseless death at the hands of Adolf Verloc repeats in dramatic novelistic fashion Apollo's psychological erasure of his son. Stevie's stumble toward obliteration resonates with young Konrad's sudden fall into the confusion, guilt, and anxiety of his father's grief, which was so thoughtless of the boy's needs. In this respect, the explosion can be seen as what happens to the sons of thoughtless fathers, and as reflecting how Konrad had been left to himself to reconstitute the fragments of his own emotional life.

The novel's descriptions of how the force of Stevie's death leaves Winnie mute and desolate, and of how primitive rage allows her, in turn, to murder Verloc, seem to draw intensity from Conrad's effort to bind his own rage at Apollo, and at himself-as-father. News of Stevie's death and Verloc's complicity had, we are told, "the effect of a white-hot iron drawn across her eyes; at the same time her heart, hardened and chilled into a lump of ice, kept her body in an inward shudder, set her features into a frozen, contemplative immobility addressed to a whitewashed wall with no writing on it" (*SA*, p.199). And then, struggling with the shocking recognition that Verloc, the trusted father, had betrayed her, Winnie loses herself (her sanity) by merging with her dead brother, infused with his rageful compassion for slaughtered innocents. "As if the homeless soul of Stevie had flown for shelter straight to the breast of his sister, guardian, and protector, the resemblance of her face with that of her brother grew at every step, even to the droop of the lower lip, even to the slight divergence of the eyes." Of the fatal knife-thrust we are told, "Into that plunging blow, delivered over the side of the couch, Mrs. Verloc had put all the inheritance of her immemorial and obscure descent, the simple ferocity of the age of caverns, and the unbalanced nervous fury of the age of bar-rooms." But in the end Stevie's primal passion drains from her, as the blood trickles down the knife-handle and drips on the floorcloth "with a sound of ticking . . . like the pulse of an insane clock." Letting go of the knife, Winnie is dispossessed. "[H]er extraordinary resemblance to her late brother had faded, had become very ordinary now" (p.215–17).

Bernard Meyer reads this mysterious moment in the text, in which Stevie's "soul" returns home to Winnie's body, as consistent with the theme, rooted in Conrad's biography, of the murderous rivalry between fathers and sons. He explains that "a family of three—man, woman, and boy—constitutes [for Conrad] an inherently intolerable situation demanding the elimination of one of the males in order to permit the remaining two to enjoy an unmolested mutual possession." When Stevie is killed in the bomb explosion, Verloc "triumphs." But when Verloc is himself murdered, Stevie has rejoined Winnie in "mystical corporeal union" (*JCPB*, p.191). I agree with Meyer that Conrad is powerfully attracted to the fantasy of a maternal figure fiercely devoted to only one male, whether the object of this devotion is a father or son figure, but disagree that the novel depicts an "unmolested mutual possession" by either male figure. Meyer overstates the case that Verloc ever achieves anything like secure possession of Winnie. And while the case might be made that Stevie enjoys with Winnie this fantasied "mystical union" after death, Meyer does not explain why Winnie needs to kill Verloc (she might simply have left Brett Street and created a "paradisial" home for Stevie in the privacy of her madness), or how her vengeance actually fails to erase the reality of Stevie's death. In my view, Conrad holds the positions of both father and son in the oedipal triangle. He expresses wish-fulfilling aspects of himself in both Verloc and Stevie, but these aspects do not expunge Conrad's unresolved grief and depressive psychology, or the depiction of these melancholy elements in the text.

The narrator plainly tells us that Winnie is unable to mourn, that nothing can console her for the loss of her brother. The circumstances of Stevie's death "dried her tears at their very source" (p.199). For mourning she substitutes vengeance; and in enacting talionic justice against Verloc, she becomes "possessed" by Stevie's unschooled, unmediated ruthlessness. What was true of Stevie's inner life, that "the anguish of immoderate compassion was succeeded by the pain of an innocent but pitiless rage" (*SA*, p.144), now becomes true for Winnie. She then merges momentarily with Stevie; but together they create a thanatonic—not an ecstatic—union where "pitiless rage" overwhelms love and then retreats, leaving behind desolation.

Because mourning is not an option for Winnie, Stevie's death marks an unsurpassable suffering, and vengeance becomes the only rejoinder to deprivation. But does the narrator understand that mourning offers an alternative to retaliation, that speaking violence introspectively can replace doing violence as a strategy of restitution? There is no explicit discussion in the novel of the imperative of mourning. What the narrator repeatedly tells us instead is that grieving is a resigned mental posture that in itself brings no relief. When, prior to killing Verloc, Winnie mentally assumes "the biblical attitude of mourning," the narrator observes that "her teeth were violently clenched, and her tearless eyes were hot with rage, because she was *not a submissive creature*" (*SA*, p.203, my emphasis). Perhaps the narrator is being ironic by, in effect, pointing out that hopelessness should be endured quietly rather than protested violently. Perhaps for him the only proper course would be to submit and accept that the world is deaf to one's suffering. This kind of distanced despair is in keeping with the narrator's nature, and with the paradoxical posture of "serene despair" offered up in Conrad's 1885 political letter, where he tells us that there is no earthly remedy for earthly miseries. Yet in the novel, the narrator also admires and sympathizes with Winnie's "maternal and violent" sensibility because it *refuses* to submit. He tells us that "She had to love [Stevie] with a militant love" (p. 203); and even more dramatically, the narrator finds "the very cry of truth" in Winnie's lament that her life should be "without grace or charm, and almost without decency, but of an exalted faithfulness of purpose, even unto murder" (p.243). Where we are invited to identify with Winnie's "faithfulness of purpose" and "richness of suffering" there seems to be little separation between the narrator and Conrad. Moreover, the exaltation does not include a caveat about murder as an inefficacious solution to the problem of loss. There are, then, only two alternatives for the narrator and for Conrad: on the one hand, internalizing unmourned loss, and, in a state of permanent bitterness, slowly killing the self; and on the other, enacting violence—murder and suicide—from "the age of caverns," or at least affirming the faithfulness of purpose such violence serves. By means of the narrator's inability to acknowledge the need for, or possibility of, mourning, and by Winnie's brief thanatonic merger with Stevie, we begin to see Conrad's phantasmatic position as disconsolate and angry son who revisits and rectifies instead of accepting, grieving, reconstituting.

While the narrator identifies with Winnie's amoral heroism, he nevertheless condemns her, though more for the lapses in maternal vigilance that led to murder than for the killing itself. Verloc is not the only one who bears responsibility for Stevie's death. According to the narrator, Winnie's "constitutional indolence" and her failure to get "fundamental information" from Verloc about his plans for Stevie make her responsible (*SA*, pp. 144, 158). And in Verloc's view, though he is to blame for Stevie's death, it is also Winnie's doing (p.212). Winnie's having entrusted the most valued person in her life to Verloc "without troubling her head about it" (p.199) is tantamount to her having abdicated her role as Stevie's maternal protector.

Neither Verloc nor Winnie meant for Stevie to perish, but each, acting out of characteristic stupidity, carelessness, and furtiveness, brought about the boy's death. Conrad makes it seem as if Verloc's murder and Winnie's suicide are but links in a chain of events moving inexorably toward a kind of poetic justice—fitting retribution for the sacrificed child.

Parental abandonment is irreducibly linked in the novel to the defectiveness of the child and to his destruction—and, for the still-grieving son of Apollo and Ewa, to the experience of object-loss as self-loss, as a loss of efficacy, worth, and trust in one's ability to love. Thus, abandonment becomes the impetus for attacking the failed parent, for parceling out blame for the child's emotional devastation. In this novelistic configuration of childhood grief, while the parents are punished with death, it is retribution purchased at the cost of the child's life. This aspect of the text reveals a central element of depressive dynamics: the projective assault on the other (the parent) requires a corresponding punishment of the self (the child), and vice versa. As Julia Kristeva explains, there is "a see-sawing between self and other, the projection on the self of hatred against the other and, vice versa, the turning against the other of self-depreciation."[48]

In depressive grief, the bond of dependency between child and parent is spoiled and becomes a bond of anger and guilt that inhibits differentiation between self and other. In dissociating oneself from feeling the object's absence, and in the often violent dance of identification and disidentification that occurs as one tries to gain control over the experience of loss (and over the lost object itself), the self too easily becomes confused with the other. In this respect, one can feel ruthlessly used by, and can in turn ruthlessly use, the lost object. The dynamics of melancholia often include both versions of ruthlessness—the terrible wounding of the first, and the punishing guilt that follows from the second. Hence, in Conrad's portrayal of the union between Winnie and Stevie (the flight of his soul "for shelter"), Stevie seems to infuse Winnie with his indignation and rage (make her his avenger). And Stevie's death seems to pay for Verloc's murder in advance, just as Winnie's vengeance must in its turn be counterbalanced by her eventual suicide. This flight into a depressive fantasy-structure of revenge and spoilage (ruthlessness against other and self), and into overt enactment (rather than symbolic restitution), is but a substitute for grieving. Conrad's bleak rendering of Winnie's inexorable fall from twilight to darkness suggests to what extent he was himself pulled down by the gravity of his own childhood traumas, and how far he was from being able to take possession of his own love and hate in a productive experience of mourning.

The unresolved tug-of-war between love and hate, the ambivalence that lies at the core of depressive grief, is what most directly establishes what I believe to be an unconscious identification on Conrad's part with the character of Stevie Verloc. Stevie is agitated by feelings of "immoderate compassion" and "pitiless rage," and is powerless to control this inner combat, which always ends in his having "turned vicious" (SA, p.144). It may be that readers of the novel, especially Conradians, will find it hard to accept the claim that Conrad himself is, even in part, emotionally connected to Stevie. After all, imaginative creations are not always self-referential ones, particularly when the character in question is dim-witted, gullible, and inarticulate. Stevie would seem to have no referential purchase on his brilliant and eloquent author-creator. I readily concede that Conrad is in many respects all that Stevie is not. Though Conrad has crystallized in Stevie many of the novel's psychological themes and patterns, what of connections between these patterns and Conrad's own life? We have already seen one such biographical moment when Conrad throws his son's baby clothes out the window of a moving train, an impulsive act consistent with the belief that Conrad harbored hostile feelings toward his male children, and consistent also with his having been himself "thrown away" as a child. In addition, the depiction of Stevie is based on the imbecilic nature of a tenacious need, a trait suggestive of the idea that Conrad, like Apollo, confuses a child's "pining" with his "stupidity." Conrad has a strong, though almost certainly unconscious, psychological affiliation with Stevie. In order to solidify this interpretation, I want to look at another biographical moment that illuminates Conrad's relation to this earnest, passionate, witless, and wronged child.

In 1904 Conrad's wife Jessie had knee surgery, and at some point during the three-hour procedure, as he awaited the outcome of her "adventure with the [surgeon's] knife," Conrad acted very peculiarly. Jessie relates how Conrad told her that "he must have acted subconsciously part of the time he waited, and when he found himself he was standing in front of an old dray-horse with his arms literally round the animal's neck" (JCC, p.90). Jeffrey Meyers has pointed out that this biographical episode is partly responsible for one of the novel's most important scenes (JCB, p.237), when Stevie pleads with the night cabby not to whip "the infirm horse," and then is overcome with a bizarre longing to take the cabman and the horse to bed with him, just as "his sister Winnie used to come along, and carry [Stevie] off to bed with her" (SA, pp. 135–144). The scene echoes throughout the text. Just as Stevie plaintively cries "Don't" when the cabby whips the horse, so Verloc utters the same word "by way of protest" when

Winnie plunges the knife between his ribs (pp. 135, 236). Thus Stevie's compassion (in the cabman scene) and his rage (acted through Winnie in the murder scene) are clearly joined by this expression of refusal or protest; and the "don't" indicates how the seats of rage and compassion have shifted, and how it is a shifting that suggests sameness, not transformation. So while the murder seems to offer some resolution of Stevie's inner emotional battle—the vanquishing of love by hate through the thanatonic union between Stevie and Winnie—it leads us nowhere. Additionally, Stevie's scene with the cabby, and perhaps Conrad's embrace of the dray-mare, are importantly connected to Dostoevsky's *Crime and Punishment*, specifically to Raskolnikov's anguished dream of the old mare whipped to death by its owner—a further example of complex ties in Conrad between literature and biography.

Conrad's biographical episode with the horse shows him in a strangely anxious and dejected state. During the interval of his wife's surgery, Conrad seems to wander from dissociation to pitiful abjection, as if Jessie's "adventure with the knife" signaled a permanent loss of the much needed Jessie herself. Conrad's confusion, wherein temporary and permanent absences become indistinguishable, is congruent with the irritation and fear he felt when he threw his son's clothes from the train—because whether in surgery (needing to be cared for herself), or preoccupied with her children, Jessie is not there for Conrad, a felt absence which causes him to lose his ability to know that she will almost certainly return. For Conrad, her absence or presence becomes absolute. As we know, leavetakings have had this inflection for him from early childhood. Both episodes—his dissociated, quasi-psychotic wanderings at the hospital, and his jettisoning of the baby clothes out the window of a train—are deeply suggestive of how crises in Conrad's emotional relationship with Jessie return him to the original loss of the mother, and to longing, anger, and dejection. Such feelings held an astonishing control over Conrad even in response to seemingly minor losses or perceived inconstancies. Inasmuch as Conrad imbued his portrayal of Stevie with his own condition during Jessie's surgery, the character surely becomes an unconscious repository for the ambivalence of Conrad's childhood grief, and a fictive exploration of ambivalence turning into a depressive bond. For Conrad (as for Stevie), love turns into hate, the needed other is either present to the point of fusion or absolutely absent, and hence "ongoing" selfhood cannot find sustenance or sustain its own middle ground, where presence and absence are codetermining and in balance.

At a more intentional level, this episode probably became part of *The Secret Agent* because the outlines of the event recalled for Conrad

Raskolnikov's dream in *Crime and Punishment*. Conrad first read *Crime and Punishment* (along with Dostoevsky's other political novels) in French translation in the 1880s.[49] And he closely modeled Stevie's compassionate protest on Raskolnikov's vision of himself as a child "about seven years old" protesting the killing of "a small, skinny, grayish peasant nag." Dostoevsky describes the boy in the dream: "With a shout he tears through the crowd to the gray horse, throws his arms around her dead, bleeding muzzle, and kisses it, kisses her eyes and mouth . . ."[50] The scene would have special resonance for Conrad, since the suffering child in Raskolnikov's dream, like Conrad at the time of his mother's death, is seven years old. This coincidence wouldn't necessarily surface except that Conrad's anxiety about Jessie's surgery most likely triggered an association to Dostoevsky's text, and to the part of Conrad that resonated with this scene. Once Conrad had found his way back to the pages of *Crime and Punishment*, then the insistence of loss and the struggle against loss in Conrad's mental life, as much as any deliberate artistic aim on his part, induced Conrad to revisit the Russian writer, and rewrite him in *The Secret Agent* and *Under Western Eyes*.

In Dostoevsky's novel, Raskolnikov rejects the child's anguished pity, interpreting the dream as a terrifying and seductive portent of his own murderous act, the killing of the old pawnbroker. However, in the end Raskolnikov is brought to an acceptance of his actions and of himself through his confession to Sonya. The love embodied in the child of the dream, the kind of love that precedes understanding or articulation, returns through her; and Raskolnikov is cleansed of the arrogance and hatred that led him to murder. In contrast, compassion is figured by Conrad as part of Stevie's hapless impotence, and ultimately as the accelerant in his self-immolation. Pity therefore is stillborn, undone from the beginning by the cruelty human beings incessantly visit upon one another. Conrad's depiction of Stevie's "universal charity" seems deliberately to mock Dostoevsky's ideas of human pity and divine forgiveness. And Conrad seems to locate in Dostoevsky's longing for redemption through faith (as also in the secular idealism of someone like Wells) spuriously optimistic illusions about ending suffering and evil.

While Conrad's relationship to Dostoevsky figures prominently in *Under Western Eyes*, there are only two basic observations that need to be made here regarding Dostoevsky and *The Secret Agent*. First, Conrad's assault on Dostoevskian charity is part and parcel of Conrad's sense of estrangement from his social world, of his inability to find convictions or ideals that afford him some sense of mastery and stability in a world so infected with dispute and conflict. A main theme of "Autocracy and War" is Conrad's fear of a great conflict breaking out in Europe, and his lack of confidence in the ability of the European political leadership to avert this disaster. Conrad's pessimism about Europe in general is interwoven with his experience of, and prejudices about, things Russian. When one thinks of the role Russia played in Conrad's early life, it is not really excessive to characterize his revisiting of Russian themes in these later works as a kind of return of (or to) the repressed. Not surprisingly, Dostoevsky figures centrally in Conrad's anomic construction of the world. Second, Conrad reads Dostoevsky not simply with contempt, but with fascination. For in attacking Dostoevsky for his idealities, Conrad also exposes his own psychological affinities with a protagonist like Raskolnikov, a character who epitomizes the melancholy person's "seesawing" movement between hate projected and hate internalized. Conrad intellectually objects to the ending of *Crime and Punishment*, but is himself psychologically stuck somewhere in the lost center of the novel, unable to find his way clear, and hence destined to struggle with Dostoevsky about ultimate meanings.

In the end, the character of Stevie Verloc, this figure of primitive attachment, inarticulate love, self-immolation, and murder, is a metonym for the depressive dynamics of the novel, and hence a fictive condensation for Conrad's own story of unresolved grief. For Conrad, the provocations of here-and-now experience—the social that evokes his anxieties of "the double evil" of revolution and counterrevolution, and the personal that evokes his vulnerability to feelings of abandonment—revive the conditions of massive childhood loss. He immerses himself, at times loses himself, in what Freud called the suffering of reminiscences; but Conrad also resists the possible sense of his recollections. His refusal to accept undifferentiated attachment love as a part of himself, and his seeming embrace of the talionic law as a substitute for mourning, both suggest how Conrad repeats the conditions of early bereavement without working through the loss. Further, he uses an impregnable irony in order to fend off what is unbearable or repugnant: Conrad relocates in Dostoevsky his own unacceptably primitive desire for love and reunion, and then scathingly dismisses the Dostoevskian miracle of compassion; and he avoids his own sense of powerlessness, and his constitutional aversion to change, by attacking Wells's futurism. Such bald optimism, such extravagant illusion, are easy targets for Conrad's irony. Attention to the others' folly allowed inattention to his own losses, especially of mundane but necessary sources of light as a child. In this, Conrad reveals his situation of melancholy impasse: he cannot go forward to an acceptance of what in life has been taken from him, and what he has spoiled; and he cannot return to childhood illusions of innocence, trust, and hopefulness. Such illusions were driven deep underground by the deaths of his parents. Conrad's irony buries them again by demolishing their extremist avatars and fictional embodiments (e.g., Dostoevsky/Stevie and Wells/the Professor), as if he were engaged in writing an obscurely yet fiercely devotional text, bearing witness to the events of past love and suffering. He will not allow trauma to be diminished by idealities, and so his only recourse is to pessimistic illusion. In this respect, I would argue, he needs to set up the narrative "I" as a prescient authority on human darkness, to depict the world as if it were without any light, and always to know this darkness as humankind's truest color.

CHAPTER SEVEN

Conrad in Relation:
Wells, Galsworthy, Dostoevsky

Conrad experienced the dominant social forces of his age through rela- tionships with three figures who in retrospect can be seen as "emblematic" of these forces. He had until 1909 regularly communicated with H. G. Wells, the Social Imperialist and utopian Socialist, and was intimate friends with John Galsworthy, whom the literary historian Samuel Hynes has described as an establishment Liberal with an acute sense of social injustice but an inability to do more than simply sympathize with the poor. These living relationships were supplemented by the equally emblematic but purely literary one with Dostoevsky. When, for political reasons, "things Russian" began to preoccupy prewar Britain, and when the literary estab- lishment acquired a new taste for the Russian realists—Tolstoy, but espe- cially Dostoevsky—the Polish-Russian ethnic prejudices so important to Conrad's early life were resurrected, and Conrad was reminded of his own boyhood and the forces that shaped it.

Wells, Galsworthy, and Dostoevsky each had a special character and place in Conrad's cultural world. Wells embodied the problematic nature of Edwardian radicalism; Galsworthy was representative of Liberalism; and Dostoevsky was at the forefront of the "Russification" of British liter- ary culture, and became emblematic (especially for Conrad) of the general irrationality of the age. The meanings that these figures had for Conrad did nothing to inhibit, and everything to encourage, his forbidding assess- ment of the modern world. Like Wells and Galsworthy, Conrad was aware of social fragmentation and injustice, but tended to regard his friends as symptomatic of these problems rather than as agents of remediation. More hurtful still, these optimists and progressives, aiming "at a direct grasp on humanity," moved the same reading public that Conrad despaired of ever reaching. Not only was Galsworthy terrifically popular, but his play *Justice* led Churchill, the Home Secretary, to lobby for prison reform (one of the few instances in which his writing was socially effective); while Wells, of course, commanded a huge and devoted following, including the Chancellor of the Exchequer (Lloyd George).[1] Wells, in Conrad's view, had willed the future, and succeeded in putting "the impress of [his] personality" upon it, whereas Conrad's conservative, skeptical, and chronically disenchanted view had prevented him from making any such mark.[2] Frederick Karl notes that in what many Edwardians confidently regard as the new age of liberalism and international idealism, "Conrad was the sole novelist of stature and breadth to tell the English that their goals as well as the texture of their lives were melancholy matters, not reasons for celebration" (*JCTL*, p.626–27). In context, the word "melancholy" seems something of an understatement. The tide of political events left Conrad isolated and cynical, and in one way or another his associates and friends were (in his view) contentiously countermanding both his political views and his character.

Further, during the late-Edwardian period Conrad's texts were badly misinterpreted, and even worse, he found himself regularly categorized by British reviewers as a Slav rather than an Englishman. It was an unbearable affront for Conrad, who had spent the years between late adolescence and mature adulthood constructing a British identity, to be told that he was and would always remain an alien in the world of English letters—that he would have been better off had he written in his native Polish, for example. Thus, the 1905 Revolution and 1907 Anglo-Russian pact, which brought Russia to England as never before, may also have reinforced for Conrad his status as a foreigner and his feelings of dispossession by the country he had adopted as his own.

British awareness of Russia followed from "Bloody Sunday" in St. Petersburg and, afterwards, from the continuing European diplomatic involvement in Russian affairs. Although Russia had traditionally been Britain's enemy, by 1904 it was a beaten giant. The decisive defeat at the hands of Japan (1904) led directly to the 1905 Revolution; and the St. Petersburg massacre converged with, and may even have to some extent inspired, political idealism within Britain. The leadership of the Conservative party found alarming parallels between the events in St.

Petersburg and the election of a Liberal government in Britain. In Sir Arthur Balfour's words, the Liberal Prime Minister "is a mere cork on a torrent he cannot control, and what is going on here is the faint echo of the same movement which has produced massacres in St. Petersberg."[3] In contrast, progressive ("new") Liberals saw the Russian workers' program as "a combination of Trade Unionism, Constitutionalism, and a mild kind of Fabian Socialism" that would, should it succeed, not only "find affinities . . . with liberal England," but might lead to "the definite overthrow of European imperialism."[4] And looking expectantly to the Russian strikers, the working-classes in Britain also began to clarify and radicalize their own position. For example, the editor of the Marxist weekly *Justice* would write, "Let the propertyless attempt to use all [their] glorious liberties in order to assert their elemental right to live—and then—why then there is nothing to choose between London and St. Petersburg."[5] In short, political and social classes—wealthy Unionists and Liberals, working-class Labourites—each construed "Russia" according to their interests and ambitions.

In 1907, the treaty, aligning Briton and Slav against Teuton, tended to quell British Jingoist fears about imperialist rivalries. However, the alliance angered the progressives, who rightly saw that the Foreign Office was propping up the doddering Tsarist regime and hence condoning massive oppression. The political left understood that the agreement with Russia was an expedient and inexpensive way of maintaining Britain's imperialist interests. At this time, Tolstoy became a moral authority on British colonial practices. The Tolstoyan Alymer Maude invoked the Russian writer's statement that "Laws are rules made by people who govern by means of organized violence" as a pointed denunciation of the "organized violence" of British imperialism.[6] Ironically, only a few years after signing the Anglo-Russian treaty—itself instrumental to the Foreign Office's strategy of defeating Germany by means of diplomacy, and hence containing its expansionism—Germany forced England's hand. In 1911, German gunboats attacked the Moroccan port of Agadir, and the Liberal government was able to defuse the crisis only by feeding the German appetite for African colonies. Smarting at this injury to national pride, Lloyd George called it "a peace without honour." This crisis then paved the way for a new patriotic consensus in Britain. In the years that followed, the Social Imperialists and other jingoist groups stepped up the din of bellicose ire that shifted public opinion from left to right, and hence made inevitable Britain's entry into war. In his 1905 essay "Autocracy and War," Conrad had rightly anticipated that "alliances based on mutual distrust" and on the "material interests" of the European imperialist powers would eventually undermine any true peace, having indeed modeled peace on the very image of war ("AW," pp. 143, 146).

Beginning in 1910–11, Dostoevsky surpassed Tolstoy in the popular imagination. It is striking that while Dostoevsky's sympathy for suffering humanity was no less affecting than Tolstoy's, Dostoevsky was in his maturity an intemperate political reactionary. By 1910, in addition to the reviews and short commentaries on the Russian novelist by Edward Garnett and Arnold Bennett, two major books had been written on Dostoevsky: *A Great Russian Realist* by J. A. T. Lloyd and *Landmarks in Russian Literature* by Maurice Baring. And between 1912 and 1921, Constance Garnett translated virtually all of Dostoevsky's major texts. For Lloyd and Baring, who wrote when civil society was destabilized by massive waves of striking British workers and the *Kaiserreich* was contesting England's imperial standing in the world, Dostoevsky was truly a prophet. In Baring's words, Dostoevsky, "the Christian opponent of revolution," appeared to have correctly predicted the revolutionary "Hooliganism" of the first decade of the twentieth century; while Lloyd observed that "Dostoeiffsky and not Tolstoy divined the symbolic force of the New Byzantium"—which, for him, meant the mystical awakening of a people to its national destiny.[7] Dostoevsky seemed to open up for a British audience the irrationality that imbues the inner lives of individuals during times of external stress, and to answer their fears and desires with his religion of suffering and his mystic conception of the national idea.

Given Conrad's insecurities about the authenticity of his cultural identity and art, the irrational religionist and Pan-Slav Dostoevsky could only create trouble. Not only did Dostoevsky find fertile soil in the aggressive nationalism prevalent at this time, but he brought religion to bear on primitive psychic conflicts that Conrad could only approach obliquely and with an ambiguity, and ambivalence, that precluded faith in the restorative powers of mysticism. Conrad forthrightly repudiated religion (there could be no "heaven of consoling peace," as he put it in *The Secret Agent*, that was not at the same time an invitation to self-annihilation), and continued in his letters to rely on secular rationalism and English moral piety to counter the unruly impulses and ambitions characteristic of humankind. However, Conrad's moralisms were breaking under the strain of his perception of "the madness" of his age, and were increasingly incapable of containing his sense of despair over the wrong turn British culture was in the process of making.

For both cultural and personal reasons, Conrad's chronic sensitivity to dislocation, loss, and ambivalence was revived with special urgency in the years 1906 to 1908, when he was attempting to finish *The Secret Agent* and gestating *Under Western Eyes*. It might be recalled that, during his wife's postpartum recovery, when Conrad took his family to Montpellier, he was suffering from feelings of rejection and abandonment. But this was only the first downward step in Conrad's descent into a period of serious depression. After a month at Montpellier, and faced with the grave illness of his oldest son Borys, Conrad decided to move his family to the spa at Champel near Geneva. Conrad had taken the water-cure at Champel after returning half-dead from the Congo in 1891. After this family visit, however, the city of Geneva, which once had been Conrad's refuge, would be associated with Borys's illness and the deterioration of Conrad's own physical and mental health. From Champel, Conrad wrote that "the place is odious to me; and the whole thing [the European trip] with its anxieties and expense sits on me like the memory of a nightmare."[8] This nightmare seems to have gone on for more than a year. For in December of 1906 Conrad turned 49, the age at which his father, Apollo Korzeniowski, had died. During Conrad's trip abroad, as well as after returning to England, and perhaps as late as January of 1908 (five months after the stay in Champel), Conrad reenacted in various ways his father's depression prior to death and, in ways to be explored more fully later, placed his own son Borys in the position of his childhood self. This series of psychobiographical events—in fact, several chapters in an anguished mid-life crisis—repeats Conrad's experience of the Korzeniowski family's Russian exile. Jessie's postpartum recovery period evoked in Conrad strong feelings of rejection and anger; while Conrad's gout and depression (first in Geneva, and then back in England) reenacted his father's self-absorption and morbid decline in the wake of Ewa's death.

Conrad's middle-age misery grows in significance when seen in its larger psychosocial context. His fears about social change—the loss of a familiar world, the feelings of being rejected by and at odds with British literary culture over all things Russian, the seeming futility of his writing career, the ambivalence he felt toward an England in social turmoil—intersected with memories of his own depressed, self-absorbed father as he tilted irrevocably toward death, and as the ten-year-old Konrad closely, quietly watched. Conrad's contemporary social context in conjunction with his personal past illuminates the thematics of breakdown in *Under Western Eyes*—the novel that began its conception in the "nightmare" city of Geneva, and whose story was ultimately set there. It also brings to light possible reasons for Conrad's lapse in 1910 into a transiently psychotic depression upon completing the manuscript.

In what follows, then, I want to investigate Wells, Galsworthy, and

Dostoevsky as figures who directly bring to Conrad's life political, cultural, and literary themes that were in countless ways (both public and private) pervasive and effecting. I also want to describe Conrad's tortured reenactment of his dying father's experience and demeanor in order to explore how personal process was aroused by social process, and thereby to suggest how deeply the interaction between the psychic and the social might have affected Conrad during this time. My ultimate aim, however, is to elaborate a coherent psychosocial framework for interpreting *Under Western Eyes*.

Wells and Conrad

Wells had been instrumental in calling the public's attention to Conrad through generally favorable reviews of his early novels (*Almayer's Folly* and *The Outcast of the Islands*) and, in 1908 and 1909, by helping Conrad obtain a pension from a government literary fund, which eased some of Conrad's financial troubles and put him to some extent in Wells's debt. But by the end of 1909 the relationship between the two men was all but over. When Hugh Walpole returned from Russia in 1918, Conrad explained to him why he and Wells had gone their separate ways years earlier. Conrad's report has him saying to Wells, "You don't care for humanity, but think that they are to be improved. I love humanity but know that they are not."[9] Though, as one of Wells's biographers says, "the words have the ring of a post-discussion *bon mot*,"(*HGW*, p.167) it is still true that Wells and Conrad disagreed fundamentally. From Wells's standpoint, Conrad was an object of humor. He found disagreeable Conrad's old-world aristocratic mannerisms, his Victorian proprieties (held in place in spite of the fact that his ménage always seemed beset by illness and on the verge of financial ruin), and his conviction that, in the final analysis, humanity must work very hard simply to retain a veneer of civilization. But from Conrad's point of view, Wells's vision of society as a logical machine controlled by expert officials, and his utopian dream wherein pain and individuality might be surpassed because "it is all of it only real in the darkness of the mind,"[10] must have seemed intolerably naive and inauthentic. It was not simply what they thought, but who they *were* that made the relationship untenable.

Conrad was disturbed by both sides of Wells's radicalism—the impulse to imprison fallible humanity within systems of control, and the opposite impulse toward anarchistic rejection of societal and human limit. In Wells, anarchistic refusal of constraint serves as a promise for a self-aggrandizing social vision, since the only social scheme that is acceptable to him is the kind imposed on others by the reformer.

Yet due to Conrad's very real need of assistance from Wells, his letters to Wells probably only hint at his actual feelings. In general Conrad was bothered by Wells's "cold ferocity," his intellectual and political "exclusiveness," and his easy dismissal of social and psychological realities in the conviction that men ought to be "improved." Conrad typically casts himself in the role of sufferer and portrays Wells as riding herd on mankind. In a 1903 letter, for example, Conrad says to Wells, "There is a cold jocular ferocity about the handling of that mankind in which You believe that gives me the shudders sometimes"; and of himself, "I'll do the sighing and slobbering and lamenting and sneezing—or whatever it is I am trying to do—and never getting done."[11] While Wells's tone is "jocular," Conrad deplores how Wells imposes his will in the name of virtue, how he despises even existential limitations and longs for an absolutely realized ideal humanity, which is from Conrad's point of view but another way of denying life. Though Conrad slobbers and laments and leaves unfinished, he is fulfilling his humanness. What is most essential to Conrad's self-experience—pessimism, dejection, irresolution—seems at times either invisible or repugnant to Wells. The theme that Conrad clearly associates with Wells, the juxtaposition of "progressive" social ideals with a narcissistically driven social agenda, shaped Conrad's portrayal of the Professor in *The Secret Agent*, as if Conrad were hoping to warn or to challenge Wells about the disturbing connection between anarchism and authoritarianism. This troubling aspect of Wells would inform all of Conrad's thinking on radicalism, including his depiction of Russian revolutionaries in *Under Western Eyes*.

In September 1906, not long after Wells's utopian fiction *In the Days of the Comet* came out, Conrad wrote to Wells: "The day of liberation may come or may never come. Very likely I shall be dead first. But if it does come that'll be the day I shall marshall my futile objections [to *In the Days of the Comet*]."[12] One senses that Conrad would rather "be dead first" than face such a liberation, or explain to Wells its meanness. For the novel shows Wells's arrogant emancipatory interests at their worst, without qualification or self-interrogation. It is not born from Wells's "scientific" tendencies, an aspect of personality that seems at times to have intrigued Conrad—at least insofar as it encouraged Wells to struggle with the divide between human actualities and idealities, and this despite Wells's ultimate aim to regulate individual responsibility and idiosyncrasy out of existence. *In the Days of the Comet* relinquishes any such tie to reality, and is based on purely magical thinking. The text shows the Wells who utterly denies the friction between reality and desire, and it is especially important to my understanding of Conrad's relation to Wells precisely because of its wholesale, anarchistic negation of the present.

In Wells's story the German invasion of Britain intersects with the passing of a comet whose "green vapours" (an extra-terrestrial but natural primordial magic) dissipate the urge for war while liberating people from traditional sexual norms. By resolving human catastrophe via this deus ex machina, the novel shows men and women transcending temporal and cultural constraints to discover their sexuality on the cushions of a perfect interpersonal and social harmony. But Wells's protagonist, Willie, is really a bundle of resentment, adolescent need, and self-pity ("I was a man who stood for the disinherited of the world. . . . I stood for the lost imaginations of the youthful heart. . . . I would make my protest and die."[13] This portrait, along with Wells's unironic presentation of it, suggests that the novel is in fact serving childish fantasies, and that the liberated culture emerging from the green vapors is actually an opportunity for Wells to assert the possibility of a grandiose self who has no need of rules and is driven only by anarchic impulses and the fantasy of their untroubled expression.

In the Days of the Comet appears to be about releasing human potential and recreating in the flesh a lost harmony; but its real subject, as Raymond Williams says, is human powerlessness. "[The comet] saves or destroys us, and we are its objects. The displacement of agency is significant." The novel's primary passion is to liberate us from constraint in general, to express and make obsolete the frustration of having to tolerate social limits. "I wish at times," says the protagonist, "[that something] would indeed strike this world—and wipe us all away." (*IDC*, p. 28). So intense is the desire for a leveling that the only alternative to the comet (and the utopian totality it brings) is apocalypse. Maximalist commitments are not gratified by partial incarnations. An ideal humanity that is absolutely imagined requires absolute negation as its counterpart, for the one entails the other, and neither is governed by a realistic sense of limit or real hope of human agency affecting the world. Like Conrad's Professor, Wells's protagonist withdraws into himself and into the recesses of an omnipotent fantasy in which others exist only to play a part devised by the self. Williams remarks that, with "no chance or hope of changing [the system] collectively," Wells devises " 'a minority culture' [that] has to find its reservation, its hiding-place, beyond both the system and the fight against the system."[14] Wells's fierce anarchism is more fantasy of escape than revolutionary ideal. When Conrad remarks that he will probably be dead long before liberation comes, he is rather subtly bringing the inevitability of Thanatos to bear on

Wells's dream of Eros—his world without death, conflict, or time. For Conrad, Wells's ideal is a bloodless romp that denies our helpless humanity, and makes dangerous those who believe too surely.

The utopian side of Wells, which was similar to what Conrad describes in *The Secret Agent* as "personal impulses disguised into creeds," was something that grew out of Wells's impatience with the pragmatic and the possible. The utopian writings are a clear move beyond the scientific romances (or a regressive refusal of their difficulties), at least in the psychological sense that Wells overcomes all conflict by means of projecting, as Linda Anderson puts it, "an untrammeled space of mind"—a space in which Wells is able to impose his individual dream or desire on society and to absorb the world into his own image.[15] Even though the depiction of Michaelis in *The Secret Agent* shows us that Conrad knew that radicalism could equate with dialectical materialism, radicalism for Conrad more deeply resembled the fascistic and grandiose utopias being concocted by Wells. Conrad's antipathy to the idea of revolutionary movements, especially as elaborated in *The Secret Agent* and *Under Western Eyes*, was rooted at least in part in his revulsion over Wells's vision. Conrad's "sighing, slobbering, and lamenting" was grounded in the realities of pain, loss, and uncertainty, core subjective truths that the Wellsian day of liberation would deny.

Galsworthy and Conrad

While Conrad was disturbed by the authoritarian and self-aggrandizing tendencies of utopian radicalism, he was equally distressed by establishment Liberalism, and struggled to tolerate the amorphous views of the humanist John Galsworthy, whom Conrad called "a moralist" who *betrayed* rather than revealed "the very truth of things."[16] In *The Edwardian Turn of Mind*, Samuel Hynes holds Galsworthy up as the epitome of ineffectual compassion, and of a cloying reluctance to translate sentimental feelings toward the downtrodden into effective social values and progressive reform—in fact, the same imaginative failures that characterized the Liberal leadership in the practical politics of the day.[17] Even at the height of Galsworthy's Edwardian popularity, one reviewer remarked that his books revealed "the liberal mind to be a sour, dour, superior affair, full of kinks and ill-disposed to mankind at large. . . . We find him posing as a helper of the poor and as a sympathizer with the pains of life. Yet all the time one feels that his sentiments are of a bitter and almost brutal kind."[18] Conrad levels similar charges at Galsworthy's novel *Fraternity* (1908).

From Conrad's point of view, *Fraternity* enacts certain abhorrent blindspots in the liberal sensibility. His struggle with Galsworthy over moral courage, and over *Fraternity*'s lack of it, is representative of Conrad's larger disappointment with the doyens of liberalism, and specifically with their failure to uphold principles of moral rectitude, right conduct, duty, and sacrifice to the commonweal—principles that fell on them as obligations, due to their positions of leadership. Moreover, the sorts of liberal confusion and cowardice that Conrad found in Galsworthy play an important role in both the thematics and narrative design of *Under Western Eyes*.

While ostensibly a satire about a group of educated upper-middle-classers who are intellectually aware of lower-class poverty but emotionally terrified of actually engaging the poor, *Fraternity* was for Conrad an exhibition of the sheer perversity of Galsworthy's protagonist Hilary Dallison. In the novel, Hilary becomes philanthropically interested in a Cockney girl (never named), who poses for Hilary's altogether superior, artistic wife Bianca. Hilary buys "the little model" a new set of clothes, including underwear, thereby arousing the suspicion of his family and the jealousy of Mr. Hughes, the violent and philandering husband of a servant in the Dallison household. Hilary's final defeat comes when he discovers that his own interest in the girl is far from philanthropic and that she has developed a dog-like devotion to him. He is horrified by the prospect of a sexual union with someone whose class difference so repulses him. In the last scene Hilary, who has broken from his loveless relationship with Bianca, embraces the young woman, promises to take her away, but then abruptly abandons her. Her mere physical presence (the scent of "her stale violet powder" warmed by "her not too cleanly" flesh) outrages his sensibilities.[19]

In a carefully argued letter to Galsworthy, written in 1908, Conrad communicates his keen displeasure with the story, and especially with the last scene.

> I don't think . . . you have realized the harrowing atrocity of his [Hilary's] conduct. You have refined and spiritualized that poor wretch into a remote resemblance to those lunatics—there are such—who try to cut off the locks of women's hair in the crowds. He is a degenerate who is completely satisfied with the last scene with the girl and therefore with incredible villainy and a total absence of moral sense. . . . The strain on the reader is tremendous and the whole thing borders on the intolerable. . . . Morbid psychology be it always understood, which is a perfectly legitimate subject for an artist's genius. But not for a moralist. . . .

All the way along you show him as absolutely betraying his class in the whole course of his inner life, of his intimate relations—in thoughts, in half-speeches, in his silences. Why? For what object? (except as a secret gratification). . . . He is perfectly faithless. He is so from the beginning. He ends by betraying by an unparalleled atrocity of this same impotence . . . the hope—the supreme hope—he himself had put into [the girl's] heart. [The betrayal] is I take it an ultimate instance of the evil of class . . . But by that time we can no longer believe in the instance. We feel—or I feel—that class is just the mask of impotence, and your attack misses its mark.[20]

First, what are we to make of Conrad's view that Hilary is a fetishist? He rules out the issue of class as an explanation of Hilary's behavior because, he says, were Hilary a social snob beholden to the conventions of his class, tyranny of breeding would "have stopped him long before [he betrays the girl]—*effectually* stopped him—which it has not done." There is some truth to Conrad's response. What is most problematic about Hilary is the contradiction between the aesthetic tenderness and concern he has for the young woman, and his total disregard for her feelings when revulsion to her "otherness" sends him fleeing. This contradiction reveals a self-dissociative element in him. The split we plainly see in Hilary between overt compassion and covert (but disowned) erotic manipulation (the devaluation of another person into a thing) is characteristic of perversion, even if the fantasy of sexual control is not pornographically acted out. Hilary's social status facilitates the fantasy, but it does not necessarily cause it. Erotic power over the model is motivated primarily by his loveless relation to an uncaring wife. His liaison with the young woman is an opportunity to expunge his sense of impotence. (As Conrad says, "class is the mask of impotence.") Hence, the novel is not at all an indictment of the ways in which hypersensitivity causes the upper classes to abuse the lower. It is instead an apology for the hidden sexuality of well-bred men which excuses their bullying of resourceless women, and a demonstration of a kind of false fatedness—a facile way for Galsworthy to seem to condemn the rich without having to look critically at the protagonist's manipulations, or explore the victim's suffering with sensitivity.

As Conrad rightly intuited, Galsworthy was essentially a custodian of traditional liberalism in its senescence, of diffidence and recalcitrance toward democratic virtue in a democratic pose. He was a sort of real-life counterpart to the lady patroness of *The Secret Agent*, with her sentimental sense of social injustice and an inability to imagine how real social change could possibly affect existing class arrangements. Hynes puts it this way: "Galsworthy's hostility was not directed against privilege but against an attitude towards privilege. He does not suggest that a redistribution of the good luck would be desirable or possible . . . [and] would have been content if only men and women had been kinder to one another" (*EFM*, p.81). Similarly, the generosity of Conrad's lady patroness does not extend to "a redistribution of the good luck."

Conrad's demand for moral stiffening from Galsworthy, and his passionate disappointment over the absence of firmness, raises interesting questions about Conrad's need to see his own ideals realized in those around him. The point is especially intriguing given the pervasive irresolution of central psychosocial conflicts in Conrad's own work (and the resulting vitiation of clear moral truths). Yet in order to vouchsafe his view of English identity as a rampart against "morbid psychology," Conrad feels he must rectify the deficiencies of its upper-class character, which, in its puzzling timidity and confusion, cannot find, much less defend, a social faith.

Dostoevsky and Conrad

Dostoevsky was Conrad's bête noire and alter ego. As both a Pole and a Briton—Conrad called himself "Homo-Duplex"[21]—he reserved a special fury for Dostoevsky, who was in Conrad's eyes a committed enemy both of Poles and of Western culture. Dostoevsky was for him the quintessential "other," in part because otherness always necessarily arouses questions of sameness as well as difference, and because Dostoevsky so uncannily plucked the strings of Conrad's inner world. Elaborating the view of many of Conrad's more psychological readers, Jeffrey Berman explains that Conrad had an "intense unconscious identification with the hated Russian novelist, and [used] denial as a defense against the repressed Dostoevskian parts of his own self."[22] I have extended this line of interpretation in order to claim that Conrad's intertextual argument with Dostoevsky—that is, his purposeful borrowing and transformation of Dostoevsky's novels in composing his own—is (more deeply than Berman appreciates) a matter of shared psychic conflicts and of projective defense against such conflicts. Much of the power and ambiguity of both *The Secret Agent* and *Under Western Eyes* grow out of Conrad's use of Dostoevsky to disguise, and perhaps dispel, what remained unresolved in himself and in his work—most centrally Conrad's ambivalent relation to his father Apollo, and to Apollo's ideal of restoring a European Poland.

The Polish Uprising of 1863–64 was a seminal event in the lives of both Conrad and Dostoevsky. As Keith Carabine has pointed out, Apollo Korzeniowski (born in 1820) and Fyodor Dostoevsky (born in 1821) were exact contemporaries, whose "lives and works were closely identified with rival [nationalist] traditions."²³ More specifically, part of what Apollo believed was that the old Polish Commonwealth was in essence European, having enshrined in its constitution the political values and freedoms of the West. And while Conrad's father and Dostoevsky would have been political adversaries, they also shared in common the Slavic tradition of messianic nationalism. The ideological representation of the nation as a crucified Christ, destined for resurrection and thus for moral and political leadership, worked at one and the same time to give hope to Polish sufferers of Muscovite Oppression, and to legitimate Russian Panslavism.

In 1863, Apollo's revolutionary politics had already been handed an elemental defeat, and his son and family were living the martyr's life in exile, deprived of the most basic security. In 1863, Dostoevsky, having spurned revolutionary politics and begun to read the reactionary Khomyakov, had become morally awakened to Russia's mystical leadership role among the nations. Dostoevsky embraced Khomyakov's doctrine of "Slavophilism," which condemned Western civilization and placed all hope in the redeeming genius of Russian institutions (such as the Orthodox church). "The Polish war," he wrote in the winter of 1863–64, "is a war of two Christianities—it is the beginning of the future war between Orthodoxy and Catholicism, in other words—of the slavic genius with European civilization."²⁴ Thus, the Polish Uprising marks "the future war" between Dostoevsky the "Slavophile" and Conrad the Slavic defender of Western institutions.

It would have been impossible for Conrad to read Dostoevsky except through his father and, with this, all that his father (the martyred patriot) entailed. Thus, Dostoevsky's religious politics (his belief that Russian Orthodoxy endowed the Russian people with a special destiny to regenerate the world) necessarily implicated itself in Conrad's personal suffering at the hands of his father's brand of Slavic messianism. At age 14 (three years after his father died) Conrad rejected Christianity outright. "It's strange," Conrad wrote to Edward Garnett in 1902, "how I always . . . disliked the Christian religion, its doctrines, ceremonies and festivals. Presentiment that it would someday work my undoing."²⁵ Even Conrad's juvenile sensibilities recognized and recoiled from the messianic and the mystical. And later, in "Autocracy and War," in a thinly veiled allusion to Dostoevsky's reactionary turn, Conrad scorns "some of [Russia's] best intellects" for "having thrown themselves at the feet of a hopeless despotism as a giddy man leaps into an abyss"; and he attacks the triumvirate of Autocracy, Orthodoxy, and Nation to which Dostoevsky had pledged himself, as "a half mystical, insensate, fascinating assertion of purity and holiness ("AW," p.132). There is a "double think," as Carabine puts it, in Conrad's assault on Dostoevsky, since the same christology, mysticism, and messianism that characterized Dostoevsky's political faith were also part and parcel of Conrad's father's Polish nationalism ("CKD," pp. 11, 15). But I would argue that more than double-think is involved here. Conrad unconsciously projects his father's faulty faith onto Dostoevsky, scorning this religiosity as a form of Russian barbarism in order to protect his father from the disdain he felt for him, and hence to not betray him.

While Dostoevsky serves as a useable receptacle in which Conrad can carry his burden of unconscious (displaced) rage at his father, and at his father's self-destructive messianic politics, it is also true that Conrad needed to find ways to idealize Apollo. In his editorial commentary to *Conrad Under Familial Eyes*, Zdzislaw Najder plainly describes Conrad's father as a democrat and "Red" conspirator.[26] However, Conrad angrily rejected the idea that Apollo was in any sense a political subversive. Conrad writes: "My father was . . . [not] working for the subversion of any social or political scheme of existence. He was simply a patriot in the sense of a man who believing in the spirituality of a national existence could not bear to see that spirit enslaved."[27] Hostility and deprivation could only be repressed or reworked by Conrad's emphatic insistence that Apollo was a patriot, and, moreover, that his patriotism was in nature rational and responsible—to the exclusion of mystical dreams.

In Conrad's 1917 "Introduction" to Edward Garnett's study of Turgenev, Conrad characterized Dostoevsky as "the convulsed terror-haunted" Slav who wrote of "damned souls knocking themselves to pieces in the stuffy darkness of mystical contradictions."[28] Conrad's feelings toward Apollo surely might have resonated with the "terrror-haunted" *Brothers Karamazov*, for example, where the foil for Alyosha's absolute faith is Ivan's skepticism ("all is permitted"), which in turn gives Smerdyakov tacit permission to murder their father. There was too much in Dostoevsky to arouse the ire that Conrad as dutiful oedipal son had tried so mightily to repress. Further, Conrad would have been confused by Apollo's desire (as he said) to "throttle" Tsardom as it had "throttled one generation of Polish Patriots after another," a desire that at times even spurned death. Apollo writes of his trial and eventual exile: "I am going to depart from my country: everything I stood for would be torn from me. Nevertheless I was not

sad. Even if [my trial] had led me to the gallows, [it] would have been a triumph for the national cause."[29] Significantly, Apollo was consumed by his
own all-or-nothing struggle—either to destroy the Russian father (the Tsar)
and thereby realize his rightful identity, or to be destroyed and fulfill himself in death in a kind of mystically sanctioned act of protest. What might
it mean to a hostile oedipal son for his father to define himself as the champion of all victimized Polish sons against the bad father? Or for that same
father to welcome his death as if it were a divine dispensation and realization of his enduring power? Confusing and contradictory, indeed. Apollo
had from the first left little Konrad's oedipal strivings without an adequate
opportunity for resolution. Insofar as he was like his father (a victimized,
hostile son), and equally insofar as his hostile feelings would only lead to
his father's greater power and glory (in death), Conrad's hatred could only
be experienced as *self*-destructive. Conrad wanted to minimize Apollo's radicalism—his role as Tsar-killer—as if hoping to mute the potential conflict.
And in a sense, Apollo could be preserved as patriot because Dostoevsky
loomed so large for Conrad at the interface between European order and
Russian "terror," and was so replete with "mystical contradictions" that, one
was given to understand, could be transcended only through suffering.

Thus Conrad, perhaps unavoidably, transferred to Russia and to
Dostoevsky the Slavic political affiliations that he found unacceptable in
himself and his father. His 1905 essay "Autocracy and War" is in many ways
infused with this ethnocentric projection, even as Conrad tries to renew his
belief in—actually, his idealization of—Europe's political traditions and
dynastic principles. By viewing European (and British) monarchy as supporting nobility, security, and order, Conrad was identifying with Apollo's
secular faith in the Europeanism of old Poland, and hence remaining faithful to his father's ideals. Conrad, conservative and traditionalist, asserts in
the essay the value of dynastic and national identity. "The old monarchical
principle stands justified . . . by the evolution of the idea of nationality as
we see it concreted at the present time." And just as monarchical standards
unify nations, so they seem at least for the moment to provide the ground
for international accord. "This service of unification [provided by the standard of monarchical power] . . . has prepared the ground for the advent of
a still larger understanding: for the solidarity of Europeanism" ("AW," p.
129). The problem, however, is that given Conrad's realistic perception of
imperialist economic rivalries among the European states—contests that
perpetuate the aggressive nationalisms he opposes—he himself is left dis-
believing in the efficacy of the "monarchical" or "conservative" principle:
"the plausible imitations" of the common conservative principle have "never

been very effective" and, besides, these imitations "disappeared long ago" ("AW," pp. 148–49).

In the end, Conrad is left with a fantasy of a kingly protector—of "the monarchs of Europe [who] have been derided for addressing each other as 'brother' "("AW," p. 140)—which has no purchase on modern politics. I would characterize this as an archaic need as much as a political position. It is the sort of need that psychoanalyst Peter Shabad describes as a self-encrypted demand, symptomatic of the compulsion to repeat trauma—a need "in search of an affirming recognition of one's impossible-to-fulfill wishes and the bitter story of their disillusionment."[30] Conrad's impossible-to-fulfill wish is that Apollo could have been (and could still be, in the timelessness of the unconscious) "the good father"; and his story of disillusionment tells how the absence of "the good social father" entails both the childhood trauma of exile and its recapitulation in social leaders who plunge the state—if not the world—into political turmoil.

"Autocracy and War" allows us to see clearly the nature of Conrad's paternal ideal, that is, how he carries this idealization forward from childhood and sustains hope of its recovery by means of his Western identifications and, by extension, his lifelong struggle to establish a fit between himself and his adoptive country (Britain). Ironically, that Conrad unintentionally reveals the ideal's archaic nature (through his bitter complaints against the world for not upholding the principles of the good monarch) also tells us that what is most needed is also fracturing under the strain of its own contradictions. The unraveling of Conrad's idealization, and with it his use of the ideal as a defensive strategy to disguise his burden of unconscious aggression against Apollo, seems correspondingly to make Conrad (in "Autocracy and War" and in the subsequent fictions having to do with Russia) more rigid and more sweeping in his hatred, and not just toward Dostoevsky, but toward all things Russian.

If Conrad would have nothing to do with Dostoevsky's politico-religious Slavophilism, he also would not have affiliated himself with most other Slavs of his father's generation who appreciated or were indebted to Western culture—for example, Bakunin, or even the Polish republicans—since in addition to adopting many Western ideas they were also revolutionary enthusiasts, possessed by the idea of the universal church of human freedom. Conrad almost certainly would have been contemptuous of Bakunin for his instrumental role in the abortive Polish Uprising (which led to Apollo's death). And in Conrad's view, the Russian and Polish populists of his own generation simply provided cannon fodder for autocratic reactionaries ("AW," p.128).[31] Wherever Conrad turned in his Russian-Polish experience, whether to despots or revolutionaries, he seemed to encounter the same result—death by suicide, or by murder. It was a legacy that prompted Conrad to refuse ever to consider that Russian political thought might at any time move beyond the ungrounded social faith of his father's generation.

From the time of Conrad's years in exile to that spent in the Austrian-held city of Cracow, Conrad unavoidably had at least some commerce with Russian- and German-speaking people. Yet Conrad always insisted that he knew neither Russian nor German.[32] Perhaps this is another instance where ambivalence demands a simplifying forgetfulness, especially when Russian or Polish insurrectionists were seen as suicidal, political fathers were experienced as murderous, and one's own real father was both at once. Committed allegiance to mystical nationalism, whether that of Russians or of Russified Germans or Russified Poles, was surely a dangerous if not impossible business. Conrad may have had to misrecognize the other-destructive and self-destructive aims of all such aggressive nationalisms, and may have done so by obscuring the extremity of Apollo's creed, and by vociferously condemning the politico-religious formulations of both revolutionaries (like Bakunin) and reactionaries (like Dostoevsky).

Conrad asserted in 1912 that it would have been impossible for him to write fiction in any language except English: "All I can claim . . . is the right to be believed when I say that if I had not written in English I would not have written at all" (PR, p. v). Undoubtedly, Apollo's career as a Polish author of revolutionary tracts and poetry has something to do with Conrad's refusal to write in his native tongue. At the age of 12 Conrad irritated his elders with boasts that he would become a great writer (like his father), but by 17 he had repudiated this identification and decided on a seafaring career.[33] Only after the death in 1895 of his uncle, his last living male relative, did Conrad begin writing—in English. Adoption of the English language and an anglicized surname may have allowed Conrad to follow his father's vocation without becoming like his father (or consciously identifying himself with catastrophic passions). Conrad's immersion in English culture was not simply a retreat from his Polish past, but also the condition for his writing at all—including following in his work the relational thematics of his youth, which would haunt him throughout his life and inform his fiction to the end of his career. Language itself provided distance: English made manageable what was otherwise too dangerous to evoke directly, using the sounds and inflections that connected him to the affective currents of his Polish past.

Thus, Dostoevsky's popularity with the British public was very probably experienced by Conrad as invasive. For Dostoevsky was a foreign writer (something Conrad refused to be) who was embraced by the British imagination in ways Conrad was generally denied. In the contemporary frame of reference, Dostoevsky was certainly Conrad's competitor. He was a rival who enjoyed great favor with the political and literary establishment and who, in Conrad's view, exercised a corrosive effect on all British readers—for example, on Conrad's long-time friend Edward Garnett. (Garnett, incidentally, was Conrad's literary "godfather," the Chief Editor at Fisher Unwin who had recommended his first novel for publication.) Dostoevsky was inevitably experienced by Conrad as a Slavic brother, as a younger upstart by virtue of Dostoevsky's recent translation into English, and as a hated confrere whose mere existence revealed to the patriarchs of British Letters the illegitimacy of Conrad's bid for acceptance as an English novelist.

In 1908, Garnett reviewed *A Set of Six*. While the review was generally supportive, it praised Conrad by describing his creative powers as Slavic, not English. Garnett speaks for example of Conrad's humor as "essentially Slav in its ironic acceptance of the pathetic futility of human nature, and quite un-English in its refinement of tender, critical malice."[34] However well intended Garnett may have been, Conrad could only have been wounded by these remarks, since he ardently desired affirmation as a writer of English prose. He responded by informing Garnett of the enormous effort that went into crafting a style suitable for the British audience ("I had to work like a coal miner in his pit quarrying all my English sentences out of a black night"), and by touting his ability to reflect humanity in "a spirit of piety" equally foreign to the Slavic "pose of brutality" and to dilettantism. Conrad perceived dilettantism as an aberration of Englishness, or as the pose of "lovers of humanity who would like to make of life a sort of Cook's Personally Conducted Tour— from the cradle to the grave."[35] If Garnett would deprive Conrad of his Englishness, Conrad in turn would implicate him in a serious act of betrayal, which is to say that Conrad saw Garnett as having cruelly dismissed a faithful servant of English letters to chase after the fashionably exotic.

Edward and Constance Garnett's devotion to Russian culture and revolutionary exiles (Constance is reputed to have been the lover of Stepniak, the revolutionary émigré) increasingly estranged Conrad, until he could no longer comfortably visit the Garnetts at their home. Accordingly, Conrad's letters to Garnett became increasingly scornful both of Garnett and, of course, of Dostoevsky. Conrad worked hard to be accepted by his adoptive

culture, but, as Karl says, Garnett, with his Russian friends and close association with Tolstoy and Dostoevsky, "kept moving Conrad back into
everything he had tried to escape" (*JCTL*, p. 650).

Garnett's tepid and at times openly critical response to *Under Western
Eyes* led Conrad sardonically to label him "The Russian Ambassador to the
Republic of Letters." Garnett was overwrought in Conrad's view, and off the
mark in complaining of his prejudice against the Russian temperament.
Conrad wrote to Garnett, "You are so russianised my dear that you don't
know the truth when you see it—unless it smells of cabbage-soup when it
at once secures your profoundest respect."[36] In this same letter, Conrad
reminded Garnett that "La Russie c'est le neant"—the words from
"Autocracy and War" that invoke the theme of Russian chaos. Conrad
would at no point admit that any essential progress had occurred in Russia;
and in fact, while he was writing *Under Western Eyes*, the country was completely destabilized by tyranny, conspiracy, and peril (as Conrad had predicted in 1905). Moreover, Conrad was not alone in regarding Russia as a
social and political abyss (un neant). Wells had written in *Anticipations* that
"Russia seems destined to become [an] Abyss, a wretched and disorderly
abyss . . . where a barbaric or absentee nobility will shadow the squalid and
unhappy destinies of a multitude of hopeless lives" (p. 216). Of course,
Wells changed his political opinions in 1917 (following the Bolshevik
Revolution); but Conrad never did. Why? Perhaps because Conrad's career
as an English novelist was self-defined as a symbolic transcendence of
Polish-Russian *otherness* and all that this meant. He had to denounce the
blindness of Slavophilic Britons to his own clear-sighted "truth" about matters Russian, not simply because he considered himself right, but because
Conrad's truth (or prejudice) also had the valence of safety, of investment
in a carefully forged and necessary identity.

Correspondingly, Conrad thought that Dostoevsky was incomprehensible—indeed, that he was unworthy of Conrad's European understanding. Following the publication of Constance Garnett's translation of
The Brothers Karamazov in 1912, Conrad wrote to Edward: "I don't know what
D stands for or reveals, but I do know that he is too Russian for me. It
sounds to me like some fierce mouthings from prehistoric ages."[37] While
other readers such as J. A. T. Lloyd were intrigued by Dostoevsky's insight
into "those stagnant depths of remote atavism," Conrad derided such fascination. Lloyd also wrote that Dostoevsky, the "barbarian with lizard eyes,"
had disclosed certain "depths which arouse the abhorrence of *good citizens*"
(*RR*, p.116, my emphasis); and Conrad can be seen employing the trite tru-
isms of his age as credentials of *his* good citizenship. Only by disavowing

feelings of "Slavic" inferiority and hate and projecting them onto his Russian confrere could Conrad, at least in his public presentation, redress the blow given his self-esteem by the British insistence on fluffing up his foreignness.

Dostoevsky's ability to arouse Conrad's ambivalent paternal identifications, and to point up his un-Englishness to British literary patriarchs, are two important aspects of Conrad's disturbing affiliation with him, but they are not the whole story. There is also the matter of the psychological contradictions or extremes that typify Dostoevsky's work. The dramatic, eschatological movement in Dostoevsky's novels from darkest hatred (toward others and self) to a condition of love and perfect harmony, where characters attempt to traverse the path from a tormented skepticism and unbelief to a condition of forgiveness and beatitude, corresponds in certain respects to Conrad's tales of disastrous anguish over the loss of secular ideals, tales that invariably remain in the indecisive middle between chronic despair and "saving" illusions (defensive distortions of, or surrogates for, what has been lost). While Dostoevsky would transform paroxysmal despair into ecstatic vision, Conrad's texts generally represent a state of suspension or ambiguity, something that is sustained by both the assertion of contradictory standpoints and the elaboration of unresolved feeling-states. In both authors, we find an abiding effort not to succumb to a loss of self. Dostoevsky's novels destabilize the self, explore the internal war and contradictory viewpoints, but then transcend dilemma by means of mystical union. But for Conrad, either isolation from or union with the ideal carries with it an implied threat of self-loss. To take but one example, from *The Secret Agent*, we see how Stevie Verloc's murderous rage (isolation from) and his "heaven of consoling peace" (merger with) follow this paradigm. The ever skeptical, ever disillusioned Conrad destabilizes traditional solutions while insisting that the hope of stability remains preserved in the tension of the "in between," where the longing for redemption is at times irresistible, but fulfillment is always deferred.

Dostoevsky's "mystical contradictions" provoked Conrad's own struggle with psychological extremes. At the level of conscious purpose and intent, Conrad makes Dostoevsky his guide to things Russian, as was commonly the practice of Edwardian observers, for whom Dostoevsky was "the national representative of the Russian temperament," and also of its social and political thought. Like other commentators of the time, Conrad conflates Dostoevsky's account of Russian political nihilism in the 1860s, or in its originary form, with all Russian revolutionary action in the nineteenth and early twentieth centuries. Conrad does so for two reasons: first, because of a preexisting prejudice to see the Russian movement in terms of the social mysticism that Dostoevsky shared with Apollo Korzeniowski; and second, because he had almost certainly read Leroy-Beaulieu, a French commentator on the Russian movement.[38] "Doctrinaire nihilism," says Leroy-Beaulieu, "has never had anything in common with the critical skepticism that compares and analyzes. Being in substance a negation which affirms itself and admits of no inquiry, it was from the first a sort of dogmatism the wrong way, as narrow, as blind as, and no less imperious, no less intolerant than the traditional creeds the yoke of which it throws off." Leroy-Beaulieu also believed that in the Russian temperament, as well as in "doctrinaire nihilism," the extremes of absolute faith and negation meet. "To the most naive veneration, political as well as religious, corresponds the most barefaced cynicism, intellectual as well as moral. . . . [Still] the Russian, whether nihilist or not, loves best to indulge in the fumes of utopia and the search for the absolute."[39]

Significantly, this Edwardian stereotype of Russian revolutionary politics is not really very different from prewar British radicalism in its utopian self-caricature. That is to say, the idea of an irrevocable coupling of wholesale "negation" and a "search for the absolute" in the totalizing assertion of revolutionary ideals might as easily apply to Wells's *In the Days of the Comet* as to Russian nihilism. Oddly, then, simplistic descriptions of Russian revolutionaries as dogmatic utopianists suggest that Conrad learned just as much about the "temperament" of those revolutionaries by observing Wells and others as by reading ostensible experts such as Leroy-Beaulieu. And Leroy-Beaulieu would also work to reinforce Conrad's existing pre-judgement on Russian political activism in 1905 as simply continuing the heady mysticism of his father's generation. Conrad was not just indebted to Dostoevsky, but to Dostoevsky via European commentators, for his sense of the sameness of opposing forces, revolutionary and autocratic, within contemporary Russian political culture. And such ideas in turn would almost certainly be reinforced by Conrad's experience of authoritarian radicalism in Britain. Indeed, it would have been extremely difficult for Conrad to step safely outside this Western hall of mirrors. Unsafe, that is, for him not to presume the rationality ("the critical skepticism that compares and analyzes") that allowed Edwardian commentators to distinguish the Western mind from its irrational Russian counterpart, even though political irrationality in the West took precisely this form, conjoining absolute negation and faith.

Conrad at the Crossroads: the Interplay
of Social and Personal Process, 1906–1908

These portraits of Wells, Galsworthy, and Dostoevsky (via Garnett) have
suggested some of the ways in which the social forces of the prewar period
impinged directly on Conrad's experience and left him feeling deeply
estranged from his adopted culture—as if the worst of his contemporaries
were filled with cold indifference, and the best were impotently naive. The
psychological thematics of Conrad's impressionable years were aroused by
Dostoevsky's popularity, and Conrad's belief in the stability of contemporary English institutions was undermined both by Galsworthy's liberal complacency and by Wells's extremism. Conrad's "friends" openly mocked or
inadvertently betrayed his values, and while pursuing their own obsessions
denied the legitimacy of his authorial identity and career. In this sense, societal factionalization and malaise colored Conrad's environment in a way
that made feelings of personal dislocation all but unavoidable. The Liberal
election and Russian Entente were not simply events Conrad followed in the
newspapers, but rather were transforming political and cultural moments in
an already "troubled time of disappearing landmarks"—recalling him to the
revolutionary perils of the past he had wanted to escape, and raising the
specter (as he had predicted) of global turmoil and war.

Conrad's insecurity is further underscored by the bad reviews that
followed publication of *The Secret Agent* and *A Set of Six*, both of which were
written directly before *Under Western Eyes* and completed only with great
difficulty.[40] One review (1908) is especially quarrelsome and stupid, and
was sure to irk Conrad by attacking *him* rather than *The Secret Agent*. The
reviewer observes: "The book might be fairly described as a study of murder by a writer with a personality as egotistical as that of Mr. Bernard Shaw,
only lacking in the wit and humour which goes some way to justify the
existence of the latter."[41] This criticism is leveled at Conrad despite the fact
that the novel mocks Fabianism (and Shaw with it), and denounces the selfishness of Wells in particular, and of Liberal culture in general. Other
reviews characterized Conrad as a foreigner, to which he responded in a
1907 letter to Garnett: "I've been so cried up of late as a sort of freak, an
amazing bloody foreigner writing in English . . . that anything I say will be
discounted on that ground by the public." Among the most astonishing
attacks on Conrad were two reviews of *A Set of Six* (1908), which anticipated Garnett's remarks, and thus questioned his career by raising doubts
about his proper claim on the English language. One reviewer says: "The
works of Joseph Conrad translated from the Polish would, I am certain,

have been a more precious possession on English shelves than the works of Joseph Conrad in the original English, desirable as these are. What greater contribution has been made to literature in English during the past twenty years than Mrs. Constance Garnett's translations of the novels of Turgenieff? But suppose Turgenieff had tried to write them in English!"[42]

While being branded an alien, Conrad was also suffering terrible doubts about his adequacy and accomplishments. In the latter part of 1906, confronted with middle age, Conrad reported to Galsworthy that he had lost direction and was "in a state of such depression as I have not known for years." He was plagued, he said, by the responsibilities "of a man of 48 with two kids and a wife to leave behind him—un beau jour." Yet according to Karl, "He mistook his own age, which was 49, but perhaps he did so because his father had died at 49 and it was a fateful number" (*JCTL*, pp. 611, 613–614). In any case, at the age of 49, and feeling beleaguered and despairing, Conrad decided to take his "fateful" six months vacation in Montpellier, France, and Geneva, Switzerland—ostensibly because he wanted "a fresh mental lease" for his work, but more deeply because he wanted to escape the difficulties of *The Secret Agent*, his long wrestle with social disorder in Britain, and human disconnection in his own life.

Five days before his departure, Conrad was stricken with fears that he might again suffer the many illnesses and physical afflictions of his child-hood. He wrote at the time, "Heart thumps, head swims—nervous break-down?—very difficult to keep it away from [his wife] Jessie" (*JCTL*, pp. 612–13). On the train trip across France, Conrad could hardly contain his frustration toward his newborn son John; and not long after the family had arrived at Montpellier, Conrad's older child Borys "began to fall into one of his terribly ill periods" (p.613), as if destiny were conspiring with Conrad's unconscious to collect negative experience into an ever-nucleating conden-sation of trauma. Borys was almost ten, roughly the age of little Konrad dur-ing Apollo's final illness. And Conrad now felt himself beset by domestic problems, a paralyzing writer's block, and a deep depression. Conrad was feeling that Jessie had failed in some measure to take care of him, and he in turn felt defeated and powerless to help himself. Borys's illness seems to have intensified Conrad's fury and guilt toward his family, and this positioned him psychologically to organize the material of his life in terms of repetition, making the trip a strange and timely efflorescence of past experience. As Karl says, "Conrad found himself with a sick, even dying, son—now dupli-cating the depressed and paralyzed Apollo with *his* sick Konrad" (p.615).

Borys contracted a series of illnesses. Karl explains that his "adenoidal condition was followed by measles, and the measles by bronchitis; and the bronchitis was feared to be tuberculosis, for the lungs were affected. Tuberculosis was the Korzeniowski and Babrowska killer" (*JCTL*, p. 615). The thought that Borys might be tubercular could only have conjured the affective accompaniments, if not the conscious memories, of childhood loss. When, during what Conrad called "the awful Montpellier adventure," Borys's condition became life-threatening, Conrad rivaled his son with his own invalidism, as if he were using physical illness to compel his wife Jessie to manage the crisis. In mid-May, following a French doctor's advice, the Conrads moved to the spa at Champel. Conrad had convalesced there before, and had succeeded in finishing his first two novels while taking the water cure. But after arriving at Champel in 1907, he writes to Galsworthy words to the effect that he is suffering a nervous collapse—feeling "hopeless, spiritless without a single thought in my head"—and also that Jessie "does everything for both [sons]. Borys who had been always so considerate is very exacting now. Nothing is right, good, or even possible unless his mother is there."[43] Conrad's attack of melancholy, paralyzing both his thinking and his will, seems to have required the ministrations of "mother," the one who makes things "right, good, or even possible." Work had to wait until Borys and Conrad began to recover.

    In the pattern of his travels, Conrad was at once repeating the past and moving toward the writing of *Under Western Eyes*, where the past is given new form. The result of the "awful Montpellier adventure"—that is, of Borys's illness—was to sweep Conrad back 40 years to the sick child he himself had been, thrown into "morbid conjunction" with an ill and desolate father. In Champel, it was inevitable that Conrad would have remembered his early struggles as an author, for it was here that he had completed his first novels; and it was just as inevitable that he would use his present, unhappy visit to Geneva to conceive the character of Razumov, the young protagonist of *Under Western Eyes* whose tragic odyssey fulfills itself in the revolutionary émigré community of Geneva. Hence, Geneva becomes the site of social disruption, ambivalent dependency on the father, loss, and despair—elements of the psychological grammar linking Conrad to his past and determining the "language" of future experience.

    There is in the circumstances and events that punctuate Conrad's life at this time an all but unavoidable unconscious pattern of reenactment, association, and significance that shaped the themes and strategies central to the fiction then germinating in Conrad's imagination. What becomes evident is a negative condensation of psychological investments, an accumulation of disturbing thoughts and feelings evoked by Conrad's reacquaintance with his childhood self through the person of his ailing son, and by an unwelcome re-identification with his father at the verge of death before age fifty. For, whether the illness and impotence of his childhood is resurrected in his son, or whether his dying father is resurrected in himself, Conrad is faced with harbingers of self-loss. We see him in Geneva standing between past and future, able to move neither forward nor back, paralyzed by a lifetime of injury and anxious accommodation.

Once returned to Britain, depressed and surrounded by piles of unfinished manuscript pages, Conrad seems to reenact Apollo's last days, when, as Karl puts it, "his father lay among unfinished projects of his own, hopes fading, son ill, the house a kind of limbo populated by ghosts" (*JCTL*, p.618). In January of 1908, when Borys had recovered and Conrad was in the midst of drafting "Razumov" (his initial title for *Under Western Eyes*), Conrad wrote to Galsworthy: "[Borys] has not a very lively time; he plays the part of the devoted son to me coming in several times a day to see whether he can do something for me—for I am very crippled [by gout] and once anchored before the table can not budge very well."[44] Illness brought Conrad and Borys together, but only to repeat together a strain of family unhappiness. Conrad had always been rather sharply critical of his son— for example, when Borys at age eight seemed unable to learn to read, Conrad had exclaimed, "Disgusting! I could read in two languages at his age. Am I a father to a fool?"[45] And now Borys had taken on the role of "devoted son" to a father who shrank from emotional contact with him, or responded to his son anxiously and depressively. Hence, Conrad had placed Borys in his old childhood role, in the position of a child who was required to care for an emotionally unavailable (a "crippled") parent, and who was, as Apollo said, "so stupid [as to] miss his father." One important difference was that Borys had Jessie, whereas little Konrad had lost his mother, and had no one but his remote, oddly poignant, unempathic father.

In "A Personal Record," Conrad recounted that his most vivid memory of the Cracow years was not of Apollo's illness, but of his father's having burned his manuscripts before he died.

> What had impressed me much more intimately was the burning of his manuscripts a fortnight or so before his death. It was done under his own superintendence. I happened to go into his room a little earlier than usual that evening, and remaining unnoticed stayed to watch the nursing-sister feeding the blaze in the fireplace. My father sat in a deep armchair propped up with pillows. . . . His aspect was to me not so much that of a man desperately ill, as mortally weary—a vanquished man. That act of destruction affected me profoundly by its air

of surrender. Not before death however. To a man of such strong faith death could not have been an enemy. (*PR*, p. xiv–xv)

While Conrad sees his father's failure—Apollo's destruction of his manuscripts suggests to his son a kind of self-destructive surrender—he also holds that, by strength of faith, Apollo transcends defeat. We glimpse Apollo's despair, but the image is quickly effaced by an assertion of his heroism. Why? After all, this scene could easily have been filled with recrimination and guilt, since Apollo had wanted his son to be a *self*-reflection (so that no otherness would intrude upon his anguish) not just of his idealities, but also of his pain. Perhaps upon leaving Poland as a young man Conrad meant also to repudiate his father's authorial vocation, to make himself different elsewhere and in a language authorized by new fathers. Now, however, he was in danger of becoming the very image of his father's failure. It's as if Conrad had to take himself to the brink, had to re-imagine his father's fate in order to witness it again in his own life, before he could find the determination to be and do otherwise.

During 1907, at the age of 49, Conrad was grappling both with the split paternal image within him, and with his own childhood self. It was a time when the dark embryo of childhood frustration, deprivation, and loss seemed to be influencing and organizing his thoughts and actions to an extraordinary degree. The re-emergence of this intrapsychic template preceded, though only by a matter of months, the attack that reviewers made on his fiction and social identity. Already engaged in an ongoing accommodation to deeply embedded childhood feelings of bereavement and depression, Conrad had to endure the parallel experience of feeling abandoned by his adoptive culture. To some extent, the patriarchs of British culture held the same place in Conrad's psychomachia as did his father, for the contradiction between needing others in order to survive, and yet being unable to depend on them, was enacted in Conrad's relations with both versions of paternity. Remarkably, Conrad did not collapse altogether when the dilemma of his dependency on an unrewarding and unreliable other, which was so central to his psychosocial identity, pressed so powerfully (from within and without) for a resolution he could not manage. What he did instead was write *Under Western Eyes*. Unfortunately, the intercession of narrative process did not resolve in any lasting way his trouble in reconciling the psychic forces that shape his novel. In fact, completion of the manuscript in January of 1910 was followed fast by delirium and a crippling depression from which Conrad felt debilitating effects well into September.

CHAPTER EIGHT

Under Western Eyes: A "Russian" Novel by "Homo-Duplex"

In his "Author's Note" to *Under Western Eyes*, Conrad makes three important but problematic remarks. First, we are told that the text is centrally concerned with the peculiar psychology of Russians, as seen through "the aspect, the character, and the fate" of the novel's main characters.[1] Second, Conrad explains that the "Russian temperament" is illuminated by a political conflict between the senseless tyranny of autocracy on the one hand, and the senseless desperation of revolutionists on the other. "The ferocity and imbecility of an autocratic rule . . . ," Conrad writes, "provokes the no less imbecile and atrocious answer of a purely Utopian revolutionism encompassing destruction by the first means to hand" (p. xvii). Finally, Conrad describes his effort to maintain fairness and objectivity toward the destructive "Russian temperament": "I had never been called before to a greater effort of detachment: detachment from all passions, prejudices and even from personal memories." And in pursuing impartiality, he employs the novel's English narrator. Conrad tells us, "the Western Eyes of the old teacher of languages . . . [were] useful to me" precisely because of the position of detachment they afforded (p. xvi). Nine years after publication of the novel, when the "Author's Note" was added, Conrad persisted in this presumption of narratorial objectivity.

Most critics have taken Conrad at his word, seeing the psychology and major political conflict of the novel as uniquely Russian. However, some readers have been more skeptical of the narrator's role, tending to view his assertion of "punctilious fairness" and timid avoidance of evaluative judgement as purposefully mystifying. For example, Terry Eagleton says that by "withholding judgement at crucial times," the narrator commits a "relatively subtle form of deception" that subverts Conrad's claim to have employed a scrupulously neutral observer.[2] Harriet Gilliam remarks that the novel self-consciously criticizes the narrator's polite English detachment from what he takes to be "inscrutable" expressions of an alien, foreign temperament. "The narrator's insistence on the nationalistic limits of human sympathy and compassion," she says, "entices the reader to realize the fallaciousness of that very insistence."[3] Though these critics are at odds with one another (Gilliam arguing that Conrad is critical of the narrator, and Eagleton saying that the narrator allows for an implicit authorial endorsement of questionable attitudes), I think both are right. The novel criticizes certain aspects of the narrator, yet depends on his fundamental lack of clear commitment—and it does so, I believe, because interested irony provided Conrad with the only means of organizing and elaborating the "passions, prejudices and even . . . personal memories" that make *Under Western Eyes* such a deeply personal book.

The novel might best be approached by addressing Conrad's agenda in the "Author's Note"—that is, by exploring the idea that the novel's underlying psychology allows one to understand central dimensions of the story's politics as well as the narrator's deceptive detachment from what he observes and narrates. I am also proposing that we further cultivate our suspiciousness about Conrad's pretense that the novel is primarily about the "Russian temperament" and its predisposition to destructive social conflict. For if the reader does not interrogate the novel's representation of foreign experience per se, she also runs the risk of duplicating the narrator's ethnocentric insistence on qualitative and essential differences between "Russianness" and "Europeaness" (or "Englishness"), and thereby of erroneously attributing to the other what also, and rightfully, belongs to the self.[4]

Conrad knew English society intimately, but understood contemporary Russia primarily through Western commentators such as Leroy-Beaulieu and through Dostoevsky. He experienced Russia directly only during childhood, when feelings of anxiety and loss—the "passions, prejudices, and memories" of Polish victimage—became his psychological bedrock. Conrad's strict narrative control by means of polar oppositions aims to contain "Russian" experience in its otherness, but the novel's rigid argument and ironic narratorial stance nevertheless indicate Conrad's underlying anxiety about being unable to separate himself neatly from his subject. Properly scrutinized, apparent moral and political distinctions collapse, allowing important aspects of Conrad's British social context and of his psychobiography to come into focus.

In order to explore these several dimensions of the text, it will be necessary to question and transform the stated intentions of the "Author's Note." I begin with Conrad's ideological argument with Dostoevsky. Conrad deliberately sets out to refute the Russian author's view of human experience and his rendering of things Russian. However, Conrad's selective reconstruction of Dostoevsky's text actually shows a Conradian dilemma of identity and difference, contradictory investments and irresolution, enacted centrally in the doubling relationship between Razumov and Haldin. Critics have generally allowed the novel's preoccupation with Dostoevsky and stereotypical Russianness to obscure the Conradian psychological narrative that underlies it. Once this is clear, I will turn my attention to an analysis of Nathalie Haldin, Peter Ivanovitch, and the English narrator, characters who teach us a great deal about the complex social context of the novel. I will want to show that the social context of political conflict and division carry double cultural referents (Russian/British). In this respect we will see, first, that Russian Nihilism (populism), which Conrad criticizes as a despotic form of utopianism, is consistent with Wellsian radicalism; and second, that the political atmosphere of constraint and spying, which is central to Conrad's portrayal of Russian autocracy, has its own Western counterparts—Russian constraint corresponding as it does to Conrad's view that liberal democracy offers only a spurious kind of freedom, and Russian surveillance corresponding to the voyeuristic strategies of the novel's Galsworthy-like narrator, the old teacher of languages. Hence the narrator's putative claim to impartiality, and his assertion of the incomprehensibility (or untranslatability) of "Russian" experience, are actually subtle defensive strategies characteristic of the equivocations of the British liberal sensibility itself. In the final section, I will employ the themes and structures derived from a psychological discussion of the novel—including the psychological dilemma described by Razumov and Haldin, and by Rasumov's isolated and dependent condition at novel's end—as interpretive guides in suggesting a secondary narrative about Conrad's biography (and psychosis). In this way, the fit between the novel and salient aspects of the life will make possible a hermeneutical moment in which the fiction reads the author as a product of his text.

Dostoevsky and Psychological Dilemma

Dostoevsky thought that Russia would become a spiritual beacon for the world once the curses of Western influence were banished and the intelligentsia returned to the people and to the God of the Russian Orthodox Church. For him, these "curses" were political doctrines based on economic values (capitalism and socialism); and such doctrines were symptomatic, in Dostoevsky's view, of what Joseph Frank calls "a moral amorality based on egoism."[5] Dostoevsky writes that "our [Russian] essence . . . is infinitely higher than the European. And in general, all the Russian moral concepts and aims are higher than those of the European world. There is a more direct and noble belief in goodness, as in Christianity, and not as a solution to the bourgeois problem of comfort."[6] In *Crime and Punishment* and *Devils*, atheistic revolutionaries and capitalists are shown to be cheats and scoundrels who claim superiority for themselves and who are willing to destroy other people if and when, as Raskolnikov puts it in *Crime and Punishment*, "these ignorant slaves" get in the way. Conrad understands the terms of Dostoevsky's reactionary ideological position—namely, the amoral egoism that taints Russia's Europeanized elite and threatens the original sanctity of the people—not as having anything to do with (Dostoevsky's reading of) Western influence, but rather as constituting the poles of the "Russian temperament" in its essence. Conrad argues that Russia is an abyss of tyranny and moral anarchy because both the rebels (like Victor Haldin) and the upholders of the social establishment (like Kirylo Sidorovitch Razumov) act on "cynical" or "despotic" motives, but disguise these motives from themselves and others with high-minded rhetoric, a "mystical" (false and disembodied) faith. Thus, Haldin explains to Razumov that, while his terrorist bombing has killed many innocent people, the successful assassination of Minister of State de P—— is a justifiable act of holy war. "The Russian soul that lives in all of us. It has a future. It has a mission, I tell you, or else why should I have been moved to do this—reckless—like a butcher—in the middle of all these innocent people—scattering death—I! I! . . . I wouldn't hurt a fly!" (*UWE*, p.14). And using the same dubious justification of Russia's holy mission, Razumov gives up Haldin to the authorities when he unexpectedly seeks Razumov's assistance in escaping the country. The narrator first tells us that Razumov "felt the touch of grace upon his forehead," and that then Razumov thinks to himself, "Haldin means disruption. . . . Better that thousands should suffer than that a people should become a disintegrated mass, helpless like dust in the wind. Obscurantism is better than the light of incendiary torches. . . . Out of the dark soil springs the perfect plant." (p. 22). Which means, of course, that Haldin himself "should suffer" for assassinating Mr. de P—, one of the thousands who must suffer for the truths that autocracy protects. Conrad uses the European stereotype of the "Russian soul" caught between the far-flung contradictions of "negation" and "faith" to fashion his idea that "autocracy" and "revolution" exemplify the same moral anarchism, though in opposite ways. And Conrad misreads Dostoevsky, who in fact criticizes those who would arrogate to themselves power over all human affairs, and who himself turns to religious faith in order to overcome the dangers of secularism. Neither Dostoevsky nor Conrad are in any sense "impartial" in their views of Russian political struggle and revolutionary activism. But whereas Dostoevsky would cast out "the demons" from Russia and project them onto the West, Conrad in *Under Western Eyes* (as in "Autocracy and War") would make Russia the wellspring of evil, and banish it from the civilized world.

Conrad's ideological assault on the mystical (mystified) evil empire is focused through a darkly ironic redeployment of Dostoevsky's novels. I would argue that Conrad had initially thought of modeling *Under Western Eyes* on Dostoevsky's *Devils*, but that Conrad's finished text relies most heavily on *Crime and Punishment*. Ever since Jocelyn Baines's discussion in the 1960s of the many ways in which the language of *Under Western Eyes* echoes *Crime and Punishment*, critics have elaborated on how Conrad's plot, characters, imagery, and dialogue correspond to *Crime and Punishment*.[7] My point is not to retrace this well-traveled path, but rather to suggest the totality of Conrad's argument with Dostoevsky and to show how the psychology of *Under Western Eyes*, though framed in Dostoevskian terms, is uniquely Conradian.

Devils is important first because Conrad borrows specific themes and ideas from it, and second because Conrad's original idea for the novel—one he did not execute—would have drawn heavily on the characters of Peter Verkhovensky and Maurice Nikolai Stavrogin. In these two characters, Dostoevsky gives satiric representation to the Nihilists of the 1860s. Possessed by a mad scheme to usurp provincial power, Peter goes to Stavrogin's elite friends in Petrograd, most notably Prince K—; and in exchange for information on former revolutionary colleagues, Peter obtains letters of recommendation to the provincial governor. Thus blinding the leading provincial families to his conspiratorial activities, Peter is free to plot a revolution that will take Stavrogin as its figurehead—the "new Ivan" or re-incarnation of the myth of the "Tsar in hiding" (the king who returns to remedy injustices). Though Peter makes a calculated appeal to a non-existent ideal, he also partly believes in the "idol" he has made of Stavrogin, though Stavrogin is just a squalid and self-lacerating voluptuary. Verkhovensky and Stavrogin do nothing to alter the balance of power, and only end up destroying their co-conspirator Pavel Shatov.[8] Stavrogin seduces Shatov's wife and leaves her pregnant with his child, while Verkhovensky convinces the other Nihilists to murder Shatov on the pretext that he has betrayed them politically. In Dostoevsky's handling, then, the nihilists are utterly bankrupt, and their doctrine is but a pseudo-idealism that leads to the arbitrary extermination of innocents.

Conrad borrows and reworks the elements of Peter Verkhovensky's contact with "Prince K——," and of informing on revolutionary friends. In Conrad's novel, however, Razumov is the bastard son of "Prince K——" and though compelled to betray the rebel Haldin, Razumov shares neither friendship nor similar political views with him. While Dostoevsky's novel denounces the manipulative workings of revolutionary "devils," *Under Western Eyes* denounces *every* aspect of Russian society. It is the fate of the unfortunate Razumov to be ground between the upper and nether millstones of revolution (Haldin) and despotism (Prince K——, General T——, and Mikulin). Conrad also borrows from *Devils* the peasant myth of Ivan the Tsarevich, the once and future King. Peter says to Stavrogin: "This democratic rabble . . . gives lousy support; what's needed is one magnificent, despotic will, an idol resting on something solid and standing apart"; and then, "I may be a joker, but I don't want you [Stavrogin], my better half, to be a joker! Do you understand me?"[9] Conrad uses similar statements to provide Razumov with a political rationale for betraying Haldin. In Razumov's view, Russia needed "a will strong and one: it wanted not the babble of many voices, but a man—strong and one!" (*UWE,* p. 22).

In a specific sense, Conrad adopts from Dostoevsky the notion that amoral egoism fuels a lying idealism. Razumov is "cynical" in having put his own life above Haldin's, and thus in disavowing the moral issue of humanity arrogating to itself the power over life and death. Razumov is therefore able to betray the rebel by means of the (pseudo) idealistic claim that Russia needs "a man—strong and one." In turn, Razumov is betrayed by cynical officials "entrusted with so much arbitrary power" (*UWE,* p.34). The difference between Dostoevsky and Conrad is that Dostoevsky believed that the Nihilists of the 1860s had no moral center and needed to return to the faith of the fathers, whereas Conrad believed that moral decision-making as such was impossible in Russia, whether in the 1860s or after the 1905 uprising.

The reader has a certain sympathy with Razumov. Though he transgresses, Razumov is under the heel of autocratic power, and is denied a social context in which to make his own moral choices. However, this sympathy would be considerably mitigated had Conrad more closely identified the protagonist of his novel with the kind of political and moral degradation we find in Verkhovensky's and Stavrogin's betrayal of Shatov. It is important to consider, then, that Conrad's initial outline for *Under Western Eyes* bears more than a distant resemblance to the double betrayal in *Devils*. In a 1908 letter to Galsworthy, Conrad explains that he has written the novel's first part (in the margin, Conrad writes "done") in which Razumov betrays Haldin in St. Petersburg; and Conrad also explains how he projects a second part in Geneva ("to do"), in which Razumov is to marry Haldin's sister, and after a time confess the betrayal to her. Conrad says "The psychological developments leading to Razumov's betrayal of Haldin, to his confession of the fact to his wife and to the death of these people (brought about mainly by the resemblance of their child to the late Haldin) form the real subject of the story."[10] Conrad would have had Razumov, in the fullness of his guilt and hatred toward Haldin, compound his betrayal of Nathalie's brother with a betrayal of Nathalie's "love." One can well imagine Razumov's scenes of confession to his wife as scenes of erotic victimage, a lurid combination of Stavrogin's erotic self-flagellation and of Verkhovensky's murderousness. Conrad's antipathy toward Dostoevsky and the "Russian" character might well have taken him to such lengths of duplication, piling one transgression upon another, but it would have meant portraying Razumov as a complete reprobate.

Already well into his initial draft, Conrad at some point abandoned his marriage plot, trading in the absolute degradations of *Devils* and choosing instead to frame his construction of *Under Western Eyes* with extensively reworked elements from *Crime and Punishment*. Inasmuch as Conrad looks for a model in Dostoevsky to frame his depiction of Razumov, he turns to Raskolnikov, who is far more sympathetic than any character in *Devils*. Most important to Conrad's choice of a Dostoevskian model is the specific psychological text of *Crime and Punishment*. This is underscored by the fact that *Devils* looks at the effects of revolutionary politics on Russian society as a whole, and in doing so is the Dostoevskian novel most relevant to Conrad's *ideological* project. Adam Gillon gives a nearly exhaustive account of the correspondences between *Under Western Eyes* and *Crime and Punishment*:

> Razumov and Raskolnikov are both fatherless students who consider themselves superior to ordinary mortals. Having committed a major transgression, they attempt to analyze it and then explain it away.

Each will be surprised at the discovery that he has a conventional conscience; each will suffer terrible pangs of remorse; each will go
through a period of . . . masochistic torment; each will demonstrate
the necessity for a moral purification to be obtained only by means of
public confession; each will engage in a duel with a fatherlike superior, representing the authorities; each must remain totally alone and
isolated; each ultimately finds his redemption through a young
woman's sympathy, faith, and devotion. In both novels, there is a sister and a mother; both mothers go mad. Razumov's encounter with
Councillor Mikulin and General T— parallels the meetings of Porfiry
and Raskolnikov. . . . The faithful Tekla of Conrad reminds us of the
humble Sonia. . . . Nathalie recalls Dunya.[11]

There are of course important differences: Razumov is not an ax-murderer
nor does he believe in the innocence of the revolutionary Haldin, whom
he gives over to the authorities; Nathalie Haldin is not devoted to
Razumov, but rather to the memory of her brother; Porfiry, the police
investigator in *Crime and Punishment*, is sympathetic to Raskolnikov, whereas
Mikulin is a cold-blooded manipulator whose only purpose is to enlist
Razumov into spying on the Genevan community of revolutionary émigrés; and Razumov does not find "redemption" as Raskolnikov does.

Some critics—notably, Carola Kaplan and Edward Wasiolek—have
observed some of the significant differences between the two novels.
However, Kaplan tends to recast these differences in the mold of similarity, while Wasiolek, seemingly predisposed to find Dostoevsky's message
more satisfying than Conrad's, doesn't explore the dense and complicated
meaning that such differences have for Conrad's project. For example,
Kaplan states that Conrad "reverses the roles of two of Dostoevsky's central characters—his protagonist, Razumov, is akin to Dostoevsky's
Razumikim and his antagonist, Haldin, is akin to Dostoevsky's protagonist,
Raskolnikov," and argues that thus Conrad demonstrates "the impossibility
of life in Russia" for Razumov/Razumikim, the reasonable man.[12] The obvious problem with this claim is that Haldin, the revolutionary martyr, is
never conflicted about his purpose, whereas Razumov is (like Raskolnikov)
excruciatingly tormented. This internal conflict isn't to be missed, for it
goes to the psychological core of Conrad's novel, and yet is elaborated in
distinctively un-Dostoevskian ways.

Wasiolek focuses on how Razumov's avowal of guilt for Haldin's
death only leads to his own pointless destruction, whereas Raskolnikov's
confession to Sonya brings him forgiveness and redemption. While it is

certainly true that Razumov is in no way changed for the better, Wasiolek misses how the non-transformative nature of Razumov's truth-telling is crucial to Conrad's scheme to ironically debunk the mystifications of Dostoevsky's religion of suffering, especially his presumptuous revelation of the true nature of love and grace.[13] However, while Conrad treats the redemptive powers of confession with vicious irony as he reworks Dostoevsky's pattern of crime, punishment, and confession, his irony remains close to the narrative surface.

My argument, ultimately, is that Conrad depicts the relation between Haldin and Razumov not just ironically, but also according to his own psychological idiom, a claim made even more salient, perhaps, by the long tradition of searching for Dostoevsky in *Under Western Eyes*. In some ways Conrad's ideological bias against Russia is mitigated by his intention "to capture the very soul of things Russian." In order to capture the Russian soul Conrad must enter into it imaginatively (thus to some extent capturing what he *imagines* to be the Russian soul); and this creative effort, unlike the more distanced commentary of "Autocracy and War," should prompt Conrad to extend himself in *imagination* toward at least an attenuated empathic linkage with his Russian characters. Thus, ironic debunking becomes complicated by the play of imagination, precisely because such play is always in some measure an empathic act.

Conrad modifies what is sympathetic in Raskolnikov in order to shape and further complicate Razumov, and does so in ways that allow him as author to take possession of his tale. He halves Raskolnikov like a loaf of bread to create Haldin, Razumov's antagonist who revolts against the system, and Razumov, the protagonist who seems to *need* to work within it. This division was necessary for Conrad. His own political and psychic conservatism would have made it impossible for him imaginatively to engage an anarchistic protagonist: Conrad's protagonist had to be, like the author himself, a social conservative with "a reasonable adherence to the doctrine of absolutism" (*UWE*, p. 58). While it is true that Razumov's "Ivan Tsarevich" fantasy demonstrates an extreme "adherence" to patriarchal idolatry, it also represents (despite its strange irrationality) a faith Conrad cultivates—at least insofar as he suborns himself (as he does in "Autocracy and War") to the fond illusion of a kingly peacemaker, a "monarch of genius" able to adjudicate successfully the myriad disputes and dangers in prewar Europe. The splitting that lies at the heart of Conrad's tailoring of the Dostoevskian text suits both his intellectual requirements and his need to organize relations in *Under Western Eyes* according to the psychosocial thematics of his own experience. And this, in turn, brings us to the central question of how Conrad elaborates himself through his use of Dostoevsky, and how an exploration of the differences in the psychological themes of the novels can help us better understand the meaning of Conrad's amputations and reinscriptions.

In *Crime and Punishment*, Raskolnikov worsens his own material circumstances "out of spite," because he is obsessed by the question of the "extraordinary person"—of whether "who can spit on what is greatest will be their lawgiver," or whether a man is "a louse."[14] From his twisted point of view, failure to be a great amoralist seems inevitable, for simply by posing the question of conscience—can one human being take the life of another?—he proves to himself that he isn't beyond good and evil, but only an ordinary mortal, and in this sense "a louse." Hence, Raskolnikov's conscience becomes tyrannical: if he doesn't murder the old pawnbroker, he despises himself; but if he dares to murder her, and in the process shows himself to be a trembling ambivalent creature, he despises himself as well. To loosen this snare of impotent self-hatred, this self-strangulation by the ligature of his own ideas, Raskolnikov imagines himself becoming a grandiose rebel, one for whom there is no contradiction between the ruthless acquisition of power and using that power as "a benefactor of mankind" (*CP*, p.419).

Raskolnikov suffers because of his "ideas," but Victor Haldin does not. By assassinating a Minister of State in order to serve an ideal, Haldin gives himself over entirely to the illusion of his own incorruptible virtue. He is the force of destiny, the incarnation of the true spirit of the motherland. When he appears in Razumov's rooms Haldin declares: "What will become of my soul when I die in the way I must die . . . ? It shall not perish. . . . My spirit shall go on warring in some Russian body till all falsehood is swept out of the world" (*UWE*, p.14). The narrator explains that, after Haldin is caught and executed, the impoverished revolutionary insurgents in Russia regard him as a Christ: "The spirit of the heroic Haldin passed through these dens of black wretchedness with a promise of universal redemption from all the miseries that oppress mankind" (p.194). Haldin's martyrdom is not merely virtuous, it is divine. In contrast to Raskolnikov, whose grandiose ambition is simply to trample on conventional rules (as all great men do), Haldin becomes one with "the Russian soul" and gains immortality through his sacrificial labors for the holy land. This self-idealization earned through sacrifice disconnects Haldin from the suffering he causes, excuses him from having to grapple with how, as the narrator puts it, the conviction of love could ever spring from "the soil of men's earth, soaked in blood, torn by struggles, watered with tears" (p. 260). Haldin never feels the reality of human pain sufficiently for *religious* mania or martyrdom to have meaning for him. Hence, Haldin can believe what Raskolnikov, merely a killer with a bad conscience, can never really believe: that one can shape the clay of humanity and keep one's hands clean.

Both Raskolnikov and Haldin are worshipped by a mother and a sister. Raskolnikov's mother, when she does not hear from her son for two months, writes to him: "You know how I love you; you are all we have, Dunya and I, you are everything for us, all our hope and our trust" (*CP*, p.30). And similarly, Victor Haldin is "all in all" to Mrs. Haldin and Nathalie. Nathalie tells Razumov of her own and her mother's grief when they learn of Victor's death: "I am like poor mother in a way. I too seem unable to give up our beloved dead, who, don't forget, was all in all to us" (*UWE*, p. 239). In both cases, a narcissistic hunger grows from such adoration.

On the one hand, Raskolnikov's arrogance and pride are fed by the attentions of his mother and Dunya; but on the other hand, he resents the fact that they have sacrificed everything for him, and feels either too great or too small to meet their conventional expectations. By his actions he seeks to undo the impuissance and rage he feels in his relations with mother and sister. In contrast, Haldin harbors no hostility toward Mrs. Haldin or Nathalie, and in this respect seems more purely and unconflictedly an extension of his mother's desires.

Haldin's self-idealization is a gift from his adoring mother. We sense this, though Haldin's family background is sketched for us in only a few sentences, when he recounts pieces of his biography to Razumov. Haldin tells of being the sole emotional support of his mother and sister, and briefly alludes to his revolutionary ambition.

> "Men like me leave no posterity," he repeated in a subdued
> tone. . . . "Look at me. My father was a Government official in the
> provinces. . . . A simple servant of God—a true Russian in his way. He
> was the soul of obedience. But I am not like him. They say I resemble
> my mother's eldest brother, an officer. They shot him in '28. Under
> Nicholas, you know." (*UWE*, p.14)

Haldin's identity depends on his being like his mother's "true" husband. Who he is is based on a disappointed repudiation of the natural father, and requires his own embodiment of the rebellious uncle, whose execution had left Haldin's mother aggrieved and seemingly unable to find the needed consolation in her husband, "the soul of obedience." We are left to speculate that Mrs. Haldin cultivated the resemblance to her brother *in* her son, because she seems to exist so exclusively *for* him. In turn, Haldin's sense of self is dependent on his capacity to fulfill his mother's desire. Once elevated to the position of husband, Haldin becomes both the son and the father. Thus, these few lines allow us a glimpse into the genesis of Haldin's "Christ" complex.

Haldin's role as his mother's redeemer finds expression in his ecstatic but impossible utopianism. He describes his likely death, which would follow the assassination, as a spiritual merger with the "soul" of his people. The underlying fantasy is of fusion with a maternal deity—Mother Russia—in opposition to the autocratic father, whom he kills in the person of the high official. For Haldin, the Russian soul, the idealized, female-inflected spirit of a "self-sacrificing" faith, leads to zealotry in pursuit of a perfect world; and his response to disillusionment in the paternal is irrational violence. Haldin seems to say, "Since I do not love my father, I owe no allegiance to any father, even to the point of overthrowing *all fathers*." His de-idealization of Tsardom, an active repudiation of patriarchy, leads to a regressive re-enchantment of "Mother Russia"; in effect, a desire to affirm himself through his own mother and render the father of no account.

There is something killing in mother Haldin's devotion to her son. When the narrator passes on to her the latest news from Russia (the assassination), she murmurs, "There will be more trouble, more persecutions for this. . . . There is neither peace nor rest in Russia for one but in the grave" (*UWE*, p.71). From her safe sadness in Geneva, she thus unwittingly pronounces the inevitability of her son's punishment and death. His resemblance to her eldest brother, which she has fostered, would now be realized. And when she later learns of Victor's death, she falls into the terrible grief that would eventually kill her. In the end Mrs. Haldin is left contemplating "something in her lap, as though a beloved head were resting there," and in this way she is envisaged as an icon of hopeless grief. "There was in the immobility of that bloodless face," we are told, "the dreadful aloofness of suffering without remedy" (p.234).

Nathalie also fails to mourn Victor, and instead transforms him into an inviolable ideal. We are told, "The concrete fact, the fact of his death remained; but it remained obscure in its deeper causes. She felt herself abandoned without explanation. But she did not suspect him. What she wanted was to learn almost at any cost how she could remain faithful to his departed spirit" (*UWE*, p.97). The terrible thought that Victor might have experienced even a moment of self-doubt or despair is lit and instantly extinguished ("But she did not suspect him"). Her refusal to accept his simple humanity, and her insistence that his identity be equivalent to his ideals, suggests the extent to which she too is loyal to the grandiose wish that is the basis for Victor's maternal relation. Nathalie's identity depends on faithfulness to the same ideals of perfection that Victor accepted from their mother. And when her brother is lost she seeks to protect herself by pledging her troth to Victor's "promise of universal redemption" (p.194). She becomes, in Conrad's handling, molded to the contours of a false faith—the very image of ideal "Russian" womanhood, but an image armored against human conflict, and even against certain basic human feelings.

Like Mrs. Haldin, Raskolnikov's mother suffers separation from her son as a narcissistic injury, and dies "not in her right mind." Unable to accept that her son is a murderer, she invents the fiction, upon Raskolnikov's removal to Siberia, that hostile circumstances have forced him into hiding, and that he will return to a brilliant career. Even while fantasizing Raskolnikov's glory, the mother, as Dunya surmises, had a "suspicion of her son's terrible fate" (*CP*, p.541). Dostoevsky suggests both that the mother *is stricken for* Raskolnikov in much the same way that he himself is stricken (defending against the ordinary murderer), and that her death is a sacrifice that upholds Raskolnikov's ultimate goodness, namely, the good conscience he earns by confessing his crime and then cultivating the pious acceptance of the miracle of Dunya's and Sonya's forgiveness.

In contrast, Mrs. Haldin never plagues herself with any thought, either latent or manifest, that her son committed an actual crime. Rather, she suffers from what she sees as Victor's emotional betrayal, his failure "to trust" her love, and hence regards herself as having been abandoned. Her irremediable sorrow, symbolized in the hallucination of holding Victor's head in her lap, seems to echo Christ's dying question to his heavenly father, "Why hast thou forsaken me?", but to alter it in relation to her missing son, "Why have you deserted me?" And it is this same sense of being "abandoned without explanation" that drives Nathalie, in hopes of recovering her dead brother, to become a strict incarnation of his faith. Of course, the reason for Victor's abandonment of mother and sister is revealed when Razumov confesses his part in Victor's death. However, knowledge does nothing to alter the course of pathological mourning, either for Mrs. Haldin or Nathalie. Conrad fixes ironically on religious iconography—in the deprivation of the narcissistic parent, and in the new faith of the sister—in order to demonstrate that the Christ-like Haldin, whether through his own violence or Razumov's necessary betrayal, brings only suffering. But ironic commentary also offers Conrad an opportunity to elaborate his own psychological thematics. Dostoevsky supplies forgiveness as ointment for the wounds of conscience, but Conrad offers only an insurmountable depression, which has nothing to do with conscience and everything to do with a part of the self, scooped away, that cannot be mourned. In turn, this bereavement without end must lean on the illusion that what is absent can be recovered.

Razumov's relation to the maternal is significantly different from Haldin's. While Haldin is thoroughly entangled with his mother, Razumov seems hardly to know his. Mentioned only once, and identified only as the daughter of an Archpriest (*UWE*, p.3), she is said to have had an illicit relationship with Prince K—, which led to the birth of a bastard son. There is nothing more of her in the entire novel. Her near absence from the text makes her fleeting presence conspicuous, of course, for it is Razumov's deprivation and anonymity in relation to her that predisposes him toward a needful reliance on Prince K—. We are told that Razumov "must get acknowledged in some way before [he] can act at all" (p.41), suggesting the extent of his continued dependence on simple recognition. There is no counterpart in Dostoevsky's novel for the sense of aloneness Razumov seems to have inherited from the circumstances of his birth.

If Raskolnikov retreats into isolation, he does so willfully. In contrast, Razumov is born without a loving connection to anyone, and must make his lonely way in the world. Consequently, Razumov's movement from isolation to guilty involvement in the social action of the novel has to be closely considered in light of the fact that Prince K— is Razumov's only familial relation. For only a precise understanding of Razumov's distant tie to his father, and of his affiliation with Tsardom, can unlock the nature of his contemptuous but confused reaction to Haldin's revolutionary zeal.

The depth of Razumov's emotional impoverishment can be measured by the fact that his relation to his natural father (Prince K—) exists more in the realm of fantasy and longing than in real interaction. The first time Razumov is permitted contact with the Prince is at the attorney's office when, as a university student, he discovers his filial relation (he is a lawyer's ward, allowed a small stipend by his father). Then, on the night he gives Haldin up to the authorities, he turns to the Prince for help, and they meet a second time. On neither occasion is Razumov acknowledged as a son, though he is himself overcome by emotion toward his father. At the first meeting, the lawyer introduces Razumov to Prince K— as a promising student, and the Prince extends his "white shapely hand" to his bastard child. "[Razumov] took it in great confusion (it was soft and passive) and heard at the same time a condescending murmur in which he caught only the words 'Satisfactory' and 'Persevere.' But the most amazing thing of all was to feel suddenly a distinct pressure of the white shapely hand just before it was withdrawn: a light pressure like a secret sign. The emotion of it was terrible. Razumov's heart seemed to leap into his throat" (*UWE*, p.7). By means of "the secret sign" and the attorney's indirect hints, Razumov is made to understand that he *is* the Prince's son, and yet that he will be forever unacknowledged. The paradox stirs in Razumov an agonizing hunger. Prince K— is awkwardly indifferent, almost reluctant to touch Razumov's hand; but for Razumov the Prince is a colossus, a wellspring. "The young man's ears burned like fire," we are told, "his sight was dim. 'That Man!' Razumov was saying to himself. 'He!' " (p.8). Razumov takes the small hints and favors that Prince K— offers him much as a starving dog takes a bone, for out of these bloodless exchanges he must draw as much nutriment as possible. From the moment of the first meeting Razumov begins "walking in the fashionable quarters," and privately linking his career goals with the Prince and his family. "Presently they [his daughters] would marry Generals or Kammerherrs, and have girls and boys of their own, who perhaps would be aware of him as a celebrated old professor, decorated, possibly a Privy Councillor, one of the glories of Russia—nothing more!" (p.8). Out of neglect Razumov fashions a fantasy of connectedness, admiration, even glory.

Of course, the Prince is no more responsive in his second meeting with Razumov, when he gives up what he knows about Haldin. Summoned to the General's office at Razumov's request, the Prince looks at Razumov with "black displeasure," but "Razumov walked in without a tremor. He felt himself invulnerable—raised far above the shallowness of common judgement. . . . [T]he lucidity of his mind, of which he was very conscious, gave him an extraordinary assurance" (*UWE*, p.27). Razumov has the assurance of a gift-bearer, his information seems suddenly to make him worthy of the Prince's recognition. Moreover, it is as if in betraying the revolutionary Haldin to the father Prince K—, Razumov were ridding himself of the intolerable patricidal wish that Haldin embodies, and in the process reconstructing himself through an idealized connection to the paternal, a connection that rests on the mere prospect of an approving gaze, and that evokes in Razumov fantasies of superiority.

Whether or not Conrad is fully conscious of Razumov's longing to make his fantasied father real, it is clear that Conrad wants us to see Razumov's "undoing" as following from an ungovernable need, a "sensation resembling the gnawing of hunger" (*UWE*, p. 29), and not just from the "irrational" external forces that influence his fate. Though many readers have said so, Razumov is hardly comparable to Razumikin, Dostoevsky's man of reason and sturdy balance, because Razumov's vulnerabilities induce him to react irrationally to both Haldin and the authorities.[15] The arch-manipulator of the novel, Councillor Mikulin, is well attuned to these vul-nerabilities. Whereas Mikulin learns just enough about Razumov to measure and manipulate him, Mikulin's counterpart in *Crime and Punishment*, Inspector Porfiry, shows a sympathetic understanding of Raskolnikov's plight and a regard for how best to help him. Porfiry snares Raskolnikov, it is true; but he does not exploit Raskolnikov as Mikulin does Razumov.

In a single encounter Mikulin appropriates his victim, coercing Razumov to spy by appealing to his vanity and longings for paternity.

> The obscure, unrelated young student Razumov, in the moment of great moral loneliness, was allowed to feel that he was an object of interest to a small group of people of high position. Prince K— was persuaded to intervene personally, and on a certain occasion gave way to a manly emotion which, all unexpected as it was, quite upset Mr. Razumov. The sudden embrace of that man, agitated by his loyalty to a throne and by suppressed paternal affection, was a revelation to Mr. Razumov of something within his own breast.
>
> "So that was it!" he exclaimed to himself. . . . And there was some pressure, too, besides the persuasiveness. Mr. Razumov was always being made to feel that he had committed himself. (*UWE*, p. 213)

Mikulin arranges for Prince K— to "intervene personally" with Razumov, and while allowing Razumov to feel that he is "one of our greatest minds" and of real interest to the elite (*UWE*, p. 205), turns this desire for praise against him. Here we see Razumov's "father hunger"—that is, his need for mirroring and idealization—that leads him toward a formal entanglement with the secret police. Though he seems at least marginally aware of Mikulin's strategy (the Prince's subtly coercive embrace provokes Razumov to exclaim, "So that was it!"), he still finds that he is unable to resist, and that his already frail sense of who he is now depends on acting according to Mikulin's directives. Such "persuasion" resonates with Razumov's inner longings for attachment and reclamation, while the pressure of despotic "coercion" arouses Razumov's fears of being abandoned to a condition of hopeless abjection. Suddenly aware of the possible consequences of Haldin's presence in his rooms, Razumov is also reawakened to an old fear—that of his strength giving way, of his mind becoming "an abject thing," and of "dying unattended in some filthy hole of a room" (p.13). Mikulin's manipulations carry with them the power to fulfill Razumov's needs, or to crush him utterly.

Autocracy is in many ways represented in the novel as the institutional embodiment of parental narcissism, which murders one's hope of independent selfhood and threatens one with abandonment if one tries to break away. Razumov's dependence on the "bad" object is familiar: it is what he knows best about the quality of human attachment. And connectedness to the paternal is above all else what Razumov wants, if not in fact then in fantasy, if not from nurture then from power and manipulation, if not good then bad. Moreover, were the object utterly absented (through revolutionary upheaval), hope of replacing the "bad" with the "good" would also be reduced to nothing. Destructive rage at the ungratifying object is psychologically suicidal when there is no better alternative object, for its loss could lead to an even more profound abjection. It follows, therefore, that Razumov must disavow any feelings of rebellion toward his tyrannical "fathers." But disavowal is not resolution, and the anger of wounded sons returns, like the return of the repressed, only now as something disguised (not-me), uncanny, and persecutory.

For Razumov, then, Haldin can only represent an extraordinary psychic danger: he is that which Razumov must deny in himself or risk his most primary internalized relations, the necessary beginnings of a half-formed self. When Haldin enters Razumov's rooms asking for help, it is as if to kill him. Haldin is called "the phantom," "the visitation" whose uninvited presence strikes at the heart of Razumov's sense of self-possession. "Razumov for a moment felt an unnamed and despairing dread, mingled with an odious sense of humiliation. Was it possible that he no longer belonged to himself? This was damnable" (*UWE*, p.209). Razumov is both ashamed and threatened by Haldin. His shame derives from having violated some private obligation to autocratic fathers, and his terror is of self-dispossession, of an "unnamed" dread of self-loss. Both are inexplicable unless the reader considers that Haldin represents an essential aspect of Razumov's psychic life, that Haldin is a double for Razumov's own inadmissible transgressive wish. Haldin's claim on Razumov is too great for it to be otherwise.

After his effort to help Haldin escape proves futile, Razumov thinks for a moment of murdering him, then despairs: "[Razumov] knew very well that that was of no use. The corpse hanging round his neck would be nearly as fatal as the living man. Nothing short of complete annihilation would do. And that was impossible. What then? Must one kill oneself to escape this visitation?" (*UWE*, p.21). Here, where simple murder seems to fall too short of "complete annihilation," Razumov's enmeshment with Haldin is clear. There are other alternatives to murder or suicide—for example, telling

Haldin to get out, to disappear as stealthily as he came—which Razumov never seriously considers, despite his "cool intellect." Razumov's helplessness in turning Haldin out is an odd problem—leaping as he does from simple eviction to murder, imagining Haldin's corpse hanging around his neck until the burden (or the loss?) has killed him. It is not merely guilt that Razumov fears. After all, shouldn't the thought of "complete annihilation" arouse guilt as well? Razumov understands too well that murder in this case also entails psychic suicide. His dilemma is that in order to be a praiseworthy son he must somehow disavow the rebellious hatred Haldin embodies, and sacrifice this aspect of himself to the idealizations he most needs. He can neither harbor Haldin nor give him up, since each alternative entails loss of self.

Though afflicted by Haldin's presence, Razumov later suffers even more at his death, as demonstrated by the delirious fantasy he has in Mikulin's office after learning of Haldin's torture and execution. First, Razumov notes that his unempathic relation to autocracy—the curse of not having his intentions "understood"—"had been brought on his head by that fellow Haldin," and he then envisions "his own brain suffering on the rack—a long, pale figure drawn asunder horizontally with terrific force in the darkness of a vault, whose face he failed to see. . . . The solitude of the racked victim was particularly horrible to behold. The mysterious impossibility to see the face . . . inspired a sort of terror" (*UWE*, p.60). The victim's identity is a mystery, leaving us to wonder: Is it Razumov or Haldin, or both? Razumov cannot recognize himself once he is connected to Haldin and to the unassimilated part of himself that Haldin represents. It is a relationship of uncanny doubling, where unconscious affiliation and otherness are held in tension. This is in keeping with the structure of a need expressed by another, outside the self, who is then disavowed.

There is of course no shortage of doubling in *Crime and Punishment*: Marmeladov, Svidrigailov, Sonya, even Raskolnikov's mother all symbolize aspects of the protagonist. Importantly, however, each of these doubles functions to resolve ambiguity rather than increase it, that is not the case in Razumov's relation with Haldin. The only doubling relation in *Crime and Punishment* that corresponds to the Haldin-Razumov relation is the connection Dostoevsky establishes between Raskolnikov's feelings of self-loathing and his assault on the pawnbroker—that is, the dynamic between Raskolnikov's having projected his self-hatred onto "the louse," and then murdered her so as to punctuate his absolute difference from her. Raskolnikov's disavowed connection with the "vile old withered woman" follows, perhaps, from the way he experiences his mother and sister as persecuting him through their sacrifices for him. However, reconciliation with mother and sister is made possible by Raskolnikov's intrinsic goodness (" 'Whatever you may have thought about me being cruel and not loving you,' " he says to his mother, " 'it's all untrue. I'll never cease to love you' " [*CP*, p.514]), and by means of Sonya's intercession, which allows his goodness a second life. The source of projective doubling is healed through Sonya (the incarnation of an ideal mother and sister), for her forgiveness permits Raskolnikov to relinquish his Napoleonic strivings and recover his authentic self.

In contrast, Haldin (unlike the pawnbroker) is not the recipient of a displaced but ultimately resolvable psychic conflict. Haldin is a noble idealist whose political fervor is directed toward a cause Razumov detests—a formidable antagonist with whom Razumov feels kinship, and yet simultaneously the representative of all that he loathes and wishes he was not. Razumov can neither entirely accept Haldin as an aspect of himself, nor entirely reject him. There is no solution, no crevice between suicidal dejection and murder by which to escape. If Razumov accepts Haldin, he commits intellectual suicide and loses all hope of gaining the acceptance of autocratic fathers. If he rejects Haldin, he protects only a sterile bond with the autocratic patriarchy that cares nothing for him and that, as he realizes on some level, has already abandoned him. They would, we are told, sentence him one morning and "forget his existence before sunset" (*UWE*, p.13). In his confession to Nathalie, then, Razumov simultaneously pursues both acceptance and rejection of his connection to Haldin, his revolutionary "soul mate."

Razumov reveals that "in giving Victor Haldin up, it was myself, after all, whom I have betrayed most basely." He thus partly acknowledges his affiliation with Haldin, but then remarks, "Only don't be deceived, Natalia Victorovna, I am not converted. Have I then the soul of a slave? No! I am independent—and therefore perdition is my lot" (*UWE*, p.250). Razumov recognizes his connection with Haldin, but he also endeavors to disclaim it in order to hold onto a view of himself as an "independent" yet loyal son of the regime. It is the same self-representation that becomes ironically inflected with the autocrat's scorn for revolutionary "slaves" when Razumov makes himself reliant on "bad" autocratic fathers who would enslave rather than deliver him, especially since subjugation is fantasized as a preliminary test on the way to ultimate reward. It is true that Razumov's love for Nathalie allows him to leave his prison of lies and no longer waste his life among those whom he sees as evident frauds. But Razumov's avowal of *independence* only returns him to his old ungratifying condition of *dependence* on an appropriating autocracy. Razumov makes a second public declaration of guilt to the revolutionary group because for him "life is a public thing" (p.36). And, fittingly enough, upon speaking out he is promptly beaten to the point of deafness by his counterpart in the autocracy, the police spy Nikita, who appears as an avatar of Razumov's irrevocable tie to the "bad" father. The revolutionists then set Razumov loose on the rainswept streets, where "a vivid, silent flash of lightning . . . blinded him utterly," and "a dumb wind drove him on and on, like a lost mortal in a phantom world ravaged by a soundless thunderstorm" (p. 255). In time he staggers helplessly in front of a tram car, whose approach he cannot hear because of his blasted eardrums. When he falls beneath it and is crippled we are hardly surprised: the moment merely affirms the autochthonous, unchangeable spiritual disfigurements to which he is born.

Razumov's fate could hardly be a more ironic reworking of the "crossroads" episode in *Crime and Punishment*, when Raskolnikov knelt down "and kissed that filthy earth with delight and happiness" in order to initiate contrition; and where shortly afterwards an apparition, Sonya's image, "flashes before him," her assurance that she would always be with him (*CP*, p.525-26). In contrast, Conrad visits terrible degradation and physical injury on Razumov without any compensatory rescue. As he lies broken and bleeding in the rain, trying to explain to the faces that hover over him that he is deaf ("*Je suis sourd*"), a woman, who we later understand to be Tekla, appears from nowhere claiming to be "a relation." She kneels, placing his head in her lap; when he is taken to the hospital "the officials had some difficulty in inducing her to go away" (*UWE*, p. 256). He has met his fate. There can be no doubt that Razumov and Tekla configure a nightmarish version, or inversion, of Raskolnikov and "little mother" Sonya.

After Razumov is reduced by confession to a state of crippled helplessness, he becomes abjectly dependent on Tekla. And Tekla, perhaps the most chronically abused character in the novel, comes to embody an anonymous, suffering maternity (she says, "I have no use for a name, and have almost forgotten it myself" [*UWE*, p.163). Her exclusive reason for living is to minister to the needs of Russian sons who are themselves so badly injured that they cannot "act at all." In the context of Conrad's ideological argument against Dostoevsky's religion of suffering, the Tekla-Razumov relation images a black parody of the Christian Pieta.

On the psychological level, confession has made external the agonies of Razumov's internal life. Tekla, in addition to imaging an absurd version of Dostoevsky's Sonya, arrives as an avatar of Razumov's absent mother, the Archpriest's daughter, who died early and left her son without "parentage." Razumov becomes the concrete embodiment of dependency on an abject maternity, a dependency he had desperately wanted to avoid; and in this way he finds his beginning in his end. Razumov seeks death ("perdition") to escape the irrevocable loss of paternal approbation, but his loss of the father now becomes manifest and permanent. Further, Conrad does not even allow Razumov the welcome relief (mercy) of suicide, but instead defers death, making suffering a process without clear conclusion, a descent without end, perhaps, in the way that Dostoevsky makes redemption a process, an unconsummated turning of the spirit in the direction of grace.

This deferral entails Razumov's re-discovery of his original solitariness and isolation, of his disconsolate original experience of Russia as "inanimate, cold, inert, like a sullen and tragic mother hiding her face under a winding-sheet" (*UWE*, p.21). The narrator relates how the revolutionists, when in Russia, visit Razumov, who is himself "ill, getting weaker day by day," and come to listen to him talk about his ideas. We are told how they make a great show of forgiving Razumov, but we are not told why. Perhaps they come out of guilt. After all, they had allowed Nikita, an informant for the state, to show his loyalty by brutalizing Razumov. The narrator offers little guidance, apart from the question, ironically posed, "who would care to question the grounds of forgiveness or compassion?" (p.263), while the reader, of course, feels the author's hand pushing her to ponder precisely these grounds. Whatever "ideas" Razumov has, they must fall on the deaf or uncomprehending ears of the revolutionists, who have come to Razumov for their own self-serving reasons; and Razumov himself is literally deaf to his interlocutors. His isolation, under the false pretense of his having at last been "understood," is complete.

Under Western Eyes certainly seems to be firmly in the grip of Conrad's ironic portrayal of Dostoevskian psychology. However, the novel's central psychological contradictions—Razumov's being caught between accepting and rejecting Haldin, between confessing and not confessing, and between finding forgiveness and remaining lost and unforgiven—are neither a function of Dostoevskian psychology, nor of Conrad's intellectual interest in subjecting Dostoevsky to ironic realignment. The clarity of Conrad's intellectual argument depends on the negation of Dostoevskian truths, but Conrad multiplies and magnifies ambiguities even as he negates. If the text ironically trades on Dostoevskian "mystical contradictions," at a still deeper level it discloses typically Conradian contradictions that end in impasse.

Like *The Secret Agent*, the central conflicts in *Under Western Eyes* involve the phantasmatic polarities of melancholia—abandonment/idealization, suicide/murder—against which Conrad defends by means of irony, whether in the form of argument or authorial posture. Razumov's primary psychodrama moves from defensive idealization of the father to the collapse of this defense into an uncanny ambivalence that cannot be dispelled, and into self-loathing, abandonment, and isolation as he traces the downward trajectory of depression. Yet by staging this ill-being within a Dostoevskian frame Conrad can label it a malaise of the "Russian soul," as if such malaise were endemic to a national type rather than a consequence of the way Conrad displaces his own psychological idiom onto that "soul." Further, Razumov in certain ways embodies both the conflicts of Conrad's earlier protagonists, Kurtz and Jim, and the Marlovian "resolution" of such conflicts. Like Kurtz or Jim, Razumov is stymied by omnipotent wishes. (Razumov's disavowed connection to Haldin reveals an unintegrated, grandiose rebelliousness; his affiliation with Prince K— reveals fantasies of idealization and merger). And like Marlow, Razumov answers or "confesses" to his situation in a way that is only partly a recognition of the truth of a kinship relation (Marlow's identification with Kurtz or Jim, Razumov's with Haldin). His response is overdetermined by the intransigent nature of the loss of a psychically necessary investment in patriarchy, and hence fated to be in some measure a concealment. One might see Razumov's failed pursuit of omnipotence as part of Conrad's ironic reworking of Dostoevskian psychological elements—that is, of how Raskolnikov successfully transcends his sense of humiliation and despair. However, this observation is complicated by the recognition that Conrad's own characters (Kurtz and Jim) are failed over-reachers who plumb the depths of dejection, and that the "pursuit of perfection" in Conrad always ends in the tension and irresolution of being in-between, of being unable to go back to archaic ideals and wishes or forward to an integrated view of self and world. Thus, Marlow never has a clear view of Kurtz and Jim, just as Razumov never has a clear view of himself. The difference between *Under Western Eyes* and the earlier Marlovian narratives is the distinct depressive inflection of Razumov's ordeal of "crime and punishment," and this is itself in keeping with the grim pallet of *The Secret Agent* and with Conrad's own prolonged mid-life crisis. Conrad's depiction of "Russian" suffering cannot be separated from the complexity and character of Conrad's own psychology. Though mediated through Dostoevsky, the novel's overarching dilemma is Conrad's familiar configuration, fixed like stars in a dark sky, only made dimmer this time by a cruelly ironic authorial hand.

Locating the Text of Europe in the Novel's Social World

The psychological narrative I have outlined yields two important observations about social conflict and context. First, the character of Haldin teaches us that revolution (as represented in the novel) is not an authentic challenge to the social order, because the revolutionary is himself an unmediated utopianist (a slave to fantasies of merger with the maternal); and second, Razumov shows that the tenuous experience of personal difference is often maintained only by disclaiming aspects of self that are reflected in a "discordant" other. The first observation helps to explain characters with "revolutionary" commitments, such as Peter Ivanovitch (the leader of the Genevan anarchists); and the second provides the key to properly interpreting the English narrator. His experience of cultural difference is predicated on disclaiming identification "with anyone in this narrative where the aspects of honor and shame are remote from the ideas of the Western world"—this despite the fact that his ideological commitments are covertly expressed through Razumov, and his deep emotional investment is obliquely represented through the intricacies of Razumov's relation to Nathalie, which he brokers.

The unconscious dynamic of the narrator's story leads us back to the essential point: that the social context of the novel is not simply or primarily Russian, but Western/English as well. As I will argue, what the narrator invariably attributes to the "inscrutable" other is also true about himself. His conventional English decency, modified by a general refusal to take responsibility, is actually the irresolute liberal response to social conflict (utopianism and authoritarianism) in the Western world. In order to explore more fully the social dimensions of the novel (in the context of the psychological), I will read Nathalie Haldin in the light of Leroy-Beaulieu's account of Russian womanhood in *The Empire of the Tsars*, Peter Ivanovitch in terms of Wells's novel *In the Days of the Comet*, and the English narrator according to Galsworthy's novel *Fraternity* and the phenomenon of Edwardian liberalism in general. Situating the finished text in relation to Conrad's manuscript, as well as to Leroy-Beaulieu's commentary (which discloses stereotypical Western political myths about Russia), to Wells's novel (which epitomizes Edwardian maximalist political fantasies), and to Galsworthy's most autobiographical fiction (which demonstrates the deficiencies of the liberal character), allows me to reconstruct the text's Western/English context.

After describing Russian Nihilism as "dogmatism the wrong way," Leroy-Beaulieu goes on to give a picture of the radicalized Russian woman of the cultivated classes. "In intelligence and power of will, as well as in knowledge and in the rank she holds in the family, the Russian woman is already the equal of the man; in some ways she seems superior to him, perhaps through this very equality which, by exalting one sex, seems to lower the other" (*TE*, p. 218). Though full of praise, Leroy-Beaulieu is plainly disturbed by these "topsy-turvy" sexual norms and values in Russian culture. "Between the Slav man and woman there is not unfrequently a sort of exchange and indeed an inversion of faculties and qualities. . . . The women, as though in compensation [for effeminate men], have, in their minds and characters, something strong, energical, in one word, virile, which far from robbing them of any portion of their grace and charm, often adds to them a strange and irresistible attractiveness" (p.219). Yet despite her strength and apparent equality, when the "revolutionary spirit" overtakes her, it cannot "fail to turn to its profit these pretensions and aspirations of a sex always more prone than the other to give way to impulse and infatuation" and to all sorts of utopian aberrations (p.210-11). He then adds, "among these votaresses [and ardent proselytes] of Nihilism, one can best see how much generous feeling and idealism thrive under the mantle of this repulsive materialism" (p.210). The political sins of Russian men are twice-visited upon Russian women simply because of their gender.

Conrad portrays Nathalie Haldin as a sensitive, generous, and intelligent young woman, but it is still remarkable how closely the depiction conforms to Leroy-Beaulieu's outline of the generic Russian woman, especially in her virility and passionate idealism. She is a cultivated aristocrat who has attended a women's college, a "Superior School for Women" [*UWE*, p.70]). To the narrator's eye, Nathalie appears thoughtful, charming, and above all masculine. He remarks, "Her voice was deep, almost harsh, and yet caressing in its harshness," and "Her glance was as direct and trustful as that of a young man yet unspoiled by the world's wise lessons," and again, "The grip of her strong, shapely hand had a seductive frankness, a sort of exquisite virility" (pp. 70, 81). Due to her brother Victor's mysterious disappearance, Nathalie alone shoulders the burden of familial suffering. The narrator focuses on how "Russian natures [as opposed to Occidental ones] have a singular power of resistance against the unfair strains of life. Straight and supple . . . she compelled my wonder and admiration" (p.122).

What is more, Nathalie is no stranger to Russian idealism, holding as she does a profound faith in a Slavic earthly paradise. For example, when told of Mr. de P—'s assassination, Mrs. Haldin predicts further persecutions. But Nathalie is carrying a prayerbook, and voices hope for the triumph of the visionary ideal. " 'Yes. The way is hard,' came from the daughter, looking straight before her at the Chain of Jura covered with snow, like a white wall closing the end of the street. 'But concord is not so very far off' " (*UWE*, p.71-72). In the narrator's view, despite Nathalie's "exquisite virility" and the equality of rank she holds within the family, "Her unconsciously lofty ignorance of the baser instincts of mankind left her disarmed before her own impulses" (p.98). In accord with Leroy-Beaulieu, he thus concludes that Nathalie's ardor ennobles "all sorts of utopian aberrations"— her "lofty ignorance" and impulsiveness blind her to the potential catastrophes and repulsive aspects of a political idealism that entails "blood and violence" (mankind's "baser instincts"). While the narrator's conservatism allows that political behavior (like the heart) has reasons that reason knows not, his ethnocentric view of Nathalie explains her grossest character flaw as simply an entailment of Russian femininity, namely, the endorsement of an irrational and sometimes fatal faith.

Turning from the female "revolutionary spirit" to the "revolutionary feminist" Peter Ivanovitch, we illuminate additional aspects of Conrad's social context. Literary critics have hitched Ivanovitch up to various possible Russian models. For example, Elizabeth Knapp Hay finds in Ivanovitch shades of Tolstoy and Bakunin, while Jeffrey Berman detects Dostoevsky's influence—specifically, Dostoevsky's articulation of the "cult of women" in *The Diary of a Writer*. In naming Peter Ivanovitch's Russian originals, however, scholars have neglected to explore the personal valences Conrad surely attached to such figures, and the relevance of these Russian literary and political figures to his contemporary social milieu.

Hay quite usefully documents "the parody of Tolstoy's titles in the works of Peter Ivanovitch mentioned in the manuscript," titles implying "the morbid character of the premises from which Ivanovitch's mystical conversion [to feminist utopianism] has sprung."[16] In addition to her observations on Tolstoy, Hay sees elements of Bakunin in Ivanovitch's "beastlike appearance coupled with a supposedly celestial nature." And like Ivanovitch, Bakunin also "made a harrowing escape to the West from a prison in Russia" (*PN*, p. 283).

However, it is important to note that Conrad almost certainly despised Bakunin for his role in the abortive Polish Uprising, and that Bakunin's utopianism (dreams of wholeness based on destruction and despotism) had much in common with socialist fantasies in Britain. These "Russian" and "English" utopianist visions were equally disturbing to Conrad. Though Bakuninism was mostly irrelevant to the 1905 Russian revolution, Conrad focused on it because for him history in Eastern Europe seems to have stopped at the time of the 1863 Polish Uprising. Moreover, Bakuninism clearly shared features with the "liberated" world that Wells envisioned in *In the Days of the Comet*, and hence Conrad's historical prejudices against Russian political activism were reinforced by what he saw in British society. Thus, Wells alone presents Conrad with reason enough to bypass contemporary developments in Russian socialism, and to invoke Bakunin as the symbol of the radicalism he knew firsthand in his own life (via his father's "red" nationalism and Wells's utopianism).

Berman focuses on Dostoevsky as a model for Ivanovitch's feminism, noting that Ivanovitch's speech on women is "a close paraphrase" of Dostoevsky's May 1876 entry in *The Diary of a Writer*. In Ivanovitch's discourse to Nathalie, he talks about receiving "the most remarkable letters" written by women, letters that "breathe noble ardour of service" and, in turn, inspire "the greatest part of our Russian hope." Ivanovitch then turns to Nathalie and pointedly advises her not to study medicine, which is for him representative of Western knowledge (*UWE*, pp. 82-83). Similarly, Dostoevsky says that he has observed Russian women "at close range" through their letters, and that "in her resides our only hope" because "the Russian man has become terribly addicted to the debauch of acquisition, cynicism, and materialism."[17]

Conrad's point is to make clear that, despite his revolutionary feminist's political difference from Dostoevsky, Ivanovitch too places "mystic phrases" in service to dogmatic causes of violence. But by making Ivanovitch virtually recite Dostoevsky, Conrad drives home his thesis that "the oppressors and the oppressed are all Russians together, and the world is brought once more face to face with the truth of the saying that the tiger cannot change his stripes nor the leopard his spots" ("AN," p. xvii). And, of course, Conrad's rhetorical violence, reducing all Russians to sameness, is often taken by readers as a valid description of Russian politics.

In these three Russian sources for Ivanovitch, then, it is possible to see Conrad modifying each, and in the process eliding important ideological distinctions. In Tolstoy, Conrad finds the hypocritical discrepancy between acting on sexual impulse and living according to Christ's teachings that is so basic to Ivanovitch's psychology, but he eliminates Tolstoy's insistence on humility, on freedom from all-encompassing rationalistic/metaphysical schemes, and on a Gospel-based pacifism. From Dostoevsky, he reworks the idealistic "cult of woman" (corroborated by Leroy-Beaulieu), and implicitly ascribes to Ivanovitch an aggressive promotion of Russian nationalism, but leaves off Dostoevsky's reactionary alignment with Tsardom. Finally, he borrows Bakunin's apocalyptic fantasies to frame

Ivanovitch's political agenda, but neglects Bakunin's devotion to the anarchist idea of a stateless society. What is more, the conflation of elements
definitely favors Bakunin's empty credo of "a universal church of freedom,"
and this imbalance transforms Ivanovitch's spiritual "cult" of Russian womanhood (the sanctity of the Russian people preached, each in their different ways, by Tolstoy and Dostoevsky alike) into a tool for
self-aggrandizement, in both the individual and political realms.
Undoubtedly, this confusing mixture allows Conrad to elaborate his view
of the social polarities of "revolution" and "autocracy" as mirror images, for
when important ideological differences are erased, "Russia" becomes a
"night in which all cats are gray."

Wells would only reinforce Conrad's prejudicial view of all revolutionists as tyrants. *In the Days of the Comet* is not just apocalyptic in the style
of Bakunin, but it centrally depicts utopia as a wish-fulfilling *sexual liberation*,
one that is premised on a grandiose erasure of human dissonances, differences, and restraints.[18] The quest for an enchanted world takes much the
same form in Wells's novel and in the revolutionary component of *Under
Western Eyes*.

In Wells's text, one might recall, the main character Willie deplores
his life and embraces radical politics because he has lost his ideal woman,
Nettie, to a male rival. Willie is made so desperate by his wounded pride
that he is perfectly prepared to murder both his competitor and his sweet-
heart (his revenge "lay in revolt and conflict to the death" [*IDC*, p.118]).
His sense of injury is further overdetermined by his earlier, frustrated
hunger for a nurturing parent. Of his mother we are told, "The existing
order dominated her into worship of abject observances" (p.38), placing
her in the position of a supplicant, prompting her constantly to thwart her
son's ambitions with her own fears, and making him feel "weak and insignificant" (p.37). Willie bemoans his fate: "Why should one sacrifice one's
future because one's mother is totally destitute of imagination" (p.36). This
"crushed hunger" can only be assuaged by female attention. Wells mends
the wound—or rather, masks the injury—since with the advent of the
comet (the deus ex machina that either destroys humankind or erases its
destructive impulses) all is magically redeemed. The tale begins with its
protagonist envisioned as the innocent victim of an inimical world, and it
ends with fantasied apocalypse allowing for a retreat into unconflicted
Eros, a disavowal of essential losses that no mere social order, however
splendid, can repair or redeem.

In Wells, cosmic forces expunge all despair from the world, and
the pretense of sexual equality and happy unions camouflage the hero's

narcissism. In contrast, *Under Western Eyes* trenchantly dramatizes the logic of Ivanovitch's lack. As with Wells's protagonist, Ivanovitch's political life follows from personal loss. In his youth he was to marry "a society girl," but she died suddenly, after which "he abandoned the world of fashion, and began to conspire in a spirit of repentance. . . ." Unlike Wells's protagonist, whose desire is blessed (by the comet) rather than punished, Ivanovitch is "beaten within an inch of his life, and condemned to work in mines, with common criminals" (*UWE*, p.83). Upon escaping, however, he regains himself through feminine insight and love. "He had become a dumb and despairing brute" until a woman's compassion, "discovering the complex misery of the man under the terrifying aspect of the monster, restored him to the ranks of humanity" (*UWE*, p.86). Just as Willie's injury is ostensibly healed by a maternal figure, so Ivanovitch's "mystical conversion" occurs by the spark of female sympathy. In both novels, then, Eros and female compassion define the male vision of a new world.

Wells imagines but then averts complete annihilation. Ivanovitch merely stresses the inevitability of destruction, telling Razumov that " '[F]or us at this moment there yawns a chasm between the past and the future. . . . Bridged it can never be! It has to be filled up,' " and that "A sacrifice of many lives could alone" accomplish this (*UWE*, p. 146). Razumov has stumbled upon Ivanovitch's vision. History is like a grave that must be stuffed with bodies in order to redress the many grievances that contribute to the revolutionist's narcissistic wound. Wells's protagonist lives a dream where all human possibilities are fulfilled, but only as an extension of his own desire. Ivanovitch's appetite for power is even more nakedly avowed. His arrogance divides humanity into the "dregs of a people . . . which ought, *must* remain at the bottom," and the elite—"the nobility"—who keep them there. Ivanovitch defines "the dregs" as the mediocre middle classes (not the peasants), while the impoverished masses are accepted by Ivanovitch only because he views them as easy-to-manipulate "children" (pp. 146,157).

Ivanovitch's underlying contempt for the very people he presumes to save resonates with Wells's scorn for humanity—something he barely disguises with the pretense of his protagonist's pity. After the comet strikes the earth (and Willie thinks everyone but himself has died), Willie sighs in pity "for all the hot hearts, the tormented brains . . . who had found their peace [their death] beneath the pouring mist and suffocation of the comet. Because certainly that world was over and done. They were all so weak and unhappy, and I was now so strong and serene" (*IDC*, p.179). This kind of "cynicism" from revolutionists is not, as Conrad would have it, symptomatic of the intrinsic moral anarchy of the Russian temperament. Rather, the willingness to rationalize death, or even genocide, marks any totalizing ideology that would suppress all thoughts of our shared humanity and doubts about the perogatives of personal power. Such disregard for human life is fundamentally symptomatic of a fascist mindset, whether its geography be East or West.

While Ivanovitch shills for the financial intrigues of his patroness, Madame de S——, he is also a sexual grifter who inhabits his own con so skillfully that there is no substance to him beyond the pretense he peddles. To the narrator he seems "hardly decent" (*UWE*, p.87); yet in recognizing Ivanovitch's falseness, the narrator only raises a more difficult question about himself. What, after all, are we to make of the narrator's own presumptions of fairness and rationality, his claims to "decency" and his self-description as a "complex Western nature" (p.80)? The narrator is in fact the very opposite of a complex intelligence, one self-consciously alive to the textures of the emotional and social life around him. Upon inspection his decency seems itself little more than a false pretense of "punctilious fairness"—a strategy of defensive detachment, ambiguous political commitment, and personal affiliation.

In an astute description, Eagleton analyzes the narrator's defensiveness according to its political meaning. What Razumov and the English teacher of languages share is a common "anti-revolutionary front," as follows from Razumov's plain autocratic commitments and the narrator's "shrinking from" revolutionary activism. In this sense, both Razumov and the language teacher are "detached" from the community of revolutionary émigrés. But unlike Razumov, the narrator thinks of himself as a good English liberal. Therefore, as Eagleton explains, "in order to avoid commitment to the cynicism and negation which underpins Razumov's detachment, the narrator must detach himself in turn from him [Razumov], stressing the Russian's inscrutability" (*EE*, p.28). Thus, the narrator engages a strategy of what Eagleton calls "double detachment": he harbors a secret contempt for revolutionary commitment; and yet by means of his profession of ignorance of all things Russian, he remains distanced from ideological predispositions that would undermine his liberal decency, his cultural difference, indeed, his good Englishness.

Just as Razumov establishes his feeling of difference from Haldin by denying in himself the desire that Haldin represents, so the narrator disavows any similarity of disposition between himself and Razumov by continually protecting his sense of cultural difference. The narrator's "complexity" follows from his need to refuse commitment to any single, clearly articulated position, while his "decency" is based on a fundamentally illusory assumption that he can fall back on a secure and coherent social position—namely, that of the "staid lovers" of Western liberty (*UWE*, p.113). In displaying an often manufactured sympathy for the revolutionary victims of autocracy, while not acknowledging his own class antipathy toward "real revolution," the narrator effectively embodies the deficiencies and indirections of Britain's liberal elite. Further, the narrator assumes a fatherly concern for Nathalie, that pitiable soul, arbitrarily robbed of "natural lightness and joy" by an "unEuropean despotism" (p.220). However, her victimization is hardly enough to turn him forcefully against the old order.

On the one hand, the narrator admires Nathalie's passion, courage, and devotion, but only as these virtues are engaged in private familial sacrifices, not sacrifices to the revolutionary cause. On the other hand, he himself possesses a disavowed desire for Nathalie, something that he enjoys through his fond illusion that Razumov and Nathalie will inevitably become lovers. At one point the narrator describes Nathalie as he imagines Razumov sees her. "It was as though he [Razumov] were coming to himself in the awakened consciousness of that marvellous harmony of feature, of lines, of glances, of voice, which made of the girl before him a being so rare, outside, and, as it were, above the common notion of beauty" (*UWE*, p.237). Razumov's feelings at this moment can only be guessed at (the documentary authority of his diary has been superseded by the narrator's first-hand impressions), and thus what the reader witnesses is to some important extent the narrator's own experience of Nathalie, and follows from the disclaiming of his desire by its projection onto Razumov. The narrator watches the couple, and indulges his desire for Nathalie by watching.

The narrator's political and personal gestures—his indirect, furtive, disavowed involvements—demonstrate a characteristic liberal sympathy-without-commitment, and implicitly reveal that his English patriarchal view of himself as a philanthropist is itself a cover for considerably less honorable sexual intentions. In the tepid, hypocritical quality of his liberalism, the "old Englishman" is like the politically equivocal Galsworthy who, while extending his hand to the defenseless, insisted that such trusteeship be painless to himself; and in this subtly erotic voyeurism conducted under a philanthropic pose, the narrator bears a rather troubling resemblance to Galsworthy's character Hilary Dallison in *Fraternity*. In the end, the narrator's Englishness is a rather sticky business, and his detachment a fraud.[19]

In *Fraternity*, the poor are but "shadows" of the wealthy: they are denied flesh and blood existence by Glasworthy's sense of propriety and

decorum ("decency"). In a similar way, the English narrator derealizes
Russian culture and then aestheticizes its strangeness. To his delicate and
conventional sensibility it assumes a lurid, melodramatic coloring, what he
calls "childish, crude inventions for the theatre or a novel," "something the-
atrical and morbidly affected," "a public play" of mere "words and gestures"
(*UWE*, pp. 75,76, 234). Those who pass before him are described as futile
ghosts issuing from "the shadow of autocracy" (p.74). His aestheticism so
derealizes human interaction that at one point he is forced to regard *himself*
as "a dumb helpless ghost . . . an anxious immaterial thing that could only
hover about without the power to protect or guide [Nathalie Haldin] by as
much as a whisper" (p.87). When left unexplained, the narrator's impotence
simply enacts his need to witness (without the sort of involvement that
would entail responsibility) the painful reality of another's existence.
Conrad's judgment of Dallison—that Galsworthy had "spiritualized" the
life out of "the poor wretch"—applies equally to the English language
teacher, who depersonalizes and isolates himself from the life around him,
and thereby reduces himself to an enervated wraith. By wanting experience
without cost, he is encrypted in the act of his own narrative telling, and he
comes to epitomize the voyeuristic rather than the transformative dimension of reading. The quality of his telling also encourages us to interpret the
human experience that the old Englishman narrates in a certain way—
which is to say, to simulate participation and remain unchanged by the
event of reading.

His use of Nathalie (the desirable female other) bears a certain resemblance to the machinations of Galsworthy's Hilary Dallison, who uses his "little model" to allay his sexual powerlessness. Just as Dallison cannot bring
himself to "touch" the little model, so Conrad's English narrator cannot
engage Nathalie without the pose of disinterestedness, and without disclaiming her relationship to disavowed aspects of his own social identity. The
English language teacher never appropriates Nathalie physically, but he lives
his desire voyeuristically and claims a voyeur's revenge on his sexual object.
His appropriation and its disavowal are more covert than Hilary Dallison's,
being those of an observer whose true desire remains always in shadow.

Moreover, the narrator attempts safely to indulge unacceptable
thoughts and feelings through the person of Razumov, who has been fatally
misperceived by both the narrator and Nathalie as an "unstained, lofty,
and solitary" existence [*UWE*, p.93]). The narrator's use of Razumov as a
kind of blank screen becomes particularly apparent just before Razumov's
confession, when the narrator tells us that Nathalie and Razumov were
drawn to each other fatally—that, having received a letter from her brother

praising Razumov, she, so ignorant of Razumov's true character, had her imagination kindled "by the severe praise attached to that one name." Similarly, in the narrator's view, "for [Razumov] to see that exceptional girl was enough" (pp. 239-40). Razumov earlier complains (quite astutely) that the narrator regards him "as a young man in a novel" (*UWE*, p.128), and here the narrator does just that. While Razumov's gaze becomes the way to romantic sentiment ("for him to see that exceptional girl was enough"), such sentiment obscures how his role is fitted to the requirements of autocracy. The narrator remains fixed on the purity of their sentimental union ("her very ignorance" and "the severe praise" attached to Razumov's name) and the melodramatic fiction that it serves. The setting of the scene, which positions the narrator on the sidelines, also makes his voyeuristic pleasure quite clear.

> To me, the silent spectator, they looked like two people becoming conscious of a spell which had been lying on them every since they first set eyes on each other. Had either of them cast a glance then in my direction, I would have opened the door quietly and gone out. But neither did; and I remained, every fear of indiscretion lost in the sense of my enormous remoteness from their captivity within the sombre horizon of Russian problems, the boundary of their eyes, of their feelings—the prison of their souls. (*UWE*, p. 238)

The irony of course is that, despite the disclaimers, the narrator reads Razumov and Nathalie as the hero and heroine of his novel, and hides himself away to enjoy the illusion without risk.

Razumov ultimately finds something sinister in the Englishman's role, and Nathalie in turn comes to recognize her own vulnerability in relation to the narrator and to wonder if he had been aware of Razumov's identity all along and done nothing. Razumov explains the Englishman's role to Nathalie in this way. "He talked of you, of your lonely, helpless state, and every word of that friend of yours was egging me on to the unpardonable sin of stealing a soul" (*UWE*, p. 248). Identifying the narrator as "the devil himself in the shape of an old Englishman," the paranoid Razumov demonizes the narrator's subtle dishonesties; but as one who knows firsthand the self-serving manipulations of father figures, Razumov is appropriately sensitive to the narrator's delicate subversions. And Nathalie herself, when she gives the old Englishman Razumov's diary, blames the narrator for betraying her defenselessness to Razumov: "And while you read it, please remember that I *was* defenceless. . . . You'll find the very word written there [in the diary]," she whispered. "Well, it's true! I *was* defenceless—but perhaps you were able to see that for yourself" (p.260). The narrator is found out, but he and Nathalie part friends; and neither abandons his or her respective fictions or disavowals. She has suffered, but to no apparent purpose; and he has participated in the tale only to tell it without explicit awareness of his own collusions.

The narrator's complicity with Razumov, from behind the veil of friendship for Nathalie, makes him something of a conspirator himself—a pale version of the informant Razumov, or even of the faceless bureaucrat Mikulin. Thus, the apparently harmless language teacher is, as Kaplan explains, a spy. "[His] prying eyes read Razumov's private journal, [his] eavesdropping ears overhear Razumov's intimate revelation to Natalia, and [his] incessant voyeurism results in the comprehensive report about Geneva's Russian colony that constitutes the text of *Under Western Eyes*" ("CNO," p.108). Perhaps it is because of his own conspiratorial activities that the narrator is so interested in what happens to Mikulin. He tells us that Mikulin's efforts to reduce Razumov to a state functionary has not guaranteed his own secure place in the regime: "It seems that the savage autocracy, no more than the divine democracy, does not limit its diet exclusively to the bodies of its enemies. It devours its friends and servants as well" (*UWE*, p.212). The narrator is the only representative of "divine democracy" in the novel, and therefore this statement might be an indirect admission of guilt for his "indecent" dining on Russian experience. Yet, the greater irony of this claim lies in the fact that the distinction between "savage autocracy" and "divine democracy"—between Russian and European political experience—breaks down, and the narrator's own position is made insecure by this collapse of distinctions.

The narrator assumes that there is a center for him, a solid, pragmatic, and sane English "place"—as he calls it, the home of "staid lovers calmed by the possession of a conquered liberty" (*UWE*, p.113)—and hence a fixed, external point from which to observe and recount the Russian turmoil. However, he is himself ample evidence of the extent to which liberal decency is eroding. What the narrator finds most disconcerting about Russian culture is also true of himself. His claim that Russians over-spiritualize and fictionalize their true (base) motives is subverted by his effort to read them according to his own deceptive strategies of detachment (spying), those complicated surface fictions that mask his secret indulgence of autocratic scorn and quasi-erotic appropriation. Conrad thus represents the world through detached "Western eyes" only in the sense that the tale is told from the position of one who cannot mediate political and emotional life in any satisfactory way, and whose pretense of commitment (its fictionalization) displaces actual engagement with real social problems. Hence Conrad, consciously or not, depicts his liberal narrator as an impotent, increasingly spectatorial member of the prewar British political establishment. This establishment was itself confronted by increasingly disintegrative social extremes (radicalism and reaction), and was willing to enter into false friendships (for example, the Anglo-Russian pact of 1907) to protect, as Conrad puts it in "Autocracy and War," its "uneasy vanity" about its position in the world—and to do so without growing at all in "wisdom and self-knowledge" (p.145). However simplistic such a straightforward analogy might seem, the fact remains that the narrator *in his essential nature* recapitulates the conditions of leadership in Britain, as well as Conrad's disaffection with European politics. The narrator's safe English place is in this respect yet another ad hoc defensive gambit.

Though Conrad seems to subject his narrator to ironic critique, he still tells us in his "Author's Note" that the teacher of languages "is useful to the reader . . . in the way of comment"—presumably meaning that the narrator provides the Western perspective which, in turn, allows Conrad to claim impartiality while at the same time cordoning off Russian experience in its otherness. But the narrator's English neutrality is a pose rather than a position, in fact an equivocal deferral of all positions. And it is so because Conrad himself could no longer defend Western institutions for their intrinsic rationality and enlightenment. Indeed, proof of this claim is found not only in the narrator's statement about "divine democracy," but in Conrad's stark vision in "Autocracy and War" that "Il n'y a plus d'Europe" (Europe no longer exists). In effect, Conrad needed to make the argument about Russian difference, but he also had no real political stance from which to do so. Hence, the narrator's assumption of political safety and cultural difference is overdetermined by Conrad's need to claim these same things, and by his very real disenchantment with the West. Conrad at once identifies with and criticizes; in effect, he leaves himself no location that is not woven from the strands of a dangerous ambiguity, wherein all political places or affiliations become susceptible to subversion by his view of a world collapsing under the weight of vainglory and duplicitousness.

Psychobiographical Elaborations

Conrad offered his version of "Russia" as authentic. However, to the extent that the preceding psychosocial arguments have weight, it follows that

Conrad's novel was formed at least in part out of his enduring Polish antipathy toward Dostoevsky (the "passions" and "prejudices" that prevent Conrad's historical imagination from moving beyond Slavic ideological positions of the mid-nineteenth century), and in part out of his here-and-now consciousness of his European and British social context. The interconnected frames of "homo-duplex"—in effect, Conrad's Polish and English experience—dominate his novel. On these grounds *Under Western Eyes* is best thought of as Conrad's most markedly autobiographical work of fiction.

The impasse created by Haldin's being not an opposite to Razumov but an uncanny reflection of him, and by Conrad's having ironically condemned Razumov to suffer for the "confession" of affiliation that he never quite makes—this structure of melancholy ambivalence seems to have a specific fit with what is known of Conrad's early childhood, and of his circumstances at the time of composition. The fiction teaches us obliquely about Conrad's life, while the life itself, insofar as it might be interpreted at all, has the status of another text. Finding a version of the author's experience in his story, and interpreting suggestive biographical facts according to the framework of the psychological themes of that story, is itself an interpretive fiction, the object of which is to illuminate, integrate, and make relatively coherent the interpenetration of three equally valid narratives: literary representation; individual life; cultural moment.

Many readers have noted that in creating Razumov, Conrad drew heavily on his own background. Besides making the character a political conservative, Conrad depicted Razumov as an orphan, a victim of autocracy, a lonely exile, and a man haunted by a sense of having disowned ("betrayed") the revolutionary part of his heritage. Conrad also made Razumov a writer—not just of spy reports, but of a personal dairy. In Geneva, where his life is composed from lies and deceit, Razumov begins writing. As the original manuscript of the novel puts it, he begins "with an idea of serving a practical purpose of another kind of knowledge," and tries to fix "the knowledge of impulses, emotions, and thoughts altogether his own, of complex feelings on a background of sombre determination as if life were a book of black science which once opened must be read to the last of its futile and accursed pages" (MS, pp. 860-61). For Razumov, the mirror provided by self-narrative is primarily "futile and accursed" rather than therapeutic; and yet it somehow furthers the "practical"—purposeful, or even necessary—process of introspective truthfulness, a process that, once begun, becomes a bleak imperative. The writer is duty-bound to investigate and narrate; his futility and purposelessness are conjoined with a purpose and determination to look at and to read, as if fatally drawn to the sharpest edges of one's own despair. Conrad, I would argue, described himself here and then excised the self-description, presumably to divorce his own writing process from the "Russian" ill-being that infects Razumov and drives him to narrate himself.

Through excision of the above passage, Conrad distanced himself from his otherwise clear kinship with Razumov. But Conrad did so only after "the horrible nightmare of my long illness," the breakdown testifying to his deeply personal involvement in his "Russian" material.[20] It is important to recognize, however, that Conrad unconsciously signals his identification with Razumov's despair not just in the original draft, but also in the finished text.

In the Genevan part of the novel, Razumov twice formulates a passive suicidal wish. The first time Razumov conveys this desire is when, just after arriving in Geneva, he walks with the narrator in the city; the second elaboration comes when he begins writing in his diary. Traversing the streets and engaging in introductory conversation, both Razumov and the narrator find the city deplorably "banal," "artificial," and "puerile"—almost at fault for not having grasped the heavy trials of the émigrés (UWE, p. 199-201); and, after a time, they stop at a bridge to look down at the smooth current rushing below the arch. The old Englishman experiences "a dread of being suddenly snatched away" by the current's destructive force; but it "had a charm for Mr. Razumov," who "hung well over the parapet, as if captivated by the smooth rush of the blue water." The narrator comments on this captivation: had the water "flowed through Razumov's breast, it could not have washed away the accumulated bitterness the wrecking of his life had deposited there" (p. 137). Razumov's fantasy attraction to the cleansing power of death comes up again—and more insistently—when he is alone with his diary on a tiny island, "named after Jean Jacques Rousseau." He becomes transfixed by "the sound of water, the voice of the wind—completely foreign to human passions. All the other sounds of this earth brought contamination to the solitude of a soul" (pp. 201-02). The enveloping murmur releases Razumov from the world and from himself; and, without actually dying, he leaves behind a "contaminating" association with other humans, gaining for the moment an encompassing security. His negative narcissism would embrace death and then magically turn death back on itself, creating the temporary salvation of an elemental, passive state of fusion, and hence turning centripetal collapse into centrifugal expansion.

This theme of perfect isolation is later echoed in Razumov's confession, when he explains to Nathalie that he "suffers horribly, but [is] not in despair," and then tells the revolutionists that he has made himself "free from falsehood, from remorse—*independent of every single human being on this earth*" (*UWE*, pp. 250, 254, my emphasis). Even leaving aside what Razumov says, the "water scenes" show us that the fantasy of inviolability-in-solitude does indeed grow out of an overwhelming despair. On the one hand, Conrad's ironic argument against Dostoevsky is bolstered when Razumov confesses only to be rewarded with suffering. On the other hand, Razumov's incoherence about his own despair suggests that confession is meant to serve the expansiveness of a malignant narcissism. Thus, twice elaborating Razumov's thanatonic fantasy, Conrad configures an unconscious narcissistic wish that exceeds the conscious ideological boundaries that he has established for Razumov's character.

Conrad could not intellectually undermine the confessional structure of *Crime and Punishment* without at the same time having that text become for him what Christopher Bollas calls an "evocative object." An aesthetic composition, Bollas writes, can be used "to 'speak' our idiom through 'the syntax of self experience,'" or to evoke from its reader certain unconscious self-states.[21] We have seen Conrad's "syntax" of thanatonic desire before in *Lord Jim*. After a life of failure (and crime), Jim's ultimate act of courage is passively to receive Doramin's bullet, and in this way to realize a fantasy of inviolability (Jim proudly says, "Nothing can touch me!"). And similarly, Razumov passively longs for a state of "independent" or untouchable fullness that would provide a wished-for escape from shame, guilt, and ruin. Through Marlow's ambiguous narration in *Lord Jim*, Conrad defers assisting or describing any mourning of the significance of Jim's death to the common culture (of imperialism). In *Under Western Eyes*, however, the author postpones any meaningful reckoning with the "accumulated bitterness" of Razumov's life by interposing an ironic structure of crime and punishment that cannot be altered by confession, however passionate—a scornful irony that on one level takes aim at Dostoevsky, but on another wards off Conrad's own identification with Razumov's despair. This ironic structure veils Razumov's narcissistic withdrawal to the lap of injury and unmournable losses, where he is cradled but never comforted. In Razumov's fate there is the familiar puzzle of melancholia, the unfinished pain that Conrad always returns to but cannot solve.

Alongside Razumov's unresolved bitterness we sense Conrad's shadow. Indeed, the Genevan sections of *Under Western Eyes* telescope or condense no fewer than four biographical frames of reference. First, there is Conrad's conscious repudiation of Dostoevsky's Slavic spirituality.

Second, we find Conrad's affectively charged, often unconscious employ-
ment of Dostoevsky's text to conjure the private linkages of his own subjectivity. Third, there are the ghosts of subjectively tinged real-life events.
We recall the elements of the mid-life crisis that Conrad endured in
Geneva and Champel, the site of his ill-fated "water cure" (perhaps something dimly echoed in Razumov's fascination with a cleansing submission
to water). In 1908, struggling horribly with his manuscript in Geneva,
Conrad was 49, the age at which his father died. A period of deep concern
for his son Borys, the child brought close to death by a lung infection, preceded Conrad's own retreat into illness. We should remember also how
these elements reconnected Conrad with the sorrow of the Cracow years,
moving him to reenact Apollo Korzeniowski's death-bed despair and to
reinhabit (in the form of his overall state of being) the illnesses, and losses,
of his childhood. Last, there is Conrad's disillusionment with the idea or
myth of an "enlightened" Europe—first expressed in "Autocracy and War"
and then metonymically refigured in the "odious" city of Geneva. What
seems especially to have brought such disenchantment home to Conrad
(and into the novel) was his own Genevan struggle to reaffirm in *Under
Western Eyes* his carefully fashioned identity as an English writer, and to give
voice to his frustration, amplified over time, with both critics and friends
for rejecting that identity.

Of course Bollas is right that close work with an aesthetic text draws
personal elements into self-revealing collaboration with that text. Conrad's
engagement with Dostoevsky stands as an unusually fierce version of this
dialectic, constituting in fact a "collisional dialectic" (in Bollas's phrasing)
between Conrad's personal idiom and *Crime and Punishment*. Dostoevsky
unavoidably leads Conrad to the revenants of his inner experience, to Ewa
and Apollo Korzeniowski, and hence evokes in Conrad all the psychological constellations associated with the unmourned or the inadequately
mourned dead. To the extent that the terms of engagement with
Dostoevsky undermine psychic stability, Conrad has to lean on paternal
and cultural idealization for narcissistic support. In a sense, he is in the
Razumov-like position of idealizing the autocratic "fathers" who cripple
him, but the content of his idealization is nonetheless distinct from that of
his protagonist.

Conrad's most needed idealization was woven from the personal
mythology that grew up around the legend of Apollo's respectable "patriotism," and from reactionary nostalgia for monarchy, the paternalism of
"Autocracy and War." Lacking this, Conrad felt cheated of something precious. It is the precariousness (not the substance) of the paternal ideal,

then, that leaves Conrad vulnerable, just as Razumov is vulnerable, to the negative transcendence of a redemptive death-wish. And to the extent that Conrad's own melancholia generates the fantasy of negative transcendence, it does so in part as a stubborn, depressed rejoinder to Dostoevskian positive transcendence—to the narcissistic support that the Russian author finds in the all-loving Father of religious orthodoxy.

It would seem that the only means Conrad has of sustaining the fragile determination to neither transcend his melancholic attachment to the dead (inclusive of dead ideals) nor wholly surrender to deepest depression is to heap scorn on Razumov's fantasy of perfect unrelatedness. Neither transcendence nor its inversion offer Conrad any oxygen to breathe. We see this excess of irony most especially at the conclusion of the novel, in Razumov's post-confessional existence, when Conrad shows him as utterly unrelated (deaf) to the revolutionists who surround him, permanently crippled and reduced to a horrible dependency on Tekla. In effect, Conrad wards off the seductiveness of transient fantasies of merger-in-death by turning Razumov's end into a living hell, and hence defers the dangerous wish by placing its withered body into the care of a hopeless disenchantment. However, Conrad also conveys the terms of the impasse to which the dialectical collision with Dostoevsky leads him. The mean irony of Razumov's condition at novel's end represents both an intellectual counter to Dostoevsky's religious notion of positive transcendence and a psychic disavowal of Conrad's own susceptibility to negative transcendence. Conrad's ironic critique of Dostoevsky is overdetermined because death must be deferred, and the mode of deferral necessarily involves punishing the protagonist, who importantly resembles the authorial self. Though Conrad's irony allows him to disidentify with Razumov, the thematics of the character's journey toward a living death are largely Conrad's own.

Razumov's childhood is marked by a maternal absence that stains his life with illegitimacy and feelings of living invisibly, of being unacknowledged. He needs to root himself firmly in the realm of the father, and feels resourceless without such a paternal union. He therefore imagines a beneficent Prince K——, an image that bears no relation to the man himself. And when the "good" idealization fails to exorcise Haldin's ghost and the torment it inflicts, Razumov is forced to assimilate Haldin as an aspect of himself that must be confessed and punished. In the process, Razumov is undone, his massive bodily injuries standing as physical analogues for psychic helplessness, inner emptiness, and centripetal collapse. This is one form of Razumov's anguish: either he relates to an idealized Prince K—— and makes himself vulnerable to manipulation and abandonment, or he is condemned (and returned) to a maternal caretaker, with whom he shares only illness, sadness, and an obsessively simulated life that, in its isolation, also inadvertently simulates death.

Razumov's dilemma of being caught between maternal absence and paternal indifference is evoked by salient features of Conrad's childhood spent in exile. That Razumov is born illegitimate, and that he experiences his connection to the "motherland" in terms of lack ("inanimate, cold, inert, like a sullen, tragic mother hiding her face under a winding sheet")—these features seem intrinsic to Conrad's conscious portrayal of Russia as a forbidding absence, the social and political abyss ("Le Neant") of "Autocracy and War." However, Conrad's depiction of the absent motherland is overdetermined by his father's acute sense of Polish dispossession and homelessness (as Apollo put it, the Poles are "on our own soil—yet dispossessed,/ in our own homes—yet homeless!").[22] For Conrad, then, the anguish of losing his mother without the possibility of properly separating from her would most likely bind him unconsciously to the dead (but not *lost*) object, an attachment experienced in his depressive sense of a self weighed down by malediction. The phrase from the novel—"a sullen, tragic mother hiding her face under a winding sheet"—is thus doubly determined, for it is at once an expression of Conrad's identification with his father's sense of national loss, and of Conrad's love for his dead mother, memorialized in feelings of hurt and affliction.

Shaken to the core of his seven-year-old soul by the death of his mother, Conrad had most likely looked to Apollo with special intensity, and probably considerable ambivalence, for protection and empathic rescue, for a presence in which to anchor himself. Razumov's absolute need for Prince K— as an ideal father, and Razumov's experience of Prince K— as elaborated in terms of the polarities of "idealization" and "abandonment," both establish a fit between the psychological template of the novel and Conrad's psychological life.

By his actions, Apollo invited his son to see him in terms of alternating polarities of good and bad, rooted both in idealities and desecrations. While Ewa lived, she remained devoted to Apollo and his ideals, and the world beyond the family confirmed that Apollo had a heroic aspect. But at the same time, there was a stunning self-absorption in Apollo's commitment to martyrdom. We must remember that when a child is unable to modulate intensely ambivalent feelings toward his or her real father, and when the father himself is unavailable (or unable) to help the child begin to view the parent openly and sturdily as a whole figure, the child often will split the paternal image between an all-gratifying father and an ungratifying one,

with the "bad" version able suddenly and absolutely to displace the "good."
To escape subjection to or deprivation by the fantasied "bad" father, the
child often tries to take defensive refuge in the ideal; and when the image of
the idealized protector fails, as it must, the child, in disappointment, often
retreats to a position of guilt and self-doubt. In turn, the sense of vulnerability to the shame and abandonment called forth by the "bad" father amplifies the need for a robust idealized protector. And on and on.

The relation to the split paternal image represents a closed universe,
something we see most clearly in the conjunction between Conrad's
repeated expressions in his fiction of an unmitigated contempt for revolutionists, and his insistence that Apollo, the avowed Red conspirator, ought
not be regarded as indulging in (what was for Conrad) this dereliction.
That Conrad rigidly defined revolutionary activism as irresponsible glory-
seeking also suggests that he was reacting to his father's narcissism by denying it. The splitting of ambivalence was necessary for Conrad, not only in
order to ward off his destructive aggressivity and protect his father from it,
but also to escape depression over maternal loss and paternal unresponsiveness. Multiple defensive interests were thus served by the preservation
of an ideal image of the father, an image aligned with the dignity of
national duty and *excluding* the ignominy of revolutionary extremism and
martyrdom.

Prince K—, a "worldly ex-Guardsman and senator" and an "aristocratic and convinced father" (*UWE*, p. 213), might reasonably be interpreted as an avatar of what we have already seen as a pattern in Conrad's
work, namely, the recurrence of an ambivalently held, defensive paternal
idealization. Conrad images Prince K— as an aristocratic public man, but
one far removed from any revolutionary connections; and he portrays
Razumov as pursuing this ideal parent, whose imagined virtues warm
Razumov in a favorable glow, and allow him to dream of an illustrious personal future. What's more, we are shown how Razumov's cultural ideal of
unified leadership follows from his personal ideal of the aristocratic father.

When Haldin first appears in his rooms, Razumov makes desperately
clear to the revolutionist that they hold no political beliefs in common.
Razumov explains that the kind of leadership that Russia has lacked all
along—in "the travail of maturing destiny" and in the work of peace—is "a
will strong and one . . . a man—strong and one!" (*UWE*, p. 22). And when
hoping against all odds to extricate himself from his predicament, Razumov
returns to the idea of the rescuing Prince: "A senator, a dignitary, a great
personage, the very man—He!" (p.27). The movement of Razumov's
thought from "a man" to "the man," from the idea of "the autocrat of the

future" to that of the princely protector, suggests the equivalency between Razumov's ideological position and his psychological need.

Of course, the logic of Conrad's irony requires that we see how Razumov has made himself a pathetic victim of wishful thinking, of his own need for "paternal affection." And when Razumov comes to understand how the Prince has colluded in the predatory manipulations of officialdom, Razumov's faith in the imaginary father unravels. "[E]verything abandoned him—hope, courage, belief in himself, trust in men" (*UWE*, p. 210). Thus, having carefully constructed Razumov's paternal idealization, Conrad catalogs its collapse, and authorial irony toward the paternal ideal comes to replace the ideal itself.

Still, one should not overlook how Conrad has formulated Razumov's imaginary father in terms of the family-romance image of the parent-as-patriotic-aristocrat, an image of the paternal that we know had influence over Conrad. In addition, Conrad portrays Razumov's yearning for the paternal protector as the cornerstone of his "adherence to absolutism." When we look at this fictional representation of the psychological genesis of a reactionary ideological stance, parallels with Conrad's biography leap out. For Conrad holds a specific, discriminating relation to Apollo's beliefs, at once endorsing his father's secular faith in European institutions, and repudiating his eschatological vision of Poland's resurrection. And on the basis of this selective paternal identification, Conrad fashions his idealized view of the European monarch of "Autocracy and War": "the monarch of genius [who] puts himself at the head of a revolution without ceasing to be king" (p.135). It seems very clear that Conrad's ideology of the strong governing hand is rooted in archaic splitting and mythmaking.

In his depiction of Razumov's pursuit of an ideal Prince K—, Conrad seems to have been elaborating a version of his own childhood wish for a protector, an internalized image that falsified the actuality of paternal disregard—in effect, disguising the "neglect" that, as Apollo himself observed, marred his parenting of Konradek. Granted, it is an interpretation complicated by Conrad's irony toward Razumov, by the fact that Razumov is "abandoned by everything," including the paternal ideal. Perhaps Conrad views Razumov from the perspective of one who knows what it is to carry a desperate wish for a lost idealized parent, and how it feels to suffer the erosion of the defensive ideal that a neglectful father comes to evoke and embody. In other words, the lucidity of Conrad's disillusionments as an adult possibly allowed him to unravel Razumov's sad grandiosities. But there is more to it.

One must also take into account that Conrad's irony is overdetermined by his intellectual argument with Dostoevsky. Prince K—, one recalls, is also a figure from Dostoevsky's novel *Devils*; and Conrad has reworked the tangential political association between the Prince and Peter Verkhovensky in *Devils* into the all-important familial connection between the Prince and Razumov. If Dostoevsky's satirical assault on the Nihilists of the 1860s significantly depends on a contrast between the false ideals of the Nihilists and the true leadership of the Tsar, then Conrad's point, contra Dostoevsky, is that Razumov is destroyed precisely because of his idealization of an ever-false, ever-malign autocracy. With this overdetermination of irony in view, it becomes possible to offer a more comprehensive reading of Conrad's consciousness (or lack thereof) in relation to the textual representation of the paternal ideal.

Conrad, I believe, elaborates a personal sense of bereftness or "abandonment" in his portrayal of Razumov's loss of the imaginary father; but the contextualizing claim against Dostoevsky also allows Conrad to distance himself from any private psychological kinship with Razumov. As is true of Conrad's irony toward Razumov's quasi-suicidal fantasy of death-as-transcendence, so here irony toward the (loss of the) paternal ideal functionally allows Conrad to simultaneously negate Dostoevsky and misrecognize his own fundamental psychology. The one thing that Conrad cannot afford to be ironic about is his own irony, because while it provides a measure of saving buoyancy and distance in his fiction, it is also a substitute for the (fantasied) sustenance of a long-lived, often reinvoked or recollected ideal, now gone.

To say that Conrad is unconsciously bereft, much as Razumov is bereft, is not yet to explain Conrad's relation to Razumov's counterfeit existence as a spy and to his maimed condition at the end of the novel. These connections between author and character grow clearer when we view Razumov's dilemma according to his ambivalent connections to both Haldin and autocratic patriarchy. On the one hand, Haldin, the rebellious son, is an image of Razumov's parricidal hostility, and hence an image with which Razumov must and must not identify. But on the other, in order for Razumov to sacrifice his inverted double (Haldin)—thereby cutting off an essential part of himself in hopes of preserving his royalist self-image and credentials—he must submit to further self-alienation as an instrument badly used by indifferent autocratic patriarchy.

The meanings that Haldin holds for Conrad are doubled, and doubled again, coming in layers that contest each other where they overlap. Haldin resonates with the figure of Apollo as both a rebellious son (struggling against the bad patriarch, the Tsar) and the bad father that Apollo became as he hewed loyally to his revolutionist ideals. Moreover, in the

novel, Haldin becomes powerful for Razumov, first, as an agent—like a
parent—who makes one's fate, and later, as the victim of Razumov's hatred
and betrayal, the memorial "phantom" of what has been destroyed and that
persecutes for that destruction. In these respects, Haldin is like the unwelcome father who first imposes his grandiose design on an unwitting son
(innocently hiding, as Razumov hides, in shadowed isolation), and who
then returns to punish the son once the guilty betrayal is done. Haldin is
Conrad's symbolic representation of the trap of "bad" paternity. The conflation of father and son in Conrad's relation to Apollo positions Conrad in
asymmetrical relation to Razumov, but it is precisely because of the multiform quality of bad paternity in Conrad's experience of Apollo that
Razumov, no matter what he does, must betray both himself and his paternity (in one of the forms that Conrad constructs for it).

The unsolvable paradox of Conrad's paternal identification is
brought into relief by Apollo's politico-religious poem, "To My Son Born in
the 85th Year of Muscovite Oppression," an epistle marking the event of
Konradeck's christening.

> Baby, son, tell yourself
> You are without land, without love,
> Without country, without people, ,
> While *Poland*—your *Mother* is in her grave. ,
> For only your *Mother* is dead—and yet,
> She is your faith, your palm of martyrdom. . . .[23]

"To My Son" crucially makes Konrad's retrieval of his birthright dependent
on following "the palm of martyrdom," the catastrophic course set down
by Apollo himself. In effect, Apollo had always already co-opted the role
of the rebellious son, and conflated this role with his own discredited
paternity. Conrad could not escape identifying with his ambiguous father,
but he also could not fight Apollo's battles. As Conrad put it in a letter
to Garnett, the legacy of Polish resistance was hopelessly doomed, since
"We have been 'going in' [to battle] these last hundred years repeatedly, to
be knocked on the head only."[24] And it was his father's ill-advised bravery
or folly that Conrad projected onto the figure of Haldin in *Under Western
Eyes*, so that Apollo's delirious enthusiasms could be punished in the surrogate of the "Russian" other. However, when Conrad refused to adopt
Apollo's way, he positioned himself to betray not only his father (and
incurring the guilt that comes with such betrayal), but himself as well. The
odd consequence of Apollo's having sacrificed everything to rebel against

a hostile paternity (Tsardom) is that when Conrad rebels against his "bad" father, he also necessarily identifies with him, for they are both, in this aspect, rebellious sons. In refusing his father he only becomes more like him. In trying to establish autonomy from the paternal, to create a separate sense of being-in-oneself, Conrad got caught up in this paradox of double identification/disidentification, which his father had never shown him how to undo.

Apollo's absolutism left Conrad, as oedipal son, with two impossible alternatives: that of assuming the martyr's fate and so renouncing the self to appease the father; or that of aggressively asserting the self over and against the father and thus, in assuming the father's destructiveness, destroying one's own plotted course toward the unique freedoms of an adult self who has mourned and made himself whole. Instead, Conrad had to juggle his love and hate for the "bad" father. That is, he had to say "yes" and "no" at the same time to the same object, and thus to position himself in-between, in what André Green calls a paradoxical "negative refusal of choice." The untenable options of either identifying or disidentifying show us that the capacity for benign assertiveness, for unambivalent doing-in-the-world, was severely compromised by Apollo's legacy. It was partly in reaction to the fact that his earliest model of effective agency was maximalist, grandiose, and self-destructive, that Conrad's belief in his own capacity successfully to do was replaced by the doing and undoing of chronic ambivalence, where every positive exertion incurred the threat of loss, and every deferral carried with it feelings of inertia, inadequacy, and failure. By leaving Poland he sought to escape the psychological snares laid for him by his father; but to the extent that he could only leave but not mourn, Conrad was left to manage the paternal paradox by recreating it in various forms, by splitting it into parts, by exiling different dimensions of his relation to his father outside of himself (now one, now another), and by reworking the thematics of this ongoing struggle in the thematics of his fiction.

Apollo's legacy was the tangled nexus that structured Conrad's novelistic genius. For had Conrad been able to claim a benign sense of self-assertion, perhaps he would have been a political hack as a writer (certainly less morbid than Apollo, but sharing his taste for patriotic propaganda), or else an uncomplicated *romancier*, as Conrad oftentimes longed to be, with a flare for seafaring adventures. His decision at age 17 to follow the sea, and his subsequent decisions to become a naturalized English citizen and novelist, all show him pursuing sublimated routes away from the psychological dangers embedded in his relation with his father. Yet Conrad never seemed to be sufficiently valorized by his sublimatory acquisitions. Throughout his two lives as sailor (1878-1894) and novelist (1894-1924), Conrad saw his achievements only as evidence of a lack of deficiencies. He was often and easily dislodged from his sense of centeredness, existing, as Karl puts it, "in fits and starts"; and he fell at times into inertness, as if he were exhausted by his psychological captivity, unable to move forward to re-establish contact with his own spontaneity, yet unable to give up the struggle with his different fathers, whether it be in bitterness or longing.

Conrad, like Razumov, can neither entirely deny nor entirely avow oedipal hostility. However, Conrad suffers his dilemma not in relation to autocrats, but in relation to the revolutionary narcissist of his boyhood, the father, who, after his mother's death, was literally everything to the son. Conrad could find no way to heal the split between his two images of Apollo (the noble but unresponsive patriot, the morbidly narcissistic revolutionary), no way to surmount the massive ambivalence that made the split adaptive and necessary. Hence, his resemblance to Razumov is governed by the logic of his own despair. Idealization, or the defensive maintenance of the "good" father (the patriot), fails to ward off feelings of injury and abandonment. The resulting collapse of defensive idealization then leads either to tormented melancholy, or to a depressive inanition, as if he had been abandoned by his internal objects. Like his protagonist, Conrad sometimes lapsed into the vicious cycle common to melancholics—hatred toward the "bad" object; guilt for hating what one also loves, or fear for hating something so powerful; and feelings of being persecuted by the bad object, often accompanied by feelings of abjection or worthlessness. Unable to mourn Apollo's transgressions, Conrad was destined to perpetuate the paternal bond as it existed for him in childhood, and was given the task of finding a way to evade the psychological dangers of his relation to the father within. The psychological trajectory of *Under Western Eyes* suggests the form and quality of that strategic evasion, intended as it is to situate the reader in between the untenable options of identifying and disidentifying with an ambivalently held father. The tale also suggests, I think, how difficult it was for Conrad to keep his psychological balance on what now seemed to be a tightrope (ambivalence) stretched over a black, netless canyon (melancholy perdition).

Razumov must contend with two imperatives—to disavow the most immediate threat to his psychological survival (Haldin), and to repair his sense of psychological impoverishment in relation to what is left. To this end, Razumov is compelled to live on the borrowed narcissism of autocratic fathers. In turn, these fathers force Razumov into further self-alienation by using him as a spy. This counterfeit identity represents a psychologically false self, since for a time Razumov's compliance to the regime sustains in him the idea that, as an agent allied with scornful autocrats, he doesn't have "the soul of a slave." This helps him avoid awareness of his truer "slavish" dependency on (and injury by) the paternal. By concretizing Razumov's needful subterfuges in the counterfeit or double identity of the spy, and by placing him at the mercy of a "bad" paternity, Conrad creates a version of the situational irony in which he found himself due to his own false or compromised position in England at the time of writing *Under Western Eyes.* Conrad was stinging from critical reviews and from the calloused responses of friends (such as those of Wells and Garnett), which had charged him with impersonating a *real* British novelist, dismissing him as a peculiar kind of joke, a freakish Slav deceptively passing for an English man-of-letters. It cannot be overlooked how Conrad shares with Razumov a double identity, and how this shared identity is shaped by ambivalence toward cultural fathers, as well as by a scornful pride, a fragile narcissistic defense against the power of fathers to mortify sons.

There was an important convergence between Apollo and the paternal role British culture played in Conrad's life. If Conrad's desire to be acknowledged and affirmed by the reigning powers of the British literary establishment was also a re-expression of his wish to recover the archaic ideal of the "good" father, then the injury Conrad felt at the hands of friends and enemies alike could only have recalled for him Apollo's unresponsive paternity. And if Conrad had hoped that monarchical Britain would at last grant him a rightful place in the world, then the perception of his disenfranchisement would represent a double loss to Conrad as "homoduplex," as a man both English and Polish. The subversion of Conrad's Englishness would have evoked for him the terrible irony of having traduced Apollo's Polishness, but only with a renewed awareness that he in fact didn't belong anywhere—that his identity was a double imposture.

Razumov confesses his guilt for betraying Haldin and is destroyed; his thought is to "confess, go out—and perish." He is first punished by autocracy. The spy Nikita, an emissary or substitute figure of Razumov's bad paternity, castrates Razumov (for his Haldin-like refusal to serve) by delivering a "degrading blow" to Razumov's ear drums. The revolutionists unwittingly assist Nikita in carrying out autocracy's retribution against Razumov by flinging him helpless into the howling night. In partial fulfillment of the second part of his plan "to go out" and "to perish," Razumov is maimed by the tram; and as he lies crumpled on the pavement, his face is so "deathlike," we are told, that even mother Tekla, who takes "his head on her lap," must avoid looking at him (*UWE*, p. 256). But finally, rather than end Razumov's pain, Conrad augments and amplifies it, condemning Razumov to speak at others whom he hates and whom he cannot hear. A de facto member of a community he has not chosen to join, Razumov withers toward death, his final days patterned on a grim parody of reciprocity.

Though Razumov has in a sense invited oedipal retribution, Conrad gives us surplus cruelty, a prolongation of injury that, in the narrative coda, moves Razumov beyond mere punishment and into the thick pain of collapse, where he is maintained in a state of aliveness as if for the sole purpose of crushing his sentient need for "understanding." With such a conclusion, of course, Conrad is punctuating his argument with Dostoevsky, offering up an ironist's version of the matador's final sword-thrust to the old bull's heart. But in a wholly unironic sense Razumov's collapse and enforced residence in the alien camp follow from Conrad's own dilemma of being Apollo's Konradek, the son of a revolutionary martyr.

Conrad elaborates the psychic annulment lying in store for him were he even partially to avow guilt for aggression against an ambivalently held father. It is as if he were envisioning himself (by means of Razumov's biography) caught in a cycle of rage at the persecuting father, of guilt over the betrayal that rage represents, and of either punishment by the father or self-punishment inflicted in the father's stead. Only suffering can ease the tension between love and anger. And in this circle of rage, guilt, punishment, and pain (which mutates again into rage), Razumov is returned to Conrad's own original wound, to the absent space where the mother should be. It is a loss that the paternal relation cannot redress or help to mourn. In her place Conrad gives us Tekla, the absent mother made present—only now disfigured and weird, always there and yet never truly there, a blank textual figure for an unrepresentable object of bereavement.

The hopeless conclusion to Razumov's fictional biography gives a not-quite tragic ending to a story from Conrad's own childhood. (In this case, irony is tragedy deferred.) In it we find the unconscious emplotment of inner constellations—the dilemma of being caught between the dead mother and the abandoning father, and that of identifying and disidentifying with the bad father—that were most threatening to Conrad's stability. Kristeva has said in relation to the poet Gerard de Nerval that in Nerval's poetic life-writing, "the melancholy past does not pass." The same might be said of Conrad. Endeavoring nonetheless to escape this "melancholy past," Conrad ruthlessly *inflicts* irony on his protagonist. Irony is used as either a protest against self-loss or a means of taking in psychological oxygen; but in either case it is employed with the hope that we, as Conrad's readers, will rise above the intractable contradictions of felt experience, become irony's partner in our superiority to the fatedness of Razumov's madness as a son of "Russia," and hence collaborate in Conrad's prophylaxis.

* * * * *

Around the time of *Lord Jim*, Conrad defined his writerly vocation in this way: only in the writer's "verve" does life, this "barren struggle of contradictions," take on "the dignity of moral strife"; and all the while," our consciousness powerless but concerned [is] sitting enthroned like a melancholy parody of eternal wisdom above the dust of the contest."[25] If, by the time of the harrowing contest of *Under Western Eyes*, Conrad was himself this "barren struggle," then irony, the paradoxical invention of superiority from deprivation, was the ultimate parody of mastery, which Conrad defensively put into play when the dignity of moral strife was drained off by a relentless series of personal and professional crises. However much Conrad's intellectualizing had allowed him to control the artifice of the novel, it did not ensure his own psychological well being, which, it seems, could not be disentangled from the dark world of lost objects.

After writing the last words of the unrevised manuscript in January of 1910, Conrad suffered a complete breakdown. Jessie Conrad provides many details of her husband's illness, from his grave physical symptoms to his delirious ramblings. And Conrad's own letters, written after "coming back to the world" in mid-May, suggest madness and enervation. Conrad wrote toward the end of June: "I feel like a man returned from hell and look upon the very world of the living with dread."[26] According to the speculations of psychiatrist Bernard Meyer, a fever ushered in an "acute phase" of emotional disturbance, in which Conrad became paranoid and possibly delusional. This psychotic phase was followed by "a protracted phase of convalescence," lasting for three months, in which Conrad regained a semblance of health, but continued to experience "depression, inertia, and childish behavior." Emotional stresses, which had been intensifying for some time, outlasted physical invalidism. Hence, Meyer theorizes that "febrile illness" did not generate mental disturbance, but did "hasten to uncover a gathering emotional storm."[27]

Apparently, the full trauma erupted just after an argument over money. Conrad had labored slowly and fitfully for two years at *Under Western Eyes*, and had accrued a staggering financial debt to J. B. Pinker, his literary agent. Pinker stipulated that he would pay only £3 for every thousand words of completed manuscript, and then threatened the novelist with entirely ending their business arrangement. Conrad, at once highly resentful of his agent's unceremonious dismissal of him, yet agitated by the prospect of financial ruin, made a pilgrimage to Pinker's London office to try to patch things up. Their exchange quickly became heated. Furious, Conrad broke the back of a chair, then lapsed into incoherence; and an exasperated Pinker snapped that "he should speak English, if he could!"(Pinker in JC, p.373) Conrad altogether lost his composure—in part because Pinker had threatened him financially and insulted his Englishness, but also because both Pinker and Conrad anticipated that *Under Western Eyes* would be negatively received. Once again, Conrad's success or failure as an English novelist would be weighed on the scales of (possibly hostile) public feeling. Upon returning home from London, he was overcome by feverish delirium.

The episode in Pinker's office was the last of a series of disenchantments, frustrations, and injuries that had worked to subvert Conrad's fragile peace of mind. His biography from 1906 onward reads like one of his most pessimistic novels, and he, the protagonist, is subjected to serial distress: the dreadful vision of political and social instability and antagonism in Britain and in Europe; the disastrous trip to Montpellier and Geneva, punctuated by feelings of rejection and defeat; the disruption of family relations by serious illness and straitened finances; as well as the disappointed ideals, estranged friendships, and betrayals of homo-duplex, the double-man living between worlds, between selves. No single disturbance would have necessarily resulted in a complete breakdown.[28] However, Conrad experienced manifold losses: his social framework had shifted around him, depriving him of requisite communal affiliations and ideological supports; and his professional and personal agonies at midlife inevitably reawakened the bereavements of his childhood. Present losses evoked past ones, and he became overwhelmed by his inner burden of melancholy. Christopher Bollas, in a psychoanalytic study of trauma, observes that, when trauma prevents a person from articulating a unique sensibility, life assumes the quality of fatedness and in effect becomes governed by "a repetitive intrusion of fateful events." For the trauma-evolving person, life is defined by "the sense of [being] inside a structure imposed on the self rather than derived from it."[29] Bollas's description is apt, for in being captured by "a repetitive intrusion of fateful events," Conrad is at once isolated from others and cut off from himself.

Indeed, the portrait we have of Conrad in Pinker's office is of a person who feels dominated by circumstance without any means of redress. He had fallen into incomprehensibility, either speaking English incoherently, or lapsing into the language of his boyhood, Polish, or perhaps into some private language. When he thus lost contact with his interlocutor,

Conrad was alone. Pinker's failure to support the novel and then its desperate author probably drew Conrad back to the abandonments of his past, for such threats would have affected him, a man stripped of necessities, with the force of a Razumov-like marginalization. Beneath the betrayals of bad fathers, I would suggest, lay the pain of losing connection with human succor. Conrad was perhaps appealing to Pinker in the language (momentarily garbled by panic) his mother had once used to comfort him, to allay the signs of her illness, perhaps to make the quiet, unkeepable promises that dying mothers often make to beloved children. This is speculative to be sure, but it is also what people do when they are panicked. In a moment of extreme stress, Conrad was returned to the time, frozen in his consciousness, when love was lost.

According to Jessie Conrad's report, on his return to their cramped cottage in Aldington, Conrad was ill with a fever of 104°, and was also disoriented, mixing his "own language" with "fierce words of resentment against Mr. Pinker." The internal dialogue with Pinker suggests not just anger over money, but also shame. He declared: "Speak English . . . if I can . . .what does he call all I have written? I'll burn the whole damned . . ." He then trailed off "almost in a sob."[30] Conrad aligned Pinker with the persecutor in his internal drama, and Conrad himself became once again the deficient child, worthy only of parental abandonment. If Pinker thought he was a stupid Pole who failed properly to "speak English," then Conrad doubly affirmed the insult. He would, if only in thought, burn "the whole damned" manuscript of *Under Western Eyes*, or even "all that I have written." Moreover, Conrad was again remembering and identifying with his father at the time of his death, when Apollo had ritualized his own defeat by committing his papers and manuscripts to the fire.

The question directed at Pinker ("what does he call all I have written?") reveals Conrad's abiding belief that his personhood, which hangs always by a fine thread, is legitimated above all else by his identity as an English writer. If writing was Conrad's primary, if not his only, means of deferring what Jessie calls his "hypersensitivity," or his lack of trust in his own perdurability, then Conrad's loss of faith in his creativity, the spoiling of the imaginative energies of self-constitution, would make him especially susceptible to his inner burden of persecution. Indeed, his response to Pinker shows how suddenly Conrad's world became crowded with tormentors, and how "breakdown" was in fact a rupture in the protective envelop of creative expression, as well as a blurring of the already unstable boundary between primitive fantasy (such as Conrad's fear of absolute impoverishment) and the reality of his interactions with other people.

During the next days and nights Conrad chattered away in Polish. Jessie Conrad tells us that "his mind was evidently back in the past," and that he was "seriously and critically ill."

> Day and night I watched over him, fearful that if I turned my back he would escape from the room. I slept what little I could on the couch drawn across the only door. More than once I opened my eyes to find him tottering towards me in search of something he had dreamed of. . . .
>
> He seemed to breathe once when he should have done at least a dozen times, a cold heavy sweat came over him, and he lay on his back, faintly murmuring the words of the burial service. (JCC, p.144)

She also relates in a letter to *Blackwood's* editor David Meldrum that Conrad, though he lacked the capacity to work on the manuscript, had a desperate need to keep it by his side: "There is the M.S. complete but uncorrected and his fierce refusal to let even I touch it. It lays on a table at the foot of his bed and he lives mixed up in the scenes and holds converse with the characters."[31] Thus, *Under Western Eyes* courses through Conrad's delirium.

Before and during the years of the novel's composition, Conrad was in manifold ways unconsciously gathering himself, or being himself gathered, around evocations of the traumas that most profoundly shaped his sensibilities both as a person and as a writer; and this process was reflected and reconstructed in the writing process itself. And to an extent that was surely unintended, Conrad configured in the space of the novel the "inscape" of his own largely disavowed traumas, but without the defensive ballast of the positive personal and social ideals of his earlier work. *Under Western Eyes* then became the space of trauma, the intermediate space (between fantasy and reality) in which he relived the hazards and conflicts, the unfixable dilemmas, of his early life. Creativity had always provided the protections of irresolutely, equivocally named existence. However, in illness, the *symbolic* dimension of literary artifice was apparently lost, and the distance upon which subject and object depend was collapsed into the dimensionless indistinctions of the unconscious. Conrad was now literally "inside" his text, not dreaming at the limits of melancholy affect and meaning, but living amidst loss and death.

He "spoke all the time in Polish"; his "mind was back in the past" and "searching" for something; and, one night as he lay on his back, he was "faintly murmuring the words of the burial service" (JCC, pp. 142-44). Conrad, of course, had long ago rejected his father's Catholic religion, and even ridiculed it in *Under Western Eyes* through his atheistic dissection of Dostoevsky. But now, in his delirium, he mouthed the prayer for the dead, invoking the very religion that he had consciously and repeatedly disavowed. What does this tell us? One might see a merger with his parents here at the threshold of death, a return to the Catholic childhood in which Conrad's own grave illness (now and as a boy) is conflated with the deaths of both mother and father. Perhaps "the burial service" has a double aspect. Perhaps Conrad's mutterings reflect encryption in the intermediate space of trauma, where his illness becomes interchangeable with the illness of mother and father, and their deaths become interchangeable with his. He and they have come to reflect each other, as if in a mirror.

Conrad, as I have argued, needed to mourn his parents in order free himself from the burdens of the past, but was unable to do so. His creativity had allowed him endlessly to shift between his inability to mourn and his abiding need to mourn, between his unconscious complicity with the dark forces nested in his personal history and his struggle to overcome those same forces, and thereby to rid himself of an intolerable sense that something necessary was lacking in him and in the world. When the carefully interarticulated ambiguities of Conrad's creativity were spoiled and he was driven to wanting to burn his novels rather than write them, he could no longer psychologically balance himself in between the failure and the imperative to mourn. Conrad's mouthing of the requiem signals a self-position where loss had become a habitation, a dwelling, rather than an event or a moment that might be thought about, reworked, overcome. In the aftermath of writing *Under Western Eyes*, Conrad, the melancholy subject, had finally collapsed into his own dark objects, trapped there by the lightless gravity of a love that survived for him primarily through the power of a complicated, unsolvable sadness, and by his devotion to its endless re-expression.

Notes

Introduction

1. I use Fredric Jameon's organization of the field of psychohistory into older and newer models in "Imaginary and Symbolic in Lacan," but argue against Jameson's endorsement of Lacanianism by using his categories to make an opposite point. See "Imaginary and Symbolic in Lacan: Marxism, Psychoanalytic Criticism, and the Problem of the Subject," in *The Ideologies of Theory* (Minneapolis: U of Minnesota P, 1988).

2. Erik Erikson, *Young Man Luther* (New York: Norton, 1962); Jean Paul Sartre, *The Family Idiot*, trans. Carol Kaufman (Chicago: U of Chicago P, 1981).

3. Fred Weinstein and Gerald M. Platt contest Erikson on this point. See *Psychoanalytic Sociology: An Essay on the Interpretation of Historical Data and the Phenomena of Collective Behavior* (Baltimore: Johns Hopkins UP, 1973), pp. 65–66. All subsequent references to *Psychoanalytic Sociology* are cited parenthetically in the text with the abbreviation *PS*.

4. With this notion of relational subjectivity, I am not proposing "a method"—that is, a body of rules that when followed produces a particular kind of reading. Rather, I want to suggest that already-existing methods of psychoanalysis and ideology critique can be made hermeneutically consistent with each other, and hence can be used to map the complex interactions between the various contexts of an authorial situation.

5. Peter Homans, *The Ability to Mourn: Disillusionment and the Social Origins of Psychoanalysis* (Chicago: U of Chicago P, 1989), p. 230. All subsequent references will be cited parenthetically in the text with the abbreviation *ATM*.

6. Heinz Kohut, "Creativeness, Charisma, and Group Psychology: Reflections on the Self-Analysis of Freud," in *The Search for the Self: Selected Writings of Heinz Kohut, 1950–1978* (New York: International Universities P, 1978). Also see Didier Anzieu, *The Group and the Unconscious* (London: Routledge and Kegan Paul, 1984).

7. Conrad's representation of this problematic is especially timely given that, in England, many factory towns and key industries retained traditional systems of authority well into the 1880s. See Patrick Joyce, *Work, Society, and Politics: The Culture of the Factory in Later Victorian England* (New Brunswick: Rutgers UP, 1980).

8. Richard Rorty, *Contingency, Irony, and Solidarity* (Cambridge, England: Cambridge UP, 1989), p. 97. Paul Ricoeur gives a succinct description of the hermeneutical conception of the subject as "a being which discovers by the exegesis of [her] own life, that [she] is placed in being before [she] places and possesses [herself]." See *The Conflict of Interpretations: Essays in Hermeneutics* (Evanston: Northwestern UP, 1974), p.74.

9. Stephen A. Mitchell, *Relational Concepts in Psychoanalysis: An Integration* (Cambridge, MA: Harvard UP, 1988). All further references to this text will be cited parenthetically with the abbreviation *RCP.* Mitchell develops his integrative project in several later books. In addition, many other theorists are part of this movement toward either integrating the insights of British and American schools into a relational model, or rewriting existing models along more dialogical lines. Notable contributors include Jessica Benjamin, *The Bonds of Love* (New York: Pantheon, 1988); Roy Schafer, in several books, including *Retelling a Life: Narration and Dialogue in Psychoanalysis* (New York: Basic Books, 1992); Thomas Ogden, in several books, including *Subjects of Analysis* (New York: Jason Aronson, 1994); Charles Spezzano, *Affect in Psychoanalysis: A Clinical Synthesis* (Hillsdale, NJ: Analytic P, 1993). The journals *Psychoanalytic Dialogues* and *Contemporary Psychoanalysis* are important "relational" venues.

10. Lacan's psychoanalytic thinking deployed quasi-Heideggerian elements prior to "The Function and Field of Speech and Language in Psychoanalysis," the lecture in which structuralist views of language and culture became central to Lacan's developing conception of the symbolic. See his *Écrits* (New York: W.W. Norton, 1977), pp. 30–113. Peter Dews stresses the Heideggerian influence in Lacan's descriptions of the analysand's movement from "empty" to "full" speech (See *The Logics of Disintegration* [London: Verso, 1987], p. 67). But "full" analytic speech seems to rely on an assumption of transparency. Hence Lacan, in his continuing meditation on the signifier, had effectively moved from fullness to opacity, virtually bypassing the Gadamerian claim of the universality of interpretation, and of relative truthfulness within dialogue.

11. See Brett H. Clarke, "Hermeneutics and the 'Relational' Turn: Schafer, Ricoeur, Gadamer, and the Nature of Psychoanalytic Subjectivity," in

Psychoanalysis and Contemporary Thought, vol. 20, no. 1 (1997), pp. 3–68; Donnel B. Stern, "A Philosophy for the Embedded Analyst: Gadamer's Hermeneutics and the Social Paradigm of Psychoanalysis," in *Contemporary Psychoanalysis*, vol. 27 (1991), pp. 51–79; Louis A. Sass, "Humanism, Hermeneutics, and the Concept of the Human Subject," in *Hermeneutics and Psychological Theory*, ed. Stanley Messer, Louis A. Sass, Robert L. Woolfolk (New Brunswick, NJ: Rutgers UP, 1988), pp. 222–271.

12. Claude Lefort, "Outline of the Genesis of Ideology in Modern Societies," in *The Political Forms of Modern Society*, ed. John B. Thompson (Cambridge, MA: MIT UP, 1986), p. 191, pp. 206–07.

13. Cornelius Castoriadis, *The Imaginary Institution of Society*, trans. Kathleen Blamey (Cambridge, MA: MIT UP, 1987), pp. 145–49. All further references to this text will be cited parenthetically with the abbreviation *IS*.

14. Joel C. Weinsheimer uses the term "being in between" to explain Gadamer's idea. See *Gadamer's Hermeneutics: A Reading of Truth and Method* (New Haven, CN: Yale UP, 1985), pp. 236–37.

15. Bhabha uses his concept of "discursive liminality" throughout *The Location of Culture* (London and New York: Routledge, 1994).

Chapter 1

1. Joseph Conrad, "Letter to E. L. Sanderson" (May 3 1897), in *The Collected Letters of Joseph Conrad, Vol. 1*, eds. Frederick R. Karl and Lawrence Davies (Cambridge: Cambridge UP, 1983), p. 354.

2. Joseph Conrad, "Letter to R. B. Cunninghame Graham" (December 14 1897), in *Collected Letters Vol. 1*, pp. 422–23.

3. Albert Guerard, "The Nigger of the "Narcissus"," in *Conrad the Novelist* (Cambridge, MA: Harvard UP, 1958), pp. 100–25; Marvin Mudrick, "The Artist's Conscience," as quoted in Ian Watt, *Conrad in the Nineteenth Century* (Berkeley: U of California P, 1979), p. 102.

4. Ian Watt, *Conrad in the Nineteenth Century*, (Berkeley: U of California P, 1979), p. 102. All further references to this text are cited parenthetically with the abbreviation *CN*.

5. Robert Foulke, "Posture of Belief," in *The Nigger of the "Narcissus" : An Authoritative Text, Backgrounds and Sources, Reviews and Criticism*, ed. Robert Kimbrough (New York: W.W. Norton, 1979), p. 314.

6. William Bonney, *Thorns and Arabesques: Contexts for Conrad's Fiction* (Baltimore: Johns Hopkins UP, 1980), p.161. All further references to this text will be cited parenthetically with the abbreviation *TA*.

7. David Manicum, "True Lies/False Truths: Narrative Perspective and the Control of Ambiguity in *The Nigger of the "Narcissus"*," in *Conradiana* vol. 18, no. 2 (1986), pp. 105–18.

8. Marshall W. Alcorn, Jr., "Conrad and the Narcissistic Metaphysics of Morality," in *Conradiana* vol. 16, no. 2 (1984), pp. 103–23.

9. Lawrence Hawthorn, *Joseph Conrad: Narrative Technique and Ideological Commitment* (London: Edward Arnold P, 1990), p. 128. All further references to this text will be cited parenthetically with the abbreviation *NI*.

10. For an insightful discussion of the stereotype, see Bhabha, *The Location of Culture* (London and New York: Routledge, 1994), pp.66–91.

11. Terry Eagleton, *Criticism and Ideology: A Study in Marxist Literary Theory* (London: New Left Books, 1976), p.135.

12. David DeLaura, "Carlyle and Arnold: The Religious Issue," in *Carlyle Past and Present: A Collection of Essays*, ed. K. J. Fielding and Rodger L. Tarr (London: Vision P, 1976), p. 136. All further references to this essay will be cited in the text parenthetically with the abbreviation "CA".

13. James Clifford, *The Predicament of Culture, Twentieth-Century Ethnography, Literature, and Art* (Cambridge, MA: Harvard UP, 1988), p. 106.

14. George Eliot as quoted in ibid.

15. George Eliot, "Address to Working Men by Felix Holt," as quoted in Robert Young, *Darwin's Metaphor: Nature's Place in Victorian Culture* (Cambridge: Cambridge UP, 1985), pp. 193–94. All further references to Young's book will be cited parenthetically in the text with the abbreviation *DM*.

16. This idea is derived from Philip Dodd, "Englishness and the National Culture," and Robert Colls, "Englishness and the Political Culture," in *Englishness: Politics and Culture 1880–1920*, ed. Philip Dodd and Robert Colls (London: Croom Elm, 1986).

17. F. H. Bradley, "My Station and its Duties," in *Ethical Studies* (Oxford: Clarendon P, 1876), pp. 180–81.

18. Joseph Conrad, *The Nigger of the "Narcissus"*, ed. Robert Kimbrough (New York: W. W. Norton, 1979), p. 55. All further references to this work are cited parenthetically in the text with the abbreviation *NN*.

19. Joseph Conrad, "Letter to Marguerite Poradowska" (September 15 1891), in *Collected Letters, Vol. 1*, p. 95.

20. Joseph Conrad, "Letter to R. B. Cunninghame Graham" (December 20 1897), in *Collected Letters, Vol. 1*, p. 425.

21. Richard Harvey Brown, *Society as Text: Essays on Rhetoric, Reason, and Reality* (Chicago: U of Chicago P, 1987), p. 101.

22. Oswald Spengler, as quoted in Gertrude Himmelfarb, *Darwin and the Darwinian Revolution* (New York: W. W. Norton, 1959), p. 418.

23. Friedrich Nietzsche, *On the Genealogy of Morals* (New York: Vintage Books, 1969), p. 84.

24. Joseph Conrad, "Letter to R. B. Cunninghame Graham" (January 31 1898), in *Collected Letters, Vol. 2*, p. 30.

25. Joseph Conrad, "Letter to R. B. Cunninghame Graham" (December 14 1897), in *Collected Letters, Vol. 1*, p. 423.

26. Jeffrey Alexander, "The Dialectic of Individualism and Domination: Weber's Rationalization Theory and Beyond," in *Max Weber, Rationality,*

and Modernity, ed. Sam Whimster and Scott Lash (London: Allen and Unwin P, 1987), p. 195.

27. Joseph Conrad, "Autocracy and War," in *Notes on Life and Letters* (London: Dent and Company, 1921), p. 142.

28. Emile Durkheim, *The Division of Labor*, as quoted in Dominic LaCapra, *Emile Durkheim: Sociologist and Philosopher* (Chicago: U of Chicago P, 1972), p. 143.

29. Thomas Carlyle, *Past and Present* (Chicago: Henneberry Company, n.d.), pp. 164–65.

30. Conrad uses arresting images of the mortuary and the graveyard to describe the *Narcissus* (pp. 4, 18). This depiction of the ship as a space of death is exemplary of the confusions of Conrad's secular theodicy. The historical source for such imagery is almost certainly the reformist speeches of the M.P. from Derby, Samuel Plimsoll, who during the 1870s led the movement to unionize sailors. See Plimsoll as quoted by R. H. Thornton, *British Shipping* (Cambridge: Cambridge UP, 1939), p. 84. Though Conrad alludes to Plimsoll himself as an officious meddler, he still uses Plimsoll's imagery.

31. Both Guerard and Watt have debated the meaning of a nonsensical qualifying phrase that appeared in the third-person narrator's paeon to work (the beginning of chapter four) in the earliest editions of the tale. "Through the perfect wisdom of its grace they are not permitted to meditate upon the complicated and acrid savour of existence," was followed by the phrase, "lest they should remember and, perchance, regret the reward of a cup of inspiring bitterness, tasted so often, and so often withdrawn from their stiffening lips." The question, of course, is how can "existence" be repeatedly given as a "reward" and then "withdrawn"? (See Guerard, p. 232; Watt, pp. 97–8). But "existence" in the third-person narrator's reasoning is bound to work-as-salvation. The idea of the phrase seems to be that work, which entails the forgetting of our thwarted desires, allows us "the life," in effect, the "reward" in the theological sense of the word.

32. Georg Lukács, *History and Class Consciousness: Studies in Marxist Dialectics* (Cambridge, MA: MIT UP, 1968), p. 335.

33. Perry Meisel, *The Myth of the Modern: A Study in British Literature and Criticism* (New Haven, CN: Yale UP, 1987), p. 33.

34. Charles Masterman, *In Peril of Change* (New York: B. W. Huebsch, n.d.), pp. 305–06, p. 304, and p. xii.

35. This statement paraphrases Marshall Berman, *All That Is Solid Melts Into Air: The Experience Of Modernity* (New York: Penguin, 1988), p. 100.

36. C. H. Pearson, *National Life and Character. A Forecast*, as quoted in Colls, p. 48.

37. Michael Tausig, *Shamanism, Colonialism: A Study in Terror and Healing* (Chicago: U of Chicago P, 1987), p. 215.

38. Sandor Gilman, "On the Nexus of Blackness and Madness," in *Difference and Pathology: Stereotypes of Sexuality, Race, and Madness* (Ithaca, NY: Cornell UP, 1985), p. 141. For similar ideas of black decadence or

degeneracy see Christine Bolt, *Victorian Attitudes Toward Race* (London: Routledge, Kegan, Paul, 1971), p. 92.

39. Samuel Weber discusses how the subject identifies with the "violater" as the subject's "emissary " or "agent" in "Ambivalence, the Humanities and the Study of Literature," in *Institution and Interpretation* (Minneapolis: U of Minnesota P, 1987), p. 22.

40. Søren Kierkegaard, *Repetition*, trans. Howard and Edna Hong (Princeton, NJ: Princeton UP, 1983), pp. 314–15, 326.

41. Robert Hampson argues against psychoanalytic understandings of literature in general, and of Conrad in specific. But the result is that he completely misses how the crew, by means of projective identification, attributes "power" to James Wait. See *Joseph Conrad: Betrayal and Identity* (New York: St. Martin's P, 1992).

42. Peter Brooks, "The Idea of a Pyschoanalytic Literary Criticism," *Critical Inquiry* vol. 13, no. 12 (Winter, 1987), p. 340.

43. Roy Schafer, *A New Language for Psychoanalysis* (New Haven, CN: Yale UP, 1976), p. 45. All further references to this text are quoted parenthically with the abbreviation *NL*. This sort of psychological experience is also well described in Thomas Ogden's discussions of the paranoid-schizoid mode. See for example his *The Matrix of the Mind* (Northvale, NJ: Jason Aronson, 1986).

44. André Green, *The Tragic Effect* (Cambridge: Cambridge UP, 1969), p. 67.

45. Wilfred Bion, *Experiences in Groups and Other Papers* (New York: Basic Books, 1961), p. 121.

46. See Guerard, *Conrad the Novelist*, pp. 114–15; Robert Hampson virtually recites Guerard in *Betrayal and Identity*, p.105.

47. Roy Schafer, *The Analytic Attitude* (New York: Basic Books, 1983), p. 70.

48. D. W. Winnicott, *Playing and Reality* (London: Tavistock Publications, 1971). Versions of this idea appear in the work of Melanie Klein, Margaret Mahler, Otto Kernberg, Harry Guntrip, Jessica Benjamin, Thomas Ogden, and many other theorists/practitioners influenced by either object-relational or Kleinian thinking.

49. W. R. D. Fairbairn, "Psychoanalytic Studies of the Personality," as quoted in Morris Eagle, *Recent Developments in Psychoanalysis* (Cambridge, MA: Harvard UP, 1987), p.113.

50. André Green, *On Private Madness* (Madison,WI: International Universities P, 1986), p. 49. All further references to this text are quoted parenthetically with the abbreviation *OPM*.

51. See Morris N. Eagle, *Recent Developments in Psychoanalysis: A Critical Evaluation* (Cambridge, MA: Harvard UP), p. 188.

52. Jessica Benjamin, *The Bonds of Love: Psychoanalysis, Feminism, and the Problem of Domination* (New York: Pantheon, 1988), p. 41. See also Winnicott, *Playing and Reality* pp. 1–25.

53. Jane Flax, *Disputed Subjects: Essays on Psychoanalysis, Politics, and Philosophy* (London: Routledge, 1991), pp. 122–23.

54. See Green on symbolic mediation in *On Private Madness*, pp. 287–96; Thomas Ogden's discussion of Winnicott's "intersubjective subject" in Ogden's *Subjects of Analysis* (Northvale, NJ: Jason Aronson, 1994), pp. 33–60; and Sheldon Bach's discussion of sadomasochistic relations, the lack of symbolic internalizations, and the inability to mourn, in *The Language of Perversion and the Language of Love* (Northvale, NJ: Jason Aronson, 1994).

55. Allistoun's means of enforcing his authority is to take charge of Wait. On the one hand, Allistoun banishes Wait to his quarters for not working; but on the other, he tells his immediate subordinates in private that Wait needs to stay in his quarters because his death is imminent (*NN*, p. 78). Allistoun's pity for Wait comes at the expense of his truthfulness to the crew. Denying that Wait is ill, but accepting his refusal to work, allows Allistoun to avoid clarifying the crew's legitimate conflict with authority. And the sequestration, which seems to the men to give Allistoun control over Wait's death, enacts the crew's wish to be rid of (to kill) their persecutor, while allowing them to disavow this wish.

56. Conrad emphatically embodies and exorcises the crew's asocial tendencies in Donkin, the self-interested "labor organizer" and shiftless ruffian with no one below him on the social ledger except for Wait (*NN*, p.65, p.83, pp. 93–94). The text depends at crucial moments on using Wait and Donkin as scapegoats, and thus depends on the ideological translatability of domestic and colonial otherness. At the time of the mutiny, Donkin's punishment prevents the angry row from becoming outright rebellion. The crew is able to split Donkin off from Wait, allowing official authority to punish transgressive otherness in Donkin, while also continuing to indulge transgressive otherness in relation to Wait. And at the time of Wait's death, Donkin has a perverse communion with him, which acts out the crew's infantile narcissism. He feeds hungrily on biscuits stolen from Wait's trunk, and in the process, imagines that Wait dies for and in place of himself. Thus, Donkin shoulders the ignominy, and the rest of the crew is absolved by being absent from the scene.

57. René Girard, *Violence and the Sacred*, trans. Patrick Gregory (Baltimore: Johns Hopkins UP, 1972), p. 125.

58. Sigmund Freud, quoted in P. De Mare and R. Piper, "Larger Group Perspectives," in *The Individual and the Group*, vol. 1 (New York: Plenum P, 1982), p. 372.

Chapter 2

1. Ian Watt, *Conrad in the Nineteenth Century* (Berkeley: U of California P, 1979), p. 153. Further references to this work are cited in the text parenthetically with the abbreviation *CN*.

2. The structural relation of the "Preface" to the work itself, and the personally and historically situated nature of Conrad's aesthetic statements, are interpretive questions that few Conradians have considered in any depth. Some recent criticism, in fact, moves in an opposite formalist direction. For example, the whole point of Richard Ambrosini's discussion of the "Preface" is to concentrate on "the text itself" as "the author's statement of his control over the evolution of his art." Apart from seeming outdated, this iconic approach, which identifies master tropes and describes their masterful execution, routinizes a complicated text. See Richard Ambrosini, *Conrad's Fiction as Critical Discourse* (Cambridge: Cambridge UP, 1991), pp. 18–20.

3. Joseph Conrad, "Letter to Edward Garnett" (November 29 1896), in *Collected Letters, Vol. 1* ed. Frederick R. Karl and Lawrence Davies (Cambridge: Cambridge UP, 1983), p. 321.

4. Review of *The Nigger of the "Narcissus"*, in *London Daily Mail*, Demember 7 1897, in *The Nigger of the "Narcissus": Authoritative Text, Backgrounds and Sources, Reviews and Criticism*, ed. Richard Kimbrough (New York: W. W. Norton, 1979), p. 215.

5. Frederick R. Karl, *Joseph Conrad: The Three Lives* (New York: Farrar, Straus, and Giroux, 1979), p. 115. Further references to this work are cited in the text parenthetically with the abbreviation *JC*.

6. Joseph Conrad, "Letter to Edward Garnett" (January 10 1897), in *Collected Letters, Vol. 1*, p. 330.

7. Joseph Conrad, "Letter to Cunninghame Graham" (August 5 1897), in *Collected Letters, Vol. 1*, p. 370.

8. Joseph Conrad, "Letter to Edward Garnett" (October 5 1897), in *Collected Letters, Vol. 1*, p. 392.

9. See André Green, *On Private Madness* (Madison, WI: International Universities P, 1986), p. 82. All further references to this text are cited parenthetically with the abbreviation *OPM*.

10. Albert Guerard, "The Nigger of the 'Narcissus'," in *Conrad the Novelist* (Cambridge, MA: Harvard UP, 1958), p. 238.

11. Joseph Conrad, "Letter to E. L. Sanderson" (26 March 1897), in *Collected Letters, Vol. 1*, p. 347.

12. William Veeder, *Henry James—The Lessons of the Master: Popular Fiction and Personal Style in the Nineteenth Century* (Chicago: U of Chicago P, 1975), p. 16.

13. Mark Conroy, *Modernism and Authority: Strategies of Legitimation in Flaubert and Conrad* (Baltimore: Johns Hopkins UP, 1985), p. 88. All further references to this text are cited parenthetically with the abbreviation *MA*.

14. Joseph Conrad, "Preface" to *The Nigger of the "Narcissus"*, in *The Nigger of the "Narcissus": An Authoritiative Text, Backgrounds and Sources, Reviews and Criticism*, p.146. All further references are to this edition of the "Preface" and are cited parenthetically with the abbreviation *P*.

15. Julia Kristeva, *The Powers of Horror: An Essay on Abjection*, trans. Leon S. Roudiez (New York: Columbia UP, 1982), p. 45.

16. Terry Eagleton makes this point in *Criticism and Ideology: Study in Marxist Literary Theory* (London: New Left Books, 1976), p.135.

17. Joseph Conrad, "Letter to Edward Garnett" (September 16 1899), in *Collected Letters, Vol.* 2, p. 198.

18. In a letter (August 28 1897), Conrad thanks Garnett for suggesting the deletion ("Thanks many many times for your sympathetic and wise letter. . . . I do not care a fraction of a damn for the passage you have struck out"). Editors Karl and Davies have included the excised paragraph along with the letter to Garnett. See *Collected Letters, Vol.* 1, p. 377.

19. Ian Watt, "Conrad's 'Preface' to *'The Nigger of the 'Narcissus','*" in *The Nigger of the "Narcissus": An Authoritative Text, Backgrounds and Sources, Reviews and Criticism*, ed. Robert Kimbrough (New York: W.W. Norton, 1979), pp. 162–63. I cite this original version of Watt's analysis of the "Preface," because in *Conrad in the Nineteenth Century* Watt tells us that the slippage of the referent is unimportant, that Conrad wanted to end dramatically and simply misspoke himself. "The meaning was muddied, and Conrad ended the preface on a note of elevated but eventually obscure finality" (*CN*, p. 85).

Chapter 3

1. Howard Stein, "Cultural Change: Symbolic Object Loss and Restitutional Process," in *Psychoanalysis and Contemporary Thought*, vol. 8 (1985), p. 315.

2. Murray Krieger, *Visions of Extremity in Modern Literature, Vol. I* (Baltimore: Johns Hopkins UP, 1960), pp. 167–68.

3. Chris Bongie agrees with Eagleton's characterization of Conrad's so-called hypocrisy. See *Exotic Memories: Literature, Colonialism, and the Fin de Siècle* (Stanford: Stanford UP, 1991), p. 164.

4. Terry Eagleton, *Criticism and Ideology, A Study in Marxist Literary Theory* (London: New Left Books, 1976), p. 135.

5. Fredric Jameson, *The Political Unconscious* (Ithaca, NY: Cornell UP, 1981), pp. 266, 276. All further references to this text will be cited parenthetically with the abbreviation *TPU*.

6. Patrick Brantlinger, *Rule of Darkness: British Literature and Imperialism, 1830–1914* (Ithaca, NY: Cornell UP, 1988). All further references to this text are cited parenthetically with the abbreviation *RD*.

7. Joseph Conrad, *Lord Jim*, ed. Thomas Moser (New York: W. W. Norton, 1968), p. 212.

8. Edward W. Said, "Two Visions in *Heart of Darkness*," in *Culture and Imperialism* (New York: Vintage, 1994), pp. 25, 29.

9. Kaja Silverman, "Too Early/Too Late: Male Subjectivity and the Primal Scene," in *Male Subjectivity at the Margins* (New York: Routledge, 1992), pp. 158–62.

10.   The phrasing here is Chris Bongie's. See *Exotic Memories: Literature, Colonialism, and the Fin de Siècle* (Stanford: Stanford UP, 1991), p. 164. However, I use Bongie's phrasing to make a point about psychic contradiction, which is quite different from his emphasis on conscious "hypocrisy" or "duplicity." Further references to this text are cited parenthetically with the abbreviation *EM.*

11.   Franz Fanon, *Black Skins, White Masks* (New York: Grove P, 1967), p. 114.

12.   Gayatri Spivak, "Can the Subaltern Speak?," in *Marxism and the Interpretation of Culture* (Urbana: U of Illinois P, 1988), pp. 271–313.

13.   James Sturgis, "Britain and the New Imperialism," in *British Imperialism in the Nineteenth Century*, ed. C. C. Eldridge (New York: St. Martin's P, 1984), p. 95.

14.   Michael W. Doyle, *Empires* (Ithaca, NY: Cornell UP, 1986), p. 296.

15.   Benjamin Disraeli, "Speech at the Manchester Free Trade Hall"; quoted by Michael W. Doyle in *Empires*, p. 282.

16.   Lord Rosebery, "Speech to the Royal Colonial Institute" (March, 1893); quoted by Bernard Semmel in *Imperialism and Social Reform: English Social Thought, 1895–1914* (Cambridge, MA: Harvard UP, 1960), pp. 54–55.

17.   The paradox of the age was that, though Britain enormously expanded its territorial acquisitions, the expansion was largely defensive. To the degree that Britain became more aggressive, more bombastic in defense of its acquisitions, it was also troubled about its waning power, and pessimistic about the permanence of the Empire. See Eric Hobsbawm, *The Age of Empire* (New York: Pantheon Books, 1987), p. 75, hereafter cited parenthetically in text as *E*; Ronald Hyam, *Britain's Imperial Century: A Study of Empire and Expansion* (Cambridge: Cambridge UP, 1976), pp. 70–134; and Ronald Robinson and John Gallagher, with Alice Denny, *Africa and the Victorians* (London: Macmillan, 1973), p. 288.

18.   Ronald Hyam, *Britain's Imperial Century*, p. 93. All further references to this text will be cited parenthetically with the abbreviation *BIC.*

19.   Helmuth Stoecker, ed., *German Imperialism*, trans. Bernol Zollner (London: Hurst and Co., 1986), p. 209.

20.   Hannah Arendt, *The Origins of Totalitarianism*, sixth ed. (New York: Harcourt Brace Janovitch, 1979), p. 130. Arendt is perhaps the first to notice this contradiction in British imperialism. To my mind, Arendt persuasively argues that twentieth-century totalitarianism could have had its "origins" in modern imperialist trends.

21.   Jürgen Habermas, *Legitimation Crisis*, trans. Thomas McCarthy (Boston: Beacon P, 1973), p. 76.

22.   William Connolly, *Identity and Difference: Democratic Negotiations of Political Paradox* (Ithaca, NY: Cornell UP, 1991), p. 3.

23.   Andrew Roberts, "The Imperial Mind," in *The Colonial Moment in Africa: Essays in the Movement of Mind and Materials*, ed. Andrew Roberts (Cambridge: Cambridge UP, 1986), p. 42.

24.   Joseph Chamberlain, as quoted by Wolfgang Mock in "The Function

of Race in Imperialist Ideologies: The Example of Joseph Chamberlain," in *Nationalist and Racialist Movements in Britian and Germany before 1914*, ed. Paul Kennedy and Anthony Nicholls (Oxford: St. Anthony's/ Macmillan P, 1981), p. 201.

25. Philip Darby, *The Three Faces of Imperialism: British and American Approaches to Asia and Africa, 1870–1970* (New Haven, CT: Yale UP, 1987), p. 39. All further references to this text are cited parenthetically with the abbreviation *TFI*.

26. J. A. Hobson, *Imperialism* (London: Constable and Co., 1905), pp. 21, 114, 48. All further references to this text are cited parenthetically with the abbreviation *IM*. Vincent Pecora suggests that because Hobson, in *Imperialism*, sometimes uses the language of benevolent paternalism in arguing against the system, his text has already been anticipated and co-opted by that larger system of meaning. Pecora's overly deterministic explanation fails to account for history, namely, Hobson's political goal of reaching an audience very largely tuned off to doctrinaire condemnations of Empire. See Pecora's *Self and Form in Modern Narrative* (Baltimore: John's Hopkins, 1989), p. 136.

27. Rudyard Kipling, "The First Sailor," in *Humorous Tales* (London: McMillan Publishers, 1931; first published, 1891), p. 62.

28. George Orwell, "Rudyard Kipling," *Kipling and the Critics* (New York: New York UP, 1965), pp. 76–77.

29. Rudyard Kipling, *From Sea to Sea, Part I* (New York: Charles Scribner and Sons, 1907; first published, 1899), p. 282.

30. Julian Huxley, *Africa View* (1931); quoted by Andrew Roberts in "The Imperial Mind," p. 61.

31. John Buchan, *Prestor John*, as quoted by Andrew Roberts in "The Imperial Mind," p. 41.

32. Charles Steevens, as quoted in H. John Field, *Toward a Program of Imperial Life: Britain at the Turn of the Century* (Westport, CN: Greenwood P, 1982), pp. 187, 169.

33. David Cannadine, "The Context, Performance, and Meaning of Ritual: the British Monarchy and the Invention of Tradition, 1820–1977," in *The Invention of Tradition*, ed. Eric Hobsbawm and Terrence Ranger (Cambridge: Cambridge UP, 1983), p. 124.

34. Ryder Haggard, *She*, reprinted in *Three Adventure Novels* (New York: Dover P, 1951), pp. 153–54.

35. James Walvin, "Symbols of Moral Superiority: Middle-Class Morality in Britain and America, 1800–1920," in *Manliness and Morality*, ed. J. A. Mangan and James Walvin (New York: St. Martin's P, 1987), p. 251. All further references to essays in this text are cited parenthetically with the abbrevation *MM*.

36. William Booth, *In Darkest England and the Way Out* (London: Funk and Wagnalls, 1890), pp. 14–15.

37. In 1883, Beatrice Webb noted that the poor "know nothing of the

complexities of modern life," and have no "complicated motives." See Philip Dodd's essay "Englishness and the National Culture," in *Englishness: Politics and Culture, 1880–1920*, p. 9.

38. Rudyard Kipling, "The Pharoah and the Sergeant," in *Rudyard Kipling's Verse, Inclusive Edition* (London: Hodden and Stroughton, 1931; first published, 1897), p. 196.

39. J. A. Hobson, *The Psychology of Jingoism* (London: Grant Richards, 1901), p. 86. All further references to this text are cited parenthetically with the abbreviation *PJ*.

40. Peter Gay, "Liberalism and Regression," in *The Psychoanalytic Study of the Child*, vol. 37 (1982), p. 542.

41. Heinz Kohut, "Thoughts on Narcissism and Narcissistic Rage," in *Self-Psychology and the Humanities*, ed. Charles B. Strozier (New York: W. W. Norton and Co., 1985), p. 148.

42. L. T. Hobhouse, *Democracy and Reaction* (1904) as quoted in H. John Field, *Toward a Program of Imperial Life*, p. 212.

43. Michael Kimmel, "The Contemporary Crisis of Masculinity," in *The Making of Masculinities*, ed. Harry Brod (New York: Allen and Unwin, 1987), p. 149. Further references to this essay are cited parenthetically with the abbreviation "CC".

44. George Santayana, as quoted in Jeffrey Richards, "Manly Love and Victorian Society," in *Manliness and Morality*, p.106.

45. H. B. Gray, *Public Schools and the Empire* (no place or publisher given, 1913), pp. 176–77. All further references to this text will be cited parenthetically with the abbreviation *PS*.

46. Alexander Paterson, as quoted in Roger Hood, *Borstal Re-Assessed* (London: Heineman Educational Books Ltd., 1965), p. 105.

47. Here I borrow from Nancy Hartsock's view that Foucault's epistemology tends to undermine his politics. See "Foucault on Power: A Theory for Women," in *Feminism/Postmodernism*, ed. Linda J. Nicholson (New York: Routledge, 1990), p. 164.

48. C. R. Nevison, as quoted in J. A. Mangan, "Upper-Class Education," in *Manliness and Morality*, p. 143.

49. Rudyard Kipling, *Stalky and Co.* (London: McMillan, 1899), pp. 249–57. All further references to this work will appear parenthetically with the abbreviation *SAC*.

50. See Peter Blos, *On Adolescence: A Psychoanalytic Interpretation* (London: The Free P, 1962), p. 194 ; and Edith Jacobsen, "Adolescent Moods and the Remodeling of Psychic Structures in Adolescence," in *The Psychoanalytic Study of the Child*, vol.16, 1961, p. 165.

51. Lionel Trilling, "Kipling," in *Kipling and the Critics* (New York: New York UP, 1965) p. 93.

52. Peter Shabad, "Trauma and Innocence: From Childhood to Adulthood and Back Again," in *Contemporary Psychoanalysis*, vol. 33, no. 3 (1997), p. 365. Further references are cited parenthetically with the abbreviation "TI."

Chapter 4

1. Marshall Berman, *All That Is Solid Melts Into Air: The Experience of Modernity* (New York: Penguin, 1988), p. 111. All further references are cited parenthetically in the text with the abbreviation *ATIS*.

2. Joseph Conrad, *Lord Jim*, ed. Thomas Moser (New York: W. W. Norton, 1968), p. 138. All further references are cited parenthetically in the text with the abbreviation *LJ*.

3. Patrick Brantlinger, "Epilogue," in *The Rule of Darkness* (Ithaca, NY: Cornell UP, 1988), p. 257. All further references to this text are cited parenthetically with the abbreviation *RD*.

4. Fredric Jameson, "Romance and Reification: Plot Construction and Ideological Closure in Joseph Conrad," in *The Political Unconscious* (Ithaca, NY: Cornell UP, 1981), pp.206–281. All further references to this text are cited parenthetically with the abbreviation *TPU*.

5. Vincent Pecora,"The Sounding Empire: Conrad's *Heart of Darkness*," in *Self and Form in Modern Narrative* (Baltimore: John's Hopkins, 1989), pp.115–75. All further references to this text are cited parenthetically with the abbreviation *SF*.

6. Captain Brierly serves as Conrad's example of those who depend on rei-fied values that won't pass the test of experience. Like Jim, he is clearly vulnerable to "criminal weakness," and his suicide is a measure of how closely he identifies with Jim's shame (*LJ*, p. 36).

7. Tony E. Jackson makes a psychoanalytic point about Jim's being "uncanny" to the sailors of the merchant marine, in that he is an essen-tial part that has to be denied in order to preserve social identity. See Jackson's "Turning Into Modernism: *Lord Jim* and the Alteration of the Narrative Subject," in *Psychology and Literature*, vol. 39, no. 3, 1993, pp. 65–85.

8. Fred Weinstein and Gerald Platt, *Psychoanalytic Sociology: An Essay on the Interpretation of Historical Data and the Phenomena of Collective Behavior* (Baltimore: Johns Hopkins UP, 1973), p. 107.

9. Jim casts "us" in the light of a doubtful morality. At the same time, how-ever, "one of us" is for Conrad and Marlow an idealized and racially determined notion, roughly equivalent to ethnic and national solidar-ity. Jim shares in this essential Englishness, never betrays such national allegiances, and hence is more worthy than the most virtuous of his Malaysian counterparts.

10. John McClure, *Kipling and Conrad* (Cambridge: MA, Harvard UP, 1981), pp. 125–26.

11. Joseph Conrad, *Heart of Darkness*, ed. Richard Kimbrough (New York: W. W. Norton, 1988), pp. 27–28. All further references to this text are cited parenthetically with the abbreviation *HD*.

12. Benita Parry, *Conrad and Imperialism: Ideological Boundaries and Visionary Frontiers* (London: Macmillan P, 1983), p. 51.

13. Conradian Reynold Humphries interprets the conceptual puns in the novella as circumventing "the super ego of capitalism," which usefully contrasts with Pecora's view of irony as a strategy of power. See Humphries, "Taking the Figural Literally: Language and *Heart of Darkness*," in *Etudes Anglaises*, vol. 46, no. 1, 1993, pp. 18–31.

14. Charles Taylor makes this distinction between discourse conceived of from the beginning as *being* control versus its *becoming* so. See Taylor's "Foucault on Truth and Freedom," in *Foucault: A Critical Reader*, ed. David Couzens Hoy (Cambridge: Blackwell, 1986), p. 83.

15. John B. Thompson emphasizes this "lack of correlation" between individuals and a culturally designated subject position. See his *Studies in the Theory of Ideology* (Berkely: U of California P, 1984), pp. 92–93.

16. Conrad genders the cultural matrix of imperialism female, and shows that it is irreducibly split between the two sinister knitters of the trading company and the Intended and Marlow's Aunt, who profer blind support for the civilizing mission. This seems an intentional irony on Conrad's part, and is consistent with the idea that one's cultural group is psychically experienced as a maternal object. See, for example, Janine Chasseguet-Smirgel, *Sexuality and Mind* (New York: New York UP, 1986).

17. Michael Taussig, *Shaminism, Colonialism, and the Wild Man: A Study in Terror and Healing*(Chicago: U of Chicago P, 1987), p. 3.

18. Brantlinger argues that Conrad meant Kurtz to represent only the colonial atrocities in the Belgian Congo under Leopold. Marlow does conveniently distinguish between English and European imperialism (*HD*, 13), but also casts doubt on this distinction. Kurtz himself is "partly educated in England" (*HD*, p.50); and his insane pamphlet is based on the "sacred trust" of benevolent paternalism, a mystified defense used by both Leopold and the English. At the story's end the frame narrator says that the Thames "seemed to lead into the heart of an immense darkness" (*HD*, p. 76). The "immense" darkness seems finally to erase nationalist distinctions.

Chapter 5

1. Sigmund Freud, "Mourning and Melancholia," in *Standard Edition*, vol. XVI, trans. James Strachey (London: Hogarth P, 1957 ed.), p. 245.

2. Hanna Segal, "A Psychoanalytic Approach to Aesthetics," in *New Directions in Psychoanalysis*, ed. Klein, Heiman, and Money-Kyrle (London: Tavistock P, 1955), pp. 389–90. I am also indebted to C. Fred Alford's discussion of the Kleinian view of the relation between the mourning process and creative fantasy. See his *Melanie Klein and Critical Social Theory* (New Haven, CN: Yale UP, 1989), pp. 111–12.

3. Peter Homans, *The Ability to Mourn: Disillusionment and the Social Origins of*

Psychoanalysis, (Chicago: U of Chicago P, 1989) pp. 306–07, p. 335. All further references to this text are cited parethetically with the abbreviation *ATM*.

4. Christopher Bollas, *In the Shadow of the Object: Psychoanalysis of the Unthought Known* (New York: Columbia UP, 1987), p. 68 All further references to this text will be cited parenthetically with the abbreviation *TSO*.

5. Homi Bhabha, "Articulating the Archaic," in *The Location of Culture* (London and New York: Routledge, 1994), pp. 123–38.

6. Peter Brooks, *Reading for the Plot: Design and Intention in Narrative* (New York: Random House, 1985), p. 248. All further references to this text are cited parenthetically with the abbreviation *RFTP*.

7. The metaphor is apt in relation to Kurtz as an image of omnivorous starvation. According to Thomas Ogden, the bulimic is unwilling "to give up the tie to the internal object mother (represented in the bulimic symptomatology) sufficiently to make room for a third. This primitive tie to the internal object-mother is not at all comparable to the tie to the father or mother in the oedipal situation. The mother of bingeing and vomiting is the mother of bodily functions who is inseparable from oneself, whom one devours, mixes with one's blood, and then partially vomits out in order not to disappear into her or be taken over by her. This is the mother to whom the patient is conflictedly loyal, enslaved, and enmeshed" (*The Matrix of the Mind: Object Relations and the Psychoanalytic Dialogue* [Northvale, NJ: Jason Aronson, 1990] pp. 126–27).

   Kimberly J. Devlin interprets Kurtz using Lacan's premise that the ego is determined by "the gaze" of the other. Her unilateral focus on how Kurtz is produced by others fails to capture the distinctiveness of Kurtz's megalomania. See "The Gaze in *Heart of Darkness*: A Symptomological Reading," in *Modern Fiction Studies*, vol. 40, no. 4, 1994, pp. 713–33.

8. Judith Lewis Herman, *Trauma and Recovery: The Aftermath of Violence from Domestic Abuse to Political Terror* (New York: Harper Collins, 1992), p. 178. All further references to this text will be cited parenthetically with the abbreviation *TR*.

9. André Green, *On Private Madness* (Madison,WI: International Universities P, 1986), p. 291. Green's remarks are in the context of a discussion of Winnicott's and Bion's insights into the negative relationship, induced by developmental trauma, which an infant can form with an absent or psychically dead object.

10. Edward Said, *Culture and Imperialism* (New York:Vintage P, 1994), p. 23.

11. Catherine Rising uses Kohut's view of healthy narcissism to read Marlow; however, she misapplies Kohut by failing to see the fault-lines indicative of self-dissociation in the storyteller. See her "Conrad and Kohut: Development Demystified," in *Conradiana*, vol. 25, no. 3, 1993, pp. 207–19.

12. Joseph Conrad, "Letter to Cunninghame Graham" (February 8 1899), in *Joseph Conrad's Letters to R.B. Cunninghame Graham*, ed. Credic Watts (Cambridge: Cambridge UP, 1969), p. 117.

13. Robert Emde,"The Prerepresentational Self and Its Affective Core," in *The Psychoanalytic Study of the Child*, vol. 38 (1983), p. 180. In ways similar, Thomas Ogden theorizes a dialectical relationship between positions or modes of experience (autistic-contiguous, paranoid-schizoid, dePive) that coexist from early infancy onward, and whose shifting balances contribute to the mood-texture and rythmicity of early self-states. See his *Subjects of Analysis* (Northvale, NJ: Jason Aronson), 1994, and *Reverie and Interpretation* (Northvale, NJ: Jason Aronson), 1997. All further references to Ogden's *Subjects of Analysis* will be cited in the text parenthetically with the abbreviation *SA*.

14. Joseph Conrad, "Letter to David Meldrum" (19 May 1900), in *The Collected Letters, Vol.2*, ed. Frederick R. Karl and Lawrence Davies, p. 271.

15. Joseph Conrad, "Letter to Cunninghame Graham" (January 23 1898), in *Joseph Conrad's Letters to Cunninghame Graham*, p. 68.

16. Authorial confusion about the anxieties "so characteristic of our civilization" inevitably raises questions about Jameson's idea of the novel, namely, that it's focus on "the individual's [that is, on Jim's] struggle with fear and courage" skirts the "real social issue" of Jim as cultural exemplar (*TPU*, p.264). But Jim's cowardice and suicidal bravery is what makes him "a social example." The problem is not Conrad's use of individual character psychology to make the critical point about the culture, but rather his failure to consistently foreground the central dialectic between *psychic* struggle and *social* lies.

17. Thomas Ogden, *The Primitive Edge of Experience* (Northvale, NJ: Jason Aronson, 1989), p. 28. All further references to this text are cited parethetically with the abbreviation *TPE*.

18. Julia Kristeva, *Black Sun: DePion and Melancholia*, trans. Leon S. Roudiez (New York: Columbia UP, 1989), p. 73.

19. I am indebted to Kristeva's *Black Sun* (p.147) for the phrase, "through the uncertainty of naming," which I use to describe Conrad's authorial position.

Chapter 6

1. André Green,"The Unbinding Process," in *On Private Madness* (Madison, WI: International Universities P, 1986), p. 342.

2. *Nostromo* again brings into relief Conrad's ambiguous vision of imperialism. The novel's most heroic figures, Gould and Nostromo (both of whom in various ways "rescue" the new state of Sulaco from chaos), are frauds, driven only by a single-minded pursuit of silver; however, their very failures suggest, as Edward Said puts it, that Conrad searches for

"a superior man, a man who . . . compels history" (see *Beginnings: Intention and Method* [New York: Basic Books, 1975], p.123). *Nostromo* is similar to *Heart of Darkness* in that, in both, disillusioning recognition leads to nostalgic longing, to a Conradian wavering between lethal emptiness and a redemptive paternal ideal. This irresolution is, as I have argued, created by Conrad's inability to mourn the losses entailed by disenchantment, so that the work of thinking through the imperialist version of reality might become the basis for the recovery of a more humane form of life.

3. Conrad, "Author's Note," *The Secret Agent* (New York: Doubleday Anchor, 1953), p. 9. All further references to *The Secret Agent* are cited parenthetically with the abbreviation *SA* .

4. Conrad, "Autocracy and War," in *Notes on Life and Letters* (London: Dent, 1921), p. 149. All further references to "Autocracy and War" are taken from this edition, and will be cited parenthetically with the abbreviation "AW".

5. I am indebted to Peter Homan's observation that "irony is the trope of mourning or, rather, of the inability to mourn." See *The Ability to Mourn: Disillusionment and the Social Origins of Psychoanalysis*, (Chicago: U of Chicago P, 1989) p. 268.

6. Much has been written about the relation between Conrad's childhood and *Under Western Eyes*, but my study is innovative in attempting to show the interplay between the social and interpersonal "present" and the social and interpersonal "past." Standard criticism connecting the biography to the novel includes the following: Jocelyn Baines, *Joseph Conrad: A Critical Biography* (New York: McGraw Hill, 1960), pp. 360–373. Elizabeth Knapp Hay, *The Political Novels of Joseph Conrad* (Chicago: U of Chicago P, 1963); Zdzislaw Najder, *Joseph Conrad: A Chronicle* (New Brunswick, NJ: Rutgers UP, 1983), pp. 351–364; *Conrad: A Commemoration*, ed. Norman Sherry (London: McMillan, 1976), which includes Edward Crankshaw, "Conrad and Ideology," and Andreas Buzja, "Conrad and Dostoevksy." A special issue of *Conradiana* (vol. 12, 1980) includes Jeffrey Berman, "Introduction," pp. 3–12, and Bernard C. Meyer, "Conrad and the Russians," pp. 13–23. Also see L. R. Lewitter, "Conrad, Dostoevsky, and the Russo-Polish Antagonism," *Modern Language Review*, vol. 79 (1984), pp. 653–663.

7. George L. Bernstein, *Liberalism and Liberal Politics in Edwardian England* (Boston: Allen and Unwin, 1986), p. 200. All further references to this text are cited parenthetically with the abbreviation *LLP*.

8. J. A. Hobson, *Imperialism* (London: Constable and Co., 1905), pp. 143–44.

9. Historians who emphasize the unity and evolutionary potential of prewar liberalism include Peter Weiler, *The New Liberalism* (New York: Garland, 1982); Kenneth O. Morgan, *The Age of Lloyd George* (London: George Allen and Unwin, 1971), hereafter cited in text parenthetically

as *ALG*; J. B. Priestly, *The Edwardians* (London: Heinemann,1970); and
A. J. P. Taylor, *English History 1914–1945* (Oxford: Clarendon P, 1965).
Also see Taylor's "Prologue," in *Edwardian England*, ed. Donald Read
(New Brunswick: Rutgers UP, 1982). Some of those who emphasize
conflict are Anthony Arblaster, *The Rise and Decline of Western Liberalism*
(London: Basil Blackwell,1989), p. 291; George L. Bernstein, *Liberalism
and Liberal Politics in Edwardian England* (Boston: Allen Unwin, 1986); Alan
O'Day, "Introduction," in *The Edwardian Age*, ed. Alan O'Day (London:
MacMillan, 1979); and Robert Scally, *The Origins of the Lloyd George
Coalition* (Princeton, NJ: Princeton UP, 1975).

10. Robert Scally, *The Origins of the Lloyd George Coalition*, p. 11. All further
references to this text are cited parenthetically with the abbreviation
OLGC.

11. "The National Health Bill," *Nation*, IX (May 13 1911), p. 240.

12. Hobson defines the new liberalism as differing from the old "in that it
envisages more clearly the need for important economic reform, aiming to give a positive significance to the 'equality' which figures in the
democratic triad of liberaty, equality, and fraternity." *Confessions of an
Economic Heretic* (London, 1938), p. 53.

13. "The State and Unemployment," *Nation*, II (March 14 1908), p. 863.

14. Paul Thompson, *Socialists, Liberals, and Labour: The Struggle for London
1885–1914* (London: Routledge and Kegan Paul, 1967), p. 170.

15. Walter Kendall, *The Revolutionary Movement in Britain 1900–1921* (London:
Morrison and Gibb, 1969), pp. 27, 26.

16. David Lloyd George, "Memorandum on the Formation of a Coalition"
(August 17, 1910), Appendix B, "The Liberals in Power," in *The Age of
Lloyd George*, pp. 150–156.

17. G. B. Shaw, *Fabianism and the Empire: A Manifesto of the Fabian Society*
(London: Grant Richards, 1900).

18. G. R. Searle discusses the Webbs' authoritarian proposals in *The Quest
for National Efficiency: A Study in British Politics and Political Thought*
(Berkeley: U of California P, 1971), pp. 241–42.

19. H. G. Wells, *Anticipations*, 1st ed., 1902 (London, 1914), pp. 250, 146.
All further references to this text are cited parenthetically with the
abbreviation *A*.

20. Alfred Milner, *The Nation and the Empire* (London: Constable and Co.,
1913), p. 250.

21. J. L. Garvin, *The Observer*, May 7, 1911.

22. J. L. Garvin, "Memo to Sandars" (November 29, December 1, 1909),
"Appendix A" in *The Lloyd George Coalition*, pp. 371–374.

23. Northrop Frye, *The Anatomy of Criticism: Four Essays* (Princeton, NJ:
Princeton UP, 1957), pp. 238–39.

24. Hayden White, *Metahistory: The Historical Imagination in Nineteenth-Century
Europe* (Baltimore: Johns Hopkins UP, 1973), p. 232.

25. John Galsworthy, "Review of *The Secret Agent*," *Fortnightly Review* (April

1908), in Frederick R. Karl, *Joseph Conrad: The Three Lives* (New York: Farrar, Straus, and Giroux, 1979), p. 627.

26. Anthony Winner reads the novel's irony as a compromise formation between being struck dumb by human calamity and seeking to protect ourselves from it ("The Secret Agent: The Irony of Home Truths," in *Culture and Irony: Studies in Joseph Conrad's Major Novels* [Charlottesville: U of Virginia, 1988], p. 76). In contrast, Paul B. Armstrong sees this same irony as educative. For him, it brings home to the reader the moral and political dangers of social condescension (the "will to power" of irony), but nonetheless endows unmediated sympathy with requisite distance ("The Politics of Irony in Reading Conrad," in *Conradiana*, vol. 26 , no. 2, 1994, p. 92). Both critics thus focus on the difficult, if not contradictory, relation in the novel between positions of detachment and fellow-feeling. However, Winner, I think, better conveys the reader's experience of capitivity when immersed in the text.

27. Martin Ray, "Conrad, Wells, and *The Secret Agent*: Paying Old Debts and Settling Old Scores," in *Modern Language Review*, vol. 83, no. 3 (1986), p. 561.

28. Frederick R. Karl, *Joseph Conrad: The Three Lives* (New York: Farrar, Straus, and Giroux, 1979), p. 606. All further references to this text will be cited parenthetically with the abbreviation *JCTL.*

29. Cedric T. Watts, "Introduction," in *Joseph Conrad's Letters to R. B. Cunninghame Graham* (London: Cambridge UP, 1969), p. 25.

30. Joseph Conrad, "Letter to Spiridion Kliszczewski" (December 1885), in *Collected Letters, Vol.1*, p. 17.

31. Terry Eagleton, *Criticism and Ideology: A Study in Marxist Literary Theory* (London: New Left Books, 1976), pp. 138–40.

32. In a letter to Cunninghame Graham, dated February 16, 1905, Conrad denounces the techno-pastoral of Shaw and Wells, and pits "folly" (what the novel exPes as Vladimir's "absurd ferocity ") against scientific reformism. "The stodgy sun of the future . . . will rise—it will indeed—to throw its sanitary light upon a dull world of perfected municipalities and WC's sans peur et sans reproche. The grave of individual temperaments is being dug by GBS and HGW with hopeful industry. Finita la commedia! Well they may do much but for the saving of the universe I put my faith in the power of folly." *Joseph Conrad's Letters to R.B. Cunninghame Graham*, pp. 161–62.

33. H. G. Wells, *A Modern Utopia* (London: Chapman and Hall, 1905), pp. 143–44.

34. Jessie Conrad, *Joseph Conrad and His Circle* (London: Jarrolds, 1925), p. 122. All further references to this text will be cited parenthetically with the abbreviation *JCC.*

35. Jeffrey Meyers, *Joseph Conrad: A Biography* (New York: Charles Scribner's Sons, 1991), p. 236. All further references to this text will be cited parenthetically with the abbreviation *JCB.*

36.   Bernard C. Meyer, *Joseph Conrad: A Psychoanalytic Biography* (Princeton, NJ: Princeton UP, 1967), p. 126, fn. p. 128. All further references to this text will be cited parenthetically with the abbreviation *JCPB*.

37.   Apollo Korzeniowski, "Letter to Karol and Aniela Zagorski" (1862), in Frederick R. Karl, *Joseph Conrad: The Three Lives*, pp. 51–52.

38.   Joseph Conrad, *A Personal Record* (Marlboro, VT: Marlboro P, 1982, first ed. 1908), pp. 48–49.

39.   Apollo Korzeniowski, "Letter to Kazimierz Kaszewski" (February 26, 1865), quoted in *Joseph Conrad: A Biography*, p. 22. Meyers offers a new translation of this letter, which I believe communicates Apollo's despair and helplessness with more force than does the original translation by Jocelyn Baines, *Joseph Conrad: A Critical Biography*, p. 16.

40.   Gustav Morf, *The Polish Shades and Ghosts of Joseph Conrad* (New York: Astra, 1976), pp. 30–31.

41.   Apollo Korzeniowski, November 1866, in *Conrad Under Familial Eyes*, ed. Zdzislaw Najder (London: Cambridge UP, 1983), p. 105.

42.   Joseph Conrad, "Poland Revisited," in *Notes on Life and Letters*, p. 224, pp. 225–26.

43.   John Bowlby, *Loss, Sadness and Depression* (New York: Basic Books, 1980), p. 15. All further references to this text will be cited parenthetically with the abbreviation *LSD*.

44.   In her book *No Voice is Ever Wholly Lost* [(New York: Simon and Schuster, 1995), pp. 52–54], psychoanalyst Louise J. Kaplan offers detailed descriptions of many of the contradictory thoughts and perplexing fantasies aroused for a child by the death of a parent.

45.   There is some controversy over whether or not children are able to mourn. More recent studies such as John Bowlby's or Louise Kaplan's (see note 44) argue that, despite certain limitations, children do engage in some version of adult grieving. In contrast, Martha Wolfenstein argues that children always avoid feelings of grief and deny the finality of loss. This claim comes dangerously close to universalizing pathology in children who lose a parent; however, Wolfenstein also argues that children often adaptively substitute for mourning by transferring love (without sadness and in a wholesale manner) from the lost parent to an acceptable parental surrogate. I have included Wolfenstein's idea of the child's transfer of love. See her "How is Mourning Possible?," in *The Psychoanalytic Study of the Child*, vol. 21 (1966), and "Loss, Rage, and Repetition," in *The Psychoanalytic Study of the Child*, vol. 24 (1969).

        Some formal psychiatric studies of children who have lost a parent suggest that the adequacy and availability of the surviving parent are highly determinative of later adult pathology. See Alan Breier et al, "Early Parental Loss and Development of Adult Psychopathology," in *Archives of General Psychiatry*, vol. 45 (Nov. 1988), pp. 987–993.

46.   Roy Schafer, *The Analytic Attitude* (New York: Basic Books, 1980), p. 119.

47. Peter Shabad, "Trauma and Innocence: From Childhood to Adulthood and Back Again," in *Contemporary Psychoanalysis*, vol. 33, no 3 (1997), pp. 354–55.
48. Julia Kristeva, *Black Sun: Depression and Melancholia*, trans. Leon S. Roudiez (New York: Columbia UP, 1989), p. 196.
49. Ralph E. Matlaw, "Dostoevsky and Conrad's Political Novels," in *American Contributions to the Fifth International Congress of Slavists [1963]*, vol. 2 (The Hague: Mouton, 1963), pp. 213–231. For more recent confirmation of Conrad's reading of Dostoevsky, see Keith Carabine, "Conrad, Apollo Korzeniowski, and Dostoevsky," *Conradiana*, vol. 28, no. 1, 1996, pp. 3–25.
50. Fyodor Dostoevsky, *Crime and Punishment*, trans. Richard Pevear and Larissa Volohonsky (New York: Vintage, 1993), pp. 55, 58.

Chapter 7

1. On Galsworthy, see Samuel Hynes, *The Edwardian Turn of Mind* (Princeton, NJ: Princeton UP, 1968), p. 83; on Wells, see Robert Scally, *The Lloyd George Coalition* (Princeton, NJ: Princeton UP, 1975), pp. 225–26, p. 246, and David C. Smith, *H.G. Wells* (New Haven, CN: Yale UP, 1986), pp. 43–49. Further references to Smith's *H. G. Wells* are cited in text parenthetically with the abbreviation *HGW*.
2. Joseph Conrad, "Letter to H. G. Wells" (September 25 1908), in *Collected Letters*, ed. Frederick R. Karl and Lawrence Davies (Cambridge: Cambridge UP, 1983), p. 128.
3. Sir Arthur Balfour as quoted in Sydney H. Zebel, *Balfour: A Political Biography* (Cambridge: Cambridge UP, 1973), p. 143.
4. H.W. Massingham, *The Speaker* (January 28 1905).
5. Theodore Rothstein, *Justice* (March 3 1905).
6. Alymer Maude, *Tolstoy and his Problems* (London: G. Richards, 1902), pp. 103–04. Commentaries from Tolstoy also figured in books devoted to the 1905 Revolution. See William Walling, *Russia's Message* (New York: Doubleday, 1908), and G. H. Perris, *Russia in Revolution* (London: Chapman Hall 1905). And, in 1906, examples of Tolstoy's visionary ethics were translated and reprinted in even the very conservative *Fortnightly Review*.
7. Maurice Baring, *Landmarks in Russian Literature* (London, 1910), pp. 140–141, and J. A. T. Lloyd, *A Great Russian Realist* (London, 1910), p. 285.
8. Joseph Conrad, "Letter to J. B. Pinker" (August 7, 1907), in *Collected Letters, Vol. 3*, p. 462.
9. Hart-Davis, *Hugh Walpole*, p. 188, quoting from Walpole's journal (January 23, 1918).
10. H.G. Wells, "The War of the Mind," *The Nation* (August 29 1914).
11. Joseph Conrad, "Letter to H. G. Wells" (November-December 1903), in *Collected Letters, Vol. 3*, p. 79.

12. Joseph Conrad, "Letter to H. G. Wells" (September 15 1906), in *Collected Letters, Vol. 3*, p. 356

13. H. G. Wells, *In the Days of the Comet* (London: McmIllan, 1906), p. 121. All further references to this work will be quoted parenthetically in the text with the abbreviation *IDC*.

14. Raymond Williams, *Problems in Materialism and Culture* (London: New Left Books, 1982), pp. 198–99, 207.

15. Linda R. Anderson, *Bennet, Wells, and Conrad: Narrative in Transition* (New York: St. Martin's P, 1988), p. 150.

16. Joseph Conrad, "Letter to John Galsworthy" (September 2–3, 1908) in *Collected Letters, Vol. 4*, pp. 114–18.

17. This is a paraphrase of Samuel Hynes's main point about Galsworthy and liberalism in *The Edwardian Turn of Mind*.

18. Lord Alfred Douglas, "Reprint from *The Nation*," by "X" in *Academy*, vol. 74 (June 28 1908), pp. 906–07.

19. John Galsworthy, *Fraternity* (New York: Charles Scribners, 1909), pp. 376, 375.

20. Joseph Conrad, "Letter to John Galsworthy" (September 2–3, 1908) in *Collected Letters, Vol. 4*, pp. 114–19; and "Letter to John Galsworthy" (September 4, 1908) in *Collected Letters, Vol. 4*, pp. 119–121.

21. In a letter dated December 1903, Conrad calls himself "Homo duplex," saying "Both at sea and on land my point of view is English, from which the conclusion should not be drawn that I have become an English-man. That is not the case. *Homo-duplex* has in my case more than one meaning." Conrad provides a further gloss on the notion of "Homo duplex" in a letter to Józef Korzeniowski (not a kinsman), February 14 1901.

> It is widely known that I am a Pole and that Józef Konrad are my two Christian names, the latter being used by me as a surname so that foreign mouths should not distort my real surname. . . . It does not seem to me that I have been unfaithful to my country by having proved to the English that a gentleman from the Ukraine can be as good a sailor as they, and has something to tell them in their own language.

Quoted in *Conrad's Polish Background: Letters to and from Polish Friends*, ed. Zdzislaw Najder, trans. Halina Carroll (London: Oxford UP, 1964), p. 240, p. 234.

22. Jeffrey Berman, "Introduction to Conrad and the Russians," in *Conradiana*, vol. 12, p. 8.

23. Keith Carabine, "Conrad, Apollo Korzeniowski, and Dostoevsky, " *Conradiana*, vol. 28, no. 1 (1996), p. 3. All further references will be cited parenthetically with the abbreviation "CKD."

24. Fyodor Dostoevsky quoted by Joseph Frank, *Dostoevsky: The Stir of Liberation, 1860–65* (Princeton, NJ : Princeton UP, 1986), p. 274.

25. Joseph Conrad, "Letter to Edward Garnett" (December 22 1902), in

Letters from Joseph Conrad, ed. Edward Garnett (Indianapolis, Bobbs-Merrill, 1928), p. 185.

26. Zdzislaw Najder, *Conrad Under Familial Eyes* (Cambridge: Cambridge UP, 1983), p. 17.

27. Joseph Conrad, "Author's Note" to *A Personal Record* (Marlboro, VT: Marlboro P, 1982, first ed. 1908) p. xiii. All further references to this work will be quoted parenthetically in the text with the abbreviation *PR*.

28. Joseph Conrad, "Introduction" (to Edward Garnett's *Turgenev*), collected in *Notes on Life and Letters*, pp. 61–66.

29. Apollo Korzeniowski, "Poland and Muscovy," in *Conrad Under Familial Eyes*, pp. 76, 83.

30. Peter Shabad, "Resentment, Indignation, Entitlement: The Transformation of Unconscious Wish into Need," in *Psychoanalytic Dialogues*, vol. 3, no. 4 (1993), pp. 481–94; and Paul L. Russell's commentary on Shabad, "The Essential Invisibility of Trauma and the Need for Repetition," in the same volume, pp. 515–22.

31. One might further consider Conrad's antipathy toward Bakunin. This lover of conspiratorial enclaves had become part of the Russian Revolutionary National Committee for the 1863 Uprising. While this committee was fully sympathetic to the Poles, they had astonishingly neglected or discounted the hatred for Poles of the Russians whom they relied on for help with the insurrection. See E. H Carr, *The Romantic Exiles* (London: Victor Gollonz, 1933) p. 237.

32. About Conrad's knowledge of German, Karl writes: "Conrad always insisted he knew no German, but Borys [his son] tells us that in an emergency his 'father spoke at considerable length and with great fluency' " (*JCTL*, p. 758). And of Conrad's knowledge of Russian, Lewitter says that it is "an affectation of ignorance in the teeth of abundant evidence to the contrary, internal and external" (p. 654). See also Zdzislaw Najder, *Conrad's Polish Background*, p. 238, and Keith Carabine, "Conrad, Apollo Korzeniowski, and Dostoevsky," pp. 9, 21.

33. Robert Armstrong, "Joseph Conrad, The Conflict of Command," in *The Psychoanalytic Study of the Child*, vol. 26, 1971, pp. 488–93.

34. Edward Garnett, "Review of *A Set of Six*," quoted by Karl in *Three Lives* (Farrar, Straus, and Giroux, 1979), p. 650.

35. Joseph Conrad, "Letter to Edward Garnett" (August 28 1908), in *Letters from Joseph Conrad*, ed. Edward Garnett, p. 214.

36. Joseph Conrad, "Letter to Edward Garnett" (October 20 1911) in *Letters from Joseph Conrad*, pp. 232–33.

37. Joseph Conrad, "Letter to Edward Garnett" (May 27 1912), in *Letters from Joseph Conrad*, p. 240.

38. In 1905, Conrad probably read Anatole Leroy-Beaulieu, *The Empire of the Tsars and the Russias*, first published in 1893. In a letter dated January 14 1905, Conrad asks H. D. Davray about Leroy-Beaulieu. "I need a book

on Russia—recent—serious. Is Leroy-Beaulieu any good? . . . I want
something on the political and social aspect of the White Empire, from
the French point of view." *Collected Letters, Vol. 3*, p. 204.

39. Anatole Leroy-Beaulieu, *The Empire of the Tsars and the Russias* (London:
Putnam, 1905), p. 204.

40. Karl makes plain Conrad's difficulty in finishing *The Secret Agent*. See
Three Lives, pp. 619–21.

41. Review by "Z" quoted by Karl in *Three Lives*, p. 626.

42. Joseph Conrad, "Letter to Edward Garnett" (October 1907), in *Letters
from Joseph Conrad*, p. 205. The review, by Robert Lynd in the *Daily News*,
is quoted in Karl, *Three Lives*, p. 648.

43. Joseph Conrad, "Letter to John Galsworthy" (May 6 1907) and (March
5 1907), in *Collected Letters, Vol. 3*, p. 436, p. 416.

44. Joseph Conrad, "Letter to Galsworthy" (January 6 1908), *Collected Letters,
Vol. 4*, p. 12.

45. Jessie Conrad, *Joseph Conrad and His Circle* (London: Jarrolds, 1925), p.
104.

Chapter 8

1. Joseph Conrad, *Under Western Eyes*, 1911, first ed. (New York: Signet,
1987). All further references to this text will be cited parenthetically
with the abbreviation *UWE*.

2. Terry Eagleton, "Joseph Conrad and *Under Western Eyes*," in *Exiles and
Emigres: Studies in Modern Literature* (London: Chatto and Windus, 1970),
p. 23. All further references to this text will be cited parethentically
with the abbreviation *EE*.

3. Harriet Gilliam, "Russia and the West in Conrad's *Under Western Eyes*," in
Studies in the Novel, vol. 10 (1978), pp. 218–19.

4. According to Avrom Fleishman, there is a "strain of racism" in Conrad's
political thesis (see *Conrad's Politics* [Baltimore: Johns Hopkins UP,
1967], p. 223). However, Fleishman apologizes for this strain, and does
not investigate either the terms or the meaning of Conrad's ethnocentricism. As I have already said, an importantly ethnocentric text that
figured in Conrad's construction of Russia is Leroy-Beaulieu's *The Empire
of the Tsars*. All further references to this text are cited parentheticially
with the abbreviation *TE*.

5. Joseph Frank, *Dostoevsky: The Miraculous Years, 1865–71* (Princeton, NJ:
Princeton UP, 1995), p. 146.

6. Fyodor Dostoevsky, "Letter to Apollon Maikov" (March 1, 1868),
quoted by Frank in *Dostoevsky: The Miraculous Years*, p. 253.

7. Jocelyn Baines, *Joseph Conrad: A Critical Biography* (New York: McGraw-
Hill Publishers, 1960), p. 370. Further references to this work are cited
in the text parenthetically with the abbreviation *JC*.

8. R. L. Lewitter, in "Conrad, Dosteovsky, and the Polish-Russian Antagonism" (*Conradiana*, vol. 12), says that Razumov's fate "distantly resembles" that of the nationalist Shatov, who "finds that he no longer shares the convictions of his associates, [and] that he is accused of being a spy and an informer and is murdered," but Lewitter overlooks the fact that Peter Verkhovensky is actually the informer, and that he betrays revolutionary friends (like Shatov).

9. Fyodor Dostoevsky, *Devils*, 1st ed. 1871, trans. Michael Katz (Oxford and New York: Oxford UP, 1992), p. 596, p. 602.

10. Joseph Conrad, "Letter to John Galsworthy " (January 8, 1908), in *Collected Letters, Vol. 4*, p.9.

11. Adam Gillon, *Joseph Conrad* (Boston: Twayne Publishers, 1982), pp. 124–25.

12. Carola Kaplan, "Conrad's Narrative Occupation Of/By Russia in *Under Western Eyes*," in *Conradiana*, vol. 27 (1995), p. 101. All further references to this text will be cited parenthetically with the abbreviation "CNO."

13. This is a paraphrase of Edward Wasiolek, "Conrad and Dostoevsky, and Natalia and Sonia," in *International Fiction Review*, vol. 17 (1990), p. 101.

14. Fyodor Dosteovsky, *Crime and Punishment*, 1881 ed., trans. Richard Pevear and Larissa Volokhonsky, pp. 417–18. All further references to this text will be cited parenthetically with the abbreviation *CP*.

15. See Carola Kaplan (note 12). See also Anthony Winner, "Irony and Women's Strength," in *Culture and Irony: Studies in Joseph Conrad's Major Fiction*, p. 94.

16. Elizabeth Knapp Hay, *The Political Novels of Joseph Conrad* (Chicago: U of Chicago P, 1963), pp. 283–84.

17. Jeffrey Berman and Donna Van Wagenen, "*Under Western Eyes*: Conrad's Diary of a Writer," *Conradiana*, vol. 9 (1977), pp. 269–74.

18. The original manuscript stresses Ivanovitch's belief in a self-appointed conspiratorial elite ("a conspiracy with the direct object to seize power") as the way to subvert the "dead" institutions of liberalism, namely, its "ideals of grinding competition and government by discussion" (Original manuscript in the Joseph Conrad Collection, courtesy of the Bineke Library rare book room, Yale University, New Haven, CT. All further references are cited parenthetically with the abbreviation MS). Though Ivanovitch's penchant for cabals recalls Bakunin, there is an even tighter parallel between Wells and Ivanovitch, since Wells's *primary target* was an exhausted liberalism—to be destroyed, as he puts it in *Anticipations*, by an "outspoken Secret Society" (H. G. Wells, *Anticipations*, 1st ed., 1902 [London, 1914], pp. 238, 257).

19. In manuscript passages revised out of the finished text, Conrad's narrator reveals his desire, rather too baldly, to "guide" Nathalie's life; and his advice about her political aspirations—that she might devote herself "to looking after the families of political prisoners," thereby "doing good" in a philanthropic way that "everybody understands"—is really

about what she could best do to make of herself (and by implication for him) a good English wife (MS, pp. 523–24). Further, the idea that guiding Nathalie is meant to bolster the narrator's sense of patriarchal prerogative is corroborated by his bewildered discomfort with his English-Canadian niece—who, as he tells, is confident that her marriage to a journalist would not interfere "with her usefulness to the community," and that each partner "would preserve an intact personality" (MS, pp.615–16).

20. Joseph Conrad, "Letter to E. L. Sanderson" (September 2 1910), in *Collected Letters, Vol. 4*, p. 364.

21. Christopher Bollas, "Aspects of Self Experience" and "The Evocative Object," in *Being A Character: Psychoanalysis and Self Experience* (New York: Hill and Wang Publishers, 1992), pp. 11–47; the citation is from p. 21. See also *Being a Character*, pp. 59–60 for the idea of a "collisional dialectic" (discussed later in the chapter).

22. Apollo Korzeniowski,"Before the Thunderstorm," quoted by Jeffrey Meyers in *Joseph Conrad: A Biography*, p. 8.

23. Apollo Korzeniowski, "To My Son Born in the 85th Year of Muscovite Oppression," quoted by Jeffrey Meyers in *Joseph Conrad: A Biography*, p. 10.

24. Joseph Conrad, "Letter to Edward Garnett" (October 8 1907), in *Collected Letters, Vol. 3*, p. 492.

25. Joseph Conrad, "Letter to *The New York Times* 'Saturday Review' (August 1 1901), in *Collected Letters, Vol. 2*, p. 349.

26. Joseph Conrad, "Letter to Norman Douglas" (June 28 1910), in *Collected Letters, Vol. 4*, p. 345.

27. Bernard Meyer, *Joseph Conrad: A Psychoanalytic Biography* (Princeton, NJ: Princeton UP, 1967), p. 207.

28. According to Keith Carabine, Conrad was guilty for having abandoned his father's Polish messianism, and that this betrayal "finally did undo him" See his "Conrad, Apollo Korzeniowski, and Dostoevsky," *Conradiana*, vol. 28, no. 1, 1996, p. 18. However, Carabine fails to consider how acutely vulnerable Conrad was to the natural sequelae of feeling he had betrayed Apollo, as Apollo had betrayed him. Carabine also neglects how, in surveying Conrad's breakdown, one must consider his vulnerability to loss, and the dynamic entanglement of present and past experiences of loss in his life. Without deploying this dialectic, Carabine comes perilously close to the reductionism of Gustav Morf in *The Shades and Ghosts of Joseph Conrad*. Morf traces every crisis in Conrad's life, and all dramatic conflicts in his novels, to "the guilt feelings he must have had for deserting Poland" (p. 150). It is time to be done with this mono-causal thesis.

Meyer, in *Joseph Conrad: A Psychoanalytic Biography*, believes that Conrad's wrenching quarrel with Ford Madox Hueffer in the summer of 1909 was the single most important factor in subverting Conrad's emotional stability—not only because Ford and Conrad shared a bond of trust for 11 years, but because Ford had been Conrad's collaborator and had helped him to refine his writing talent. In addition to the unfixable breach with Ford, Meyer suggests that Conrad's personal involvement with the Russian material of the novel was "possibly contributory " to the breakdown (p. 210–11); but, remarkably enough, Meyer does not reflect on the dynamic connection between the Russian material, on the one hand, and the ending of significant relationships and the deaths of parents, on the other. In my view, the break with Ford was difficult, but it was one part of a much larger and more complex constellation of dislocation.

29. Christopher Bollas, *Cracking Up: The Work of Unconscious Experience* (New York: Hill and Wang Publishers, 1995), pp. 114–15.

See also Paul L. Russell, "The Essential Invisibility of Trauma, and the Need for Repetition," in *Psychoanalytic Dialogues*, vol. 3, no. 4 (1993). Russell puts defensive constraint in the context of mourning, saying that while the processing of trauma requires "a particular kind of grief," this processing is often avoided because the pain accompanying such grief is so extreme (p. 518).

30. Jessie Conrad, *Joseph Conrad and His Circle* (London: Jarrolds, 1925), p. 142. All further references to this text will be given parenthetically with the abbreviation *JCC*.

31. Jessie Conrad, "Letter to David S. Meldrum" (February 6 1910), *Joseph Conrad: Letters to William Blackwood and David S. Meldrum*, ed. William Blackburn (Durham, N.C.: Duke UP, 1958), p. 192.

Index